JAMES AYLOTT

Tales Of

WHISKEY TANGO
From
MISERY TOWERS

A NOVEL

Beautiful Arch — St. Louis

First Publication 2024

Hardcover ISBN: 979-8-9876812-1-3
Paperback ISBN: 979-8-9876812-2-0
E-Book ISBN: 979-8-9876812-3-7

Library of Congress Control Number: 2023946768

United States Register of Copyrights TXu 2-335-982

First printing edition 2024

Beautiful Arch LLC
St Louis, Missouri.

"The fifth night we passed St. Louis, and it was like the whole world lit up."

Mark Twain, *Adventures of Huckleberry Finn*

With Thanks

Editing

Robert Aylott

Joyce Hogan

Donatella Montrone

Sharongay Pearline

Roger Plackemeier

Lance Shaffer

St. Louis Research Assistance

Ronald Kirkwood

Lawrence Muskin

Claire Wedemeyer

Beta Readers

Lorraine Raggio

Cliff Renfrew

Eleonora Scholz

Lennert Scholz

A Declaration of Fiction

Dedication

This one is for River; the little guy who is named in honor of the mighty Mississippi.

Contents

August 2019

Welcome to M-i-s-e-r-y!

Nick Pipeman was far from poetic but always thought fellow Missourian T.S. Eliot should have known better: August, not April, is the "cruellest month." In the city of St. Louis, mid-August, with its sweltering heat and stifling humidity, is the cruelest part of that cruelest month.

For the first forty-plus years of his life, Nick had admittedly been, aside from romantic endeavors, a blessed guy. This lifelong lucky streak had not only ground to a screeching halt but a truck-sized load of bad luck had been directed his way. A hardy man like Nick could've easily taken a little bit of personal tragedy or misfortune in his stride. However, the effect of forty-two years' worth of jinxed crap luck coming tsunami-style in a minute stretch of time had now spiraled wretchedly out of control. The compounding effect from the hex on his back had led St. Louis, an ever lawless city, to the brink of total anarchy.

On this sticky Friday night, with air temperatures lodged in the high 80s, Nick was precariously standing on the southern side of the Eads Bridge looking down at the Mississippi River. With both hands, he grasped a large heavy urn full of pennies. Nick's brain was spinning and his mind raged with anguish.

How could one single action lead to this? He contemplated for the infinite time. To anyone who by chance witnessed Nick standing on the walls of the bridge, it looked as if he was on the verge of ending it all.

The noise of a roaring car approaching from the St. Louis side of the river made Nick raise his eyes from "the big muddy" to see what was coming his way. Cars speeding over 100 mph were a dime a dozen on the wild streets of St. Louis. What was unusual about this ride was what it *was*, rather than what it *wasn't*. In these parts, racers were typically Dodge Chargers, sans muffler and plates, and they usually came with heavily tinted windows, a stench of weed, and the thud of urban beats. Pipeman, in all his four decades, had never seen on any highway a gray nineties Chrysler LeBaron with a very much out-of-place speed flap lifted from a Lotus Esprit doing a buck twenty. The open-top Corinthian leather-upholstered roadster was piloted by a determined, ragged-looking man who held onto the steering wheel for dear life. From the car's stereo a tune by Roxette blasted into the air. As always with racers on St. Louis city streets, the specter of law enforcement was nowhere to be seen.

*   *   *

Colton Chesterfield III awoke to find himself in a nightmarish predicament. His most pressing concern wasn't that he was trapped inside a locked coffin with no apparent way to escape. For Colton knew, due to the make of this particular coffin, one of the flimsy ones his former company imported from China, that this piece of junk, unlike its marketing promises, quickly collapsed upon burial. So he was certain about one thing – this coffin was, for now, above ground.

The dreadful situation he was about to endure was initially made apparent by a rumbling stomach and the feeling that he was going to need, in a rather short period of time, an emergency bathroom pit stop. A man like him, in his early thirties, by this age has a solid radar on two important things in life. First, he instinctively knows the kind of partner he would like to bump the nasties with. And second, he has a precise awareness of the nature of stool he is on the verge of delivering. Colton Chesterfield III was a hundred percent sure he did not have a run-of-the-mill crap on the brew, but he was about to conjure up one of those turd salvos that, like night follows day, come rapidly after a blowout breakfast at Denny's.

Colton mentally played out the full permutations of his current state of affairs. He was trapped in a coffin alive and was about to shit himself in a tight and confined space the mother lode of ca-ca. Now, for a man who had spent a lifetime charming his way out of sticky situations, this was a daring concern like no other he had faced. All Colton could hope for was that this coffin was about to be rolled into a crematorium, or buried. At least that would be a relatively quick and painless end to what he deemed a glorious, triumphant life. The alternative of being trapped in a coffin and slowly being suffocated to death by one's own shit was a nightmare within a nightmare. Colton Chesterfield III began ferociously banging on the coffin lid and screaming as loudly as he could, "Get me out of here!"

*　　*　　*

With a rapid swipe of his smartphone, Mike Love a man who was a doppelgänger for Bruce Springsteen in his mid-eighties prime, unlocked the first scooter in the nest. He put one foot firmly on the electric vehicle's deck and the other on Washington Ave. He had come to a fork in the road of life. It was about a woman, or more accurately, a choice between two.

Seven blocks southeast was the prodigal manic pixie dream girl that once shattered his heart and now enticed him with a get-out-of-this-town runaway adventure. She was a quirky beauty molded like a Tarantino muse poached from Central Casting. This siren of enticement offered to take him to Los Angeles – a new start, an escape from being just another "forgotten man" of the Trump hinterland. The sex they had in high school was dynamite and he had no reason to believe that a decade on, if he still had the stamina, it would be anything less than the same. The future she presented was lucrative, unplanned, and breathtakingly exciting. This was the American dream of the movies, and what was on offer was a starring role.

Four blocks north awaited stability, domesticity, and the natural order of life for a regular guy like Mike. It wasn't all boring, and in the plus column she was a natural beauty with a head-turning, non-traditional Midwestern physique. Odds on this life route would be speedy marriage, church-approved sex and in short shift a batch of children numbering at least three. Obligatory on the goals front would be a tidy house in Ballwin, Fenton, or some other outer-ring St. Louis suburb. Proudly sat in the drive of this lushly landscaped, cookie-cutter cottage a pair of practical minivans. This scenario, although the woeful

4

predicament for the antiheroes of Springsteen dirges, could be argued as an understated American dream.

Plotted out on paper for most even-headed men like Mike was a tough decision to make. Both life-changing choices had jaw-dropping pitfalls and much in the way of enticement. Certainly the options to decide between were more nuanced than a simple follow-your-head or follow-your-heart call. However, for Mike Love, a man who agonized over the simplest of tasks, it was a surprisingly easy decision to make. Mike opened up the scooter throttle and raced along Washington Ave. as fast as his ride would permit.

*　　*　　*

Daris Ballic downed a shot of Pusser's Rum and looked out the wall of windows that wrapped around his apartment. Missouri Towers might not be the flashiest city address any longer, but it did possess some of the finest views in all of the Midwest. Daris, as long as he breathed, could never get tired of gazing at Eero Saarinen's marvel of mid-century engineering. Tonight there had been a constant buzz of helicopter activity in the city and he noted three currently hovering around the St. Louis Arch.

Daris walked into his kitchen and placed the shot glass into the upper portion of his Fisher & Paykel dishwasher. He opened a drawer and took out two 9mm pistols. He slipped the first into the small of his back and the second into an ankle holster. He was by choice a one-gun kind of guy but his attire tonight, a three-piece suit from London's Henry Poole & Co, looked unsightly with extra ammunition stuffed into the pockets. Guns and the British are not the most natural of partners, so it wasn't a surprise that his finest bespoke suit, the one he only wore for grand occasions, wasn't at all practical for said occasion. James Bond, who was never short of bullets, obviously frequented a different Savile Row tailor.

Meet Go = Be 8 tonite pinged the text from the receptionist at the dentist's office. Daris, who had started learning English in his native Bosnia, if given the choice preferred using the Queen's English. Just like the way he had learned at school in the old country. The only thing he detested more than dumbed-down American English was the lazy text slang of tiresome millennials. He texted back, *Please thank Dr. Gold Tooth and I will be in your company promptly.*

Locked and loaded, Daris left his apartment. As he rode the elevator down to street level, he knew that whatever went down tonight there would be no modern-day, "peace for our time" kind of Munich Agreement. And that certainly he would, "Never Surrender." This dental appointment for Daris Ballic was more akin to a round in Thunderdome than a check-up and clean. The likely outcome of this late-night appointment was, two men would enter, only one man would leave.

*   *   *

On the eastern side of the Mississippi River at Mound City Gentlemen's Club, Butterfly was about to go on stage. She might well by now have a corpse in her car, but that wasn't something she would let distract her workplace focus. At fifty-two, Butterfly was by far the oldest dancer at the club. Only her professionalism to the trade and exceptional "customer service" would defy the odds and gravity, and keep her tight grip on a lucrative Friday night dancing slot.

A scantily clad Butterfly strode onto the stage to her signature namesake Dolly Parton song. Her heart raced as she scanned the audience for familiar faces. *He had kept his promise and was here.* Butterfly only wished that he had put some casual garb on, or at least taken his hat and tie off. Strip clubs invariably attracted an eclectic clientele, but a man dressed in full funeral garb was not enhancing the ambiance of erotica.

*   *   *

It was hard to believe that it was hotter inside City Museum than it was outside, but Gloria McKendrick felt like she was melting in her dressing room. Try as you can, but keeping what was a hundred years ago a shoe factory to 21st-century American cooling standards was impossible.

Gloria stared into the mirror, perfect prom queen curls and possibly a little too much stage makeup discreetly defused the recently appearing lines on her face and occasional pesky gray hair. Although old enough to be a grandmother in Missouri, she knew she was still young and beautiful. As she studied her reflection carefully, Gloria decided she really did look like Molly Ringwald's character Andie Walsh from *Pretty in Pink*. As confident as she was, the idea of throwing herself back into the dating game at the age of thirty-two drowned this confidence with a deluge of dread. Tinder swipes, lengthy "getting to know you" texts, awkward encounters and, of course, just as you got to fall for Mr. Perfect there was the modern-day plague of being "ghosted." The other major predicament was that as soon as suitors learned she was a trapeze artist, it was like shining a "Bat Signal" in the air and drawing in the crazies. The awe of "flexibility" is what they all said when Gloria questioned their kinky second-date requests.

Settling down, marriage and children; in the space of one week those dreams had been snatched once again from her. Her man wasn't perfect but who is? She thought they made a great team and had envisioned their future together. Gloria could run away again but she had been bolting from something or other all her life. Escaping the farm, running away and joining the circus, escaping the circus, and running away to St. Louis to work at City Museum. She couldn't keep on running. For all of her running, Gloria knew in her heart she was just a Kansas girl who, whether she liked it or not, would end up one day back on the farm.

*   *   *

Tyrone Booker's instinct told him the gunshots were coming from a southerly direction. With nineteen years of experience in the St. Louis Metropolitan Police Department, he knew it was the sound of small arms popping. He pedaled his police bike against traffic down 9th St. towards Market St. This part of the city was relatively quiet for now. Most of the protesters had congregated in groups outside City Hall or the police headquarters six blocks north. Constantly scanning his surroundings as he rode, Tyrone didn't see anything or anyone out of place. He pulled up outside the abandoned AT&T building on Pine St. This is where the shots had originated. There were no bodies lying in the street, nor any visible pools of blood – both common sights in America's most murderous city. *Likely some punk shooting at windows,* he thought to himself.

St. Louis is a fatalistic northern city in perpetual decline, lodged in a southern-looking state cursed with never-ending racial problems. A city with de facto segregation that apartheid-era South African politicians could admire as a model of urbanist planning. Tyrone could feel a tension on the streets tonight that was hard to decipher. Anger had evolved since the Ferguson shootings five years before. Those events seemed like the beginning, the start of a rise, a genesis for change. Of course nothing had changed since then. All the Ferguson unrest had managed to do was put a national spotlight on a tragic regional problem.

Tyrone had only one year until retirement. He was going west to Colorado. He just had to survive twelve more months. Tyrone checked his phone and looked at the *St. Louis Tribune* digital edition. Somehow they always managed to spin the news in order to emphasize the M-I-S-E-R-Y in Missouri. He knew the mantra: if it bleeds it leads. But there had to be something decent happening out there some of the time. And not just a daily roll call of murders, racial challenges, and civic corruption. There was no update on the condition of Devonte Jones. In this instance, no news was good news. He knew it wasn't his fault but he did feel a personal connection to the event.

The rattle of gunfire came from the east. Tyrone pointed his bike in that direction and with caution went to investigate. The cop tonight was pulling a double shift and would be on duty until 6 a.m. He had a feeling this was going to be a long and dangerous night.

*   *   *

On the rooftop observation deck of Missouri Towers – or Misery Towers as residents affectionately tagged it – a lady by the name of Madison Stone lit up a cigarette and took a sip of iced white wine from an oversized tumbler. Hot and drunk always, she was never situationally aware, and nor did she care.

Half a dozen blocks behind her she could hear the sound of a city fighting for its life. Police sirens raging, helicopters circling, flash bangs exploding, small arms popping. On the other side of what T.S. Elliot called the "Strong Brown God" was the modern wasteland of a once bustling East St. Louis. Beyond this hollowed-out city, Madison could see flashes of lightning. She counted the seconds down until she heard the accompanying thunder. High overhead in the sky an airplane flew en route between the left and right coasts.

Eight days earlier...

Apartment #1011   Born to Run

The old-school analog alarm clock alerted Mike Love that it was officially 7 a.m. – although the hot sun beating in through the 10th-floor window of Missouri Towers had made him aware that it was rise and shine time long before any bell rang. St. Louis in the summer feels at best like a slow hot drowning, but the blistering heat of the last few days was above the usual level of misery. "Maybe global warming is real," Mike muttered. His father had always talked about the winters being colder.

Possibly in New York it would've been considered a large living space, but by St. Louis standards Mike's studio apartment was more room-with-a-view than comfortable living. Mike looked out of his lone window. A freight barge was heading south on the Mississippi, in the direction of New Orleans. Tourists, even at this early hour, were descending on the Gateway Arch. The big office meeting was at 10 a.m., three hours away, so he had time to kill.

After showering Mike sat himself at the office desk positioned on the opposite side of the room from his bed. Hung above this desk was a large poster displaying the cover of Bruce Springsteen's seminal 1984 album *Born in the U.S.A.* Blessed with robust Germanic genes, Mike had an athletic build for Missouri and a fine head of dark black shaggy hair. He seldom strayed far from Walmart when shopping for clothes and owned a wardrobe primarily consisting of blue-collar basics. Today, like most days, Mike had dressed himself in a pair of faded blue Levi's and a white cotton T-shirt that was a little too tight for comfort – a style copied straight off the poster hanging directly above him. If Mike wanted to look smart he would break out a vintage straight-cut dark suit paired with a crisp white shirt and bolo tie. This dressed-to-impress ensemble was artfully inspired by the cover of Springsteen's great but understated album, *The Tunnel of Love*. With a little bit of nature and a generous amount of purposeful nurture, Mike Love looked and dressed eerily similar to his hero Bruce Springsteen in his eighties glory days prime.

They healed your pain, broke your heart, held you back, and got knocked up at the most inconvenient of times. These, of course, were the ladies of every Springsteen ballad. Mike's very own dress-swaying, screen-door-slamming Mary was a lady by the name of Gloria McKendrick. Hailing from Kansas, this perky thirty-one-year-old had all the jaw-grinding niceness of a keep-your-bed-warm-at-night Midwesterner packaged within the body of a ballet dancer.

They had met at Missouri Towers. She resided two floors above him, and at certain angles when looking from his window Mike could see Gloria on her balcony. With the building's gym mothballed, the pool rarely open due to a constant losing war with algae, and the underground garage frequented by muggers, the elevators were the only safe place to casually encounter a fellow resident. However, as much as he had wanted to he would never serendipitously bump into Gloria while riding the elevators. When they did finally meet, he thought Gloria might be a little too much to handle, but thankfully it all worked out in the end.

Gloria lived in a positively spirited two-bedroom apartment, along with a tiresome perma-single roommate by the name of Zoe. The girls spent a considerable amount of their downtime sitting on the sofa eating ice cream from the tub while binge-watching eighties rom-coms. They shared the annoying habit of reciting lines from Molly Ringwald flicks. It could've all been worse, at least Gloria and Zoe didn't feast on *Gilmore Girls* reruns.

Gloria worked as a trapeze artist and instructor at the inappropriately named City Museum. This sprawling former factory in the Downtown West neighborhood of St. Louis was brimming with slides, mazes, trains, and repurposed pieces of industrial Americana. The offerings were one giant playground for people of all ages, and in no way conformed to any notion of what you would think to be a traditional museum. City Museum also housed a small circus arena and training school; it was here where Gloria worked.

Mike was under constant pressure to move in with Gloria and take their relationship to the next level. Pointing to her ring finger she would say, in the purest of accents which only those from Kansas speak, "We've been dating for two years and you need to make a COMMITMENT!" To be fair to Gloria, two years was a long time to be courting in the bible belt without a walk down any aisle. Gloria had hit her thirties, a panic-inspired age (especially in this part of the country), where if you don't already have children it's assumed there's a problem. This was also an age that made her a veteran in her industry. Most trapeze artists retired by twenty-five. Gloria, to her credit, still rocked a sequin leotard, used her flexible prowess in the realm of nocturnal pleasures, and was very much a master of her high-flying craft. She certainly wasn't ready to be pensioned off and Mike liked the fact that her job was also her passion.

However, on the home front, Gloria wanted to settle down, have carefully curated, autumnal couple pictures taken, get engaged, plan a big wedding, rear children, buy a house and enjoy all the other trappings of an Instagram-worthy life. Mike could definitely help with purchasing the home part of Gloria's goals, since he worked as a realtor at local brokerage Spitfire Real Estate. And even though he wouldn't actually qualify for a mortgage for *any* house with his current earnings, he could certainly find one. It's the rest of the commitment package that scared Mike to death.

The real estate business is all about being positive, Mike had to remind himself, as he drank the day's first cup of coffee while checking for voicemails. He couldn't kid himself: being positive wasn't as easy as the motivational podcasters peddling their foolproof home-selling techniques made it sound. The real estate business at its essence was like a brutal contact sport. It has that same thrill of victory and that same grueling agony of defeat. Of late Mike had no wins to brag about, with only losses on the score sheet.

For the first two years of Mike's Spitfire career, he had been a member of the agency's top-producing Play-Worth team. Love was good at what he did. He kept his phone on, knew the local inventory by heart, remembered his contract law, never missed a ticked box on lead paint forms, deciphered even the most brutal of chicken scratch names left at open house log books and, unlike most millennials, turned up to appointments on time. This was good when Mike was being trained and getting leads delivered by his team bosses. However, since striking out solo with the hope of keeping more of his commissions, he had crashed and burned.

Mike's dad would say, with a re-engineered Woody Allen quote from *Annie Hall:* "Those who can't do, teach. And those who can't teach, teach gym. And those that can't teach gym get a REAL ESTATE LICENSE!" In a way his dad was right. One in a hundred people in the United States hold a real estate license. So everyone will ultimately know someone who can represent their real estate needs. Mike had heard that in San Francisco there were three cars for every two parking spots, and drivers were continually fighting for a place to put their cars. It was the same in the world of selling real estate. There were more licensed agents beating the streets than transactions to be had.

Realtors send you flyers, magazines, birthday and Christmas cards. They join the boards of charter schools, run gardening clubs, organize trivia nights, and even host kindergarten parties. They are simply trying to find a way to inject their usefulness into your life. A big elaborate hustle to grab a slice of your next housing purchase or sale. Mike's dad was a union HVAC technician – the kind of job that's well-paid and recession-proof but boring and not worthy of any runaway dreams.

If there were two things Mike found to be of educational merit in Springsteen's back catalog they were first, be careful what you do down at the lake, and at the very least when making out near any body of water, double-bag your Johnson. Second, and of more dramatic importance to Mike's own future, nothing good ever comes from staying in your hometown.

Mike's older brother had never left Missouri. The highlight of his life was owning a 700-square-foot, vinyl-sided house on a floodplain that hosted in the driveway a beaten-up minivan laden with child seats. Mike's friends from high school who had stayed around had jobs at places like the lumber yard, the refinery, in factories. The fresh-faced, slender girls they took to prom and then married had long ago, with the excuse of children, let themselves go. Mike didn't envy their shabby toy-strewn homes in generic suburbs. This wasn't his idea of any promised land and he vowed to not end up like his brother or any of these friends.

Gloria had a decade prior packed up and run away from small-town farm life in Kansas, and before moving to St. Louis she had toured all over America with a famous circus. Mike, in contrast, had never spent more than two consecutive nights of his life farther than an hour's drive from his childhood home. There was a chance that if Gloria and Mike stayed together in St. Louis he would forever resent her for not allowing him to escape and follow his dreams. They constantly argued about their different visions for the future.

In Springsteen songs, they tore up roads in suicide machines, pink Cadillacs, Chevy stock super eights and chrome-wheeled classics. The highways were dusty, empty, lonesome and forever thundering. With or without Gloria riding shotgun, Mike had always known his manifest destiny was much like a Springsteen song – to escape. His goal was to be able, at short shift, to fit everything he owned into a car and drive away. For this reason he lived life as a minimalist.

However, the problem he currently faced wasn't that he had too much in the way of possessions but that he drove a sub-compact 2012 Chevrolet Sonic. This car was so tiny you could barely fit enough luggage in it for a weekend at Lake of the Ozarks, let alone consider it practical for transcontinental migration. Mike, at heart a romantic dreamer, was in his head a practical guy brimming with Midwestern sensibilities. He would settle for a utilitarian late-model Toyota SUV over any supercharged hot rod. And he would happily take the gas mileage advantage that I-70 yielded over cruising whatever was left of Route 66. However, Mike's finances were running on fumes and he didn't have the cash to upgrade the Sonic.

Selling real estate was still a way to make it big and a profession he could take with him to a larger market like New York or Los Angeles. Further failure in this business though would take him straight back to working at the tire shop. He had done that grueling gig for eight years after graduating from Meramec Community College with an Associate's degree in sociology. There was no way he wanted to return to the garage, and there wasn't anything he could do, aside from flip burgers or work at Walmart with this low-level qualification. Capitulation wasn't an option. Mike knew he had to get the transaction pipeline flowing fast.

Mike had zero voicemails. He then checked his creaking computer for emails. The credit report he was waiting for hadn't arrived. This prospective rental application was the closest thing he had to a transaction. His commission payout would be just $250, but at least it would make a dent in the delinquent office fees he owed. Aside from invites to numerous open houses that overly busy Spitfire agent Tracy Trampleasure was hosting on Sunday, Mike's inbox contained nothing but junk. He couldn't afford the pay-to-play listing referrals pitches offered and wasn't in need of hair regrowth remedies or bigger pecker girth. He batch deleted the unread junk e-mails.

"Hopeless?" Mike shouted loudly as he put his computer to sleep. With nothing in the way of constructive work on his planner, he decided to venture up to Gloria's apartment for his second cup of coffee that day.

Mike exited apartment #1011 and bolted down the musty, poorly-lit hallway towards the elevators. Missouri Towers had three very slow operating elevators but only one car currently stopped at his floor. One elevator was exclusively reserved for the commercial spaces that filled the building's first nine floors. The second elevator serving the residential condos between levels 10 and 20 was out of action due to flood damage several months ago. With the commercial sections less than thirty percent occupied, the residents of the upper floors had tried to commandeer this elevator for shared use. Unfortunately, the sparsely populated lower levels housed a bunch of frothing-at-the-bit lawyers. They were quick to send a barrage of "fuck off and die legal threats" to the management company and nip this idea in the bud.

When the elevator finally arrived, the smell of cheap perfume alerted Mike before a visual was made that he had hijacked someone else's ride. He sheepishly shuffled over to the elevator controls and hit the 12th-floor button; a maneuver performed while looking down in an attempt to avoid eye contact with whoever was standing next to him.

"Seriously, you couldn't walk up two flights of stairs? You kids these days are really fucking lazy," barked his elevator companion when she realized Mike's destination.

She did have a point, Mike thought, as he raised his eyes to look at his fellow rider. There was indeed a set of stairs that some of the healthier-looking residents had been using since the gym was shuttered last year. The woman opposite him was someone he'd previously met. She looked like a poor man's Dolly Parton with what you could politely call a robustly manufactured bosom and matching derriere. Within her canyon-sized, gravity-defying cleavage she sported a faded butterfly tattoo, noticeable to even the most casual of onlookers. Mike had talked to her once before. He recalled she was in her fifties, originally from southern Missouri, and owned a condo on the 15th floor. He knew she wasn't planning on renting, selling, or buying real estate in the near future. Hence, no business to be had, and due to that Mike had long ago scratched her name from an inner newsfeed entirely focused on prospecting. Gloria had tagged her "cheap shower-fume lady" as she reeked like a Chinatown knock-off perfume store. Oddly, she was now using a walker.

"Did you have an accident?" Mike asked in a concerned tone to move the conversation away from his own laziness.

"Did it dancing," she replied. Mike gave her an obvious up-and-down look. *She isn't performing with the Bolshoi Ballet!* He internally contemplated, and before he could ask her what kind of dancing, she added, "I dance in Sauget." This was an aha moment for Mike. The small Illinois town of Sauget's entire raison d'être was to provide a friendly business environment to bars without closing times and anything-goes strip clubs.

Mike, looking at the walker and the aging lady it propped up, decided this hot mess had incurred what the realtor training manual labeled, "A life-changing event!" And due to that fact, this woman would shortly be in need of "professional real estate services." With a Gatling gun velocity plucked from Willy Loman's wet dreams, Mike pulled out a business card and made his pitch.

"Downtown market is super hot. It's a great time to sell, especially now that you're retiring!"

"Who's retiring?" she replied before adding, "This is my last day with the walker. I'll be back at work next week!" She then handed Mike a business card for Mound City Gentleman's Club with the name Butterfly printed on it. The lady then roared, "Honey, I make more money in four hours shaking my ass than you do in four weeks breaking your ass, and I'm not retiring as long as my titties are hard and I can still grip a pole."

The drunk homeless guy permanently stationed on Tucker and Pine St. made more money collecting change than Mike did working, so he didn't take this as a genuine put-down or a sign of her own personal wealth.

"Looks like a nice place, maybe I'll swing by next time I'm in Sauget."

"I have a pole in my living room, come over for a special. Apartment #1511!" she shouted, as Mike made a timely escape at his elevator stop.

In this situation, the training manual said something about not stepping over dollars to pick up dimes and instead move on to the next client. However, Mike was intrigued by Butterfly and put her business card in his wallet. He would enter her details into his customer database for a follow-up call.

The 12th-floor hallway was identical to his own, aside from the walls being painted in a nasty green shade instead of a disgusting blue hue. Mike decided both colors must have originated from a deeply discounted paint sale during the Nixon administration. He rang Gloria's doorbell with his signature three pushes in quick successive bursts.

The door opened to reveal Gloria's roommate, Zoe. She was a big, tall white woman of a somewhat athletic build. Just a decade older than Mike in years but a middle-aged fogey in terms of mannerisms, Zoe was dressed in gray sweatpants and a baggy St. Louis Cardinals T-shirt. Mike would tell Gloria that Zoe was a "green-tea bitch of the highest order." And she was certainly fulfilling that prophecy with a cup of something hot and herbal gripped in her hand.

"Gloria isn't here," Zoe said, standing in front of the door to block him from barging in.

"Do you know where she is?" he asked with concern due to the early time of day.

"Running. Us girls need to stay in shape for the sake of our careers."

"Why aren't you with her? Or are party clowns not required to keep fit?" Mike replied in a pithy manner.

"Mike, you know I'm a circus clown, not a party clown. We have talked about this before. There's a big difference, and you are making me mad!"

Zoe was once a circus clown with a big-name troupe from Montreal. She had been "red-lighted" for getting a little too cozy with the ringmaster. His wife, who was also the show's executive producer, became aware of the relationship and set Zoe adrift in St. Louis. Mike didn't want to push the clown category issue but he knew that Zoe did the occasional Bar Mitzvah in Ladue, and that was certainly party clown turf.

"Can I come in and have a coffee until Gloria's back?"

"She only just left and it's not a good time," Zoe replied.

"Does the clown lady have COMPANY?" he asked in an enquiring way, to someone in all the two years he'd known her had, to his knowledge, never been on a date.

"No Mike, I'm still waiting for "MR. RIGHT!" No company is here. If you really want to know, I'm shopping for winter boots."

"It's not even 8:30 and it's 81 degrees outside. How can you even think about winter boots?"

"It's a girl thing, you wouldn't understand," she replied.

Mike knew this wasn't necessarily a "girl thing" but possibly a "St. Louis girl thing." It was as if every lady out there was itching for summer to end and fall to start. Mike noticed when that first sub-80-degree September day with low humidity arrived that every other woman he saw was proudly sporting new boots. So it made perfect sense to him that during the hottest week of the year, when the local lady faire should be still thinking about summer bikinis, they're busy browsing for winter boots.

"Actually, I have something for you," Mike said, as he extracted several small items from his pocket and handed them to Zoe.

"These are amazing!" Zoe said as she received half a dozen shell casings. After a close inspection, she added: ".223 bullets from an AR-15. Beauties!"

As well as being a professional clown, Zoe had a side hustle making jewelry. Her brand, STL Hoodlry, created necklaces, bangles, earrings, and bracelets – all crafted from bullets, shell casings, and the occasional ammo magazine found on St. Louis streets. She marketed herself as, "a sustainable, female-owned business" that produces "artisanal, hand-crafted, small-batch, 100% recycled eco items for the sophisticated urbanist wanting to embrace the gritty side of gentrification." PETA hadn't any qualms with the possibility humans may have been killed by pieces used in her product line when they gave her bling a coveted, "Cruelty-Free" certification. With St. Louis this year overtaking Chicago and Detroit and reclaiming the "Murder Capital of America" tag, demand for her products had only increased. However, it had now become hard, even in downtown's bullet-sprayed streets, to find enough supply to meet demand. As much as Zoe annoyed Mike, he knew she had banked a pile of cash from selling her baubles and had a down payment in place to buy a house. Picking up the spent bullets he found on his daily encounters was the least he could do to keep her sweet in an effort to be the agent for that deal.

Mike, enjoying a rare détente between himself and Zoe, decided to seek his second coffee of the day somewhere else and left the clown lady in peace to continue shopping. While waiting for the elevator he thought about calling Gloria, but knew she wouldn't have her phone with her. Gloria, along with Warren Buffett and your typical American justice via drone-strike-avoiding terrorist, must've been the only people in 2019 without smartphones. She always complained that her bulky Motorola didn't fit into any of the pockets in her running gear. So she left it at home.

The opening of the elevator doors revealed that he would be riding down to street level with Daris Ballic. This was the one person who lived in Missouri Towers that he didn't, albeit briefly, want to be trapped in an elevator with. Daris, as well as being one of those irksome first-generation, overly successful done-well-for-themselves immigrants, was not only his landlord but also his boss at Spitfire Real Estate. As usual, he was dressed in a smart three-piece suit and clutching a Burberry man-bag.

"Mr. Love, we meet again! I presume you will be attending the meeting today?" said Daris in his British-sounding accent.

"I'll be there."

"This is a "do or die day," Mr. Love. Our futures depend on it."

"Got it." Mike replied.

"While I have your undivided attention, your rent check didn't arrive, and you are behind on office fees."

"Working on it," Mike said, after a pregnant pause. "I'm juggling multiple deals."

"Don't let me down!" Daris responded.

They rode the rest of the journey in silence. Daris exited Missouri Towers and darted into an awaiting classic convertible Jaguar. The bossman had long ago stopped walking to the office and liked to arrive with pomp and style.

Mike, after pretending to check his mailbox to give himself some distance between Daris, exited Missouri Towers. With a blast of morning heat he was standing in the belly of a city beast that had seen better days. For a brief period of time in the early 20th century, St. Louis was a global city that could hold itself against London, New York or Paris. The Olympics, the World's Fair, and one of the biggest train stations in America all put St. Louis on the map during this era. 7-Up, the ice cream cone, and the world's first purpose-built gas station were all St. Louis firsts. History, on a relentless march west, took with it much of St. Louis' energy, talent, commercial riches, and half its population.

St. Louis' decline was briefly interrupted in the 1950s and early 1960s with a burst of civic vigor. City leaders wanted to bring back the spirit of that early 20th-century metropolis. The Gateway Arch and other gems of futurist mid-century architecture arose from both the bulldozed city slums and the freshly developed western prairies. Almost as soon as the last piece of the arch was carefully welded into place, the urban rot once again accelerated. By the early 21st century, the city's population had fallen in half from the zenith of its gilded age. St. Louis had gone from being the fourth most-populated city in America, and a hotbed of innovation, to the 21st largest city, with a claim to fame for toasted ravioli, pizza topped with Provel cheese, and out-of-control gun crime.

Mike made the short walk between Missouri Towers and his favorite diner on 5th and Pine. He entered a restaurant that had barely changed in nearly fifty years of business and sat at the counter next to a middle-aged man in a suit. On the jukebox played a cover of Bruce Springsteen's *Thunder Road*. The woman singing was sultry and emo and Mike thought did great injustice to a fine song. Mike picked up the menu and seeing the guy next to him eating pancakes decided to make small talk. The realtor training manual said there are clients to be found everywhere. A guy wearing a suit, far enough from the courthouse to not be on trial, was a solid lead.

"How are the pancakes?" Mike asked.

"Good," the man mumbled.

"Do you live around here?"

"I'm not buying what you're selling!" the man shot back.

Mike wasn't sure what to say. The training manual certainly had advice for these situations, but in the heat of battle, he didn't recall what it was.

"How do you know I'm selling something?" he finally replied.

"I've met you before, and I knew you were about to try talking me into buying a loft." The man then went back to eating his pancakes.

0-2 on conversions today, thought Mike, tallying up his sales attempts.

Mike scanned the menu. His counter-friend then added, after drinking the rest of his coffee: "Last time we met you were telling me about a great deal on a place on Washington and Jefferson. That building had a double homicide last week. I'm moving to Eureka as soon as my lease is up. I'm not sticking around downtown, so don't try to hawk me anything. Let me finish my food in peace."

Now Mike remembered this potential client. He had tried to convert him from a renter to a buyer on the patio of the coffee shop located in City Garden. The condos he was talking about were branded as being, "Not just a loft, it's a lifestyle!" That wasn't the most fitting slogan for a residence that just had a double homicide. Although double killings are common in St. Louis, double murders with single-headed Ottoman battle axes aren't. This particularly gruesome slaying had even made national news. Mike was sure there was a marketing department somewhere ready to offer a needed rebranding package to the building as soon as the blood-spattered walls had been patched and repainted.

Mike's second failed conversion of the day paid his check and left the diner. Not wanting a third failure before 10 a.m., Mike decided to halt the sales pitches for now. He grabbed a copy of the ever-shrinking *St. Louis Tribune* newspaper from the far end of the counter. Taking up the lion's share of the front page were stories about nationally known, locally born celebrities. These stars, like anyone with money and options, had relocated from St. Louis years ago. *Mad Men* star Jon

Hamm had been stung by a jellyfish on a beach in Hawaii, and sports presenter Joe Buck was having a bad hair-plug day.

Mike glanced over this banal non-news and moved on to the next page. Buried at the bottom of page three was a two-paragraph article about a triple murder in North City. This was typical of St. Louis' local media. Expat St. Louisans, who only come to town for Thanksgiving or to turn on the Christmas lights, do trivial nonsense and get front-page treatment. Meanwhile, in the real world a few miles from City Hall, three people are brutally gunned down and barely get a sliver of coverage. Mike opened up his smartphone and added these murders to the log he was keeping: 130 killings so far this year.

A raspy-voiced waitress, who had passively smoked a pack a day for two of her three decades on the job, took Mike's order. He chose the bacon and egg combo and, more importantly, was finally served his second coffee of the day.

Mike continued to flick through the newspaper, there was a grim story about a local child accidentally shooting his father with a gun found under a bed. Now, if death by accidental shooting was an Olympic sport, Missourians would make up the bulk of the American team and every spot on the podium.

The business pages focused heavily on "Infrastructure Week," although it was a little like *Groundhog Day*, for this must have been the third time the Trump administration had touted "Infrastructure Week."

Mike liked the direction Trump was taking the country in, and the president made him feel proud to be an American. Gloria hated Trump so they steered clear of political discussions. They had only been dating for a few months when the presidential campaigns were in full swing. On election night Mike and Gloria had a blowout argument that nearly imploded the relationship. Mike had been telling her for weeks that Trump was going to win. "The people are too smart to let that happen," was Gloria's comeback. However, Mike could see exactly how he was going to win. Hillary Clinton was out of touch with real America. He watched her close out the campaign with celebrity-packed parties in California. It was obvious that she was already looking ahead to the presidency. Trump, on the other hand, was busting his ass off in the square states with a compelling, "What do you have to lose?" message. Gloria didn't realize places like St. Louis had been left behind for decades by national politicians.

Gloria was still relatively new to St. Louis and had yet to grasp the fact that she was living among a populace obsessed with a self-ordained exceptionalism. For St. Louis wasn't just visibly divided by race but also subtly defined by a fascination with status that wasn't always evident to outsiders. Mike had heard that in England you are immediately judged by the way you talk. Within two spoken sentences, the English can tell the region of the country a fellow citizen is from, and whether they're upper, lower, or middle class. In St. Louis, the first question anyone asks a new acquaintance is, "Which high school did you go to?" Your reply, much like accents in England, will delineate your position on the totem pole of local parochial life.

If you graduated from a high school in the city, you are most likely a minority. If you graduated from a public high school in the county, you are most likely white. These demographic quirks are not an accident of geography but a casualty of Civil Rights legislation. When city schools desegregated in the

1960s, many who didn't agree with what was happening packed up and left. Of course not all public schools outside of the city are equal. Schools in the wealthy suburban towns of Clayton, Ladue, and Webster Groves are traditionally going to be better funded than schools in poorer areas like Maplewood or University City. Rich people cluster together in their enclaves and direct taxes toward their offspring.

Missouri was always a reluctant partner in the process of the Federal desegregation of schools. Another legacy of this is that St. Louis has more private schools per population than any other city in America. There are schools for Jews, Lutherans, Catholics, single-sex schools, co-ed schools, and even a few with a wokey curriculum and a carefully curated, somewhat subsidized, hand-picked "diverse" student body. However, absolute power in St. Louis is concentrated in the hands of graduates from a select number of ritzy schools: Priory, Westminster, John Burroughs, SLU High, and Chaminade, to name just a few. These alums socialize at exclusive country clubs, marry each other, and do business deals together. If you don't have a diploma from one of these institutions, you aren't going to become a big shot in St. Louis.

Mike graduated from suburban South County High – deemed a "good school" by parents, mostly on the basis that the majority of the student body is white. The minority kids within its ranks were deemed "the right kind." As good as South County was academically, Mike was always going to be a second-class citizen in a town with a social and merchant aristocracy groomed for greatness by the top private schools. Donald Trump spoke directly to people like Mike, forgotten men of the heartland held back by an unfair, rigged system.

Placed opposite the story about all the shiny new airports, bridges, trains and highways promised by "Infrastructure Week" was a full-page ad promoting New Berlin Real Estate. This upstart brokerage had recently opened a downtown office. New Berlin touted itself as the hi-tech, fresh face of 21st-century real estate. Mike had peeked through the windows and its interior looked like the Death Star command deck. He had heard via the coconut telegraph that they charged discounted commissions of no more than five percent. More shockingly, he had also been told that their roster of agents looked as youthful in person as they did on their corporate headshots. Daris Ballic had seen the opening of this new office as a blatant act of aggression, and today's meeting was a call to arms to repel this threat.

After flicking through the rest of the realtor ads, Mike progressed to the weather report. A further week of high temperatures was predicted. This heatwave had been dragging on and had made life miserable. Looking through the paper today and seeing the crime stats, weather forecast, and small-town nature of what makes front page news, Mike was again reminded of why he needed to leave St. Louis.

Mike began the long sweaty trek to his office. He always loved walking down Washington Ave. This main thoroughfare was once home to a collection of bustling shoe and garment factories. In the early 2000s, many of the decommissioned empty shells were converted into residential lofts. The scale of the buildings and the canyon effect they created was inspirational. Twenty minutes later and half a pound of sweat lighter, Mike had made it to 1202 Washington Ave. – the headquarters of Spitfire Real Estate.

Spitfire's majestic office space was situated on the ground floor of a former dry goods warehouse. Like many of the old industrial buildings, above the commercial space were residential lofts. The office's revolving door entrance was topped with flags of the United States, the city of St. Louis, and rather eclectically, to honor the office's Spitfire plane mascot, the ensign of Britain's Royal Air Force. In the gleaming windows were an abundance of real estate listings and a rogues' gallery of stuck-in-their-prime realtor headshots. The biggest photograph in the middle of this splendid imagery was an authoritative portrait of Spitfire broker-owner Daris Ballic.

Mike pushed open the doors and entered the spacious office. It was heaving with agents. He looked for a free spot to park his overly moist body. His eyes connected with Mindy Playpus, his old co-boss from the Play-Worth team. She waved him over, moving her Gucci handbag from a seat next to her she'd been saving for him. Undoubtedly, Mindy wanted to see how life on the outside of their team had faired for Mike.

Mindy, a former air hostess for TWA, decked out in all her power-suited glory, was a fine-looking woman for her vintage. She was expensively groomed with a Princess Diana-like feathered haircut that neatly complimented her trademark cat-eye glasses. Her look hadn't been updated since the late eighties when she ran the first-class cabin on flights to Europe. In her prime, Mindy had been a rampant bed-hopping sky girl. With little prompting, she alluded to many carnal encounters at the pointy end of the plane. Her favorite kiss-and-tell, always told with a sly wink and nod and never verified as gospel, was about how she may or may not have inducted Phil Collins into the Mile High Club. So the myth goes, after Live Aid in 1985, Phil needed to be in Paris for a video shoot. Collins, famous for flying Concorde, wasn't going to risk taking "Air Chance," as Air France, with its questionable safety record, was then known. He opted for TWA's flagship New York to Paris flight. "We may have been flying subsonic but he was supersonic for me," she quipped when recounting their supposed dalliance. Mindy bragged that they still exchanged Christmas cards. Playpus had used the same seductive techniques to get her realtor business off the ground after TWA went bust for the second and final time.

As Mike sat his perspiring body next to Ms. Playpus, she – as quick as a gunslinger – pulled out a small tube of air freshener. She sprayed it unashamedly around him. "Stuffy in here," she said, as if she was once again airborne, trying to repel the odor that drifted from the great unwashed in economy class towards her side of the curtain.

"How's business?" she smugly added as she put the air freshener back in her bag.

"Plenty of irons in the fire!" Mike replied unconvincingly. Truth was, all his leads had gone dry, aside from a rental listing in Benton Park and the tenant whose credit report he was waiting for on another property.

Julie Titsworth, the other half of the Play-Worth team, sauntered over with a local Kaldi's iced coffee in hand. Not wasting any time to make her point, Julie said to Mike, "Your volume since you went solo is garbage. Do you want to come back with us? We can make space for you. The door is always open for an agent with POTENTIAL!"

Mike had never really liked Julie. As well as being an annoyingly successful real estate agent, she was the premier national spokeswoman for early menopause sufferers. Titsworth, in cringeworthy style, never failed to mention upon meeting new people that she was barren by the age of thirty. She had an entire TED Talk-worthy presentation that brought the women, and some men, in every audience to tears.

Mike imagined that in her younger years, those out-of-order eggs could've been quite the turn-on for your average red-blooded male. Who wouldn't want to have a roll in the sack with a good-looking woman who, as much as you screw her, is never going to hound you for child support? At this point, though, with Julie creaking into her golden years, nobody needed to hear about her ovaries. It wasn't merely the instant expectation that by her age she should be as dry as cracker juice. It was that Julie had about as much maternal warmth as Hillary Clinton. And no matter what status her reproductive parts were in, she had no business ever having children.

Before Mike could rustle up a smart-ass answer to Julie's impromptu offer to rehire him, hotshot realtor Nick Pipeman came bounding over and sat on the other seat next to him. Nick, in his early forties, made up for the lack of hair on the top of his head with a mugshot-worthy bootstrap beard and a counter-culture soul patch that might have been briefly fashionable during the early aughts.

Dressed in a light-blue suit with an eighties vibe, Nick was a fellow resident of Missouri Towers. Like Mike, he listed on his company bio that he "specialized in buying and selling lofts." Those two similarities were where the parallels between them started and ended, for Pipeman was highly successful and month after month made bank. Nick was a master of peddling even the grubbiest and most outdated condos in the most fiscally challenged buildings. On top of his high volume of transactions in both buyer and seller representation was a unique ability to upsell home warranty plans to one hundred percent of clients. For each of these policy pushes he was paid a sweet kickback.

For once Nick didn't have his mutt Rollo with him. This ugly little sausage dog had the amazing knack of finding buyers for Nick. Like Lassie could sniff Timmy stuck in an abandoned well from a mile away, Rollo could smell the scent of someone who was in need of real estate services. The dog would lead Nick to people who were on the hunt for a home. Mike was technically Nick's downtown rival at Spitfire, but in reality and realty they were light years apart in their books of business.

Breaking the uncomfortable silence between Mike and the Play-Worth team principals, Nick interjected a cheeky but observant wisecrack loud enough so all around could hear, "Looks like Puss and Tits are wanting Love again!"

Play-Worth was the official team moniker for the Mindy Playpus and Julie Titsworth-led team, but the nickname they were tagged by all was, "Team Puss & Tits."

Before anything else could be said on the subject, Daris Ballic took to the floor and started his very important meeting.

Apartment #1111   Broad sunlit uplands

Daris Ballic was fifteen years old when he arrived in America, accompanied by his sister Sara and mother Hana. Daris's early teenage years were spent living in refugee camps. Before that, all he could recall was living in a Bosnia decimated by war. His father had died during the early days of the ethnic cleansing and mass genocide that had ravaged his homeland.

They gave you a choice. Do you want to go to Chicago or St. Louis? In films America is New York, Los Angeles, on occasion Chicago – but never St. Louis. America of the asylum seeker doesn't offer up any of the perceived glamorous destinations. Daris's mother picked St. Louis for them; she said it was because of a photograph of the beautiful Arch she'd seen in a magazine. That was her official story but actually, she associated Chicago with organized crime, violence, and Al Capone. After watching Yugoslavia's bloody disintegration, the least she could do for her children was move them somewhere deemed safe. Daris's sister Sara was ten when they landed and her life up until then had been spent living in Red Cross shelters waiting for a ticket to America.

Upon arrival, they "give you" a voucher for short-term housing and $1,500 in cash. In truth, they don't *give you* anything. It's not a handout but a loan to be paid back to the

United States Treasury within six months. Their new life in America started off in a rundown motel in The Ville area of north St. Louis. Hana thought Bosnia's war-torn towns were in better shape than the buildings in this part of the city. The family moved as soon as they could to the Bevo area. With all the new immigrant arrivals, this part of St. Louis had been tagged Little Bosnia. It wasn't in much better physical shape than The Ville, but at least drug dealers weren't popping warning shots in your direction at the playground.

As an immigrant, it's about being accepted by your new country, even if your new country doesn't really accept you. Being dumped in an American high school, and speaking only basic English, was hard for Daris. The local kids didn't want to give you the time of day, and hanging out with other Bosnian immigrants wasn't assimilation. Can a first-generation Muslim ever become a real American? Can a Bosnian become anything in America? These were all questions that Daris agonized over during his first few months at school.

By junior year Daris was fluent in English but still had an accent and wasn't settled in his new country. He didn't feel Bosnian, but neither did he feel he could ever be American. Waving flags, pledging allegiance, going to prom, baseball and apple pie just didn't feel right. But he knew that America was a land of opportunity, where anyone with enough skill, luck and bullshit can find their way to a seat at the top table. He started working on his path to the American Dream.

The state of Missouri prides itself on its many historical firsts. Native son Harry Truman was the first, last and so far only person to wage war with atomic weapons – and this is a badge of honor the Show-Me State has exclusive bragging rights to. So, as it could be said that with the dropping of the "Fat Man" and "Little Boy" a Missourian ended World War II, it could also be said that the Cold War was declared in the state of Missouri. In March 1946, at Westminster College in Fulton, Missouri, former British wartime leader Winston Churchill gave his famed Iron Curtain speech, and with his spirited words officially kicked off the Cold War.

For Daris, a senior year school trip to the National Churchill Museum in Fulton would ultimately be an essential step on his journey of life. Winston Churchill wasn't someone Daris was familiar with before this visit. The teaching of 20th-century history was limited at the refugee camps, deemed too delicate a subject to teach a group of people who were making their own cameo in a dark part of Europe's latest history. And in America, the teaching of history at his own school was insular. The narrative rarely left the continent or strayed from homegrown exceptionalism. So, as Daris studied Churchill's life story on the walls of the museum, he became fascinated by a man who, until then, he knew little about.

Daris learned that Churchill, with his blend of plucky American blood and diluted English aristocratic DNA, had always managed to beat the odds. On his road to greatness, Churchill crashed and burned on numerous occasions but somehow always came back stronger. Journalist, politician, army officer, statesman, wartime leader and historian – roles crammed into a life that bridged the Victorian age and modern era. Churchill was an enigma, both a staunch booster of aggressive imperialism and a furious champion of freedom for all. Although he was charged with running a country, he was himself fiscally inept and permanently in debt. These were just some of the paradoxes of Churchill's life that opened and intrigued Daris's mind.

Upon returning from his excursion to Fulton, Daris went to the library and devoured every book written about and every speech written by, Winston Churchill. By high school graduation Daris had become an expert on Churchill and had found himself a hero who would ultimately inspire his life.

Now out of high school, Daris needed to find a career. He knew wealth in Europe was largely based on an old aristocratic order, with money passed down over generations. The richest people in England owned land and titles that had been given to them 900 years prior. In Germany, Italy, and France, family fortunes made during the Renaissance were still held by their heirs. The dubious methods and violent ways this old money was derived had either been long forgotten or were now only known through a sugarcoated recounting of history.

In America, money and wealth, much like the nation itself, were relatively new by comparison – so recent that you could trace the modern holders of fortunes to the exact act of thievery, con or hustle that their money had originated from. In both the old world and the new, Daris realized the common denominator for the creation and preservation of wealth was the owning of real estate assets. If he was going to make it in America, real estate was going to be his best chance.

With little money, zero connections and an accent deemed strange, Daris had few options available. Making his fortune in real estate was his goal, but like most new immigrants in his situation, he was forced to start at the bottom. Plucked from the classified pages of a newspaper, Daris's first gig was selling timeshares, or "fractional ownership interests" as they had been rebranded, for a Lake of the Ozarks' development. This job was without salary and paid solely on commission.

Peddling a product that common sense states you don't need, and financial sense says you should never buy, isn't an easy task. For Daris, this job was made all the harder due to him being an oddly dressed immigrant with low confidence and a strange way of talking. Daris realized quickly that the people who succeeded in this job had model looks, Yankee orthodontics, uber-confidence, and certainly didn't sound like a New York cabbie – as he did. After three weeks of work, zero sales, no earnings, and failure not an option, Daris urgently needed a new plan.

With three years of American residency under his belt, one thing Daris had learned was that faking it often went hand in hand with making it. Jews changed their last names, Hollywood stars got plastic surgery, people in Missouri who'd never been out of the country had winter tans, eighty-year-olds had blond hair, and every teen had a million-dollar smile. With a tiny budget and a limited amount of time, Daris began to scheme. Being dressed throughout his school years from the aisles of Goodwill stores, he knew that you could get everything you needed, and much that you didn't, from thrift stores. At the nearest Goodwill, he quickly found himself a cheap pinstripe suit, a bowler hat, a walking stick, a British flag and an inflatable bulldog. Armed with his extensive knowledge of Winston Churchill's life, and a butchered accent that to most Missourian vacationers passed as the Queen's English, Daris started pounding the streets of Osage Beach as a timeshare-selling Winston Churchill lookalike.

As anyone knows, the trick to selling timeshares is dragging someone into the office. Then the free buffet, that beautiful model of the new development on display, and a hard sales pitch will work their magic and get the misguided risk-taker to sign his life away. With his wacky outfits, strange props, aristocratic way of talking, and newfound confidence, Daris now had the right blend of showmanship magic to get people through the office door. Within two weeks of his quirky rebranding, Daris had become the highest-earning timeshare salesperson in all of Osage Beach.

An energetic attempt to sell a timeshare to a visiting St. Louis realtor got Daris an introduction to a downtown brokerage. If he could succeed in selling timeshares, he would certainly be able to sell houses, his new boss told him during his interview. Within his first year of work, Daris became one of the top producers at this office. He doubled-down on his Churchill shtick and bought himself a top-of-the-line suit, handmade British shoes, a vintage MG Roadster, and a real-live bulldog. He also took acting lessons and perfected an English accent. With the help of roadside billboards and television advertising, by the age of thirty Daris was one of the best-known realtors in town. He was *"the guy on TV with the bulldog!"* people would say when they saw him on the street.

With his sales commissions rolling in, Daris was in a prime position to buy the downtown brokerage he worked at when the owner retired. He renamed the newly purchased business Spitfire Real Estate, in honor of the testy fighter plane that had defended Great Britain during World War II. The marketing icon he used for the office stationery was a Royal Air Force roundel. For a corporate motto he went with, "Reach for the Sky." This was the title of a classic Battle of Britain film. Daris converted a back room in his downtown office into an operations and planning center he tagged, "The Bunker." Inside this command center, he had a giant table map of the entire St. Louis region. Daris placed miniature house figures representing company listings on this map, and from The Bunker ran his real estate business like he was waging a never-ending war. Daris was married to his work so he never had time to date, let alone find true love. He did, though, take care of his family. He bought his mother a condo in South Florida and paid his sister's way through college.

The Great Recession housing slump lasted longer in St. Louis than in many other parts of the country. But Daris turned this national economic pain into his own personal gain. He bought several bankrupted local independent brokerages and absorbed them into a growing empire. He called these offices – just as Churchill had Australia, New Zealand, Canada, and South Africa – "The Great Dominions." Daris upgraded his car to a Jaguar, his wardrobe to suits tailored in London, and, just like Churchill, began smoking Cuba's finest Romeo y Julieta cigars. His bulldog died, and not having the time to deal with animals Daris had it stuffed and put in a glass case on a shelf in The Bunker. In his free time, Daris watched documentaries about Churchill and read books on World War II. Like a crazed method-acting Daniel Day-Lewis never getting out of character while on set, Daris hid himself away in a Churchillian shell that he rarely ever left.

The business of being a realtor is selling houses and making a living from the commission derived from each transaction. The business of being the owner of a chain of real estate offices is all about collecting desk fees from the agents who work under your brokerage umbrella. As long as your agents are selling enough properties to pay your fees, you're good. Churchill may have believed that the British Empire would last a thousand years, but Daris knew the business side of selling and buying houses was ripe for disruption in a much shorter span of time. Travel, newspapers, shopping, and a host of other legacy industries had been turned on their heads and fundamentally altered by Big Tech. Smartphone apps and brokerages with venture capital funding that could afford perpetual losses were slowly making their way from the coasts toward the heartland. It was only a matter of time before Silicon Valley figured out a way for consumers to avoid forking over six percent of the biggest asset they owned when it came time to sell it. And so it was only a matter of time before owning a brokerage and collecting fees from agents was no longer a viable business.

As Daris knew he was on borrowed time, he was constantly preparing for the new world order to come. He had been consistently pouring his brokerage profits into purchasing physical properties. He had been a strong believer from his timeshare-selling days up until now that owning real estate was the key to continued wealth. Daris's current area of interest had been buying up individual condominiums in Missouri Towers. The master plan was to purchase every unit that hit the market and eventually own the building outright. Once in full control, with the aid of generous city, state, and Federal tax credits, he would remodel and upgrade Missouri Towers. The completed project would be a mixed-used building, containing mostly high-end residential rentals, a limited amount of upscale commercial space, and a small boutique hotel. He would rename the new complex Spitfire Towers. On the roof deck, Daris planned to place a giant replica of a Spitfire plane that at night would be illuminated by World War II-era, anti-aircraft searchlights.

Daris was some way off of gobbling up the entire building but presently owned all of the 11th floor and forty or so other units scattered throughout various levels. Daris himself called home an enormous apartment that had been created by combining several residences into one unit. From this abode, he had wrap-around views of the Gateway Arch, Mississippi River and downtown skyline. He leased out the other units while patiently waiting to buy up anything he didn't already hold a title on. Daris envisioned that the redevelopment of Missouri Towers would spur downtown regeneration and transform the surrounding area from a bleak and dangerous wasteland to an awesome metropolis of positivity.

Life was good for Daris; the agent's fees were rolling in for now and the local real estate brokerage quasi-cartel had managed to avoid disruption so far. However, in recent months Daris had encountered some local difficulties that were beginning to challenge the status quo. A brokerage with unknown ownership called New Berlin Real Estate had emerged from nowhere and entered the market. By the looks of their aggressive operational tactics and the placing of their premises, this was bad news for Daris. In the last month, they had unveiled a flagship office on Locust and 11th St. – a mere 400 yards from his own headquarters. Daris had until this point owned the only brokerage with a physical downtown location. New Berlin had also opened up multiple satellite offices, all within blocks of the other Spitfire locations.

Daris, not wanting to be seen as weak or scared by this, hadn't visited any of the rival premises in person. He had, though, sent spies on reconnaissance missions to gather intelligence. The images, video footage and notes brought back were disturbing. The New Berlin offices, in contrast to Spitfire's ramshackle appearance, were sleek and modern, with the look and feel of Apple stores. They were kitted out with ergonomic designer furniture, slick flat-screen computers and not a piece of paper anywhere to be seen. Spitfire offices in contrast were old-school, with piles of paper, clunky computer monitors and vintage heavy wooden desks.

Images showed that New Berlin office support staff were dressed in hip black uniforms and looked like they could've been runway models if they had chosen the road less traveled. In complete contradiction, Daris's crew made the cast of television's *The Office* look glamorous. Even the coffee served was a microcosm of how this new brokerage compared with his. Spitfire gave clients truck-stop coffee in polystyrene cups. New Berlin was pouring organic Hawaiian brews in china mugs, and from what his intel gatherers reported, the coffee was awesome.

On the business front, New Berlin was offering house sellers a flat commission rate of five percent. A full one point less than every other brokerage in St. Louis. Technically, in order to avoid violating anti-trust laws, commission rates weren't fixed by competing brokerages. However, by some magic, everyone seemed to independently set their rates at six percent.

At times there had been slip-ups, and it had been found out that individual agents or brokerages were going below this "standard rate." At the agent level, this was dealt with by a speedy yanking back into the office and a heavy course of retraining. At the brokerage level things were a little more severe and it could get nasty. The result was always the same and everyone charged six percent once they had been coerced or retrained back to acceptable industry norms.

At its heart, the real estate business is a people business. You can have a slick office serving tasty coffee and offer discounted commission rates, but if you don't have a backbone of good agents it all means nothing. Annoyingly, though, New Berlin Real Estate was at the top of their game, even with this part of the business plan. Like Leonardo DiCaprio browsing the "new faces" pages of the LA Models catalog on the lookout for dates, New Berlin had headhunted nothing but easy-on-the-eyes realtors. Of course, they also happened to be some of the best producers in town. Through the grapevine Daris had heard there were some hefty signing bonuses dished out to lock up this talented-on-all-fronts team. Daris might have had some amazing agents on the books, but in the appearances department most looked nothing like the frozen-in-amber headshots they used for promotion. Hence, he hadn't had anyone swiped by New Berlin Real Estate. Not yet anyway.

A delegation of brokerage principals and owners of national franchises based in the region had made an approach to this newbie agency for a parley. The agenda for this meeting was to discuss "concerns about the New Berlin Real Estate business model." What they really meant to say but couldn't was, "You better stop charging five percent pronto!"

Thomas Trinkenschuh, the broker of record, was quick to fire back chapter-and-verse government legislation citing uncompetitive and illegal business practices. He added in a to-the-point teutonic, straightforward manner that any further dialog on these matters would be immediately reported to Federal trust-busting authorities.

The exact ownership or financial backing of New Berlin had yet to be established by anyone, but whoever it was they certainly hadn't got the memo that the entire industry was propped up by six percent commissions. On all fronts New Berlin Real Estate looked like a force to be reckoned with. If nothing else it was certainly aiming its guns directly at Spitfire.

Daris, at the best of times, treated business like war, but the threat posed by New Berlin Real Estate, if not yet a war, was certainly a gathering storm that needed to be prepared for. Daris Ballic had spent days holed up in The Bunker with his top management team trying to determine the threat level from this upstart agency. Was it a stealth move by Big Tech? And where was the money coming from? Who owned the operation? Why had they opened an office downtown? These were just some of the questions he was unable to answer. As Churchill said, "Everyone has his day, and some days last longer than others." Daris Ballic was of the opinion that his day was far from over and he was ready to fight.

"Attention, attention, everyone!" said Daris, who had earlier ditched his civilian attire and dressed for battle. He now donned a striking khaki siren suit with matching beret.

He looked at the crowd in front of him. It was a massive turnout of agents similar to the mandatory diversity training day. The only negative about the crowd was a few too many people in the audience sucking down on their 52oz Quik Trip cups. Nothing screamed Midwest morning meeting more than the sound of soda being slurped through ice.

Daris's power five top agents were all in attendance. Sat in the front row from the Central West End office was big-hitter Alexi Coklande. A prime beauty in her early thirties, Alexi was dressed conservatively in a dark-blue power suit with freshly tresseled hair, snooty mascara, and a French manicure not suited for hard work – the kind of long, unpractical nails in a less-muted hue that any post office counter clerk would be proud of. On Alexi's finger sat a rock so big it alerted anyone with lusty intentions that bedroom ownership had been snatched via a hefty dowry. With sharp elbows and endless mailbox flyer carpet-bombing, Alexi had stormed her way into being the top listing agent for the grand turn-of-the-century Central West End area houses. Streets like Portland Pl. and Washington Terrace were her domain. She closed just under $20 million in sales last year and was a much-appreciated member of the team.

To her left from the Clifton Heights office was Clint Cummings, a strange beady-eyed man, short in stature, who'd claimed he was 58 for what seemed like the last decade. He was a top producer who never failed to bring in $15 million in annual sales. This blue-blooded Georgian, who by birthright should never have had to work, was disinherited by his family for his homosexuality. Clint hated the idea of selling things but once bounced from the family trust fund was in need of cash to maintain his decadent lifestyle. In his illustrious career before selling real estate, he had sold computers, cars, and for a short time in the eighties, tanning beds.

Clint, never without his Spitfire Real Estate lapel badge and always impeccably groomed, would tell anyone who cared that there was a "real estate circle of life." Barking in a raspy Southern drawl, he would say: "People like to fuck, they then get engaged to that special partner, get married and many in time reproduce. Some will divorce and some of those divorcees will then remarry, and of course ultimately everyone dies. In every one of these circle-of-life events there's a real estate transaction to be made."

Most agents would be happy to be the guy to clinch the deal at each of these great passages in life. However, what Clint would never tell anyone is that he had worked out a multiplier. Cummings was always quick on the draw and with great diligence would find the client "a very special home." However, on purpose he never managed to find the buyer the true, *perfect home.* The secret sauce was, about two years after a transaction was made, he would sweet talk these former clients into selling the great house they lived in and buy something else that was "more suitable for their needs." During every transaction he managed to make the buyers and sellers feel like they had made bank on their last property, and how lucky they are now to find an even more "amazing home than the last." The trick to his continued success was to make the buyers and sellers feel like winners. Clint, the king of stats, had calculated that his rinse-and-repeat system, although somewhat ethically questionable, had created fifty percent more transactions over the span of his career.

Positioned with a strategic amount of space next to Clint in all her pearl necklace and pant-suit glory was buyer specialist Roxie Johnson. Daris knew that former air hostesses, with their ability to work under pressure and a mastery of happy face masquerading before the most pesky of clients, in the most turbulent of situations, made excellent realtors. Two categories of discharged trolly dollies could pull off a successful career switcheroo from aviation's friendly skies to the terra firma of peddling homes.

In one group were those former first-class cabin crew, many of whom were pink-slipped when St. Louis lost its hub status and legacy international flights. These impeccably dressed beauties were like fine wine and only got better with age. They were well-traveled, up-to-date with current affairs, and had honed that skill of gracefully engaging in any conversation with people from all walks of life. This crème de la crème from up front of the plane are master of getting listings in every price range and one way or another getting these homes sold. The backbone of the snobby brokerages of West County consisted of a strong cohort of these former dames-of-the-air.

In the second group, mainly from the back of the plane at budget airlines, are the dressed-for-comfort, roll your-sleeves-up, logistically orientated, six flights a day, demobilized cabin crew, quick to toss you a packet of peanuts, hand you a sick bag and yell across the aircraft that you cannot go to the bathroom barefoot. They know more about Justin Bieber than Jakarta and would most likely think Concorde is that quaint suburb in South County than the only possible way to have lunch in both London and New York on the same day. Roxie Johnson was solidly in this category. The poor girl had her wings clipped when she became too wide to glide down the aisle of a 737 Max. Roxie might teeter on heels and never be without a Big Gulp diet soda in her hand, but she was one of Spitfire's top producers and her desk a hub of transactions.

Sitting a row behind in Roxie's broad shadow was rising Spitfire star Mandy Tuggnutt. With softly curled television hair, the face of an angel and the body of an expensive escort,

Mandy held claim to many of the assets needed to succeed in this industry. For the occasion of this staff meeting, Mandy had slipped into a little black dress that hugged her body tighter than Joe Biden at a ten-grand-a-seat fundraiser.

Aside from Mandy's stunning looks, another dimension to her deal-making prowess was her marriage to the third-generation owner of a string of appliance stores. Daris was amazed at how connections to the merchant aristocracy in St. Louis yielded so much business. The broker could only imagine what it would be like to get one of the Busch brewing family, or someone from the Schnucks supermarket clan, licensed. The volume of business that would follow them through the door would be sensational. Mandy called the downtown headquarters of Spitfire Real Estate home.

The bedrock and lead agent at Spitfire was Brad "Puffman" Thrust. In his late forties, Brad was built like a fire hydrant with a square chin, a subtle hint of cleft and the full-throated voice of an overly energetic NFL playcaller. His mop of badly dyed hair illustrated a not-so-graceful defiance of aging that was common among real estate agents' headshots.

Brad was affectionately nicknamed "Puffman" for his legendary wordsmithing of listings blurb. His creative, flowery writing skills could spice up the appeal of even the crappiest of properties. This was a well-needed trait as Missouri had a copious number of ugly houses that by merit alone should be unsellable. Price point was not seemingly a factor in these brutal inventory offerings. Options ranged from gaudy custom-built millionaire McMansions in well-heeled Ladue to fugly-ass tract homes in blue-collar Maplewood. It was as if something in the DNA of the state designed and constructed the most aesthetically unpleasing housing stock in all of America. With creative "puffing" and a touch of photographic magic, Brad was able to make the ugly houses of St. Louis look beautiful and sound amazing.

Puffman had a gushing pipeline of listings that never ceased to flow. With two decades of experience in the business, Brad had a brag book that was believed to be less than six degrees of separation from every metro area house worth over four-hundred grand. Brad was part drill instructor, part team leader, and part office talisman. He was the consummate salesperson and the kind of living legend that rookie real estate agents aspired to be.

Daris lowered the lights in the room and fired up the PowerPoint projector. Beamed onto the wall was a map of the St. Louis region with the various Spitfire offices highlighted by icons depicting the brokerage's airplane mascot.

"Agents standing before me, I have nothing to offer but blood, toil, tears and sweat," said Daris, starting his speech with office manager Pam Hardings by his side. He then pushed a button on his wireless clicker. On the projector map popped up small black iron eagle icons representing the recently opened New Berlin Real Estate offices. They were menacingly all next to the Spitfire icons.

"Competition drives our business to do great things. I'm all for a healthy and level playing field, but we have a new upstart in town with unknown backing and uncertain ambitions. AND they are not playing by THE RULES!" said Daris in an accent sounding heavily mid-Atlantic with a dash of Balkan.

Daris pushed his clicker and a huge flashing "5% commission" graphic filled the screen.

There were gasps and groans throughout the room. "They can't do that!" shrilled Roxie Johnson at the top of her voice.

"Five percent today, four percent next, it's a slippery slope!" said Brad "Puffman" Thrust.

"Five percent isn't going to take care of my Mercedes E-Class payments," said Alexi Coklande, who cherished her flashy, leased realtor ride more than anything else.

In a spontaneous outburst, all the agents in the room started chanting, "Six percent, six percent, six percent...!" until office manager Pam Hardings called the room to order.

"Our industry has grown and flourished over the decades, thanks to every brokerage peacefully co-existing and living in harmony with each other. And within our rules," said Daris, as he started off a long presentation about the history of the real estate business and how it found its natural equilibrium with its commission rate structure. There was a hefty amount of time devoted to detailing the wonderful and sometimes thankless service that realtors are expected to give their clients, and why they are not only worthy of charging six-percent commissions but really should charge more. It was during this point of the presentation there were a few whispers in the room about the horizontal refreshments Mindy Playpus had delivered to clients over the years as part of her full-service, six percent package.

Daris reiterated this discount rate promotion could be a temporary marketing splash. However, he wasn't actually sure as no local brokerage owner had been able to find out who ran or owned New Berlin. Daris warned there was also a strong chance this brokerage had intentionally gone renegade and was operating outside of the system. There was a genuine concern they might also be the vanguard of a Big Tech push into the St. Louis market. Whatever and whoever was behind this shadowy operation, it was causing headaches for every brokerage in town and every agent sitting at this meeting.

"The scenario we find ourselves in is a "phoney war!" said Daris, trying to liken New Berlin's provocative actions to those undertaken by Hitler before he went to war with Great Britain. Daris said he could still see optimism and was himself trying to get other brokerages to form a coalition of the willing to get New Berlin to play by the rules. Charging less than six percent, though, wouldn't be acceptable. At this point no shots had been fired but he wanted to tell the entire Spitfire team that he had their backs, and that management was ready for everything and anything. Daris also firmly suggested to all his agents that they should resist any solicitations from New Berlin. He warned that, with the money they were spending on advertising, office space and recruitment, they could be out of business by Christmas.

Daris finished off the hour-long speech with true Churchillian fighting words. "We shall go on to the end, we shall fight them in the city, we shall fight them in the county, we shall fight them on the Hill, in Lafayette Square, Maplewood, Kirkwood and Central West End, and all other areas of St. Louis, and we will fight them in the streets, we will fight with growing confidence, we shall never surrender. This will be our finest hour!" The angrier Daris's speech became the more authentically English and less Balkan he sounded.

Daris gave a V sign with his fingers and shouted, "Victory at all costs!" He then descended into The Bunker, flanked by Brad "Puffman" Thrust and Pam Hardings.

Daris thought his speech had hit just the right balance to get his twin messages across. He wanted to fire up his agents so they would fight for their commission rates like their lives depended on it. He also wanted to infuse them with a little fear so they wouldn't be tempted to jump ship to this shiny new brokerage with all its tempting offerings.

"What do you make of that?" Nick Pipeman whispered to Mike at the back of the room once Daris was out of earshot.

"Sounds batshit crazy to me!" Mike replied.

"I don't know what to make of this. Not sure what's more bizarre, New Berlin Real Estate's business model or our fearless leader dressed like he is off to war. Anyway, can you do me a favor? I need to do a client preview on a house in Soulard tomorrow. Can you come and take a peek with me? It looks way overpriced, I want your opinion," Nick asked.

Mike jumped at the chance to tag along with Nick and was flattered by the request for his professional expertise. "No problem," he replied.

"I've gotta go. I have a Realtor Continued Education class on gender-inclusive pronouns and I'm running late. Can you do me another favor and book tomorrow's showing?"

"Are you having a gender identity crisis?" Mike asked.

"She/him, they/them, I have no idea what it's all about, gotta stay relevant. Everyone on the coasts uses a pronoun;

that means sometime in the next twenty years Missouri will catch up and we'll all be using them too!" Nick pipped back.

"OK, what's the address?" Mike shouted as Nick was by now halfway across the office.

"916 Ann St.," he yelled back.

Mike was busy booking the showing on his phone when he felt breathing down his neck. He looked up and it was Mindy Playpus.

"Phil Collins is in town next week performing at the Enterprise Center. Do you want to come with me? I have great seats and we could talk about you rejoining the team," she said, standing a little too close for comfort.

Phil fucking Collins ran through Mike's mind. Mike recalled from a high school history class there were quite a number of tragedies during the eighties: AIDS, the hole in the ozone layer, famine in Africa, and that Soviet nuclear meltdown, to name a few. But to Mike, the fact that a prick like Phil Collins was the bestselling artist of the decade was the biggest tragedy of them all. The notion of sitting front row with Mindy Playpus watching Phil Collins belt out *Sussudio* to a bunch of women sporting a dated Jill Collins hair bob (Phil's wife from a few previous marriages and mother of actress Lily Collins) wasn't at all appealing.

"I hate Phil Collins and I'm not coming back to the team!" Mike shouted back.

He had possibly made a big mistake with such haste, as a lot of agents making no money would love to be part of a high-flying group. It was, however, the thought of spending two hours of his life listening to the music of Phil Collins that had made him so impulsive.

*   *   *

Mike left the office and walked back towards Missouri Towers in what was now 102-degree heat with just enough humidity not to rain. He found one 9mm bullet casing on the route and collected it for Zoe. Unfortunately, though, the chorus of *Sussudio* was now stuck in his head.

As Mike arrived at the front of Missouri Towers, he saw a woman in her mid-twenties standing in the searing heat with two suitcases. In one hand she held a crumpled piece of paper, with the other she was unsuccessfully punching the entry keypad trying to access the building.

"Are you looking for someone?" Mike asked.

"Marty in #1311. He gave me the building code and has left a key under his doormat," she replied in an unfiltered hillbilly accent. Mike didn't place this dialect as being anywhere from Missourah, as national politicians call the more rural parts of Missouri when trying to win their votes.

Mike took a better look at her. She was a pale woman with pinkish dyed hair. Her small somewhat saggy boobs were squeezed into a white tube top that fit badly enough to reveal a glimpse of a pink bra. The rest of her thin frame was dressed in a short denim skirt and her small feet were slipped into a beaten-up pair of laceless, blue canvas sneakers. Mike, from this closer inspection, knew she'd lived a tough, hard life.

"I'm not supposed to let non-residents in, but I know who you are here to see. So come in with me," Mike said, as he opened up the building door and accompanied the woman to the elevator.

There was no Marty on the 13th floor, but he knew exactly who she was meeting. Sam Robinson was his name; he was a shabby-looking fortyish guy who worked at an Illinois packaging factory. Sam had a hooker habit that Charlie Sheen would've been proud of, albeit on a more frugal budget. Mike had ridden the elevator with several of his lady friends and knew that Marty was the fake name he gave when booking.

However, the woman he was now standing in the elevator with was nothing like Sam's standard faire. Mike had established via his brief chats that these regular ladies could be put into two distinct categories. There was a college-aged girl whom he believed Sam was a sugar daddy to. Mike had learned that the smart, super-attractive, overly-obliging sugar babies were making over $20,000 a month. Sam's factory salary evidently wasn't landing him those top-notch pickings. The one on his payroll was an unhealthy-looking lady dressed in third-tier university-branded clothes. Mike knew part of the deal with sugar babies is that they become your friends. Mike could only imagine the deep pillow talk occurring between a middle-aged, blue-collar guy like Sam and a twenty-something fifth-year senior forever a few credits away from graduation.

The second type of escort, and from Mike's surveying more frequent visitors, was a selection of hardcore, straight-down-to-business working girls. Often they were dropped off by mean-looking pimps and before getting down to the nitty-gritty stopped to have a last-minute cigarette at the Missouri Towers front door. These women dressed lightly for easy disrobing and traveled sparsely with only small bags. Mike, who had zero experience with whoring but was armed with a fertile imagination, decided the bags held cigarettes, rubbers, lube, mints, perfume, and possibly but not definitely extra panties. Mike could tell that aside from deep conversation and kissing, every twisted fantasy fulfillment and dirty kinky request was available from these girls, at a price.

"How do you know Marty?" Mike asked.

"Friends from work," she said, giving the same standard reply all the women gave.

"You're not from around here," Mike said, looking down at her luggage before adding, "Most of Marty's friends travel more lightly."

"You ask a lot of questions stranger," she replied.

They rode in silence until they got to Mike's floor. Seeing he was exiting, the woman added, "I'm in town from Kentucky."

"Welcome to Misery," Mike threw out, as he left the elevator.

Very odd! Mike thought as he headed into his apartment for his third cup of coffee and second shower of the day. He was hoping that the combination of the two would eradicate the strains of *Sussudio* that were stuck on a loop inside his head. Although now he was wondering exactly what the story was with the visitor to the 13th floor. The only thing he did know was that this wasn't Sam's usual type of friend, and so far this day had been bizarre.

Apartment #1211   Are the voices in your head calling Gloria?

In the Pantheon of Midwestern states, Kansas is viewed as the most quintessentially American of them all. Think of Kansas and it conjures up visions of small tidy towns, endless wheat fields, wholesome cheerleaders, uncorrupted high school sports, patriotic state fairs, nuclear families, and of course pure and innocent Dorothy with her ruby slippers. In contrast in that same Pantheon of states, Missouri would be tagged the ugly redheaded stepsister, complete with chipped meth teeth and bad tattoos. Say Missouri to a national audience and they'll have visions of rustbelt towns, bad weather, gun violence, obesity, prom queens that long ago ditched their purity rings and hicks like Huckleberry Finn. Mike Love viewed Gloria McKendrick as the embodiment of all that's good about Kansas. With his questionable but sturdy Missouri stock and her exquisite Kansan DNA, they made a fine couple.

The early morning light reflecting off the Arch glowed on the wall just above Gloria's head like a halo. Mike thought she was at her most beautiful when she slept. The sun rises fast in August and the angel effect moved on as quickly as it came. Mike didn't want to wake her up so he rose slowly and quietly, put his clothes on, and snuck out of her bedroom. As he closed the door, the vision of her sleeping on the bed made him feel proud and content. He tiptoed to the kitchen area and switched on the coffee machine. A ping alerted Mike to an incoming email. Finally, it was the credit report for Gary Smith that he'd been waiting for.

"Shit!" he shouted out.

Gary had a 590 credit score and a general rating of C. As well as some of the student loans that Mike knew about, Gary had unpaid medical bills and numerous maxed-out credit cards. He had also failed to truthfully disclose the full amount of accumulated college debt. Mike thought the few thousand he had shelled out for his time at Community College was steep. But Gary's degree in Celtic Mythology from an under-endowed chic-named Vermont liberal arts school had cost him over a hundred-thousand dollars. All that outlay resulted in Gary landing a measly thirty-eight thousand dollar a year job at an art museum with a billion-dollar endowment.

Mike had shown eight apartments to Mr. Smith, and when he finally rolled up to showings, at least ten minutes late each time, he was never without an iced drink in one hand and a slice of avocado toast in the other. Instant gratification and easy access to credit was the plight of a generation whose only hope and eternal dream was a Bernie Sanders-backed bailout. Asim Ur, the hard-nosed Tunisian landlord with a portfolio of properties bought out of foreclosure for cents on the dollar, wasn't going to take a chance on this bad credit knucklehead. He instantly rejected Gary's apartment application.

Mike texted the unfortunate news to Gary and sent him a link to the financial self-help blog *Our Great Life*, hosted by Penny and Dave Rosebush. These two cheery millennials with gleaming teeth had many helpful ways to assist in budgeting. They themselves had retired at twenty-eight and were part of the FIRE quit your job movement. Mike had consumed much of their informative content and finally figured out exactly how Penny and Dave were able to catch their dreams. They sold all their possessions, including Dave's prized Pokemon card collection, downsized from a Philly metro apartment to a trailer in rural New Mexico, cut cable, shopped only at thrift stores, bought discounted groceries near their expiration date, qualified for free healthcare, got all their books from the library, and with a fundamentalist zeal collected credit card points, relied on rainwater for bathing and vowed never to adopt pets or have kids.

Mike, with a little skepticism, had seen through the smoke and mirrors and worked out that the secret wasn't the obvious, what they didn't spend money on, but the very obvious, that they spent eighteen hours a day producing and pimping out monetized social media content. This was an additional revenue stream on top of a $478,000 stock account they had inherited from a great-aunt. "Never touch the principal, live off the dividends!" Dave would say, in a "don't break the golden rule" way, as he showed followers the monthly income derived from his portfolio. So, technically, they were self-made, carefree and retired as advertised. In reality, they now worked harder and for longer hours with their side hustles than they did when they both "worked for the man" at their old city jobs. The Rosebush team also had a nice slice of luck from that timely inheritance.

Now Mike could see how Penny and Dave lived well with their frugal lives, and respected the snake oil salesman tricks they used for promotion. But there was always one piece of the puzzle that he didn't understand: how did Dave end up with Penny? Dave was a bald man with dated frat-boy facial hair and a horrifying taste in normcore clothes. He tossed out a not-so-funny selection of catchphrases and had a bizarre eye tick. Penny, on the other hand, was drop-dead gorgeous, with model looks, and in every sponsored barely-there bikini try-on video posted to their site looked amazing. You only had to look at the click counts to see that Penny shaking her ass in a two-piece was getting more traction than Dave doing a step-by-step on how to change your own car oil. Dave was well out of Penny's league. So, unless Dave had an anaconda tucked into his dad jeans, Mike didn't see how he had snagged this woman. Mike was waiting for Dave to either write a book on how to date unicorn girls that shouldn't give you the time of day, or be arrested for kidnapping Penny and holding her captive all these years.

Gary texted back and apologetically said he had forgotten about the medical bills and didn't realize his credit was so bad. He appreciated the work Mike had done, and when he was finally in a position to move out of his mother's basement he would certainly call him. That was fifty percent of Mike's business out the window. He did still have the rental listing in Benton Park, but that was it.

"Morning," said Zoe, Gloria's roommate, as she came out of her bedroom door dressed in a robe.

"Did I wake you?" he asked apologetically.

"Not at all! I'm used to the nightly lullaby of gunshots, screeching cars racing, and the couple in #1212 making monkey love noises through the thin walls. I can sleep through just about anything these days. I'm up to ask you about something else... actually someone else."

"Fire away," Mike shot back with anticipation.

"Nick," she said without adding anything.

"Nick Pipeman?"

"Yeah, that Nick. I've bumped into him a few times in the elevators over the last couple of weeks. He's a charmer. Do you know if he's seeing anyone?" she asked.

"He's not, and never is for more than one date, but you should stay well away from him."

"Why's that?"

"He's strange."

"I have never met a real estate agent who isn't bizarro in one way or another. Gloria told me that he's the top realtor in all of downtown. How strange can he be?"

"That's true, he certainly can sell a property, but trust me he's a weirdo," Mike replied.

"In what way exactly is he weird?" she asked.

Mike pretended not to hear her and started looking at the latest housing inventory on his phone.

"Don't worry, I'll still use you to buy a home. All I'm asking is for you to see if there's any interest. There's something about him I like."

"I'll ask."

Mike didn't want to divulge to Zoe what made Nick such a freak to be on a date with. Zoe would immediately tell Gloria and he didn't need her to find out about Nick's eccentricities. Mike made his excuses to Zoe, took his coffee to go, and did the short walk of shame down the stairwell to the 10th floor.

Gloria McKendrick woke up in her oversized bed alone. She stood in her pajama shorts and pink cami top and gazed out of her bedroom window. The Mississippi River water level was high and the sky above the Arch looked as clear as a dream.

The two most common ways that people end up living in St. Louis are: first you are born there and never leave. Or second, you marry someone from St. Louis. Your spouse then takes you away from whatever wonderful place in the world you are residing in and drags you back. Off go all those bright young things from St. Louis, venturing to places like New York, Chicago and Seattle. All with hopes, dreams and aspirations, only to end up exactly where they started. The reason given for returning to St. Louis is always from the same shortlist: to be closer to family, availability of good schools, and an affordable cost of living. As Gloria stared out of the window she wondered if the real reason people obediently returned was that there was a super magnet buried deep under the Arch, and its pull brought anyone back who had gone too far, been gone for too long.

To be fair, it was the ladies who dragged the husbands home, and not the other way around. These St. Louisan women should come attached with a caution label when they are offering themselves up into the wife pool in whatever new city they have ventured into. The warning would state in big red letters: "Beware! Marry me and in short shrift I will take you back with me to St. Louis, Missouri!" In much smaller and harder-to-read print underneath the disclaimer would continue: "Your future home of St. Louis ranks first in the nation for gun violence, second for the percentage of habitants with an STD, and most of the city is racially segregated – even the hair products at your local pharmacy!"

There is, of course, one detail that the future wife won't tell you as she is selling you the dream of a life in Missouri's largest city – that because you didn't go to high school in St. Louis, you'll always be treated as an outsider. And even more annoying, you'll forever be bumping into, and having to make nice with, all her ex-boyfriends, whom you'll encounter on a daily basis in your new hometown.

Now, how Gloria McKendrick ended up in St. Louis was a whole different tale. She wasn't born in St. Louis, she had no family in St. Louis, and although she often wished it had been the case, no one had romanced her and brought her home to live with them here.

Gloria was born in Kansas and raised on a farm in the Great Plains. Her town had one stop light, a Walmart, and not much else. Life for her was very flat and extremely boring. Curiously, though, there was a Minuteman nuclear ICBM silo at the end of the farm that technically had the ability to showcase a one-off rocket show of epic, end-of-days proportions – although even this had been mothballed by the time she was a teenager. So, aside from a brief time having front row seats to a nuclear strike, rural Kansas didn't offer Gloria much in the way of excitement. This is why she always sympathized with Clark

Kent for flying away from the farm and taking up residence in Metropolis to avoid his own rural Kansan life.

By the aughts, and in contrast to previous eras, farming was less about digging and plowing and more about science, technology and possessing business skills. Gloria was a smart cookie, excelled at high school, and was destined for college. Although she would've liked to have done a *Felicity* and run off to NYU to study art, the expectation from her family was that she would do something that would help manage the farm. Instead of following her dreams to Manhattan, New York City, Gloria followed her head to Manhattan, Kansas and enrolled at the State College of Agriculture.

Gloria's head was always in a dream. A romantic dream to be precise. She mentally escaped her mundane life on the farm by watching Hollywood movies. The ones she obsessed over most were the teen comedies from the eighties directed by John Hughes. These provided a perfect distraction for a girl stuck in rural middle America. However, the result was that Gloria had expectations that she herself would be swooped off her feet by a wealthy man with thick hair, a fast car and a repertoire of romantic gestures. Unfortunately, life isn't a movie and she found herself having to do most of the amorous chasing. One day, as part of the pursuit of a dreamy boy from Topeka, Gloria joined her college's Flying Circus Club. She didn't get far with that particular man but she did find in high-wire acrobatics a pursuit that she not only excelled at but also enjoyed.

Gloria was a natural at walking the tightrope and in no time had a part-time job at a regional circus. A scout from Ringling Brothers watched her perform at one of these weekend gigs.

He was impressed by her showbiz talents and all-American looks. He knew that with a little in-house nurturing she could be a star. For Gloria, the thought of graduating college and going back to the farm filled her with dread. Best-case scenario was being married off to a neighbor's son that was set to inherit a swathe of prime sunflower-growing land. She knew she would be fine and was more than capable of running a farm, but this wasn't the life she wanted. So, just a semester short of graduating, Gloria fled her course in agricultural technology management and took a full-time seat on the Ringling Brothers train. The circus was heading west and she had a tight knot in her stomach until reaching the Rockies, and with it the reassurance that she wasn't in Kansas anymore.

Safely across state lines, Gloria broke the news to her family. They flipped upon learning that their little girl had run away and joined the circus. They did agree to keep open lines of communication with the hope that eventually their prodigal daughter would return. Gloria thought they had actually taken this shocking news quite well.

Life in the circus was tough but exhilarating. Gloria was well-schooled by the head of acrobatics and quickly perfected her craft. The money she made wasn't excessive but living with the circus was an economical way of life. By the conclusion of her first season, she had $10,000 sitting in her checking account.

Gloria had fiery romances with co-workers but never met anyone she wanted to take home to meet her family. Of course, part of the problem was that she was holding out for a Blane McDonough, Jake Ryan, or some other idealistic heartthrob that's only ever found in 80s movies. One by one her circus friends got married and started families. By the age of twenty-six, Gloria was a veteran trapeze artist and looking around at her peers she was starting to feel old, lonely and in need of a soulmate.

One spring day, she was sitting alone having lunch in The Pie Car, as the Ringling Brothers dining carriage is called. The circus train was traversing the Canadian prairie a few hundred clicks from Calgary when in walked a new cast member she hadn't met. Lion tamers, in Gloria's experience, were overly cocky, overly paid, and very much oversexed players of the circus ecosystem. They were well-known for chasing local women at each performance stop. From the number of ladies Gloria saw exiting the lion tamers' sleeping car, dating profiles that included pictures of men with wild beasts and whips were in high demand. For this reason, and to avoid betrayal and heartbreak, Gloria gave the lion tamers a wide berth.

This new lion tamer, who ever so politely introduced himself to Gloria, was from a different breed indeed. Advik Devesh was a charming and good-looking man who had recently joined the cast from an Indian troupe. Advik had arrived with his own lions, something he explained assisted the visa process. His English was perfect, with a rich transatlantic accent that sounded more like a 1940s movie star than the owner of the Kwik-E-Mart in *The Simpsons*. The two of them quickly hit it off and within days were immersed in a hot and heavy romance.

Over the next few months, Gloria felt like she was living a dream and would pinch herself daily. Their relationship had the best elements of workplace dating with the added bonus of the scenic backdrop to a never-ending holiday romance. At each stop the circus made, Gloria and Advik would run off hand-in-hand to explore the new city. Holding hands at the top of the Empire State Building in New York, swimming on the beaches of California, and taking in the museums of Washington, DC were a fraction of the adventures they had on their transcontinental travels. For a man from a third-world country, Gloria was amazed at how culturally enlightened and sophisticated Advik was. She had never before been taken on a date to the ballet, nor to an opera. Her time with Advik flew by too fast and she wished this circus season would never end.

As the train made its way to its winter home in Sarasota, Gloria knew that Advik was, *Her One.* Gloria, as anyone would during the waning days of a passionate vacation liaison, frantically tried to work through the solutions they could act upon to stay together. Advik was from a poor country and had a short-term visa that was non-renewable. He would soon return to India and wouldn't be allowed back to the United States. The only workarounds were: she could go with him to India, or they could get married so he could stay in the country. But marriage would potentially cause Gloria another set of issues. Her family had about as much diversity in it as the first three seasons of the television show *Friends*. Taking a brown boy home wouldn't be acceptable to them. They had so far grudgingly gone along with her life choices, but she knew Advik would be the final straw. Gloria was too much in love. No matter what she had to do, even if it meant living in India, or being disowned by her family, she was going to stay with Advik at all cost.

The Ringling Brothers season was over and Advik had put his lions on a ship bound for India. He was due to fly out from Miami in two days. Gloria and Advik would drive across

Florida and spend the rest of their time together holed up in South Beach. En route, they pulled over at Alligator Alley's scenic rest stop. As the two of them looked into the swamp for gators, Gloria started to talk about the future. She confessed to Advik that she didn't want their relationship to end. She said she would happily go back to India with him and suggested they could even get married so he could remain with her in America.

"You are very sweet. I love you dearly!" replied Advik, as he held Gloria's hand tightly.

They chose the News Cafe for their dinner destination on that final night. This South Beach restaurant was famous for being Gianni Versace's favorite eatery and the last place he visited before he was murdered. December in Miami is wonderful and a warm wind was blowing in from The Bahamas. Gloria in this moment loved Advik more than she could have imagined.

They were halfway through their main course when his phone rang. He got up and waved to a couple standing over at the hostess's desk. Upon catching sight of him they walked over.

"My son, it's great to see you," said a well-dressed Indian woman.

"Advik, you are looking good. And who is this nice lady you are having dinner with?" asked a suave man with an almost British accent that Gloria realized was Advik's father.

"Mom, Dad this is my friend Gloria," said Advik, introducing her to his parents.

"Good friend!" Gloria replied. Her head began to spin.

"Advik is such a shy boy. He never told us he had made American friends," said his mother.

It quickly became clear that Advik, who hadn't mentioned to Gloria that she would be meeting his parents, had also never talked about her to them. Over dinner, Gloria came to realize that Advik wasn't quite who he had told her he was. The circus he worked for in India was owned by his family. Working as a lion tamer for him was a bit like Jeff Bezos having his kid placed at an Amazon fulfillment center shipping boxes for summer break. Advik's family was from an incredibly wealthy dynasty that traced its roots back to serving the Mughal Emperor. Through thuggery, diplomacy and the greasing of palms, their fortune had survived the British Raj and India's post-Independence flirtation with socialism. She knew Advik's family had a house in Bombay (he always called it that instead of Mumbai), but she didn't realize they also owned a mountain retreat in Shimla, a beach house in Goa, and a dozen condos in Dubai. As the evening came to a close, the one thing Gloria realized was that Advik had not once this evening mentioned their relationship to his parents. She was confused, almost speechless, and wanted to cry.

After dinner, Gloria and Advik walked the beach together.

"You never told your family about me," she said with tears in her eyes.

"You are correct, my sweet Gloria."

"Why not? I was willing to do anything for us. Move to India, lose my family. Why did you lead me on for the last nine months?"

"For a moment I thought it might just work. But it couldn't." Advik said with an air of finality.

"So this is it! You're dumping me?"

"Gloria, our time together has been magical and I will never forget you, but I have commitments. We are a powerful family in India and it's just not possible for me to marry a white American." With that, he kissed Gloria on the cheek and left her in tears on the beach.

That didn't happen to Molly Ringwald in any movie! Was the first thought that came into Gloria's mind as she sat alone crying.

Advik was never planning a future with Gloria. For him, their relationship was nothing but one glorious, elongated holiday romance. It also turned out that Advik's family were more racist and less tolerant than her own.

Gloria, not ever wanting to see a lion or a lion tamer again, told Ringling Brothers that she wouldn't be back next season. She wasn't quite ready to give up on life and go back to the farm, so she looked for a job. City Museum in St. Louis, with its self-contained circus operation, was a place she had previously heard of. Gloria applied for a position as an acrobatics and trapeze instructor at its in-house performance school. With her strong resume and Ringling Brothers references, she was hired. The salary wasn't great but she thought life off the road might help her mentally. Not knowing anyone in this new town, she found herself a roommate and decided to make this strange city her new home.

*   *   *

Missourians will watch a thunderstorm as if they're watching their favorite television show. Add the screech of a tornado warning and you've got all the makings of a primetime event. Drive through any city street when the apocalyptical siren and the barely audible message is advising taking immediate shelter, and what you'll see is that this has the opposite effect, for everyone has instinctively but unnaturally gone to their front porch or onto the street to see what Godly form of destruction is on the way. It's as if the sirens were really saying that now is a great time to make new friends, the perfect moment to acquaint yourself with a neighbor you've never spoken to before. Maybe the impetus was the inclement weather presenting a finite window of talk time and with it an easy set of choices. If you like the direction of the conversation with whomever you're talking to, then you've got the option of taking shelter together and elevating this relationship to the next level. If the conversation is going south, you can make your excuses and scuttle off to your basement to hide without fracturing any code of Midwestern etiquette.

In St. Louis, you would be amazed at how many people meet their future husband, wife or best friend while waiting for imminent twister destruction to come. At Missouri Towers, when the warning sirens wail, everyone naturally looks out their window or stands on the balcony of their apartment. It was in this exact manner two years ago that Gloria formally introduced herself to Mike.

One Saturday night in late spring, Gloria heard the tornado sirens rage to life. She turned on the local news just in case the alert was warning of a real-life version of *Red Dawn*. It must have been a rural Great Plains thing, as her dad had instilled in her that if the Commies ever invaded, the attack would be spearheaded through the heartlands. After seeing the Russians weren't on their way, she did the next most obvious thing and walked out onto her balcony. The sky was a dark, moody green, but Gloria couldn't see any twisters on the horizon. What she did see in every direction was Missouri Towers' residents either standing on their balconies or sticking their heads out their windows. From the corner of her eye, Gloria sensed someone looking up at her. She gazed downwards. As their eyes briefly met, the person looking at Gloria pulled his head back into the window.

Zoe then came out onto the balcony with a bottle of wine and two glasses. She filled the flutes and both girls sat down to share a drink. With the din from the sirens it was hard to talk, so they watched lightning forks fight it out in the sky.

After a few minutes, Zoe shouted over to Gloria, "Don't look down but there is a creepy guy staring up at us."

Gloria of course did the opposite. As soon as their eyes met for a second time, the man who'd been staring moved his head back inside the apartment. He then closed his window firmly shut.

"There are no balconies on that floor. I'm going to invite him up to have a glass of wine with us and watch the storm," Gloria said to Zoe.

"You're crazy! He might be an axe-murdering rapist for all we know!"

Gloria ran back into her bedroom and began to make herself presentable. Bras at the best of times she labeled "shackles of patriarchy." Besides, when you don't have much to put in them, they are an optional item of attire. However, if she was inviting company over she thought it best to at least dress properly. Gloria put on a pair of Daisy Dukes, a Ringling Brothers T-shirt, and for the occasion of making new friends a brassiere. She brushed her short, curly Molly Ringwaldish hair back into a bun and walked down two flights of stairs.

Following Gloria's dumping by Advik and subsequent rolling into St. Louis, she hadn't had much luck dating. To put it bluntly, the offerings in her age group were a selection of damaged individuals and caddish desperados. Most of her love matches had ex-wives, children, bad credit, rap sheets and prison tattoos. She once dated a man with potential, a doctor from California, but during their third date, he sprung it on her that he would only *commit* to a polyamorous relationship. She told him she wasn't sure "commitment" and an "open relationship" were compatible as she broke things off. Gloria figured out quickly that St. Louis was going to be a tough place to find *Mr. Right*, although that hadn't stopped her trying. Inviting a cute neighbor up for drinks was her latest attempt.

Mike lived in apartment #1011. It was two floors directly below hers, although the floor plan was totally different. Gloria rang the bell and nobody came to the door. She gave it a minute and then rang it again. Still nobody answered. Finally, she rang the bell three times and banged hard on the door.

A man dressed in a white sleeveless T-shirt and faded blue jeans opened up. Before he had a chance to say anything, Gloria blasted at a mile-a-minute pace, "Hey neighbor! I'm Gloria, I saw you looking up at our balcony. The 10th floor doesn't have outside space, but I do. We're having a tornado-viewing party. Would you like to be our guest?"

"Is that safe?" Mike asked, not knowing what to make of this overly forward woman.

"Of course the safest place to ride out the storm is the basement. But the basement in this building is a muggers' and murderers' paradise. So I'll take my chances on the balcony," said Gloria, making a pitch for the first date she'd had all year that didn't involve an algorithm.

"I'm actually a little bit busy with work tonight," said Mike, not sure what to make of this odd woman who had minutes ago been feverishly pounding on his door.

"What kind of work do you do?"

"Realtor."

"What a coincidence, I wanna buy a house!" lied Gloria, whose salary certainly wouldn't qualify her for any form of home ownership.

"I can always find time to talk to a neighbor about the virtues of buying a home. Give me ten minutes and I'll be up. Mike Love is the name, real estate is the game!" said Mike recycling a cheesy phrase from a rival agent's billboard advert.

Ten minutes later, Gloria's doorbell rang. She opened the door and standing in front of her was Mike. However, now he looked totally different, having changed his outfit. He had switched out the jeans and T-shirt for a dark suit with what she believed was one of those strange ties worn by Texans. He'd brought with him two bottles of mineral water and a stack of paperwork. It became quickly apparent that Gloria's flirty bedroom eyes had been misread, and that through the din of the tornado sirens, Mike was trying to sell her real estate. Zoe, not wanting to be a spare part, made her excuses and left Mike and Gloria together on the balcony.

Gloria studied Mike more closely. He wasn't as good-looking as Advik, but he was cute. She filtered through the bombastic sales pitch a few details about him. He was locally born, single, never married, had no children, no prison record and didn't even know what the word polyamorous meant. Mike came across to her as good-natured with a sweet sense of humor. He was also genuinely interested in hearing about her life on the farm and her time with the circus. Another positive was that he was like all good salt-of-the-earth St. Louisans, a huge fan of City Museum. Gloria, within a brief span of time, found herself to be genuinely intrigued by this neighbor she'd only just met.

The twister never came, the lightning fizzled, and the sirens stopped just as suddenly as they started. Gloria promised Mike she would contact his mortgage lender for a loan pre-approval and that they should meet again to discuss her home-buying options. She set the date for Wednesday, right after her last high-wire performance of the day. She handed Mike a complimentary pass to City Museum and told him to arrive early so he could see what she did for a living. In return Mike presented Gloria with a Buyer Representation contract to sign, a Missouri Brokers Disclosure document to initial, and a Spitfire Real Estate business card to put in her purse. As Gloria let Mike out of her apartment she felt a warm and fuzzy feeling inside that she hadn't experienced for a long time.

Gloria, with a solid track record of initiating romance, knew how to play the game. Mike may have thought setting the meeting point at her place of work was for convenience, but Gloria had ulterior motives. A hard-bodied girl in a tight-fitting leotard doing twists and turns on a rope has the amazing knack of getting a man's blood flowing to all the good places. After fifteen minutes of watching Gloria doing her acrobatic tricks, Mike's mind was no longer thinking about subdivisions and sales contracts but about how to woo this girl.

On the walk between City Museum and Missouri Towers, they stopped off at Bridge Tap House for an impromptu dinner. Over bowls of mac and cheese, they tried to get to know each other better. Why had she run away from the circus? Why hadn't he married his high school girlfriend like everyone else did in St. Louis? These were just some of the get-to-know-you questions they each avoided fully disclosing until now, what was technically their first proper date.

Towards the end of dinner, they both sensed there was the possibility of a genuine connection. They agreed to meet again, although they couldn't decide where the next date would take place. Gloria wanted to cook Mike dinner at her apartment and then watch the film *Pretty in Pink*. Mike wanted to take Gloria to the lake, as in his words, "All the magic in the Springsteen songs happens at the water." They flipped a coin and he won. The date would be a picnic at Lake Carlyle in southern Illinois.

Mike detailed the Sonic, loaded up a Bruce Springsteen mixtape and packed food for their date. Mike seemed to know exactly where to park, so Gloria knew she wasn't the first special person romanced at this body of H2O. The evening air was crisp and the sky clear enough to make out the zodiac constellations. They each opened up a little more about their pasts and their hopes for the future. Mike hadn't married his high school sweetheart as she had broken his heart by dumping him and running off to California. Gloria shared her own heartbreak of being let go by what she said was, "The man of her dreams." Their shared experiences of gut-wrenching heartbreak gave them a strong bond. Mike confessed to wanting to leave St. Louis. Gloria admitted to Mike that she wanted marriage and to start a family. They talked openly and honestly about big-picture plans and future aspirations – the kind of topics broached easily with someone you've only just met but become much harder to discuss as a relationship matures.

Gloria, who had experienced recent dating hell, and Mike, who hadn't been on too many dates of late, both realized that night at the lake that they had each met someone special. In a city where many people have made their complete friend list for life by first grade, Gloria, born and bred in Kansas, brought to Mike a touch of regional exoticism. He may not have sold her a house but he had closed a deal on something better. Gloria might not have found her dreamy rom-com heartthrob, but it didn't matter. Gloria was happy, content and, more importantly for the first time since her fizzled romance with Advik, was in love.

Two years on and Gloria and Mike were going strong, although Gloria thought they should have moved in together by now. Mike felt that they lived so close to one another they practically *did* live together, and anyway, his micro-apartment was more like an office than a home. She also thought he should've put a ring on her finger by now. Gloria sensed that ring could be coming any day, so that would be progress on one front. She was patient but she was now thirty-one and her biological clock was ticking loudly.

Mike talked less these days about leaving St. Louis, but she realized it was always on his mind. In the back of her head she worried that Mike was still aching a little bit from the girl who had dumped him. Gloria assumed their life plans were on hold until Mike had made progress with his real estate career. Since Mike struck it solo, business had been rough. But he was working his ass off every day and she knew he would eventually make it – he just needed a little bit of luck. Once his career was settled he could divert attention to their futures. For now she was there at his side and supporting him all the way.

Gloria loved her job at City Museum. Since starting she had been promoted and part of her role was now as a creative director. She did, though, still have plenty of acrobatic action. The money wasn't great but she loved what she did and that in itself was a form of compensation.

Gloria had settled into the rhythm of life in St. Louis. Toasted ravioli, gooey butter cake, and pizza made with cheese that easily gets stuck in your teeth were all local foods she now adored. St. Louis had a small-town feel for such a big city, which made for an easy place to live. The St. Louis Blues hockey team had recently won the Stanley Cup. The energy their sensational run had created for the city was like nothing she had experienced before. Unfortunately, though, they had adopted the eighties pop song *Gloria* as their motivational anthem, which had led to months of people singing the song at her whenever she uttered her name. During peak Blues euphoria in June, it had become unbearable. The irony was that her parents had named her after the Van Morrison tune *Gloria* and not this disco hit. Although in a bizarre twist, the lyrics of Laura Brannigan's iteration eerily spoke to her own life story. It had now gotten to the point where Gloria couldn't listen to the song anymore as it was messing with her head. She turned the radio off if it came on, which it did often.

Gloria got herself dressed and went into the kitchen. Zoe was sitting on the sofa watching the 1960s film, *The Graduate*. Zoe was a great roommate but by the age of thirty-one, anyone outside of San Francisco or New York is too old to be cohabiting with random people. Gloria was going to have to talk with Mike this week about getting on with their lives like grownups and getting a place together.

"Morning Zoe," said Gloria as she took a Pop Tart out of a cabinet and put it in the toaster.

"Mike called me a party clown yesterday," said Zoe, who, due to their schedules, hadn't seen Gloria for a day.

"I will talk with him."

"It's fine. He did bring me some awesome bullet shells which will make a stellar pair of earrings, so I'll forgive him this time," said Zoe.

City Museum didn't open until 10 a.m. Gloria had some time before she had to leave for work. She joined Zoe on the sofa and watched the movie. Dustin Hoffman's character Benjamin Braddock, was walking through the Los Angeles airport to the soundtrack of a Simon and Garfunkel classic. Hoffman's facial expression summed up the same sense of worry and hopelessness that Gloria had recently been feeling. *It will all work out just fine!* said the loud voice talking inside Gloria's head.

*   *   *

Daris had spent all night in The Bunker, readying his business empire for any eventuality. He had already made a few tweaks to operations. *Keurig* machines had been ordered for all the offices as an upgrade from the usual low-grade coffee offerings. Pam was working on a company-wide memo detailing that this fancy coffee was for "clients only" and that agents needed to bring their own pods if they wanted to use the machines. Daris was also going to green-light a uniform for the office support staff – although exactly what it was going to be he hadn't decided. Daris wanted camo battle fatigues while Puffman was angling for black boiler suits like those worn by James Bond foes. Overnight Spitfire had three listings swiped by New Berlin. Daris updated his battle map moving these losses off the table.

Pam Hardings, as prompt as ever, rolled into the office at 9 a.m. "Morning sir!" she said.

Pam, with her logistical expertise and Rottweiler ability to get bills paid, was the backbone of Spitfire's operations. She was a no-nonsense Indian Sikh immigrant in her fifties who nobody wanted to get on the wrong side of. Daris had admired how the Sikhs were instrumental to the British in running their own Empire when he hired Pam.

"Any updates?" asked Daris.

"Bad news sir!" Alexi Coklande defected.

"To New Berlin?"

"Yes, she called me this morning. They offered to pay her Mercedes lease payments. I tried to sway her and said we could work something out but she was set to go. As well as the car payments, she said they were a better fit for her business."

"Bitch," said Daris. Alexi, a heavy hitter and easy on the eyes, was just the kind of agent New Berlin had been poaching from other brokerages. Daris took her picture down from the wall in The Bunker covered with active agent headshots.

"The Cok has gone! Alexi and that bloody big Merc!" said Daris with a heavy heart and the realization that he'd lost one of his biggest stars.

"You know what they say?" said Pam, who, after getting no reply from Daris, added, "One day you're cock of the walk, the next you're a feather duster. Let's go out of our way to turn Alexi into a feather duster as quickly as we can."

"I like your spirit Pam! We'll play Alexi at her own game. We're going to carpet-bomb her areas of specialty with a three-salvo postcard of direct hits. Make those flyers big and beautiful and out of the finest quality paper. Put lots of market stats on them – everyone loves stats. The pretty new hire with the hot librarian vibe. Use her as the face of this mailer blast."

Pam looked at the wall of headshots until she found the agent Daris was referring to. "Dolores Jilling," said Pam.

"That's her! Let's make Jilling a star!"

Pam left The Bunker and headed to the print shop. Daris went back to his battle map and moved Dolores Jilling's pin marker to the areas of specialism now controlled by Alexi Coklande. He tried to anticipate New Berlin's next move. Still, the biggest unanswered question was, exactly who were the masterminds behind this outfit?

*   *   *

As Mike was at home packing his bag for the showing on Ann St. his phone suddenly alerted him with a notification. "Oh no!" said Mike, as he read the alert's title: "A very sad message from *Our Great Life.*" A teary-eyed Dave Rosebush, in that cringe-worthy millennial way, was promising a "transparent, honest, open, special message" to the "Greaters," as he, branded his followers. Penny had left Dave and their trailer in the "Land of Enchantment" for a new life in San Diego. He said she had become tired of the "hard work" and constant "self-promotion" that comes with being a professionally retired person. She found a new "life partner" who is rich enough to allow her to properly retire in a real city and not a barren wasteland in the middle of nowhere. Although evidently not quite rich enough for California living, when Penny blindsided Dave with the breakup, she demanded half the stock portfolio, a buyout for her share of the trailer and full title to the 1997 Toyota Corolla with 270,000 miles on the clock. Dave was also served a legal writ requesting seventy percent of future *Our Great Life* royalties in perpetuity. The larger portion of revenue she claimed was because the bikini videos starring a solo Penny were the site's biggest revenue generators.

Mike, although happy to have finally found balance restored to the universe of sexual matchmaking, did feel bad for Dave.

Mr. Rosebush had confessed to having to dust off his resume, rejoin the workforce, and leave retirement in the rearview mirror. He would soon start as a manager for an electronics store. Mike knew lightning wouldn't strike twice for Dave on the woman front, and it was going to be all downhill from here in the post-Penny new world order. If there was one bright spot it seemed this whole ordeal had cured Dave's nervous tick eye twitch.

With keys in hand, Mike Love waited outside a tidy-looking townhouse on Ann St. He could hear the growl of Nick Pipeman's Porsche approaching long before he could see it. Many agents have flashy rides, but none aside from Nick boasted a Porsche 911 previously owned by actress Courteney Cox. Living in a town that's far removed from Hollywood, and where anyone with connections to Hollywood has removed themselves far from this town, Pipeman's car, with its butt groove connection to Tinseltown royalty, had become a minor local celebrity.

Nick and the Porsche were invited annually to participate in the St. Louis Independence Day parade. Not only did the car provide an open-top mode of transportation for Miss Missouri to greet the crowds from, but it also had another important task. It was deemed the perfect parade buffer vehicle to separate the diverse cheerleader squad from inner-city school Vashon High, and the very non-diverse cheerleaders from a rural Missouri district that still used a Confederate Colonel as their mascot.

With The Killers blaring from the car stereo, Nick pulled up and parked in front of Mike's Sonic. He bounced out of the Porsche wearing a light tan suit that would have been the height of fashion for a Talking Heads fan circa 1983. On his head he wore a trilby hat and, bizarrely, a blue surgical mask on his face.

"Why are you wearing that strange face mask?" Mike asked.

"Pandemics," he replied, in a slightly muffled voice due to the mask fully covering his mouth.

"What are you talking about?"

"Global pandemics, my friend. Bill Gates says this will be the biggest catastrophe Earth will face in the next decade. He claims we will have no cure, millions will die, and it will bring unimaginable consequences."

"Ooo—K, sure Nick. If Bill Gates says it, it must be right," Mike replied sarcastically.

"Dude, it's scary stuff. I listened to a podcast all about it. Houses are full of botulism. This face mask could be the difference between life and death," Pipeman replied earnestly.

"If the world's going to end, I better stock up on food and toilet paper in case we have panic buying," Mike said, going along with Nick's grim prediction.

"That's exactly what Bill Gates said!"

"Let's go and see this house before armageddon strikes," Mike said, as they both walked towards the entrance.

Mike banged on the front door and shouted out to see if anyone was home. The two men entered the property.

It was a pretty, historic house that had been gutted about five years earlier. Looking at some of the finishes it was more Hoosier-hab flip than painstaking restoration. The property wasn't staged but had been decluttered and showed well. The details sheet verbiage roared, "PREPARE TO BE STUNNED" and boasted "SOARING CEILINGS" and a "SUN-DRENCHED DINING ROOM." This was a bit of a stretch, the dining room was a north-facing nook with little direct light. The ceilings were indeed on the high spectrum, but not exactly soaring.

"It's priced at $300,000. That seems high!" Mike shouted over to Nick, who was now studying a living room wall covered with photographs. Nick said something back, but it was hard to decipher through the face mask. Mike walked over to where he was standing.

Hung on the wall were numerous pictures that told the life story of the homeowners. The lady of the couple was in her early thirties, had white gleaming teeth, and shampoo ad hair. The husband, a few years older, had a rugged look that was somewhat feminized by a russet hairstyle and a wardrobe overly plucked from the gender-neutral aisle of JC Crew. Also on the wall were engagement pictures taken in front of the St. Louis Arch, and snaps from numerous exotic locations around the world. The wedding itself was a little pretentious, with the bride and groom saying their "I do's" in a balloon floating over the Grand Canyon. The latest additions to the pictures were a portrait shot at Lafayette Square Park, with the woman sporting a well-developed baby bump and next to it a snap of the happy couple holding their bundle of joy.

Mike always liked to know why an owner was selling a property before writing up a potential buyer's offer. The baby photo answered this question. Everyone flees the city in search of good schools as soon as they have children. Just above the top of the pictures were the framed his-and-hers dentistry school diplomas. That explained to Mike where the travel budget, funding for the over-the-top wedding and perfect pearly whites all derived from.

"I always tell clients to take down the personal photos when they are prepping to list," Mike said to Nick, who was currently staring a little too hard at a picture of the couple on a beach in swim attire.

"So who are these buyers we are doing the preview for?" Mike asked Nick.

"Out-of-staters, internet inquiry," was the answer Mike could just about make out through Nick's mask.

That isn't like Nick! was the first thought that came to Mike's mind.

Nick usually only worked on solid referrals, or with past clients. He avoided getting sucked into potential time-waster situations with random strangers found on the web.

Mike went into the kitchen. Subway tiles, stainless steel appliances. It would be an awesome selling point. He opened up the fridge. Stuffed with basic bitch food all purchased from Whole Foods. He hated to see people spend money on the same items they could get elsewhere for less. He took a peek out the window. Cute garden with a fire pit and Weber grill.

Shit! Mike thought. He had forgotten to ask Nick if he had any romantic interest in the crazy clown lady. Setting up dates wasn't usually his thing. But Zoe was a potential buyer and the realtor training manual did talk about, "Going beyond the call of duty for a client."

Mike shouted from the kitchen towards the direction of the living room: "Nick, you've met Gloria's roommate Zoe a few times. Oddly enough she has been asking about you. I think she would like me to set up a date between the two of you."

There was no reply. Mike couldn't see Nick anywhere on the ground floor, so he went down to the basement. Nick wasn't there either. He went up the stairs to the second floor and opened a door. It was the baby's bedroom, nicely decorated, but Nick wasn't in it. Mike could hear noises coming from the master bedroom and walked that way. He was admiring the exquisite crown molding as he cruised down the hallway into that bedroom. The sight in front of him must have broken every rule in the Realtors' Association's Code of Ethics.

Nick Pipeman was sitting on the owners' bed. Laid out before him was an extensive collection of what was presumably the sellers' sex toys. From the look of some of the more bizarre instruments of pleasure, the man of the house on occasion doubled-up as the lady of the house. Piled high next to the numerous sex toys, some of which Mike couldn't even begin to contemplate what you did with them, was a fully emptied-out laundry basket. Nick, now without the face mask on – the thing that only ten minutes prior was the thin line of protection between life and death – was intensely sniffing the gusset of a pink pair of lacy thong panties.

"What about that end-of-days pandemic?" were the select words a stunned Mike could stutter as Nick's nose moved from the crotch area to the butt string part of the undergarments.

As Pipeman took a long satisfying exhale, he replied, "That was heavenly, and if it kills me it was worth dying for." He then threw the soiled undies towards Mike, and with a perverted look on his face yelled, "Take a sniff yourself."

Apartment #1311   Only the Lonely

The key was, just as Marty said it would be, under the doormat. Alice Jones let herself into the small 13th-floor studio apartment. After her journey she was exhausted. She sat herself down on a beaten-up sofa that doubled as a foldout bed. The drapes were drawn but had Alice chosen to open them she would've been amazed by the view from the window.

Alice turned on the television via a remote control she found in the middle of a sad looking coffee table. Marty didn't have cable, so there was nothing she could find worth watching. The apartment was clean, almost too clean for a bachelor pad. The aroma of bleach blended with a whiff of mold from the air-conditioning pipes gave the place a creepy odor. Looking around at the barren clinical residence with its unique smell Alice worried she might've been enticed into a serial killer's lair. She took a peek in the fridge to see if there were severed heads in plastic wrap. Nothing sinister, just whole milk, processed food and white sliced bread. The staples of any poor person's diet.

She found a note in the Kitchen: *Help yourself to anything!* Oddly, it also read underneath, *Apologies my name is Sam not Marty.* "Guy has been lying to me all this time," Alice muttered to herself. There were more specific instructions on the note's flip side, but she was ignoring them for now.

From the freezer Alice took a microwave mac and cheese and nuked herself lunch. She slipped off her sneakers and tucked into the meal. If there was one dish Alice could make from scratch it was mac and cheese. She could easily improve on this sorry excuse of a meal. As white trash as Alice was, she gave microwave meals a wide berth. Alice washed down lunch with a can of Dr Pepper retrieved from a shelf in the fridge designed for eggs.

Alice started thinking about her journey to St. Louis. Fourteen hours on a Greyhound bus wasn't a trip for the faint-hearted. The man sitting across the aisle from her had been gazing at her legs all night. It must've been the short skirt she was wearing. Or maybe it was the belly flesh on display. More likely it was the way she squeezed her thighs together in a rhythm synchronized to the bus's motion. Alice knew that any escaped guttural whimpers were masked by the drone of the bus's air-conditioning. This rider's nonstop staring had empowered Alice; she felt like she had control over this man. She enjoyed that feeling.

Alice noticed that the guy she had just ridden the elevator with had been checking out her cleavage. "There are sinners everywhere," she whispered to an audience of none as she clutched her Jesus on the cross necklace.

Elevator man was cute. Why didn't she ever have boyfriends like that? He was age-appropriate, he likely had a good job and a normal family. I bet he wouldn't have strung her along with a fake name for weeks. And she would put money on him not

94

expecting to be orally pleasured on a first date, or demand rough, sadistic sex by the second. Elevator man might even be the kind of person to pay for dinner and take her to a musical. A chaste date would be novel, something to build a relationship on. Alice had been treated like crap by men all her life. Someone who wasn't drunk, high, or abusive was the least she deserved.

Alice unpacked her two light suitcases. As per her prior conversations with Sam, she placed her clothes in a drawer that had been emptied for her. She had enough items of clothing for a week. That was as long as Sam said he could afford her.

Alice was in need of a shower. Wash away the grime of the bus. Wash away the coal country dust she had dragged from home. Wash away her sins. The water was hot, the shower pressure strong. She had thoughts of self-love which were doused by her unknown surroundings. She had no idea if there were hidden cameras. The last thing she wanted was to end up as an artifact of voyeur pornography. If that happened Alice would have to leave her church. She put on a fresh outfit. Yoga pants with a long T-shirt should keep the creeps at bay. The clean garments hugged her body tightly and felt good.

Sam seemed like a sweet guy from their numerous conversations. Alice was under no illusions about what he wanted from her, and he had sent her money upfront. This alone demonstrated a level of trust. $200 a day plus expenses is what they had agreed. Alice had no idea if that was the going rate or if she was overcharging. All she knew was that this was the amount the private investigator charged in *The Rockford Files*. If nothing else this was all an adventure, a trip to a big city, an experience to be had. Something you probably wouldn't be in a hurry to tell your grandchildren about, although maybe the purpose of the journey she would.

"Every day we stray further and further from God's light," Alice said aloud as she looked in the mirror and tied her now clean pinkish hair into a ponytail. She was twenty-five years old but looked more like thirty-five – and a hard-living thirty-five at that. It would be understandable if she was a meth head, but unlike her peer group, she didn't have chemical hobbies. Just work, chores and church filled her days.

She'd lived a life of rural poverty – orphaned young, and left to raise two siblings as best as she could. But there's only so much a checkout clerk at Family Dollar can bring home to support a family of three. Alice did what she could. She did what she had to. Coming to St. Louis was in her head a business trip; working for God and maybe a little extra to keep for herself.

Sam said he would be home later that night; he was doing a double shift. His instructions for what he wanted her to do were specific. Alice walked over to the window to see what the weather was like outside. She pulled the curtains open. "That must be the prettiest thing I've ever seen!" she said, upon realizing the view from Sam's apartment was the iconic Arch. She drew the rest of the drapes. *These are open as long as I am here. This sight is too good to hide!*

On the side counter was $200 in cash and directions to the MetroLink station. This was extra money and not part of her fee. *YOU DON'T NEED A TICKET* was written next to the name of the station she would be getting on at. Sam had told her that nobody bought train tickets in St. Louis as there were no entry barriers or inspector enforcement. He was very clear he wouldn't be reimbursing her the $5 that a return ticket to a suburban strip mall would cost if she purchased a ticket.

Alice left Missouri Towers and descended into the blistering heat. The weather was not like this at home. She was now regretting not wearing less clothing. She felt sticky and gross after walking a single block.

The soaring buildings around her were inspiring, in a church spire kind of way. Alice stopped for a few minutes to take in the architecture. She had noticed most of the ground floor commercial spaces were vacant. Now it made sense why she had to trek out to the burbs to do her shopping.

Next to the train station was an understocked convenience store that stunk of cheap incense. Alice bought from it a dozen condoms. Disease was on her mind, and not preventing or interfering with God's plans – whatever they might be. Alice wouldn't ask Sam for repayment for these. She put them down to the cost of doing business. And anyway, she was genuinely intrigued by the ones that promoted themselves as "Ribbed for her pleasure." For she had never experienced anything like that before.

She made her way down the escalator to the station. There were, just as Sam had claimed, no entry gates. Standing at the platform she thought there would be more people around. Aside from a homeless man resting on a bench, she was alone. The first train was heading for the airport and Alice let that pass. The next train was the one she needed. Apart from a sleeper with what must have been all his possessions, the carriage was empty. In the movies, city trains are crammed. Her worry had been fending off frottage, not sitting in a deserted car.

NO CONCEALED WEAPONS read a sign at the front of the carriage. *How would anyone know if you had a concealed weapon? The sign is redundant. Who's checking for weapons? Nobody's asking for tickets, let alone frisking for guns.*

After a few stops the train left its subterranean route, and from the window Alice got a glimpse of the city. In every direction it looked broken. Even the graffiti adorning the crumbling buildings was artless. They passed by an old rail depot that was once one of the busiest in the world. Now all its concourse housed was an abandoned shopping mall. At Grand Station, several passengers boarded. They looked shady and smelled of weed and poor hygiene that had fermented in the heat.

Alice watched as a man with long dreads and sagging pants ambled through the carriage offering drugs for sale. The dealer stared her down. Alice felt like she could read his mind; she tightened her body into a ball. She felt the dealer's evil. He smiled at her revealing a mouthful of gold teeth. The train pulled up to a station called Skinker. A security guard boarded, and like cockroaches in the light everyone else exited the carriage. Alice now breathed easy as she sat in the empty car.

The train rolled through a more pleasant area. From the windows she viewed pretty brick houses on leafy streets. At the university, students boarded. She watched as they talked to each other or stared into their phones. She could only dream of going to college. She had responsibilities and no money.

Alice was envious of these students. Their Thursday evenings were going to be dinner with friends, studying at the library, or going to a party. Her Thursday evening was going to be whatever Sam wanted it to be.

Alice exited the train at Sunnen and followed the directions Sam had jotted down. After a short walk across a busy road, she was outside her destination: Ross Dress For Less. "I can do this," Alice said loudly.

Alice walked into the store. On the sound system a song by eighties band *The Motels* played. She browsed the clothes racks. Sam had an exact list of what he required her to buy. A place like Ross is a post-industrial bizarre, and possibly the only store where you could find everything on Sam's inventory.

Alice could sense she was being watched. She looked over her shoulder. A store associate was standing behind her.

"Can I help you find something in particular?" asked the employee.

"I'm not gonna steal anything!" Alice shot back.

"I never said you were ma'am; I was just trying to help!" the now on-defense woman replied.

Alice looked at the lady. She was broader than she was tall but had a friendly disposition. *She doesn't even know what I've done in my past. I'm paranoid. She's just being friendly. Trust in God.*

Alice handed the employee her shopping list and thanked her for the offer of assistance.

"Oh dear!" said the woman as she scanned the piece of paper. Her eyes darted around in all directions as she tried to figure out if they stocked any of the items. "This is quite specific!"

"It's for my boyfriend. He's detail-orientated," said Alice.

"You two must be going somewhere special. Let's give this a try! See what we can get," she responded with enthusiasm.

"Thanks," said Alice as the two ladies began their quest.

*   *   *

Sam Robinson wasn't always the man he is today – a single guy, working a lowly paid job, living in a small studio apartment with a pay-to-play sex habit he couldn't afford. Sam was once happily married, owned a home in the burbs, had a solid career at the local water utility, and never dreamed of paying for intimacy.

Sam married Becky, his teenage sweetheart straight out of high school. Together they bought a home in the St. Louis suburb of Richmond Heights. The Robinsons agreed early on they didn't want to start a family and lived a mundane low-octane Midwestern life. Sam was an asset to his bowling team and in his spare time organized trivia quiz nights. Becky had a part-time job at the mall, gardened ferociously, ran a book club, and with a no-prisoners-taken attitude kept order in the home.

All was good until Becky, out of the blue, requested a divorce. No real reason was given, she simply wanted something different for her life. Sam pleaded for Becky to change her mind but he couldn't stop her. He was heartbroken.

They sold the house, divided up the jointly held assets and went their separate ways. Sam had no idea where Becky moved to, she just vanished. He suspected somewhere with a better climate, as over the last few years she had complained about the winters. Sam moved downtown thinking the change of scenery would do him good. With his proceeds from the home sale, he lost all motivation to work and quit his job.

Sam vowed to find love again. He hadn't dated since high school and even then had only been with Becky. The dating world had evolved and looking at the plethora of apps invented to find soulmates, he figured landing a girlfriend wouldn't be a challenge. In reality, the abundance of choice was a curse, especially when you're a pudgy, balding, jobless forty-something.

The girls Sam tagged on the dating sites didn't reciprocate the interest. Sam broadened his parameters and upped the age range and body types to those more similar to his own. Finally, his profile got some traction, although he quickly began to wish it hadn't. Sam's mutual matches spent hours messaging him. They asked deep questions and shared their hopes and dreams in painstaking detail. Sam didn't own a computer and typing long wordy texts via a cell phone was burdensome. These back-and-forth chats would go on for days. And then all of a sudden his potential love match would vanish. At the same time, the personal profiles stacked with thirst trap portraits and profound quotes also disappeared. All the energy Sam had invested in building up a rapport was wasted. He had been introduced to the world of "ghosting."

The one and only time Sam managed to convert a cyber match into a physical date, he knew he was done with this game. The woman who presented herself looked nothing like the pictures she had enticed him with. Sam felt like Michael Douglas in *Falling Down,* when the Whammy Burger handed to him is a "sorry, miserable squashed thing" and not what was advertised. As Sam sat at the table with this woman, he wondered if she was even the same person as presented in her profile's professional-quality photos. She was also the most boring woman he had ever encountered, with a personality light years away from her colorful "about me" prose. Sam figured dating was overrated; besides, what he really wanted was sex. And if he had to pay for it, so be it.

Sam's first attempt at finding love for hire was a trip to a brothel. Now, if he was in a Nevadan cathouse on a Friday night the ladies available would be an array of seductive beauties. Missouri is no Nevada and the gals stood before Sam at a rural Jefferson County brothel on this particular Tuesday afternoon were a motley crew. Sam looked at the line-up of strumpets and wondered how, with their quirky looks, they could even eke out a living.

He had a big heart and did what he would have done if he were at the kennel rescuing a mutt that, without his divine intervention, would be destined for euthanasia. He plucked Kendra, the most unattractive lady available, on the basis that she must need the business. From Sam's estimation, this woman was the wrong side of thirty, and with crooked teeth and a porky little nose had a quixotic look. However, what she did have going for her was a gigantic pair of breasts. Kendra led Sam by the hand to her room in one of the sketchy-looking double-wides the girls worked from.

Sam wasn't in the mood for drawn-out negotiations. He told Kendra that he had $123 on offer and asked what she would do for that. "Anything you want, but for that price you get thirty-two minutes max!" Kendra said as she took his crumpled notes. *That was easy!* Sam thought as he stripped to his underpants.

Kendra took her shirt off and released the hounds. They were huge, but not necessarily in a good way. There was a considerable amount of sag and her nipples were overly puffy in a freak show oddity manner. With Kendra half-naked, he now noticed she had a C-section scar.

"You have children?" Sam asked.

"Had a daughter. She died, drowned at the lake," replied Kendra.

"Sorry," Sam said wishing he hadn't asked. He was now feeling greater sympathy for Kendra than he had during the line-up parade.

Kendra, with her free-flowing boobs, edged nearer to Sam and moved her hands on top of his boxer shorts. She began to massage his member.

"What are you requesting, mister?" she asked.

"Nothing special, just regular old-fashioned sex. You see, my wife left me last year and it's been a while."

"I'm sorry," said Kendra, who hadn't asked for a backstory.

"Still don't know why; she just walked out of the door one day."

"How about we start with a titty-fuck," said the bawdy-house worker, trying to change the subject.

"Sounds like a plan," replied Sam, looking at Kendra's rack.

"We need to get you fired up!" she said with a cheeky smile that fully revealed what a mess her teeth were. Kendra tugged at Sam's penis, which was still placid.

"Why not take your underwear off?" she suggested in the hope airflow would improve blood circulation. Sam slipped them off.

Kendra continued to stroke Sam's love stick. One of her specialties was hand jobs. Most amateurs yank at a pecker like it's a joystick for a game console. As a pro, Kendra always treated her client's cock like the yoke of a helicopter. A bit of pitch, a little yaw, and plenty of throttle usually got the "John" elevated within seconds. However, as much as Kendra cranked up the speed Sam was not getting off the ground.

"Nerves!" said Sam, who could see his bordello pilot was going beyond the call of duty in terms of effort.

"Let's try this a different way," Kendra suggested.

Kendra pushed Sam back onto the bed and wrapped her breasts around his floppy penis. She squeezed the tits over his spirit stick and went through the motions of a diddle ride.

It was all to no avail. As much as Kendra tried, she couldn't get Sam erect.

Sam may have picked Kendra out of sympathy but by the end of their thirty-two minutes together, it was she who felt sorry for him. As well as apologizing for his performance issues, Sam wouldn't stop talking about his wife leaving him.

On the ride home Sam realized he had found himself to be that classic cliché – a man who went to a brothel and couldn't get laid. Sam assigned his technical difficulties down to Kendra's funky looks and the strange surroundings of the whorehouse. He should have also stayed away from talking about her family life. If a hooker came to his home he would be more relaxed and thus able to enjoy the experience. If he found himself a sexier offering, his biggest problem would be shooting his load too quickly and not any erectile dysfunction.

As Sam started the process of bringing a for-hire woman to his apartment, he knew he was out of his depth. There was an entire glossary of terms he needed to familiarize himself with. Drive me to you, fly me to you, 50-50, girlfriend experience, pornstar experience, no kissing, no daty, Greek surcharge, multiple shots on goal. It was overwhelming for a man like Sam who was a newbie to these dark twisted realms.

Although there was an array of options available, as with all things in life, it became apparent his resources would define his choices. Some of these women were charging a staggering $4,000 an hour. Sam decided the exotic, website-based ladies were off-limits. He picked up a copy of the scrappy local alternative weekly and caroused its back pages. At this juncture of his ongoing adventures, he had accepted that whoever turned up to his doorstep would unlikely resemble their marketing materials. A girl by the name of Jennifer, though, Sam felt had promise, and so he contacted her. For his own safety, Sam would go by the alias Marty.

And just like calling in for a pizza, two hours later Jennifer was banging on his door. Jennifer was about his age, not that there was anything wrong with that. She carried with her a small bag and was dressed minimally in sweatpants and a T-shirt.

Jennifer promptly lost her shirt and stripped off her pants. She was now standing before him in a pink lingerie set that had seen better days. Sam, however, liked the look of what was on offer and had no hesitations on what his next move should be.

He moved closer to Jennifer. "Hold on buddy, we need to talk terms," she bleated in a raspy voice.

Sam explained that he had never done anything like this before (the brothel disaster was more like an exhibition game and he decided it didn't count towards his record). For the next fifteen minutes, Jennifer and Sam, or Marty as she called him, conducted exhausting negotiations. They agreed there would be a flat fee of $175, and depending on how things went bump up rates for more adventurous activities.

Jennifer handed Sam a condom. He saw it was medium-sized. With her years in the business, she was likely able to estimate a client's pene dimensions without even seeing the goods. Sam struggled to get it on his floppy organ.

"How about I put it on with my mouth," she suggested. That would cost Sam an extra $10, but under the circumstances, he felt was money well spent.

Sam was amazed by Jennifer's tongue agility, but it didn't do anything to resolve his situation.

"I have a few tricks up my sleeve," Jennifer said. This lady was certainly a professional but nothing she did worked. After an hour of messing around, Sam conceded defeat. He liked Jennifer's level of effort and apologized for his woes.

"I'll come back tomorrow and bring something with me. We can try again," she said.

Jennifer returned the next day. Sam thought she could have worn something other than the sweatpants and the same T-shirt but he didn't complain. She once again stripped off, this time revealing buttercup yellow lingerie that was in a sorry state. Jennifer brought with her a bigger bag and from it produced a scary-looking penis pump.

"You owe me $60 for this," Jennifer said, as she passed the contraption to her client.

Sam excused himself, went to the bathroom, and skimmed through the instructions. He then put his wang inside the tube and began to crank. It was hopeless; if anything his dong shrunk. Sam paid Jennifer for her time and sent her away.

Sam consulted a doctor to discuss his problems; $200 later, and with a Viagra prescription in his pocket, he had new hope. Jennifer, who was always happy to take someone's money, came back the following week. Not knowing how long it would take for the medication to kick in, Sam booked her for a two-hour session. He also purchased a gift for Jennifer – brand-new, black lingerie.

Sam took his blue pill while Jennifer was in the bathroom changing. She charged him an extra $25 for wearing the outfit, which she stated to be a "costume request."

Sam sat on the sofa in his underpants. Jennifer sat beside him in her new panties and bra set. They both waited for the marvels of medicine to make the magic happen.

Unfortunately for Sam, nothing was stirring in his underpants. Even more unfortunately for Jennifer, she was having the exact opposite effect. She had suffered a bad allergic reaction to the new lingerie's fabric and had broken out in a very noticeable and very itchy rash around her vagina and down her legs.

A furious Jennifer exited Sam's apartment, cursing him for curtailing the rest of her day's business. She texted him the following day demanding compensation for lost work. Jennifer sent a picture of her inflamed cooch as proof to back her claim. Sam sent Jennifer five-hundred dollars to make her whole.

The Viagra had been worthless, but not ready to concede defeat Sam decided maybe it was Jennifer. He had liked her looks but it could be she wasn't the right match for his mental needs. Over the next several months, Sam called in numerous different escorts. He tried all shapes, sizes, and races hoping to find a compatible match. Nothing meshed.

The final straw came when a North City harlot bluntly commented while straddling Sam, "Homie this ain't working for ya! It's like trying to put a marshmallow into a parking meter."

At that point Sam knew he needed a different playbook.

"No personal connection!" Sam concluded that was the problematic element of his limp-dick plight. He decided that procuring a sugar baby would bridge the girlfriend-prostitute divide and cure his intimacy issues. Sam signed up for a service that brokered this style of companionship. There were model-calibre stunners on the books, but the compensation wants were beyond his budget.

After some back-and-forth messaging and a little haggling, Sam officially became a sugar daddy. For the princely sum of $1,000 a month, Sam arranged weekly rendezvous with a lady called Mary. Monday evenings would be his regular slot. One minor problem, Sam was running low on cash. He hadn't worked for months and his outgoings for hookers, the penis pump, and the Viagra prescription had hit him in the pocket. To cover his new sugar daddy responsibilities, Sam took a job at an Illinois packaging plant.

Prior to their first meetup, Mary laid out a couple of ground rules. The initial date would be getting to know each other at a public place. She also stated that oral sex wasn't something she did under any circumstances and Sam was never to ask for it. She explained that she had four extra molars and this led to a dangerous gag reflex issue if too much of anything entered her throat. Sam told Mary he respected her boundaries and they would have a relationship of mutual respect. Mary also expected to be treated to a full meal on each of their "hangouts" and in addition, she appreciated gifts. "Treat me like a princess!" was an expression she frequently tossed out.

Their first meeting was at a downtown pizza restaurant. Mary walked over to Sam and greeted him like a friend rather than a client. He instantly felt this was a different experience in contrast to his call-girl faire. Sam presented Mary with a dozen roses. She thanked him for the flowers, made a few remarks about the weather, and then immersed herself in the menu.

Mary was in her early twenties, a nursing student, and carried a few extra pounds that weren't disclosed on her resume. Mary explained she was working this hustle to help pay off student loans. She had been a sugar baby for just two months and was still learning the ropes.

Mary had quite a healthy appetite and ordered a starter, main, and dessert. "Those four additional teeth were good for something," Sam muttered as she waddled off for a bathroom break. Mary washed down her three-course meal with several exotic cocktails. Two hours and $157 of food later, the date was over. As Mary got up to leave she said, "The flowers are nice but bring me a gift card next time. Amazon or Starbucks please." It was mentioned in the sugar daddy manual that gifts on top of the service fees are expected. "No problem princess," Sam said, as he took care of the tab.

For the second date, Sam and Mary attended a *Cardinals* baseball game. With beers north of $11 a pop and Mary's aggressive thirst, this was another expensive night. Sam suggested she visit his apartment afterward but Mary said, "I need to get to know you better before that happens."

Mary wasn't too deep on the questioning front and Sam thought it was going to be hard for her to ever know him well. She was chatty enough about herself and apparently liked watching reality television and shopping. *Easily done with all the gift cards she's collecting!* Sam figured. Mary had let it slip she had four sugar daddies and that it was now almost a full-time job.

Sam had mixed feelings about Mary. Her relative youth compensated for her weight, which as the weeks went by with all her paid-for meals ballooned. The personal connection element of the sugar-daddy sugar-baby arrangement he did enjoy, though. As uninterested as she was in his life, he liked the updates about what she was studying at school. However, Mary was becoming a pricey habit and Sam had to take on more shifts to support his newfound responsibilities.

As expensive as his dates with Mary were, she had now become his most exciting weekly event. To be fair, he didn't have much else going on; he'd long ago quit bowling and trivia nights. Sam's workplace was boring and nobody even talked to each other. They just listened to music on headphones as they worked. Mary, as much of a phony as she happened to be, was the nearest Sam came to having any real friends.

Sam paid for a second month of Mary's companionship. The relationship seemed to be advancing and she had agreed to visit his apartment for dinner. Sam wasn't the best cook so they grabbed Thai to-go. Mary had warned him before they went up, "I'm a romantic girl and don't have expectations of anything happening – not yet anyway!" Sam detected from this sentence a hint of possibility.

Sam and Mary ate their noodles against the backdrop of the setting sun reflecting a magnificent glow onto the Gateway Arch. With this beautiful view and Mary downing at least four cans of beer, Sam figured this was an opportune moment to make an advance. Sam began massaging Mary's feet. She didn't say no, so he carried on. "You are very sweet Sam. I like that in a man," she said, as he worked his magic on her toes.

Mary closed her eyes and was clearly enjoying the attention. Sam looked at her face; she was a funny-looking creature but that wouldn't stop him. He relocated his hands from Mary's feet to her shoulders and then gave her a neck rub. Mary leaned into him and rested her head on his torso. Sam could now smell her hair conditioner brand. He placed his arms around Mary and in the process accidentally brushed her breasts. They felt wonderful. Mary didn't protest in the slightest. Sam's heart was beating fast and he was trying to plot his next move when something magical happened. Biology was once again working and Sam felt himself getting hard.

"Mary I want to make sweet love to you," whispered Sam into her ear.

"I think I would like that," she replied. Sam was trying to figure out if he was going to fold out the sofa bed or do it on the floor when Mary added coldly, "That will be an extra thousand."

"I don't have that!" said a stunned Sam as his pecker deflated faster than a popped balloon.

"Let's pick up where we left off next week," said Mary with her business hat firmly in place.

Mary said their time was up and she left the apartment.

The only thing that had thwarted mission accomplished was Mary's mercenary traits. However, Sam felt born again. He took out a payday loan and had Mary's fee ready for their next meeting. Sam spent the week preparing for this appointment and was like a kid counting down the days to Christmas.

The date they agreed would be a brief dinner out before going back to Sam's place to finish what they had started last week. Sam waited for Mary at a bar on Washington Ave. He could already feel the anticipation of tonight's plans rumbling in his pants. He was ready for action.

Mary, however, was a no-show. Sam called her but the phone went to voicemail. *Ghosted!* Sam figured. Although there must be a rule in the sugar baby handbook about ditching a sugar daddy without adequate notice.

Sam headed home with a heavy heart and turned on the news. It was at this moment he found out why Mary hadn't made it.

Mary had died in a bizarre and tragic way. The news item skirted around the more graphic details but the poor girl had choked on her own vomit while engaging in a sex act. The story made general allusions to the exact circumstances but hinted that she was an escort girl.

"She wasn't lying about her inability to perform blow jobs," Sam grunted, as he turned off the television. Evidently, one of the other sugar daddies hadn't treated her like a princess and the resulting forced oral copulation had led to her untimely demise.

For a brief moment, Sam was sad. If only because Mary had brought him close to regaining his sexual mojo. In the bigger picture, however, Mary was rapidly bleeding him dry. Sam decided her death wasn't a terrible outcome as ultimately she would've bankrupted him.

If kooky Mary with those extra molars could raise the Titanic, Sam knew so could another gal. He conducted an unscientific triage of his recent failures. From this wreckage, he plucked the elements he believed would help. Sam had no problem paying for sex. If any man was honest, one way or another you end up paying for it anyway. So why not bite the bullet on the front end. Sam decided his ideal partner should be younger and more attractive than he himself was. "Punch above your weight and all that!" Evidently, the personal connection with Mary had worked, so that would be a certain. Then there was a time element to his encounters. An hour or two wasn't enough of a window to get his mechanics fired up. He was a slow-burn man and needed days to make the magic happen. Most importantly, Sam needed all these elements delivered to him within a tight budget.

Sam now realized what he was looking for. He needed a Julia Roberts style *Pretty Woman* on the payroll for a week. His ex-wife Becky loved that flick. Sam recalled Richard Gere's dashing character paid tens of thousands for his hooker Vivian. Where and how could Sam get himself a Vivian type girl for a full week? A hooker that would let him do anything and everything. A person with a willingness for unbridled debauchery. No meter running, no surcharges, and nothing off-limits. "Where could he find her?" was the question he asked himself over and over again.

He woke up in the middle of the night to find himself in the midst of a "eureka" moment. "CRAIGSLIST!" he screamed. This website is designed not only as a vehicle for people who want to get rid of unwanted junk but also for poor unfortunate souls in need. One of those types of people in need were men like

Sam searching for booty. The other were people looking for hard cash to make the rent.

Although Craigslist ditched the de facto hookup section "Casual Encounters" years ago, there was a stealthy way to now seek obliging women – in the "Help Me Please" section. In this area of the site, at the start of any given month, you could find numerous people requesting cash assistance to make rent. If you scanned the accompanying pictures and text, these damsels in distress were not unobvious about what they would do in return for dollars.

To work within Sam's modest budget and his expansive needs – that being a live-in hooker at his full disposal – Sam scoured a Craigslist site in a region of America with a low cost of living. Appalachia is about as cheap as you get, he realized, as he trolled through the local Craigslist site. Bingo! After a deep search, he found a posting that read: "In need of rent $$$, will work for you!" The picture embedded in the listing was of a thinnish, youngish girl from a town in rural Kentucky. Although dressed in an emo-goth punky way, she looked intriguing. Her face was unfortunately obscured by the camera used to shoot the mirror selfie. But the photograph's background reeked of whiskey tango poverty and this, Sam knew, bumped up the odds of his proposition's allure. Sam made contact under his Marty alias and requested a clean face shot. The response was quick and Alice, as she introduced herself, sent him a clearer picture.

Alice, although looking a little rough around the edges, had an angelic aura. And she was for sure a league above Sam in the beauty department. As a bonus, he didn't see any evidence of needle marks or drug use. Sam briefed Alice with his very specific and detailed request and she wasn't put off.

Sam, between all the various types of working girls he'd engaged, now had a deep understanding of the legalized side of the sex business. He drafted up a contract outlining Alice's obligations. Upon getting the signed paperwork back Sam paid her in advance. He knew this was a risk but she had a trustworthy face and he wasn't worried about being conned. "Think of yourself as Julia Roberts in *Pretty Woman*," he said to her. Although Sam was upfront with Alice she knew from day one that he was certainly no Richard Gere.

As Sam entered the front door of his apartment, he instantly knew Alice was there. The usual bleach and stale AC odor was intermixed with a seductive blend of perfume and hair product. He put his keys down on a side table and walked through the hallway into the apartment's main room. The lights were dimmed so he couldn't get a good visual of Alice. All he could make out was a silhouette on the sofa watching an old black and white movie.

Upon hearing Sam enter, Alice turned off the television. The room became even darker.

"Close your eyes Sam. I'm not quite ready, a few finishing touches," Alice said with a smooth Southern twang as she darted into the bathroom.

Sam covered his eyes and didn't cheat, although it was dark enough that cheating wasn't technically an option. They had video-conferenced each other over the last few weeks, so this wasn't a total blind date. But he was curious to see what Alice looked like in the flesh and if she had managed to get anything from his list.

Alice checked herself in the mirror, adjusted her hat, and put on the new white gloves. She was almost ready and recited a preparatory prayer. Alice knew she was about to sin but asked God for forgiveness. After a lipstick touchup, Alice gave herself a final once-over. In general, she had a self-loathing nature but tonight she knew she looked ready for primetime.

Alice turned up the lights as she entered the room.

"Open your eyes," Alice said as she twirled before him in a free-flowing silk polka dot dress. "They didn't have it in brown but this was close," she added enthusiastically.

Alice was dressed in a sleeveless black and white polka dot dress that rose just above her knees. She had switched out her canvas pumps for white high heels. On her head was a straw boater hat with a band of material matching the dress's fabric. Under the hat she had dyed her former pinkish hair a deep chestnut brown. Her bright red lipstick stylishly clashed with her brilliant white gloves and matching earrings, and her usually splotchy-bumpy skin with the aid of makeup looked flawless.

"Wow!" said Sam, while taking a deep look at his special import from Kentucky.

"Never underestimate what Ross Dress for Less offers. Even better I came in under budget. I left the change on the counter," said Alice now hoping Sam would tell her what to do next.

Sam walked over to the fridge and retrieved a can of Dr Pepper. He then returned to the sofa and intensely studied Alice. *She found everything and looks better than perfect.* Sam now knew shipping in Alice was a brainwave.

Alice was now face-to-face with Sam for the first time. They had video chatted, but only on a small phone screen. In person the man who sat before her was shorter, balder, grayer, and fatter than he looked on those calls. He was wearing tired clothes from JCPenney that were decades out of style. He came across sadder and more tragic in person. Although who was she to be judgmental? Alice had sold herself for eight days for a grand total of $1,600 plus expenses. Only God knew what wicked and fiendish things he would do to her next.

Alice didn't quite know what the sex worker protocol was but decided there must be a theatrical preamble required. Alice spontaneously began to enact what she thought to be an erotic dance. She wiggled her butt and squeezed her modest breasts together, and then one-by-one began shedding items of clothing. First, the gloves came off and then the stilettos were tossed to the far side of the room. Upon losing the hat she unclipped the barrette that held back her hair. She had curled it earlier and with its new brown hue, it possessed a fresh voluminous look. Alice then unzipped her dress. As it fell to the ground she revealed to Sam a new black lacy lingerie set she had purchased, as per his request.

As Alice danced for her paymaster, she was overcome by a sense of panic. Poor Sam sitting in front of her chugging a Dr Pepper was hardly putting her in an amorous mood. She was now regretting not picking up a tube of lube while on her travels. Alice's lady parts were dry as dust and the idea of Sam thrusting one of those "ribbed for her pleasure" condoms inside her filled her with dread. And tonight was only the start. The contract she had signed was vast in scope and nothing was off-limits. *If he's some kind of crazed horndog I might be getting back on the Greyhound bus in a wheelchair!* Alice thought as she jiggled her bosoms and began to mentally focus on the soul restoration message from Psalm 23:3.

Alice carried on with her show but was searching in her head for alternatives that might be in the kitchen from which to MacGyver herself substitute K-Y jelly. From the look of Sam, Alice could tell his mind was elsewhere. *Am I not pretty? Am I a disappointment?*

She stepped closer to Sam and moved her breasts within inches of his face. She knew this was how they did it in the movies. Alice turned around with her back to Sam and unclipped her brassiere. She slung it in the direction of the window with the Arch view. Cupping her breasts to conceal her nipples she turned around to face Sam.

As she was about to reveal her naked upper-half, Sam shouted dismissively, "Stop. I've had enough."

"Did I do something wrong?" Alice said as she ran over to the kitchen to retrieve her bra.

"I'm sorry Alice. I'm tired. Double shift today. I want to rest for a bit. Maybe we can pick this up later. At this moment I need to shower and recharge my batteries!" Sam said, and abruptly curtailed Alice's one-woman show.

Sam showered and changed for sleep. In another unexpected move for Alice, he let her take the sofa bed solo.

Sam rolled out a sleeping bag on the floor for himself in the far corner of the apartment. He turned the lights off and they both went to their respective sleeping areas.

There was a saying that Family Dollar continually drilled into new recruits during training: "Even if the client is wrong, the client is right." Alice had to look at Sam like a customer at her store, she reassured herself, as she pulled a sheet over her body.

She endured a restless, sleep-deprived night. It wasn't Sam's snoring echoing off the walls that kept her awake. It wasn't spending the night in an unfamiliar place with a random man in the same room. It was the anticipation that at any minute she would find Sam pawing her. Or even worse on top of her, or trying to stick his penis down her throat. Alice knew that was what she had signed up for and that she was contracted to be an obliging partner, but it still scared her. Sam owned her for seven entire nights and she couldn't deny him any whim or demand as long as it was legal. Alice was effectively a sex slave.

In a perverse way, she wished they had already slept together. She was as ready as she would ever be. All dressed up in her beautiful new clothes and lingerie set. Sam likely had baby oil stashed somewhere in the apartment, so it wouldn't have been all pain. At least she would know by now if he was rough, gentle, or if he intended to hurt her. Alice simply had no idea what Sam was capable of. Alice lay awake in a strange bed anxiously trying to steal sleep. The uncertainty of what might happen next kept her on edge.

Somehow she finally nodded off. When she woke she still had all her clothes on. There was no evidence that Sam had laid a hand on her during the night. The microwave's clock read 10 a.m. and she was alone in the apartment. Sam had placed a note on the counter. *I am doing a double shift, will be back tonight.* Next to it was a list of touristy things within walking distance she might want to check out.

Alice showered and put on a second outfit she had bought yesterday. A pair of high-waisted blue jeans and a crisp white blouse. Standing in front of the mirror she liked what she saw. The attire was smart and certainly something that could be repurposed for church. The new brown hair with its leftover curls she was digging. Somehow the fresh color gave her a level of sophistication she hadn't previously experienced. Sam, for a strange creepy guy, had a fashion flare she liked. Alice could've sworn she was now looking closer to her age and had discovered a level of confidence previously not experienced.

After walking around downtown for several hours, Alice ventured into the sole supermarket in the area. She picked up food, flowers, and a bottle of Missouri-made wine. Home cooking, uncorked Norton grape vino and fresh flowers smothered the stale air of the apartment. In her sprightly outfit, Alice stood in the kitchen cooking dinner for her and Sam. For a split second, she felt like a suburban housewife on a husband-supporting mission. In reality she was more like a feeder mouse making herself at home in the vivarium. Her fate was known but she might as well make the best of it in the meantime before the snake got what it wanted.

With the food cooking and the table set for dinner, Alice refilled her wine glass and sat down on the sofa. She switched on the television and tuned into the local news. The report was full of crime. "These St. Louisans are trigger-finger happy.

They are good at shooting each other, themselves and anything else they can!" she said aloud upon being informed of what had been a brutal day in the region.

Alice heard the door unlock. Sam was back.

"Alice, you're still here?"

"Where do you think I would be?" she replied.

"Run off, nothing stopping you."

"We made a deal. I'm yours for the next six nights. Go clean up. Dinner will be ready in five. It's mac and cheese, my grandma's recipe. I hope you like it!"

They made small talk over dinner. Alice gave Sam the highlights of her day traversing downtown. She was amazed at the beauty of the old train station ticket office, which was now a bar. Alice had even spent a couple of hours at City Museum and watched a circus show performance.

Sam was intrigued. With her new hair color and pretty clothes, Alice was a world away from the girl he had video-chatted with to set up this trip. She certainly looked nothing like any of the harlots that had traipsed through his apartment over the last year. In truth, Alice looked just like his ex-wife did when she was the same age.

"I like the flowers," Sam said as Alice cleaned up the table.

"Trying to make the place a little more comfortable," she replied while loading the dishwasher.

There was a silence between the two of them as Alice wiped down the kitchen.

"Would you like me to put on the outfit I wore last night?" she asked.

"You're good as you are."

"What can I do for you?" She responded, knowing the business end of the day was approaching.

"Dance with me."

Sam dimmed the lights and put on a CD. Alice recognized the tune. It was a Roy Orbison classic that her grandma used to play.

A tear rolled down Alice's cheek as they danced.

"Are you OK? Did I do something wrong?" Sam asked, noticing she was crying.

"It's not you. This song reminded me of someone who passed," Alice replied, without elaboration.

They danced for the remainder of the song. At its conclusion, Sam said, "We've got a busy day tomorrow. Let's call it a night."

Alice began to unbutton her blouse in anticipation of what was about to happen. The half-bottle of wine she had downed would make it easier than it would've been last night. Sam looked on as she threw the shirt off and started unzipping her jeans. She was wearing another sexy underwear set. Her offerings were beyond tempting. Alice was everything that all his other girls were not.

"Why not change into your sleep outfit in the bathroom? You'll have more privacy. Anyone can see in," he said while looking out of the window.

Alice beautified herself in the bathroom for the final act of the day. When she was done she came out to find Sam passed out in his sleeping bag. He had pulled the sofa bed out for her and the sheets were perfectly turned.

Odd. He paid for an all-you-can-eat debauchery buffet and hasn't taken a nibble, Alice thought, as she now really felt like that mouse in the snake's cage being toyed with.

Alice was less apprehensive than the previous night but still struggled to sleep. She was plagued with nightmares of being eaten by a python.

She woke up to the smell of coffee in the pot and waffles in the toaster. She checked herself over and Sam hadn't done anything to her last night.

"Eat up and get yourself dressed. I'm going to give you a tour of St. Louis."

After breakfast Sam pulled his car out of the garage. It was an old convertible Chrysler LeBaron with a bizarre speed wing on the back that looked out of place. They spent the day driving around St. Louis. Sam even showed her North City. It was so depressed, that it made coal country look affluent.

As Saturday drew to a close, Sam again called an early night. And not the kind of early night he had paid for. Not the kind of night Alice had expected to be participating in.

For Sunday Sam planned a picnic at a local park with a French-sounding name. Alice was nearly halfway through her contracted time. She was starting to wonder if she was going to be riding the Greyhound bus back with her honor intact and a dozen condoms still in their wrappers.

Alice looked down at her Jesus on the cross necklace: "Thank you, Lord," she said. Alice could only think God was appreciative of her service and was repaying her with his protection. Although there was still a considerable amount of time on the clock, and anything could and might happen with Sam. And to be fair, what she had signed up for was unlimited in regard to obligations. It was still too early to declare that this particular feeder mouse had been scrubbed from the snake's menu.

*   *   *

Mike Love may have managed to duck the stinky lingerie that Nick Pipeman tossed his way, but he certainly didn't avoid the rest of the shit storm that followed in the wake of what he tagged, "The Nightmare on Ann St." Like everyone these days that lets random strangers into their homes, the owners had strategically placed video cameras throughout their property. They'd seen just about everything that happened and were furious. Steve Santiago, the seller's listing agent from the ritzy Madis-Bunion brokerage, was lightning-fast with an angry call to Daris Ballic. Steve demanded he launch a full investigation and filed his own complaint with the Real Estate Commission.

There was a deeper backstory to the incident that Nick confessed to Mike. The female owner of the house wasn't a random stranger but turned out to be Nick's dentist. He had apparently an ongoing infatuation with her. On top of this creepy crush, Nick was also holding a grudge against the dentist for not using him to list her home. Nick had tricked Mike into booking the showing so his own name wouldn't be part of any digital log records. The face mask and trilby hat were all part of Nick's elaborate disguise, and the pandemic backstory made it more plausible for him to be wearing the outfit. Mike thought that part of the plan was a little far-fetched and couldn't envision a scenario where anyone would wear a surgical-style mask out in public.

All this elaborate subterfuge was a front to allow Pipeman to gain undercover access to his dentist's home and then poke around her private belongings. Or, as Pipeman freakishly justified in a manner that sounded like a serial killer in training, "I wanted to get to know her a little better." Nick had told Mike that he knew all along she was a "closeted dirty minx" and suggested the naughty lingerie and kinky toys he found in the house had proven his theory correct.

Although the owners had just about seen everything, they didn't have a clear image of Nick without either a face mask on or underwear covering his identifying features. Mike told both Daris and the investigating Real Estate Commission team that his buyer was an office walk-in and had given a fake name. If it was ever found out that the panty-sniffing freak was Pipeman, his real estate license would be revoked. Daris had a pretty good idea who it was in the video but went along with Mike's story, as he didn't want to risk losing Nick. As much as Mike would like less competition downtown, he would rather play fairly. Mike knew there might be some fines coming his way, but Pipeman said he would cover them.

Mike had also found out there was some interest from Nick in the Zoe department. The panty-sniffing was the tip of the iceberg with Nick's deviant behavior and was another element of a personality that he would try to shield from Gloria and Zoe. However Mike, like a chess grandmaster, had in his head a sequence of moves planned out to advance his goals. Mike thought Zoe was always a little uptight and spent too much time waiting for Mr. Perfect. Life wasn't a John Hughes movie and the likelihood of some floppy-haired heartthrob presenting himself to an angsty aging clown was slim. If he could, as he would delicately say, "uplift her spirit via the touch of a man," Zoe might ultimately think about marriage, children, and nesting. Hopefully, this trajectory would lead to her using some of her jewelry cash to buy a house – using Mike as the agent.

With the same methodology, if Pipeman had a love interest he might refocus his current twin full-time passions of attempted debauchery and the consuming desire to sell a copious amount of homes. Simply put, if Nick was tied up with a love interest, he would not only get into less trouble but would also have less time to work. Nick, now in Mike's debt, would pass his way some of the business he didn't have time for. This was a Machiavellian play on Mike's part that Spitfire top gun Clint Cummings would be proud of.

Pipeman owed Mike big time for covering up his indiscretions. The first bone Nick tossed to Mike was giving him an open house to hold in the desirable Lafayette Square area. Statistics showed it was rare for buyers to purchase homes discovered at open houses. However, they were a wonderful tool for agent self-promotion and a good place to pick up future clients. Mike was in desperate need of new business and jumped at this opportunity. For the occasion, he donned his prized black suit and bolo tie regalia, as inspired by the sleeve artwork for Bruce Springsteen's seminal 1987 album *Tunnel of Love.*

Like every day over the past week, it was a hot one with devilish humidity. Mike planned to arrive at the listing an hour early and crank up the air-conditioning to make the viewing experience more comfortable. First step, park his Chevy Sonic far away from the house. Mike didn't need potential clients to associate him with a ride that didn't exude success. This maneuver would've been more sensible on a cooler day. By the time Mike had lugged the open house sign a full block from his car to the listing, both he and his outfit were drenched in sweat. Once Mike had set up the yard sign and mustered up the energy to inflate a few eye-catching balloons to tie on it, he let himself into the property.

"Oh crap!" he shouted loudly upon entering. The house, although with a park view and beautiful from the outside, wasn't at all beautiful on the inside. It had dirty musty carpets throughout, and looked as if nothing had been updated post Jimmy Carter relinquishing the Panama Canal. To add to the general dismay, the air-conditioning wasn't working well, and even when on full blast failed to abate the blistering heat. Between the hot temperatures and the state of the property, Mike was now sweating more profusely inside the house than he had been when dragging his yard sign down the street. He took off his shirt, jacket, pants, and bolo tie and draped them on the kitchen counter to dry off. He then gave himself a whore's bath from the sink in an attempt to freshen up.

What a house of horrors! He thought as he sat down wearing just his underpants and socks on a sofa that made a poor excuse for staging.

He grabbed his cell phone and called Pipeman. He was ready to give him a piece of his mind for not warning him about the condition of this so-called "Premier Listing."

Pipeman picked up. From the background noise, it sounded as if he was at some kind of outside event.

"Where are you?" Mike asked.

"City pool, my friend; too hot to work. Besides, this is the last weekend the college girls are still on lifeguard duty. They're back at school soon and I need to get my final fill of all those boney-assed beauties," Pipeman replied.

In mid-August, the schools and colleges started back. That meant the more nubile seasonal help was no longer available. Pools were left with an assortment of older lifeguards, many drafted from the back offices of City Hall. They didn't nearly provide the same standard of eye candy for the mental spank bank of a pervert like Nick. And certainly, no hormonal boy, with these end-of-season offerings, was in a hurry to recreate the lifeguard rescue and kiss scene from *The Sandlot*.

All this talk of girls' ass reminded Mike he needed to have a delicate conversation with Pipeman before his date with Zoe. Nick, due to a particular brand of lewd requests, was notorious for crashing and burning on dates.

"Nick, this house you touted as "a grand painted dame with sylvan views" is a shit show! I can see why you would rather be at the pool ogling barely legal girls and not sweating your balls off on this garbage heap," Mike proclaimed.

"Mr. Love, you have to realize what you have the keys to. We're at the end of the buying season and there's a limited amount of inventory, especially in the single-family home market. So let me explain the situation in a way that's easy for you to comprehend the opportunity I've given you," Nick said, reverting back from a "Peeping Tom" to a seasoned salesman.

"I'm all yours," said Mike, who was enjoying the park view from the living room window.

"Think of the late-August housing market like the Hair of the Dog bar before last orders. All the attractive ladies have been picked up and gone home with somebody. While these girls and lucky guys are engaging in glorious lovemaking, you are sitting at the bar looking for "strange." What's available? Drunk chicks falling off their stools, thicc girls who need to lay off the toasted ravioli, and Hoosier hags playing pool. Also, sharking are guys who failed to bag a lady but want to get laid."

"Where's this going?" Mike asked.

"Supply and demand in force. At the bar it's a numbers game. The girls, no matter what they look like, or how much of a lush they are, will have an option of going home that night and getting royally fucked," Nick said.

"Even the ugliest of women can look attractive with the aid of liquid courage and when viewed through beer goggles," Mike said, realizing the general direction Nick's conversation was heading.

"Especially under the constraints of an impending closing time. It's either one of those bottom-of-the-barrel ladies or jerking off to porn," said Nick.

"Indeed!" Mike replied.

"You're holding an open house and all of the people coming through the door need a place to live. You're correct, it's a pig of a house, but like the fugly gals at the Hair of the Dog, you have something that people want. Buyers need a home, just like the dudes at the bar need a woman," said Nick.

"There's an ultimate motivating fear of ending up with nothing," Mike interjected, as he watched through the window a lady in brightly colored clothing walking two dogs.

"My friend, today you're adjudicating an event in many ways similar to an evening at the bar. A barman in essence is selling the dream of sex to customers. He keeps the men and women plied with alcohol, and everyone on the premises believes they have a chance of getting bedroom action that night. The property you're standing in is like a well-nourished, beauty in the eye-of-the-beholder, in urgent need of twelve-step house version of a fugly lady at the bar. But I always say there's an ass for every chair out there, no matter how big the ass, and how fragile the chair. You need to work your magic and get someone to fall in love with that house and sell them the dream of home ownership. If not buy that house today, come back for a second look and buy it, and if they still don't want that house, show them another. Be positive young Mike, seize the moment, find your lane, and stick in it," Pipeman declared, as he finished off his rant about the grandiose, polished turd of a house he had Mike trying to sell.

Find your lane and stick in it! Resonated with Mike before being reminded by the "ass on seats" reference that he needed to have an important chat with Nick.

"Nick, on the subject of ass on seats, and more directly ASS," can we talk about your date with Zoe? I would really like... HOLY SHIT!" Mike said, dropping his phone to the ground.

Out of the window, Mike saw the most shocking of events take place. A souped-up motorbike with a second person riding on the back raced down the street and mounted the sidewalk. It proceeded to drive on the pavement before pulling up in front of the house he was in. The person sitting pillion, holding a baseball bat in his hand, jumped off the bike and started to take wild swings at Mike's open house sign, Nick's for sale sign, and for added measure the surrounding shrubbery. Several swipes later the signs were smashed, the balloons had popped, and the bushes were in tatters.

Mike, who didn't have time to put on his trousers or shirt, bolted out of the front door and screamed to the bike riders, "WHAT THE FUCK ARE YOU DOING?"

The driver of the bike flipped him the bird, and the batsman waved his attack weapon menacingly in the air as a warning to not come closer. They then dramatically rode off, leaving behind a trail of destruction. Watching not only the attack but also with a clear view of Mike without his pants or shirt on, was rival realtor Linda Lyon and two of her clients. They had been waiting for the open house to begin.

"We're a few minutes early!" Linda shouted to a disheveled and disrobed Mike. "We'll pick up coffee and come back when you are set up, have turned all the lights on and put on your tie." She grabbed her clients and walked away.

Through a blast of texts and emails, Mike found out that his open house assault was just one small part of a synchronized wave of attacks attributed to New Berlin Real Estate. All of that day's Spitfire open houses had been targeted. To add to the air of menace, New Berlin was now buzzing a company-branded blimp above the property. In the style of hybrid psychological warfare, it was blasting out from speakers the Rolling Stones greatest hits. The "Phoney War" had ended and the real war with New Berlin Real Estate had begun.

Linda Lyon returned, accompanied by her clients; they were the first party to enter Mike's open house. Linda, in her early sixties, was dressed in an age-inappropriate bright pink leather moto jacket and a matching skirt that didn't preserve her modesty when walking up stairs. With a little too much plastic surgery, and too much time spent in the tanning booth, she had a face that resembled a large dry roasted peanut. Linda and her husband Jim Rore ran a highly successful team based in the Ballwin branch of a big national franchise. As a play on their names sounding like lion and roar, their logo was a roaring lion, and their marketing slogan: "Lyon&Rore – Take a bite out of real estate with us!" Linda and Jim had an army of associate realtors working for them dubbed, "Cubs." The entire team drove around in zebra-patterned SUVs. Linda was never more than three feet away from her clients as they toured the property. She was in and out of the house in quick order, snarling "Not interested!" upon exiting.

The next thirty minutes were consumed by several sets of nosey neighbors, who between them had too much free time on their hands and many more Lafayette Square stories to tell than he needed to hear. Mike fielded their questions, listened to their yarns graciously, and made sure they all left their details on the sign-in sheet. He would make it a priority to start following up with them on Monday.

Next came a snarky gay couple to tour the property. They were frothing at the bit about all the upgrades they would need to make on this home. The man of the relationship was in the medical profession and his partner was a wannabe home-flipper. They measured the rooms, shone laser pointers at the ceilings, and thoroughly kicked the colloquial tires. After spending forty minutes plotting out their vision for making the house great again, in unison they screeched, "This house won't work for us," and walked out.

The New Berlin Real Estate barrage balloon must have run out of power or hot air, or whatever else this tool of passive-aggression ran on. It floated off towards the horizon halfway through the open house.

Mike Love wasn't much of a guy for making rules and many would label him a libertarian. In terms of fashion sense, he generally had a "no-fucks-given" attitude, best illustrated by his daily no-fuss attire. However, for a guy who didn't care much about style, and who claimed to want less government not more, he had strong opinions in one area: leisurewear. Mike thought the trend for women to wear yoga pants as a fashion statement was a modern-day, societal problem. In his opinion, they were never intended to be everyday clothing. Mike thought it was such a pressing issue that it needed immediate government intervention.

Mike figured that ninety percent of the yoga-pants-wearing population must have lived in a world with no mirrors and were committing a daily crime against humanity. He knew, though, that however bad the yoga pants looked, and however bad the people looked in them, it would be near impossible to fully ban this article of clothing. However, he did have a few restrictive riders that he said could be legislated in order to create a more civilized society. Mike said that if yoga pants are to be worn in public, outside the defined confines of a "house of exercise," then they should be in no other color than black, they shouldn't be worn by anyone old enough to legally drink, and a shirt or some other piece of clothing must be utilized to cover up any hint of the naughty bits.

Jenna, a thirty-something woman, and her tween son breezed through the doors of Mike's open house. This lady was a living, breathing example of everything that was wrong with wearing yoga pants in public as if they were acceptable clothing. Jenna, who quickly confessed to Mike that she was a single mother, had poured herself into a shiny aqua pair of skin-tight yoga pants that seemingly had the prime function of highlighting a camel toe the size of Texas. Standing in front of Mike, Jenna could be produced as the perfect "smoking gun" witness to illustrate the very cause he was campaigning for. The jury might even be so shocked that they dismiss his limited request and instead go full Taliban fundamentalist and enforce an outright ban on wearing yoga pants more than twenty feet from a yoga mat.

Jenna was asking good questions about the home, but it was hard for Mike to focus on her talking bits. And anyway, he had the feeling that she was on the prowl for a surrogate father for the fruit of her loins and not a place to call home. Mike, trying not to stare at Jenna's crotch cleavage, mentally came up with some apt marketing remarks that might assist in her quest for a new man. If Jenna was his listing, she would be "a very special home" with "good bones," albeit with some "light wear-and-tear from a previous owner." Verbiage also coming into Mike's head courtesy of the in-your-face ninja bootie was, "hardwood floors throughout" and "beautiful inside." Within agent remarks, Mike would add "motivated seller" to increase brokerage activity. To cover his ass, he would have to include in the seller's disclosures that "Jenna would demand another baby within five years."

Now what if Mike was representing the buyer's side of the Jenna transaction. If he wanted to uphold his code of ethics' fiduciary responsibility, he would need to tread carefully. Mike would warn clients that Jenna was going to need "ongoing maintenance" and value may "depreciate fast." In summary, he would suggest poor ol' Jenna would come with a "buyer beware" warning and was "better to rent than own." Mike managed to shunt Jenna and her aqua-green yoga pants out of the door and pointed her in the direction of another open house. He did feel mightily sorry for her son, though. He was at that age where if mom turned up to school dressed like she was today, he would be up for some serious grief from classmates.

It was nearly three o'clock and Mike, with a splitting headache and a desperate need to shower, was eager to finish the open house promptly. He hadn't gotten anywhere near to selling the house, and he didn't think he had found any future clients. If he was the bartender at the Hair of the Dog, he would have a mad bunch of customers who would need a cab called to "go east" and head to a strip club. This open house had been a bust.

The only slight relief for what had been a hell of a day was that Mike didn't get any newly loved-up couples on the hunt for their first home through his doors. It was easy to get jealous when these fresh off the love boat, infused with hope, optimism and often boasting well-paid jobs came bounding in. Hands were held tightly, doors heroically opened by the gentleman, rooms thoughtfully picked out as a nursery, blah blah blah. Unfortunately, all this positive energy underwent a rapid polarity reversal by the time it had drifted from "said happy couple to a jaded Mike." Maybe he thought this was why women tended to make more successful real estate agents. If you can live through monthly menstrual cramps and the pain of childbirth, you are certainly well-conditioned, no matter how bad you feel, to put on a happy face and bluff your way through sharing the unbridled joy of others.

It was now after three and Mike finally got the Indian family of five out of the door. They had zero interest in buying the house, but that didn't stop the children from fighting over which bedroom they would have if they bought it. Everyone wanted the attic suite. As much as Mike kept telling them it would be cold in winter, they wouldn't stop fighting over future ownership rights to this room. With the family finally out the door, Mike could start turning off the lights, lock up and leave.

Mike was checking that the basement windows were properly shut when he heard the sound of the front door opening and closing. He could hear footsteps traversing the living room.

"Open house is over, book an appointment with your agent to come back another day!" Mike shouted up the stairwell.

Mike wasn't in the mood to either extend the open house or answer any further questions about this wretched home. He could hear the person still walking around the house. He turned the basement lights off and headed up the rickety stairs to the ground floor. There was no one in the living room. Mike could hear noise from the kitchen. A drawer was opened and then the sound of the dishwasher door closing.

"I'm about to lock up; I have an appointment I need to be at in twenty minutes!" he shouted as he walked down the hallway towards the kitchen.

Mike Love's day so far had been a roller coaster ride with few highs and many lows. But the open house visitor now standing in the kitchen before him had added a wild, unexpected twist. So much so that Mike, though he was fully prepared for the eventuality of this moment happening, was now lost for words.

Apartment #1411 Grit and Grace

A billboard in front of the waterfront casino advertised tonight's motivational speakers. A fully loaded rogue's gallery of hustlers and hacks had been assembled. Headlining was an energetic Trump administration flunky who had been fired after twelve days on the job. This man had been living off his brief stint in the belly of the orange man's dysfunctional beast for the last year. There are only so many ways to skin a cat but this slippery New Yorker continually found fresh angles to milk from his 288 hours of Oval Office fame. For a price and a chance to plug a project, he would gleefully share anecdotes with anyone who cared. Missouri was a frothing-at-the-bit Trumplandia and the MAGA crowd had flooded into town for this evening's extravaganza.

Among the warm-up acts on offer was an engaging, easy-on-the-eyes thirty-something Missouri native by the name of Colton Chesterfield III. He was a rags-to-riches, riches-to-rags, now working his way back to riches all-American antihero. A medium-term stretch in prison had only enhanced his celebrity status and lucre-making opportunities. Colton's recently released biography had been a number-one bestseller in the Missouri non-fiction charts. As well as writing books and recording podcasts, Colton was an in-demand speaker available for corporate events. Evident from the throng of early arrivals, Colton was a popular guy, especially with the ladies who brought to this audience a rowdy Nashville bachelorette party vibe. Reginald Oakland, a man with a mission and in no need of Colton's persuasive charms, was sat at the back of the packed auditorium watching the show.

Upon filling his boots with unwanted messaging, Reginald relocated himself from the crowd to the shadows of the casino's underground garage. Car crime was prevalent in these parts, as was the practice of mugging unsuspecting gamblers of their slot machine winnings in parking lots. Most people loitering, as Reginald now was, would get noticed and subsequently busted by security, but he had thought ahead. Reginald was dressed in the full regalia of a funeral director. Although the stately hat and long coat were not ideal for the steaming August heat, it was an outfit that didn't draw questions or raise suspicion. For authenticity, he had parked up in the garage a Hearse complete with a flower-adorned casket. Out of respect, no one would dare question Reginald's presence. It was obvious to even the dumbest Missouri Hoosier that an undertaker standing alongside a coffin-laden vehicle was on the job and deserved the dignity of not being interrogated.

Reginald had been scoping a metallic blue Porsche 911 for the last two hours. Only in America could a fresh out-of-jail bankrupt be driving around in a hundred-grand ride. Only in America could a convicted felon be the author of a bestselling self-help book. "No class these days, villains become pillars of the community for turning their crimes against others into crimes committed against themselves. How does the bad guy manage an image redo and make bank rebranding himself as the victim?" muttered Reginald under his breath, angry at the turn of events that had led to him lurking in this hot garage tonight.

A car alarm chirped. Finally, the Porsche driver had returned. Reginald had a visual on the person he had been following around all day. Actually, he had been stalking this man much like a big-game hunter for months. The prey before him was tall and unashamedly handsome, with a tan that screamed country club, not manual labor. He was dressed, as he was most summer days, in a designer beige linen suit, and in his hand he clutched a Louis Vuitton man bag. *The car and clothes no doubt business assets and untouchable!* thought Reginald, who knew the person he had tracked here was meant to be paying restitution to victims, not living high on the hog – although real victims like Reginald were of course the last to ever get paid. The IRS, Missouri tax office, city, regional utility companies and other deep-pocketed entities would be made whole before the little guys saw a dime. That was the way the system worked. That's why Reginald was taking matters into his own hands.

To say Reginald was apprehensive was an understatement; this precise moment had been months in the making. Now all he had to do was execute a well-rehearsed plan. *Can I do it?*

Reginald moved nearer to the Porsche. The car's owner had laid his jacket on the back seat and was hunting for something inside his man purse. With an intensity and speed he hadn't drawn on since his high school football days, Reginald moved towards the driver. Hearing footsteps, the Porsche owner looked up to see who was approaching. Viewing the descending subject dressed in a funeral director's outfit, he knew he was unlikely to be about to get mugged.

"Evening brother!" he said to Reginald.

Cuz I am black this guy thinks I am a brother! Reginald thought with an additional DEFCON-level of rage.

On a hot St. Louis evening, a heavy funeral director's jacket is far from useful – that is unless you are trying to conceal something. Reginald was a three-point line away from the only other man in the parking lot when he pulled from under his jacket a Benelli tactical shotgun. If the sight of the weapon didn't grab the Porsche driver's attention, the sound of the gun being cocked certainly did.

"Hands up Colton Chesterfield III!" Reginald screamed as his target dropped his oversized man bag and raised his arms high above his head.

*   *   *

Reginald Oakland was a man of humble origins, infused early on with ambitious life goals. He was raised in the rural Bootheel region of Missouri once tagged "Little Dixie" for its plantation farms. Slavery, in fact, was only a few branches away in his own family tree. Reginald's father Samuel was raised by sharecropper parents in the era of Jim Crow. For Reginald himself, even in the post-Lyndon Johnson Equal Rights era, being called the "N" word throughout his fifty-plus years was something he had regularly dealt with. And he had been taught from an early age that being Black in this part of America meant keeping your head down and your mouth shut.

If there was one thing that Black people in mid-20th-century Missouri were good at doing, it was dying. Poor diet, poor job safety, poor medical care, poor police protection, poor-quality housing; insert poor into any aspect of the Black experience and it was an excellent way to cut a life short. In an era of segregated schools, pools, trains, restrooms and diner counters, white people in rural Missouri had little interest in providing funeral services to African Americans. Reginald's entrepreneurial father Samuel saw a business opportunity to be grabbed amid the tragedy of his community's limited life expectancy.

Samuel was a man with a vision, a plan, and a biblical sense of grit and grace. He knew Black people would never allow any family member to not be given a proper burial and rousing send-off. He also knew white people of that era had little concern for "the Blacks" and minimal interest in burying them. For this reason, Black-owned funeral parlors were among the few businesses the white merchant classes didn't see as competition.

As a bonus to his career credentials, Samuel possessed a calm and caring nature; an essential quality to deal with the emotions of the recently bereaved. Samuel's father rustled up seed money from friends and family and set up a small parlor in Kennett by the name of Safe Haven. Kennett was the nearest large town to his rural Missouri homestead. He marketed his operation as "Black-owned for the Black community." The enterprise was an outstanding success.

Reginald's upbringing was nothing like his father's. For one thing, it was middle-class; for another, Civil Rights legislation had technically torn up the old segregation playbook. Although rural Missouri was always a slow unwilling partner to "Great Society" reforms, and decades behind the rest of America in embracing progressive values. Even so, Reginald attended a fully integrated public school and, in a shock to his mother, dated white girls. After graduation, though, and with the approval of his parents, he married an African American woman by the name of Cynthia. The couple quickly started a family and had two children, a boy called George and a girl – for simplicity – they named Georgina.

Reginald and Cynthia took over the reins of Safe Haven after Samuel's retirement. His father had always been reluctant to market to the white community – a side-effect of having ingrained into him from birth a "them and us" separation of the races mentality. Reginald, although always heeding his father's advice to keep your head below the parapet, came to age in an era where even funeral services in Missouri had reached a post-race détente. Reginald's ultimate ambitions were to grow the business and market to not only the Black population of Kennett but the entire city.

With a loan from a community bank, Reginald and Cynthia had funding in place to reimagine Safe Haven. The way in which Reginald pitched their expansion plans to the financiers was by likening the improvements to an airport adding a second runway to facilitate extra flights. Safe Haven upgraded the utility infrastructure, tuck-pointed the building, enlarged the parking lot, expanded the reception rooms, and constructed a state-of-the-art crematorium. With investment, quicker turnaround times were possible and Safe Haven was able to conduct multiple additional funerals each day. Within this part of the state, there wasn't anything comparable within a hundred-mile range – a fact they marketed with a big advertising and public relations push.

Safe Haven's business grew expediently and the investment paid off handsomely. Reginald, thanks to his father's business acumen, his inherited calm nature, and his own grit and grace had shattered the glass ceiling of Missouri's rural racism to become a regional captain of industry – and with this newfound success became borderline rich. Reginald bought his father Samuel a condo in Florida and sent him off to continue his retirement in style. Cynthia was allowed to give up work and become a full-time, spa-pampered, mall-shopping housewife. George and Georgina were enrolled in top private schools. The Oaklands upgraded their practical cars to fully loaded Cadillac SUVs. And the greatest treat for everyone was the purchase of an Osage Beach vacation home. Reginald now had all the trappings of success but wanted more.

"The accomplishments of Safe Haven can be replicated easily," Reginald proclaimed, as he proposed growing the business further. He would constantly tell Cynthia that Safe Haven could become to the burial industry what Starbucks was to coffee shops. The only thing stopping global domination for Safe Haven was access to capital. The small community bank that had backed him for his first expansion offered an additional loan. However, it was only enough to fund what would be a painstakingly slow organic growth, that would take decades to scale. Reginald wanted to conquer the world – and he wanted to do it quickly.

A trusted funeral parlor in a small town is part of the local community's DNA. Funerals are pricey, and in rural America, people plan ahead for their final expenses, which can often amount to tens of thousands of dollars. Buying a prepaid funeral package decades before you're likely to need it is economically astute. The final costs are inflation-proofed and the payments can be spread out over years. Think of it as a layaway plan for something you will need but will never be around to enjoy. To the customer it brings peace of mind knowing that you have secured a dignified send-off and are not leaving a financial burden on family.

Since its opening day, Safe Haven had administered prepaid funeral plans. Samuel would often tell Reginald that in his business's infancy, these local trusting customers making their monthly payments was the difference between success and failure. The money received from clients for their future needs was placed in trustee accounts held at the same community bank Safe Haven used for operations. The interest they earned from these deposits was modest but the money was secure and liquid when needed, to be drawn upon for a future burial. Reginald abided by his father Samuel's insistence that the money held in trust was ring-fenced and not used for anything but its intended purposes. Over the years, for even a medium-sized operation like Safe Haven, this pot grew into a sizable amount – over a million and a quarter dollars by the time Reginald's mind was consumed with corporate expansion plans.

Most women who came through the doors of funeral parlors were either teary-eyed mourners or embalmed in a casket, ready for burial. So a pretty girl with a pulse walking into the front office serving up flirty banter wasn't something funeral directors were accustomed to dealing with. When a sweet-scented, youthful beauty stormed into Reginald's office with a timely proposition, it was a red letter day.

Janet Sodman, a micromini-wearing, cleavage-revealing stunner was the perfect tool to get Reginald's full attention.

The message she delivered was as pleasing to Reginald's ears as her looks were to his eyes.

Janet was a salesgirl representing a slick company by the name of Merlin Investments. From her cross-legged position on a comfortable couch, Janet explained that the funeral business was a tired, "broken" model. Her corporation, backed by Silicon Valley venture capital and led by a team of Wharton business school grads, was dragging the funeral industry – albeit kicking and screaming – into the 21st century.

"Warren Buffett owns insurance carriers for one specific reason," Janet said as she moved closer to Reginald. "The premiums he collects, he invests. The returns he gets from his investments are far more substantial than the profits he makes on insurance services. Selling insurance for Buffett is really about generating cash and making money from that money. What if I said to you, 'Reginald, you have been running your business the wrong way!'"

The perfume Janet was wearing was intoxicating. He wanted to ask her what it was, but he felt that would be inappropriate. "Tell me Janet, what have I been doing wrong? Before you answer, I'll say in a non-braggadocious manner that I'm a wealthy man with a nice car, a great lifestyle, and a lake house. But I am humble at heart and always ready to learn from others."

Staying on track, Janet quickly replied: "You've been doing everything right and your success is evidence of that, Mr. Oakland. But what Merlin will do is take the money for prepaid funerals that you have saved in the bank and strategically invest it. Your capital will be held in trust, just like it is now.

But instead of getting low, single-digit interest on your deposits, we will be making you returns that Berkshire Hathaway shareholders would be jealous of."

As she was making her point, Janet handed Reginald a glossy brochure showcasing Merlin's corporate board – the company's big-hitters – portraits of a bunch of smiling East Coast types with expensive educations and slick, heavy hair gel. Reginald scrolled through bios and perused the fine print. Merlin was regulated and backed by the Federal government, so it was certainly legitimate.

"What do you guys charge for this?" Reginald asked, sneaking a glimpse of Janet's teal-colored bra while she bent down to retrieve lipstick from her satchel.

"No fees. All we do is split the returns on the investments. It's a win-win for your business. Your prepaid funeral expenses are guaranteed. There are no extra administration fees, and we share the profits equally." She then handed Reginald a chart showing three years' worth of portfolio growth. It was substantially higher than the bank payout he was getting now. The kind of returns that could propel Safe Haven's ambitious expansion.

Janet handed Reginald a stack of literature and a binder full of glowing endorsements from prominent business executives, and a few Shark Tank runner-ups. Before she left, she told him that many of his in-state competitors had already signed onto the program. The sales rep listed a roll call of people he knew within the industry who worked with Merlin. Reginald's mind was instantly diverted away from Janet's never-ending legs to the desperate thought of rival parlors getting an advantage with access to the money yielded by Merlin's investment system. Janet said she would be back in a week.

In the early days of Reginald's Safe Haven stewardship, he and Cynthia ran the operation as a team. Since she had elevated herself to full-time housewife, she had not been involved in day-to-day operations. His father Samuel's own life verged on that of a never-ending Jimmy Buffett song, and he had mentally detached himself from the business years ago. Reginald was running the show single-handedly, a fact he often told himself was the reason for Safe Haven's marketplace dominance.

Janet, as promised, was back seven days later. She popped the Merlin-branded champagne as she made what they call in the world of sales, "a puppy dog close."

*   *   *

"I have money if that's what you want!" said Colton with his eyes looking down at his bag to indicate there was cash in it.

"One million, two hundred and thirty-two thousand dollars – do you have that in the bag?" asked Reginald.

"That might be a stretch, will $400 work? Plenty enough to get high."

"I'm not a junkie, $400 isn't enough," Reginald replied looking into the car.

"It's a stick shift; I'd rather you didn't take it," said Colton, who knew the cost to replace a Porsche gearbox would be ugly.

"You think I want that? I'm not a carjacker either," said Reginald, who with one hand holding onto the gun pulled out a roll of gaffer tape from his pocket with the other. "Hands behind your back," he ordered as with the skill of a magician he began to restrain Colton with the tape.

Colton obliged. For a split second, he had thoughts about grabbing the gun. But one of the first things he learned in prison was that life on the streets of St. Louis had little value. Many of his captive compadres were doing time for killing someone that needn't have been murdered. Fat finger on the trigger, dialog lost in translation, miscommunication between parties. The list of the inconsequential minutiae that was the difference between life and death was infinite, and Colton had heard every conceivable reason why someone had died for nothing. Standing in front of a likely madman brandishing a lethal firearm, Colton was smart enough not to question his capabilities or ask his motives.

After taping Colton's hands together, Reginald gagged his mouth with a St. Louis flag bandana. He then shoved the gun into the small of his back and barked, "WALK!"

Colton, via the coercion of hard metal, was prodded towards the Hearse parked at the far side of the garage.

Reginald opened a door to the second row of seats and pushed Colton into the car.

"Lie down!" said Reginald.

Colton's reply was garbled by the gag but Reginald deciphered him saying, "You want me in the coffin?"

"On the floor!" he responded.

150

Reginald proceeded to use rope ties to bind Colton so he was unable to sit up. He then threw a blanket over him. Reginald placed the shotgun in the Hearse's front seat, took his coat off and covered the weapon with it.

That was easier than I thought it would be! Although Reginald had underestimated the meticulous planning conducted over the prior months that had led to this operation's smooth execution. Hours of research went into finding out where Colton was holed up. Snagging an apartment in the same building was a cunning move. Placing a hidden camera to monitor Colton's comings and goings was slick. Tailing Colton around St. Louis was no easy feat. Reginald had been logging the man's movements for months in order to get to a situation where he could kidnap his target uninterrupted. Reginald had always worked from the shadows and not once did he ever make eye contact with Colton.

Reginald sat in the driver's position and strapped his seat belt on. He had so much business from people not buckling up that he was extra vigilant with car safety. He put the keys in the ignition and started the vehicle but it wouldn't turn over. The battery was dead.

"Shit!" Reginald shouted as he popped the hood release and sprung out of the car. This Hearse was in good shape but the poor ride since the funeral parlor shuttered hadn't been used enough. Either the battery was toast or the alternator kaput. Reginald had AAA coverage but for obvious reasons he didn't want a tow truck driver poking around.

He got back into the car and tried the ignition again. Nothing happened. He slumped into the seat trying to work out his next move. He had prepared contingencies for many elements of his plan, but not for this precise problem.

In a simultaneous blast to the senses, Reginald could smell the noxious whiff of a cigarette and suddenly felt like he was being watched. He looked to his left and there was a lady who resembled Dolly Parton peering through the side window. She pointed to the Hearse's raised hood, attempting to offer assistance. Reginald pressed the button to lower the window but nothing happened – he'd forgotten the electrics were out.

He opened the car door, "Can I help you ma'am?" he asked, as he swished away a cloud of cigarette smoke from his face.

"*I* was going to ask *you* if you needed help. And if you please, I hate being called "MA'AM." Makes me sound like an old Southern aristocrat, which I'm certainly not."

"I think I'll be OK," Reginald said, getting out of the car in a dismissive manner while trying not to suffocate on this lady's overindulgence of perfume.

"You look like you're late for a funeral," the woman said, laughing at her own soft joke.

"Thanks for the concern, but I can take it from here."

"My name is Butterfly," she replied.

Reginald ignored her introduction and stuck his head under the hood to see if he could fix the problem.

"I know you!" Butterfly added after a long drag on her cancer stick.

"I doubt it," mumbled Reginald, as he cleaned a spark plug. The woman before him looked like the kind of aging barfly that frequented redneck Honky Tonks. Reginald, until his recent falling on hard times, didn't rub shoulders with this caliber of riffraff. For this reason, he couldn't envision how he could know her.

"You stay at Misery Towers?" Butterfly said now putting the pieces together.

"I live down by Cape!" said Reginald, using the colloquial name locals call the town of Cape Girardeau.

"I've seen you riding the elevators in my building."

"You must be mistaken," Reginald replied, now seated in the driver's seat, trying to get the car started without success.

"I'm like *Rain Man* with faces," Butterfly said as she stubbed out a finished cigarette and pulled a fresh one from her purse.

Reginald took a good look at the lady hovering over him. Her outfit wasn't exactly modest for a woman who was in his age bracket. The cleavage was hard not to stare at. The Butterfly tattoo on her breast plain gross. He had encountered a lot of wacky-looking people in his trade, but this one was a hot mess he needn't get to know. He had, though, seen her around the common areas of the building he was renting short term. For good reason, he had always kept to himself and never talked to any of the residents he brushed shoulders with.

Butterfly walked around the Hearse. The clank of her stilettos echoed off the parking garage walls as she teetered.

153

"Do you have someone in the back?" Butterfly asked as she looked into the rear of the car.

"I'm en route to a funeral; there's a client in the coffin."

"I don't mean in the box? I mean under the blanket. There's something or someone moving down there." The peroxide-hair dame stated.

Reginald, sensing his mission was in danger of spiraling out of control, again grabbed the concealed Benelli shotgun from the car and aimed it at Butterfly.

"Lose the cigarette and get in the car lady!" he demanded.

"Keep your hat on man!" Butterfly replied as she tossed the butt on the ground and sat on the rear bench seat.

"Smoking will kill you," said Reginald ironically, as he held the shotgun pointed at Butterfly's head. He then taped her hands up.

Butterfly looked down at the other seat – it was obvious someone was under the blanket. Whoever it was could be seen squirming and heard making noise.

After a pause, Butterfly said to Reginald, "I thought it was strange a funeral on a Sunday night."

Reginald sat in the driver's seat of his immobile vehicle trying to figure out what to do next. He now had two people captive.

Reginald tried the ignition again but no luck.

"I think you're stuck!" Butterfly said.

Reginald now wished he had taped the lady's mouth shut.

"It's hot in this garage. Is that a problem for the body in the casket?" she asked.

"Don't worry about that," Reginald replied.

"It's a problem for me," Colton could be heard saying from under the blanket.

"Don't you need to take the body somewhere?" Butterfly asked.

"No."

Colton was shaking and squirming, trying to dislodge the blanket, but with no luck.

"I have a car," Butterfly said.

"I'm sure you do."

"It's a Tahoe. Big enough to move your coffin to wherever it needs to be," said Butterfly.

"You think I'm stupid, and I will just release you and expect you'll walk to your apartment and bring back a car?"

"It's not at Missouri Towers. It's just over there," said Butterfly pointing via a shoulder movement to the next row of vehicles in the garage.

"You drove to the casino? It's quicker to walk. It's only three blocks?" said Reginald

"Dude, it's fucking dangerous out there. I don't stroll around downtown at night," she replied.

"Danger everywhere!" said Reginald, with a tight grip on his gun.

Butterfly looked at her captor and then at the person with a blanket over them lying next to her.

"That's for sure!" she said.

Reginald slumped into the seat. Life had crashed out of control. One day he was a man who had it all – a loving wife, children who adored him, a lake house, fancy cars, money in the bank, respect from the community. Now within the space of a few years, he was penniless, his wife dead and his kids hated him. And for a guy who never broke the law before, he was racking up a rap sheet of prosecutable crimes at record speed.

Had Cynthia been in the office the day hot-puss Janet and her marketing charms walked in, things would've turned out differently. Cynthia was smart, she could spot a con. The name Merlin alone, with its hocus-pocus connotations, would've been a red flag to her. Merlin Investments was a $400 million fraud. Nothing but a big Ponzi scheme. New Merlin clients' money was paying for old clients' funeral services. That's until the cashflow stopped coming and Merlin was unable to pay out for contracted funerals. Then the proverbial shit hit the fan. Federal authorities investigated and Merlin collapsed, bringing down with it hundreds of funeral parlors.

"What had the money been spent on?" was the question Reginald and dozens of others asked the investigating authorities. For one thing, a jet-setting lifestyle for the C-suite guys who ran Merlin Investments. For another, hefty sales commissions for the army of eye candy that acted as their front-line stormtroopers. And who was the mastermind behind this scheme for the ages? Colton Chesterfield III, whom the press tagged during his trial, "the hot flamboyant Bernie Madoff of Missouri."

Reginald looked in the rear-view mirror. This Butterfly looked harmless enough. He didn't have a beef with her. He didn't want to kidnap her either. Colton was the one he was after.

"I do live in Missouri Towers, albeit a short-term residence. Reginald Oakland is my name," he said to Butterfly over the seat headrest.

"I never forget a face," she replied, before adding, "In my business, it's important to remember regulars."

Reginald gave Butterfly a long once-over. He had a pretty good idea of what she did, but he still wanted to ask due to her age. Before Reginald could pose the question, Butterfly shot back, "Dancer on the Eastside!"

"I don't judge," said Reginald.

"I have seen a lot of weird shit happen in my years, and the key to my longevity has been discretion. So how about you untie me? I give you, the person under the blanket who keeps making sounds, and the stiff in the back, a ride to wherever you want to go, no questions asked. Once I drop you all off, we go our own ways, and whatever happened tonight never happened – if you know what I mean."

Reginald contemplated the proposition. Colton attempted to communicate his input to Butterfly and Reginald.

The undertaker put the gun in the front seat and covered it. He then exited the car, opened the back door, and released Butterfly from her restraints.

"The coffin is empty. You're not going to try anything funny, are you?" Reginald asked.

"If I was going to, I'd have done it by now," said Butterfly as she opened her handbag and pulled out a pistol.

Reginald was too far away from his own gun to react and stepped back.

"Mister, I know a good guy when I see one. You've got "troubled" written all over ya face, but you ain't "trouble," Butterfly said as she put the gun back into her bag.

"What about me?" could be made out, coming from Colton.

Butterfly pulled off the blanket to see who had been her backseat passenger.

"You!" she said in surprise.

"You know Colton Chesterfield III from Missouri Towers?"

"Yes! And he was also a regular at my strip club. High spender, although he would always go for the fresh young things. Guy didn't appreciate a pro like Butterfly," she said as she lit up a cigarette.

"This man and his fraud scheme destroyed my life," Reginald said, with an air of vengeance in his voice.

"Oh yeah, we know all about that. First place he came after he was released from prison was the Eastside strip clubs to party. He didn't seem short of cash for someone who owes millions in restitution," said Butterfly.

Reginald looked into Colton's eyes and said, "One million, two hundred and thirty-two thousand dollars is what you owe me. I know you have it."

"Feds took it all," Reginald made out as Colton's reply.

"Don't believe it. Ms. Butterfly says you were spending it up the day you got out of the slammer."

"Nothing left, all gone."

"How ya pay for the 911?" Reginald asked.

"It's on loan from a friend. Strip club money was a gift from my lawyer," Colton replied now more clearly, as he had managed with his tongue to loosen the bandana over his mouth.

"There's a good story for every objection. He's lying, that I know," said Butterfly.

"I've been watching him for months and he's smart for sure. But I guess you have to be. Feds are tracking your every move. They know you have the money stashed. One slip-up and they will get it," said Reginald.

"You were never meant to lose anything. It was the securities commission that shut us down. They didn't understand our model. It was too complicated for the G-Men," Colton said smugly.

"Bullshit! It was one big fraud with honey-trap marketing," said Reginald.

"I know some Illinois guys who are good at getting people to pay up," said Butterfly, but Reginald wasn't listening.

"Missouri, the state that gave the nation Walt Disney, Mark Twain, General Pershing, Jesse James, JCPenny, and of course the greatest invention of all, sliced bread, also gave us a vile conman like you. Bootheel justice will be served, Mr. Chesterfield!" said Reginald.

With that, Reginald picked up a grave-digging shovel from the back of his Hearse and slammed it into Colton's head.

Reginald was sweating profusely in the outfit of an undertaker, with a shovel in his hand, and a man who might be dead flopped lifeless before him.

Butterfly dropped her cigarette in shock and checked to see if Colton was OK.

"He's alive – just," said Butterfly.

"That's a shame," said Reginald, who then told Butterfly the coffin in the Hearse was intended for Colton.

Butterfly showed Reginald where her Chevy Tahoe was parked. He then dragged Colton's limp body into the back of the truck and threw the blanket over it.

"I'm driving, you need to rest," said Butterfly to Reginald, who was still shaking with anger.

Butterfly pulled out of the casino garage onto Highway 55 and headed south. Twenty minutes later, they had left St. Louis city limits. Although there wasn't official signage, two hours farther down the highway, they entered Missourah, as country folk pronounced their state name. To the side of the highway, small tidy houses dotted the landscape, plenty with Trump signs proudly displayed. In this region of America, many argued the wrong side had won the Civil War and due to that society was still paying the price.

There's a saying: "People get the government they deserve." Reginald had long ago decided the same theory was in force for strip malls. The one they rolled into to grab gas, with its check-cashing store, bail bondsman, sleazy massage parlor, and dollar shop was fit for the poor white neighborhood it served. Rural Missouri offered a like rival to any failed urban core in terms of poverty and miserable quality of life.

On the journey, Reginald told Butterfly about his family business. How it had been bankrupted by Merlin Investments stealing funds that were intended to pay for customers' funerals. The community felt sorry for him being swindled. He had it all: a great business, a loving wife, financial stability. He continually blamed himself for being stupid, for being greedy. Reginald sold everything he owned to contribute what he could for impacted families, to help with their funeral costs. The cars, the lake house, his family life; it was all gone. He knew it was the stress of it all that had killed Cynthia. Technically, it was cancer, but there was no doubt in his mind what the contributing factors were. Reginald poured his heart out to Butterfly. She was a good listener. She had years of practice. The stripping business was as much about listening as it was jiggling your boobs.

Another hour later they were deep in the Missouri Bootheel. Butterfly was directed by Reginald towards Kennett, the jewel in the crown of Dunklin County. This town of ten thousand was an agriculture hub for the farming community. The roads tonight were busy with kids cruising. It was as if every sixteen-year-old boy who owned a driver's permit believed that lifted trucks with mammoth decals and no working mufflers were an enticing mating call.

Reginald continued to direct Butterfly's route until they reached their ultimate destination. At the corner of Dixie Ave. and Davis St. was Safe Haven funeral parlor. Its grounds were overrun with weeds and the building's windows boarded up. Reginald cried looking at his defunct operation. If Reginald could get the money he invested with Merlin Investments back from Colton, the plan was to rebuild. In honor of his former wife, he had wanted a name change for the establishment. Cynthia's Heavenly Home was the top contender.

Butterfly drove the SUV into the parking lot of the funeral parlor. Colton was still passed out in the back of her car. He was lucky to be alive as it was quite a hit with the shovel. The funeral home, although looking run down, was expansive. At the far end of the compound was a small cottage. Butterfly figured it must've been Reginald's home. She pulled the car up to the rear of the cottage and shut the engine off. Reginald dragged Colton from the back of the Tahoe, threw him down the steps of an old coal storage cellar, and padlocked the door shut.

*   *   *

The Alice Jones that Sam Robinson had been corresponding with over the prior weeks was a ratty-looking thing who dressed like a girl who cared little about appearances. Her skin was splotchy and her faded pink hair was better suited for a hormonal teenager protesting prom dress code than a woman in her prime. Alice wasn't the prettiest lady money could buy, but she worked within Sam's budget and didn't quibble over his terms.

The Alice that Sam met in person was in a league above what he had anticipated. She looked like a movie star, albeit an Eastern European one, where the concept of beauty was askew to Hollywood norms. When Sam told Alice after first greeting her, "You look amazing," it was the only time he had given any of his rented lady friends an honest compliment.

As Sam sat on the sofa watching Alice's divine entrance, he found himself in the strange twilight zone between being a kid in a candy store and a deer frozen in panic on the highway as a big rig approached at full steam. He didn't know what to do, although he certainly knew what he couldn't do, which was raise his flag to full mast. This time Sam put it down to being tired from working a double shift. It certainly wasn't because of Alice, as she looked phenomenal.

Sam knew there was plenty of time on the clock with Alice and no pressure to rush into things. He had many more nights paid in advance. A long window of opportunity was exactly why he'd hired her. Anyway, he was fully expecting to wake up with "morning wood," which would require Alice's attention. But the following day, like a greasy pig that always manages to escape, his schlong had unwired itself from his mind. Sam put it down to nerves.

Alice was now on her fourth day of the trip and Sam had yet to sample the goods. Although there hadn't been any intimacy, surprisingly he was having a blast. Alice, who had made herself at home in Sam's apartment, was the nearest he'd come to a traditional life since his divorce. Not only did Alice cook, clean and do the shopping, but she was a real-life person who showed an interest in him. Sam did, however, wonder if Alice was just stringing him along and faking having fun, no different from one of his harlots and the "for your consideration" performances screaming their lungs out from the slightest petting of the kitty. Could Alice be conducting one extended psychological shamgasm for his benefit?

Sam enjoyed showing Alice the sights of St. Louis and getting to know her. He was intrigued by her rural upbringing and how she had dropped everything to raise siblings. Even though she had been dealt a rough hand of cards, Alice had a plucky spirit and made the best of things. If only her landlord knew the lengths Alice was going to make the rent. Sam had seen that the mentality for the younger generations was, "Buy what you want and beg for what you need." Many others in Alice's situation would have simply stuck it to the landlord.

Sam and Alice spent Sunday afternoon at Lafayette Square Park. She packed a picnic and purchased a frisbee for the occasion. To anyone who saw them, it looked like two people who cared deeply for each other having a great time. There would certainly be no suspicion of the circumstances that had brought them together.

Apartment #1511 Butterfly

Illinois is triumphantly branded, "the Land of Lincoln," but Southern Illinois should really be tagged, "the land of teen moms and strippers." Butterfly, of course, had been both.

Butterfly's life story was much like most professional erotic dancers: raised in a trailer park, abusive upbringing, father didn't stick around, failed relationships, teen pregnancies, abortions, a pair of divorces... the misery list goes on. It's better to not go into Butterfly's backstory in too much detail as it would be like every stripper cliché rolled into one epic yarn. The more intriguing side to Butterfly's tale isn't where she came from, but what she managed to make of her life considering the circumstances of those early years.

The average career of a bump and grinder is less than twelve months. Most are lucky to last that long. Too much quick money, too much booze, too much nose candy, too many bad men, and too many poor life choices lead to an early retirement. Get chatting with your typical diner waitress in Caseyville, Granite City, Fairview Heights, or any other Metro East Illinois township and you'll find a plethora of demobilized veterans who know the geography of a dancing pole.

Butterfly, in terms of a long, lucrative and illustrious career, was the Tom Brady of bi-state peelers. She had been swinging the poles of Sauget and its hinterland communities for a staggering thirty-four years. If there was a stripper hall of fame, Butterfly would've not only been a worthy inductee but paraded as a living legend. For Butterfly, within the industry, was likened to a nodding donkey in an Oklahoma oil field. The machinery was old and functioning but the daily flow pumped a trickle compared with its heyday. But Butterfly, like a Comanche County well, was far from dry and still producing.

Butterfly's primetime dancing slots were fewer than her George H. Bush era heyday, but she was still a rabid hustler. If not swinging from a center-stage pole she could be found propping up the front lobby of Mound City Gentleman's Club with a lit Newport in hand. Butterfly, even at her vintage, was no lazy meet-and-greet fluffer but an active lady sharking for punters to sell lap dances to, and much more.

While most strippers crash and burn young, or slither into careers as lot lizards and Waffle House waitresses, Butterfly had been fiscally savvy and made bank. She might not have paid her kids' way through college (Tiffany, Misty and Anastasia all became strippers on their eighteenth birthdays), but she had invested her loot wisely. Butterfly owned her spacious Missouri Towers fifteenth-floor condo outright and had paid for it in cash. The money she carried into closing was stuffed in a dozen pickling jars that had been hidden from Uncle Sam's reach.

From her condo's expansive windows, Butterfly had commanding views of the Illinois strip club municipal fiefdoms of Sauget, Centerville and East St. Louis. As well as her real estate domain, she held considerable blue chip stock investments. If Butterfly so chose, she could live well from their dividend yields and loosen her death grip on many a pole.

America is a never-ending land of opportunity. Where else could a syrupy real estate tycoon become a TV star and then leader of the free world? Where else could a C-list celebrity like Kim Kardashian, with a plump derrière and questionable other talents, make herself into a household name, and a billionaire? On paper, Butterfly should have amounted to nothing in her life. Slouching around a trailer park with an abusive partner and a dependency on welfare checks and opioids could've been her ultimate destination. But Butterfly was a "gal done good" who had grabbed the American dream by the balls and ridden it hard.

It was late in the evening by the time Butterfly and Reginald entered the small cottage home tucked away behind the Safe Haven funeral parlor. The house was hot, without AC, and the ceiling fans didn't offer much respite. Butterfly learned that this was Reginald's father's original house and had been used mainly for storage in recent decades. That was until Reginald was forced to sell his family residence and move back into it with no other options.

While Reginald showered, Butterfly fixed up something to eat for them in the kitchen. After she cleaned herself up, they ate together. Butterfly told Reginald the story of her life. To him it was intriguing. In the funeral business, you hear a lot of puffed-out tales, mostly about those who have passed. Reginald had yet to listen to any eulogy that compared with Butterfly's for color. Reginald slept easy in his old childhood bed. Butterfly took the spare room. The din of talking insects acted as white noise against the soundtrack of the occasional car racing down the highway. They both slept soundly.

*   *   *

When Mike Love's brain computed who had just strolled into his Lafayette Square open house, he froze in panic and was stuck for words. For a nanosecond, this visitor might've seen ghosts in the eyes of the boy standing before her that years ago she'd sent away.

Time had treated the unexpected guest well and Mike could see she looked as beautiful as the last time he'd been with her. On that fateful occasion, she'd given him the cliché of all clichés, the "it's not you, it's me" declamation. Upon shattering Mike's heart with that impossible-to-counter phrase, she'd kissed him on the cheek and brutally extracted herself from his life. They hadn't spoken since. That was nine years, two months and three days ago... not that Mike was counting.

"Miss Elizabeth Winslow, welcome to 1609 Mississippi Ave. Can I tell you a little history about this wonderful Gilded Age home?" said Mike, who had extensively rehearsed for this moment to occur. However, when pressed on the spot he couldn't execute his plan, or think of anything more appropriate than this to say.

"Technically, these days it's Elizabeth Snodgrass, not Winslow, and this is a Victorian, not Gilded Age era home. You can tell by the millwork around the doors," she replied, before placing herself on the living room sofa and adding, "I would rather you call me Lizzy. Just like you always did."

Mike might not have known the exact era of the home they were standing in, but he did know Lizzy was a Mrs. and not a Miss., and that her last name was now Snodgrass and not Winslow. Courtesy of the 21st-century digital infoglut, Mike had been able to voyeuristically follow Lizzy's life post their split. In fact, he knew an extensive amount about it. Lizzy had moved to Los Angeles, married, and was now a successful realtor. The day of her nuptials had been a tough pill for Mike to swallow. As hard as he tried not to, in an exercise of self-flagellation, he sought out Lizzy's wedding website and made himself miserable via her happiness. Lizzy, with her booming career as a realtor, was churning out transactions at a frenetic pace, and with the high price of Los Angeles real estate was making big bucks.

To Mike, Lizzy's husband Levin Snodgrass was a worthless tool, and certainly not good enough for someone like her. But Mike would have said that about any of Lizzy's subsequent suitors. Levin, armed with a law degree from a third-tier institution, worked as a low-level entertainment lawyer. By stalking his social media pages, Mike knew that Levin represented various C-list celebrities and spent his downtime kite-surfing shirtless in Malibu. The appeal of his envious torso of thunder was obvious; the tragic GI Joe beard he seemingly refused to shave, not so much. How Lizzy ended up with this man, Mike couldn't comprehend. If nothing else, the name Lizzy Love had a better ring to it than Elizabeth Snodgrass. It had to be timing; everything was always about timing with Lizzy. Then again, the journey of life is dictated by timing – sometimes under your own control, but often not.

Since meeting Gloria, Mike hadn't been following Lizzy's life trajectory too closely and had almost managed to scrub his caring about the minutia of her existence from his mind. Not the easiest thing to do when the person in question was the love of your life, someone you had inexplicably let slip away. Gloria had been that perfect tonic to pull Mike out of his long, drawn-out, Lizzy-split funk.

In the near decade since Mike had last seen Lizzy, she had barely changed; if anything, she looked finer with age. This magic was even more remarkable when you consider she worked in a stressful profession that was arguably detrimental to not only mental health but also physical appearance.

"The three-year thirty," was the phrase that Nick Pipeman used to describe the results of realtors overindulging at open house buffets and downing copious amounts of lattes en route to showings. The fresh-faced, perky agent who waltzed into the office during the spring of 2016 was by the summer of 2019 rolling up to her desk with a face full of worry and an extra thirty pounds. This, Pipeman vowed, was the first stage on a slippery slope that would ultimately lead to rapidly aging agents clinging to their vintage headshots.

The Lizzy now seated before Mike had managed to maintain her slender frame. A subtly updated pixie cut highlighted her sharp bone structure and gorgeous face. Avoiding Missouri's harsh summer sun and frigid dry winter air had kept her skin as smooth as porcelain. She was always a fashionista and the cute summer dress she wore today, sans bra as always, possessed a sophistication that identified her as no longer a local. The temptations, barely hidden under the outfit, were just as they were back in high school – devilishly teasing.

From their first time making love in her father's hot tub on her seventeenth birthday to their very last moments together, she'd been pure sexual dynamite. Mike may have nearly rubbed out from his brain the pain she had caused him, but his mind had memorized, and wouldn't forget, every nook and cranny of her delights.

"Mrs. Snodgrass, are you working with an agent? And please, when you have a chance, can you enter your details into the sign-in sheet," said a Mike battling his emotions while remaining on realtor handbook autopilot.

"I have no interest in this dog-hair-everywhere house. And I don't see myself ever living in St. Louis again," she replied.

"Too good for St. Louis now?"

"You always talked about escaping yourself," she replied before singing, *"It's a town full of losers, and I'm pulling out of here to win. Oh-oh come take my hand. We're riding out tonight to case the promised land... Oh-oh Thunder Road!"*

Cutting off Lizzy's singing, Mike said, "I played that to you on our first date down at Lake Carlyle."

"You played it so much that the lyrics are hardwired into my brain," she responded with affection.

"You thankfully indulged my Springsteen mix-tapes," Mike said, his mind drifting back to the zenith of the relationship, that magical summer following school graduation.

"How could I forget our first date at the lake? I had never received a foot massage before. Not sure I've had one so good since," she threw back with a sparkle in her eye.

171

With a down-to-business tone, Mike abruptly ended the reminiscing. "So why are you here? I can only presume you happened to be walking by and saw my sign by *chance* and popped in to catch up on the last *nine years*?"

"My aunt Beth died. I'm back for her funeral on Wednesday. I did try to call and email you but I couldn't get through; my messages bounced back and the calls failed."

Mike now remembered that in a fit of anger years ago, he had blocked her telephone number, and with some nifty software redirected any of her emails to the outer rim of cyberspace. Mike hadn't actually thought she would ever reach out again but had done this in spite just in case she did.

"I'm sorry for your loss but I didn't know her well. So if you have sought me out for an invite to the funeral, I don't really think it would be appropriate that I went. Besides, your mother always hated me and went out of her way to make sure we wouldn't end up together. So I am the last person she wants to see," Mike said while loosening his bolo tie.

"Mike, you didn't really make a great impression on my Mother; you could've tried harder. It might've made the difference between us."

"Give me an example of what I did wrong?" he said now with an extra layer of sweat on his face that had nothing to do with the fubar AC unit that had made the house stifling.

"Career plans. Do you remember that dinner with my family? And the answer you gave them when they asked you what you wanted to do after graduation?"

"Vaguely," he said, wishing he hadn't gone down this particular rabbit hole.

"Telling my mother that you intended to get into the business of kickboxing wasn't the slickest move. Not only was it not a new sport with a good future and zero career longevity, but they knew you had ripped off your entire monologue from *Say Anything!*" Lizzy said.

"How could I know that was your parents' favorite film?" he countered.

"Had you repeated any other movie quote, you might just have gotten away with that bullshit answer. After that, they figured you were just a no-hoper trying to get with their daughter."

"You know better than anyone that I had no idea what I wanted to do with my life. What was I supposed to tell them? Mrs. Winslow, I'm in love with Elizabeth and want to marry her and spend the rest of my days with your daughter. One minor detail, though – I have sweet fuck-all in the way of a career, and no idea how to pay my way through life, let alone scrape up the money for a ring or a deposit on an apartment."

"Maybe not that, but you could've ad-libbed something meaningful, maybe alluded to you having hopes, dreams, prospects. Make them see a little of what I saw in you. Make them believe in what we had. Make them not go out of their way to..." Lizzy stopped herself from finishing the sentence.

There was an unpleasant moment of silence as Mike paced around the living room. Both parties were stuck for words.

"Do you know how long it took me to get over you Lizzy? It was years. From the day I met you in high school, I knew you were the one," said Mike, herding his words carefully to break the silence.

"That's very St. Louis romantic of you, wanting to marry the girl sitting behind you in high school," she replied, with too much flippancy for the moment.

A now agitated Mike tossed back: "So, you didn't come here to invite me to Aunt Beth's funeral. You aren't here to buy this "very special home." And you obviously aren't a nosey neighbor wanting to poke around this dilapidated Gilded Age dump! So, Mrs. Elizabeth Snodgrass, why exactly are you here?"

"There's a saying in Los Angeles, 'You should always know your second husband first.'"

Mike looked down at her left hand and realized there was no ring on *the* finger.

"You're divorced?"

"In the process. As I said, technically I'm still Mrs. Snodgrass, but not for much longer. It's hot in here. Would you like to take a walk in the park with me?" Lizzy asked.

Mike turned the rest of the lights off, locked the front door, and put the house keys back in the Supra box. It was roasting outside and the air was sticky. The buzz of cicadas nullified the noise of the interstate two blocks away.

Mike and Lizzy walked in silence towards a pavilion in the park that was a popular spot for taking wedding photos. As they took a seat on a bench, Mike could see, in another area of greenery, Sam Robinson with a woman. It was the out-of-town visitor he had met at the front door of Missouri Towers last week. The lady was dressed very differently today. Her hair was no longer pink but a deep brown in color. And she was wearing a hard-to-explain ensemble that made her look like all the Scooby Doo characters at once. Sam and this girl were playing frisbee together and seemed to be having fun.

Questions that needed answers began to whirl around Mike's mind. Do hookers charge more for running around the park with their clothes on than they do for delivering horizontal refreshments with their clothes off? Did Sam negotiate a day rate or a weekly rate? Could the girl really be a friend of his and not one of the usual pay-to-play harlots? Maybe Sam and the lady were just coming out for air before going back at it? Mike had an inkling this girl wasn't Sam's usual, wham-bam thank you ma'am, in-and-out, sixty-minute special.

"Do you know them?" Lizzy asked when it became obvious that Mike was distracted by the frisbee-playing couple.

"That guy lives in my building. Screwball with a strange line in friends," he replied, before adding, "What happened between you and your husband?"

"Levin cheated on me with one of the clients he represented. A yoga-teaching TikTok star, to be precise."

"Younger woman?" Mike asked.

"You have crashed and burned by twenty-four as a professional internet influencer. So, yes, she was younger," Lizzy answered.

"What was her special talent?"

"Tripod headstand with lotus legs pose in a string bikini to K-Pop music; it was more about the flesh than the yoga. TikTok is one infinite, soft-porn warehouse," Lizzy said.

Mike liked to watch pictures of car chases on TikTok but he got her drift – not that he responded to her comment with this nugget of detail.

"Levin must have fallen hard for her. He wouldn't ever lose the silly hipster beard for me, he shaved it straight off for her. If I was honest, I'm not sure we were ever that suitable."

"So why did you marry him?" Mike asked.

"He just came into my life at the right time…"

"Timing is everything," Mike interrupted.

In fact, the way Mike had first met Lizzy was down to timing. They had sat at opposite ends of their social studies class. She was moved because she talked too much to her seat partner. The teacher relocated her behind Mike. Who knows if they'd ever have become friends if she hadn't been moved that day.

"You and your timing theories Mike… as I was saying, I had been dating in LA. Most of the men were douches – finance guys, wannabe scriptwriters, hustling actors, and the like. Everyone had a dream and a scam and a lie. It never went anywhere with any of them. Actually, let me correct you, there was one guy I truly loved, but he left me for a sitcom actress. Before I knew it, I was single and twenty-six..."

"And you always said you wanted to have two children by the age of thirty," said Mike, cutting her off.

"And you would say to me, thirty? You're going to be the oldest mum in town," Lizzy replied.

"To be honest, I was relieved that you were the only girl in high school who didn't want to be married with kids by the five-year class reunion. The thought of children back then scared me. Thirty seemed safely far enough away in the distant future to not worry about," Mike said.

"Yes, I wanted children by the "Big 30." You work back the numbers. Meet a guy. Date for a year. Get engaged. Spend twelve months planning the wedding. Then get pregnant as quickly as you can. Rinse and repeat with baby number two. Add in the friction of maybe not finding the right guy straight away. Or the chance of not getting pregnant as quickly as you want. I was in danger of running out of runway," Lizzy said, emphasizing her own self-prescribed panic and the obvious fact that she was now over thirty and childless.

"You could've just had children later. All the Hollywood celebs are breeding in their forties," said Mike.

"You would hate to know what they are spending on fertility doctors. As a realtor, you are always part-shrink. I've had many a client share their tears and tribulations in trying to conceive in their late thirties. I might not want to live in St. Louis again, but I am a Midwestern gal in my heart. I always wanted the huge wedding and children. Just not by the age of twenty-two, like all our friends."

"Don't I know it," Mike said with regret at her breaking at least one part of the Midwestern mold by dumping her high school sweetheart.

"One Sunday, I was holding an open house at a Santa Monica condo, and in walked Levin. He was charming, had a good job, and we hit it off. He ticked all the required boxes."

"Happened to walk into your life at the right moment. Good timing again," Mike said.

"Yes, the right man for the right moment. Or so I thought."

The conversation was halted by a Cardinal bird sitting on a grassy area in front of their bench.

They both stared for a moment at the bird before Lizzy continued. "Less about my body count, what about you? I see you don't have a ring on your finger. Are you seeing anyone?"

"I am," he replied, without the necessary elaboration that would make her think it was anything significant.

Suddenly a second Cardinal landed next to the first. The pair of birds began to chase each other. For a silent minute, Lizzy and Mike watched the birds courting.

Lizzy then added, "I didn't even know you were a realtor until I looked you up earlier this year. When did you get your license?"

"A few years ago," Mike replied, without divulging that he had started the process after watching Lizzy get her license.

"Los Angeles real estate has been good to me. My motto is, I never overpromise, and I never take on more than I can handle. How about you Mike, have you found your lane?"

"You're the second person who's said that to me today," Mike replied.

The two Cardinal birds flew off together.

"How come you never left St. Louis?" Lizzy asked.

"I didn't find anyone else I wanted to leave with." This statement was followed by an uncomfortable pause in talking.

"I need to apologize," Lizzy said.

"For dumping me and running off with no real explanation; for breaking my heart; for fucking up my life. We'd made plans. We had our lives together plotted out. Do you know what you meant to me? What you did to me? What you took away from me?"

Lizzy reached over, took Mike's hand and began to stroke it. With her other hand, she extracted a piece of crumpled paper from her purse. She then passed it to him.

"This was the pirate's treasure map of our lives. Do you remember? We drew it together on that magical date at the lake. Straight after the foot massage," she said.

"And a few moonlight fumbles," he added.

Mike flattened out the piece of paper. In his hand was the life map they had both created when they were sixteen. In a cute twist, it had been crafted on Hello Kitty stationery.

It said, in Lizzy's overly neat handwriting:

1: Fall in LOVE

2: Move to Hollywood

3: Get married

4: Maybe have children

5: Get rich

6: Grow old together

Mike was immediately taken back to that special night when it was crafted. Tears were forming in his eyes as he stared at the document.

"Do you recall that recurring dream I always had about the two of us?" Lizzy asked as she watched the tears roll down his face.

"Sure do!"

Lizzy then went on to recant it. "The two of us were super old, sitting on a park bench, just like we are now. Back then I thought that might be about fifty years old. Now I realize in the dream we were really in our nineties. I was fat, and you were totally bald. But there we were – old, fat and bald, but still together, still madly in love."

There was more silence before Lizzy said, "Mike, come with me to Los Angeles. I have it all worked out. Our plan never had an expiration date."

*   *   *

A typical Sunday night for a real estate agency broker is busy but banally mundane. Sunday night is ultimately when all the proverbial shit hits the fan. Agents will call in a panic, with an array of deadline-induced contract questions. Do I need to write in the lion garden statues with that offer for the house in U-City? I have a hostile client, can you refer me to a good attorney before this deal spirals out of control? Is it worth submitting a backup offer for that townhouse? Remind me again how escalation clauses work. Daris would clear Sunday evenings to deal with these kinds of issues, brought to him by his cohort of agents. This was the prime responsibility for a broker. You are there to clarify contracts, get offers accepted, get listings closed, dodge legal pitfalls, and lead the team.

However, this Sunday night was like no other. Daris was not sitting on his wrap-around balcony working with a cocktail in one hand, an iPad in the other, against the backdrop of the Arch. Daris was holed up in The Bunker with Pam Hardings and Brad "Puffman" Thrust. All of Spitfire's Sunday open houses had been ransacked in a well-coordinated series of attacks. Some of the more junior agents were so traumatized they had left their postings for fear of their lives.

Daris's voicemail was jammed with complaints from other brokerages who had clients waiting outside locked open houses and owners demanding that Spitfire pay for damages to landscaping and fencing.

Daris had contacted every other regional broker to see if they had been attacked. They were all untouched; only Spitfire had been victimized.

"Any update on where the blimps landed?" Daris asked Puffman in relation to the New Berlin balloons that had been in the air at the same time the attacks occurred.

"Nothing! We had a visual on the balloons until they reached East St. Louis. No one wanted to follow them into that dangerous cesspool," Puffman replied.

"I understand," said Daris, who himself refused to go to the Illinois side of the river to avoid high gas prices and crime.

"We have ten spare yard signs in storage. I've put in an order for another thirty, just in case we need backups," said management-focused Pam.

Three listings had already been canceled by homeowners concerned about further property damage. Daris removed their little home icons from his battle map. One trainee agent had quit in sheer terror. She had a face for radio and not real estate, so she wouldn't have lasted anyway, thought Daris, as he yanked her headshot from the wall of team photos. Even with the hostilities, they had managed to get four homes under contract today. On his map, he changed the status of those listings.

"The attacks were obviously the work of New Berlin, but any idea who is the mastermind?" Puffman asked.

Daris, with his eyes focused on his battle map of Greater St. Louis, replied: "No idea Brad, but you are correct with your assumption." He then added, in a Churchillian tone of doom: "My friend, we are passing through a dark and deadly valley."

*   *   *

The offer Lizzy made Mike didn't really set in until he was back home at his apartment late that night. In many ways, it was all his greatest wishes and dreams handed to him on a silver platter, in a single serving, and with no check to pay.

Mike would leave St. Louis as soon as possible and move to Los Angeles. He would transfer his salesperson license to California and Lizzy would create a position for him on her brokerage team. "We are a powerhouse" was a phrase she repeatedly used to describe her crew. She boasted they had more work than they could handle and he would be an excellent asset. Mike would be hitting the ground running and thus avoid his current preoccupation of hunting for leads. And with the median price of a listing in her area in the six-figure range, Mike would be making the kind of commissions you could only dream of in Missouri.

Lizzy was going to take care of logistics. Trunk space in the Sonic was no longer an impediment, as she would arrange a U-haul to take his belongings. Even better, Mike could ditch his jalopy as Lizzy said she would lease him a Mercedes when he arrived. In the City of Angels, she said it was all about image. The snazzy ride Lizzy had in mind oozed success.

The unexpected blast from his past that had rocketed back into Mike's life had offered him a game-changing MacGuffin. He finally had the opportunity to flee St. Louis and the chance to make mega money. Most amazingly, he would be reuniting with Lizzy, the love of his life – a beautiful, smart funny woman, who he knew, from the first day he set eyes on her, should be his wife. Was it all a dream? Mike began to pinch himself. Whatever it was, this kind of golden opportunity never happened in any Bruce Springsteen song.

Mike's phone rang. It was Gloria.

"Shit," he shouted out loud. In his quixotic state, he'd totally forgotten he was going up to her place for dinner. He answered the call and told her he would be up shortly.

Gloria opened the front door. Before he had a chance to digest her natural beauty, she ripped into him.

"Mike, if we lived in the same apartment, it would be a lot harder to miss dinner!"

She then gave him a gentle kiss on the cheek. Gloria's scent was the perfect combination of a sweet perfume mixed with her sweat from an evening run.

"Sorry about that, I was deciphering the usual chicken scratch from the open house sign-in sheet," he replied.

"How did it go? Anything promising?" she asked.

Gloria knew holding an open house for another agent was a low-odds game and wasn't expecting much.

"Decent traffic. You never know, something amazing might have come out of it," he vaguely replied.

It was just the two of them tonight. Gloria had cooked a pot pie. Zoe was out getting her hair done before her date with Pipeman.

Mike was staring out of her huge window directly at the Gateway Arch. Although he was looking at America's tallest monument, his mind was filled with images of the Hollywood Sign.

"Are you OK? You don't seem yourself," Gloria asked, noticing he wasn't digging into his food as usual.

Mike, with his eyes looking out the window, said. "Gloria, if your dreamy Indian lion-tamer ex-boyfriend called up and said, "I've made a big mistake. My private jet is at Lambert waiting for you. Please, I beg you to board it. Let's get married," what would your reply be?"

"I would tell him it's too late, your big mistake in Miami worked out perfectly for me. I've moved on and am taken.'"

"Even though he would be offering you the type of life that's out of reach otherwise?" Mike asked, in an effort to double-check that she had thought through her answer carefully.

"Yes, I would say, 'You broke my heart. I thought it would be impossible to love like that again, but it wasn't. And as hard as I thought it might be, I found something better.' I think that would put him in his place," Gloria said.

She is perfect and really does love me, Mike thought, as he slowly ate his pot pie.

The setting sun reflected a glorious golden light off the Arch into Gloria's apartment. It was pure magic-hour illumination.

"I'm not feeling well," Mike said to Gloria.

"Can I get you something?" she asked with concern.

"It was the heat today. AC was out in Pipeman's listing. I was dying. I just need to go back to my place and have an early night," Mike said.

Mike bolted out the door and ran down the two flights of stairs that separated their places. Once in his apartment he went to the bathroom and threw up. *The timing of Lizzy's appearance today isn't good!* Mike contemplated while barfing into the toilet.

Apartment #1611   Colton Chesterfield III

In the St. Louis region, the only thing that takes precedence over high school affiliation is your family name. Ultimately, with the greasing of palms or enough charitable donations, you can buy yourself into a fine establishment of learning. What you cannot buy is heritage and pedigree. For there are only a limited number of eligible bachelors from the great Busch, Kemper, and Pulitzer families to go around. And if you're a man, the money, not the name, comes with the bride, so you will forever be a second-rank interloper who clawed your way into the clan. Being a member of the regional aristocracy in St. Louis is to be a part of a privileged club and a stealthy way to grab a license to print money.

Now Colton Chesterfield III, by appellation alone, seemed to tick all the boxes – a first name that when said aloud had an authoritative aura of greatness. Colton, a rugged name with suitable elasticity, fit for a gentleman farmer, NFL quarterback, oil baron, or C-suite tech entrepreneur. The last name Chesterfield brings forth a magical blend of old-world establishment and West St. Louis County fine living. For added status, the numerical suffix reeks of "dynastic wealth." Throw into the hat Colton being a graduate of the finest school in all of zip code 63141, and within the state of Missouri, on paper at least, this was a man who had it all. Only he didn't. Colton Chesterfield III was a living, breathing, fabrication of facts.

Colton Chesterfield III, as he is known now, made the decision early on in life to become a con man. Not just a low-level guy selling fake phone cards or broken stereo speakers out of the back of a truck, but a titan of big-time fraud. To be a balling swindler you need three essential traits: you have to be good-looking, a king of bluff, and come from a reputable family.

Colton, by some miracle, was blessed with the physique and face of a Greek god. From a glance at his parental stock you would wonder how this was possible. But evolution is a strange beast and via the kinks of genetics, the ugliest parents are often blessed with the best-looking children. Colton was tall, broad-shouldered with gleaming, perfect teeth and thick flowing hair. If this man was raised on the coasts he would've been plucked from a crowd and turned into a movie star.

The bluff part of the needed package was a by-product of his physical presentation. Colton found that his pretty smile opened doors and scored him favors. By his teenage years, he came to realize it also got him the girls. After years of refining his charms, the man who would in time become Colton had honed his bullshitter skills and lived in a world where he never heard the word "no."

The only element of the holy trinity of trickster attributes he lacked was a reputable backstory and a well-connected family. This he needed to improvise and create. His name wasn't, of course, originally Colton Chesterfield, and he was certainly not the third of any great line. Our aspiring criminal mastermind was born Nigel Sadmane and hailed from a hamlet on the outskirts of Joplin, Missouri. He knew such an uninspiring name and those humble origins weren't going to make it in the upper echelons of white-collar crime.

Nigel first needed to move himself to a bigger market from which to conduct his hustles. Looking at the map of America through the eyes of a small-town Missourian, he narrowed it down to two options: Kansas City or St. Louis. With a beady eye focused on the financial upside, St. Louis, with geographic proximity to Illinois corruption, was deemed the more lucrative market.

Next, our aspiring Lex Luther needed rebranding. After a long period of contemplation and much-humped housewife pillow-talk feedback, the improvised faux name that got him bed partners the quickest was the alias of Colton. Chesterfield, via the same utilitarian methodology, was the municipality where he snagged the highest quota of other people's wives for affairs. For a grand establishment-style suffix, he opted for III. It was the perfect slot between the stodgy old money of IV and the nouveau riche of II. With a little bit of paperwork and a few hundred dollars in application fees, Nigel Sadmane officially transformed himself into Colton Chesterfield III.

Missouri is known as the Show-Me State, but in the upper strata of St. Louis life, this is in name only. Colton was amazed how few people questioned his glorious biography or asked to see the diploma from the prestigious high school he claimed to have attended. Colton had half-heartedly covered his tracks via deep-fake stories impregnated into the web with the assistance of Belarusian hackers. But still he was amazed at just how much he got away with as he plugged away with his ever more daring cons. Via a sleek combination of dashing good looks, pushy convincing bluff, and faux aristocratic tales, Colton Chesterfield III was enabled by the local establishment to become the Bernie Madoff of Missouri.

Colton woke up with a sore head and no idea where he was. He remembered being in the casino parking lot and talking to an undertaker. Wherever he was, it was dark and dirty, and his hands were tied. In addition, he was tired and thirsty and in immense pain. Colton passed out again.

He woke up several hours later. It must have been daytime as bright light was now shining through a crack in an entryway. He realized he was in a basement or cellar. He could make out a bowl of water near him. He shuffled over to it and drank like an animal. His current predicament made jail seem like a Four Seasons resort. Both of these institutions he had personal experience being holed up in.

Colton now recalled a little more about yesterday. He had been accosted at gunpoint in the parking lot by a funeral director. He knew this man from somewhere, but where, he could not place. The person had asked for a million or so dollars. "This was nuts," Colton muttered. His head was pounding with pain.

A door opened. The light adjustment made it impossible to make out who was entering.

"Room service!" was shouted, and a Snickers bar tossed at him. The door was slammed shut and darkness resumed.

He spent the next hour trying to open the packaging of the Snickers bar – a feat difficult with his hands restrained. The good news was, he managed to get the St. Louis flag bandana off his mouth, so at least he would be able to eat if he could ever open the wrapper. By now he was putting the pieces together, and realized the grim reaper with the gun must be a pissed-off Merlin investor.

Colton rehashed the Merlin debacle to exhaustion during his prison stint. And a debacle it certainly was, only because it folded so quickly. When they planned out Merlin Investments, the founders had envisioned being able to keep the charade going for decades, not a few short years.

It was all quite the genius operation. Target an industry sitting on hard cash and run mostly by unsophisticated male management with minimal finance experience. Offer them something too good to be true. But make sure the people offering it were seductive enough to divert blood from the brains to what was resting between the legs of these decision-makers. Colton would have liked to have taken credit for hiring sales girls plucked from modeling agencies, but that wasn't his idea. That was a junior team member who would no doubt end up as a Wall Street player once his prison sentence concluded.

The press tagged Colton the Bernie Madoff of Missouri. Colton felt that didn't give him enough credit if you factored in that Bernie Madoff was going at his fraud for seventeen years, not three. And the cost of living in New York is far greater than in Missouri. In a short time, in a low-expense area of the country, the $400 million Merlin Investments had swindled was far more efficient and profitable than Bernie's infamous Ponzi scheme. He also felt if he was based in Los Angeles, New York or Miami, he would have been getting much better post-prison opportunities. "The coasts love smooth-looking criminals in a manner the Midwest doesn't appreciate. Classic flyover country snub," Colton would say.

The Snickers bar, once Colton finally managed to open tasted good. But it wasn't nearly enough food. He had, however, managed to undo his trousers and take a leak. Although the downside of that was the piss started smelling after a few hours. He still had no idea where he was but realized as the shaft of light that fed into the basement faded, that night was descending.

*   *   *

Reuniting with Lizzy Winslow after all these years had given Mike Love a sleepless night. He texted her at 3 a.m. and suggested they meet for breakfast to talk a little more about *the future*, as she phrased it.

St. Louis is one of those big cities that in essence is a small fishbowl. Everyone knows everyone, and your chances of maintaining an illicit affair for any duration would be virtually impossible. Lizzy going over to Mike's place for breakfast wasn't an option, and neither were any downtown eateries. Gloria would've been tipped off to Mike's sneaky rendezvous before he had taken his first sip of his second coffee. They arranged to meet at 8 a.m. at Tiffany's diner in Maplewood. This 24-hour hole-in-the-wall hash house was far enough off the beaten track that they could be discreet. Perfect edge-of-town kind of locale, where shady meetings happen in Springsteen ballads.

Mike sat nervously at the counter chugging a coffee. His mind was racing in fifty directions. He couldn't even drum up enough concentration to scan the *St. Louis Tribune* for yesterday's body count. He was still stuck at 146 murders for the year.

Mike's phone alerted him to a text. It was Gloria. *Coming up for breakfast?*

Mike's heart was pounding. It was partly down to him feeling like a cheating spouse, and partly down to that knot in the stomach you feel when on a first date. He couldn't figure out why he felt this way, as in reality he wasn't cheating (yet) and he certainly wasn't on a first date. Lizzy and Mike had been together for just under five years. People are married for less time than that. One of those people being Lizzy.

Mike texted Gloria: *Showing at Oregon St. Went early 2 set up.* The appointment was actually at 9.30 am. She sent back a sad face emoji with the message, *See u later xxx.* This was the first time Mike had ever lied to Gloria. He felt terrible.

The diner door opened and Lizzy stormed in wearing another impressive outfit. She was talking loudly on her cell phone, something about a zero lot buildout teardown in the Santa Monica flatlands. The lone staff member flipping pancakes gave her the, *You're not in LA anymore, honey!* dagger stare.

"It's 6.15 a.m. West Coast time. People are doing business that early on a Monday?" Mike asked Lizzy.

"The phone never stops ringing. You'll get used to it Mike," Lizzy replied as she gave him a hug and a kiss on the cheek. Her hair smelt freshly shampooed, and she'd found a new perfume since they dated.

Mike turned off his phone to avoid the lack of incoming calls being embarrassing.

He still couldn't believe that he was once again sitting next to Lizzy. For years after they went their separate ways, to even have breakfast with her would've been a far-fetched dream. Now in the moment, he didn't know what to say. He wondered if this is how it is when an actor wins an Oscar. You have dreamed about this scenario your entire career. Then you win and you are walking up the podium, only to endure a "now what" moment. At least they have a speech stashed in their jacket. Mike had no script to work with.

"Any leads today?" asked Lizzy as she browsed the menu.

"All kinds of stuff on the books. I moved things around just to make time for coffee with you," Mike said.

In fact, he had only one showing today – a rental in the perma-gentrifying Benton Park area. The booking had come in late last night. Although at least he had something concrete that showed Lizzy he was a working realtor.

When Lizzy left Mike, he was crushed. However, at the time he didn't take this as game over but a temporary setback to be overcome. Why had she left him? They had great chemistry and much in common. It had to be something else.

Moping around in the basement bedroom of his parent's home, he formulated a plan in an attempt to win Lizzy back. Working at a tire shop and not attending college, he concluded, was part of the problem. Maybe not directly for Lizzy but certainly it was an issue to her parents. They would continually tell their daughter, Mike wasn't good enough, and if they married both their lives would go nowhere. Mike ultimately found out Lizzy's California relocation was masterminded by her parents in an effort to split them up.

Mike enrolling at Community College was the first step in leveling up his own achievements to Lizzy's. The idea was that once he had enough credits earned, he would transfer to UCLA, just like she had. However, Mike struggled at Community College. Working full-time and going to school wasn't an easy task. He did ultimately graduate with an Associate's Degree, but it took five years, not the planned two. And, unfortunately, he didn't have the grades needed for UCLA.

For Mike, taking college classes was always more of a cog in the wheel of a plan than a way to learn a new set of skills. Throughout his studies, the only book he truly enjoyed was *Love in the Time of Cholera* by Gabriel García Márquez. In this novel, the antihero Florentino Ariza spends his entire life pursuing Fermina Daza, a woman who, much like Lizzy, had broken his heart. After decades of dogged obsessive pursuit, Florentino eventually wins her over. Mike took inspiration from the story and vowed to not give up on Lizzy, no matter how long it took, or to what lengths he would need to go.

Getting his real estate license was much like going to college – another tool utilized in his long game plan to win back the heart of a lost love. Mike tracked Lizzy's career choice and emulated it. For a period of time before he met Gloria, his entire raison d'être was putting himself in a position where Lizzy would want to come back into his life.

He sat at the counter with Lizzy, he was subtly mystified. She was always the power-player in the relationship dynamics and called the shots. And of course it was her that ended things between them. But here they were together again, and surprisingly it was Lizzy who had come to St. Louis to find him, not the other way around. Mike hadn't had to wait until he was elderly, like Florentino and Fermina in *Love in the Time of Cholera*, to get a second chance. Destiny had prevailed.

Over pancakes, they talked about the real estate industry in both their markets. Mike briefed Lizzy on his successes at Spitfire. She was über-impressive, talking about her own skills, in the process tossing out cool buzzwords and motivational phrases. Listening to her pitch it was obvious the business of real estate was a different game in California. For one thing, realtors didn't even set up their own yard signs, they had a whole crew of people who did that for them. Clint Cummings would choke on his oversweetened iced tea when Mike told him about this. Mike was getting excited about his prospects in Los Angeles. This move was going to be his big break.

But his mind wandered back to Gloria. How would he tell her he was going to California for real this time? Would he fill her in on the reappearance of Lizzy?

"You know I'm seeing someone," Mike said to Lizzy as the thoughts in his head turned to words.

"What's her name?" she asked.

"Gloria, just like the sappy eighties song. It drives her crazy when people sing it to her." Mike paused to sip his coffee before adding, "We met in our apartment building during a tornado. Very St. Louis thing to do."

"What's she like?" Lizzy asked as she sipped her coffee.

"Well, she's beautiful, caring, funny and a great cook. She can even breathe fire and juggle knives. She doesn't do that too much these days. She was a trapeze artist with Ringling Brothers. She now teaches at a circus school," Mike said, using multiple disjointed statements to describe Gloria.

"How long have you guys been together?" Lizzy asked.

"A few years," he replied.

"She is obviously not right for you," Lizzy said, in a matter of fact way.

"Why do you say that? She's amazing," he replied.

"Why aren't you married then?"

Mike didn't want to respond. It was a question he couldn't answer. Or maybe he could, but he would sound a little pathetic if he told Lizzy that part of the reason was her.

Lizzy didn't ask the question again. She assumed that Mike sitting down and planning a move to California summed up the status of his current relationship.

Mike looked at the wall clock. "It's ten past nine. I need to get out of here! My showing is at nine-thirty."

"A lot has changed in St. Louis, but I'm glad you can still get anywhere in twenty minutes," she replied.

"When are you back?" Mike asked Lizzy as he paid the check.

"I am driving to Jeff City today. The funeral is Wednesday. I'm seeing a few other family members out there and will be back Friday afternoon. I'm booked on a late flight to LA that night."

"Send my best to your parents!" Mike said.

"I'm my own person now. They are not a factor between us," she replied.

"Got it about your parents. Dinner Friday evening before your flight?" Mike asked.

"Perfect. I want to hear all about the contracts you are writing up and the listings you snag this week. Full report!" Lizzy then lent over to kiss Mike goodbye.

Mike pushed her away. "I have to tie up some loose ends first," he said.

"You were always so sweet and perfect. I should never have left you," Lizzy respectfully replied. Mike exited the diner and made his way to the rental showing in Benton Park.

*   *   *

During the few hours between Daris leaving The Bunker late Sunday night and his dawn return Monday morning, the Spitfire offices were vandalized. It was now just after 9 a.m. and Daris was dressed in his combat-ready siren suit, overseeing the team of glaziers replacing the windows.

Bricks, most likely from a derelict North City home, had been the weapon of choice. He had decided to get the office boarded up for now so the new windows would be protected – a defensive measure, he told the staff via email, and not any sign of weakness.

With the window work finished, Daris took refuge in The Bunker with Pam Hardings to digest further developments. He also had to come up with a response for his aggressors, although this would be more effective if he could find out exactly who was behind New Berlin Real Estate.

"More bad news! We had another agent resign and go to New Berlin," said Pam Hardings.

"Who now?" asked Daris.

"Jenny Bumdoch," she replied.

"No way! She's been with me from day one."

Bumdoch was a great operator and specialized in mid-century modern homes. She was the perfect imposter who exemplified success in the business of real estate. Behind the fake last name, twirly hair extensions, and expensive nose job, was your typical bacon sandwich-eating Jew with the ability to turn the kosher personality on or off in order to close a deal.

"First Alexi and now Jenny. I'm getting hit where it hurts!" said Daris.

Brad "Puffman" Thrust marched into The Bunker in a frenzy.

"All our systems are down. We've been hit by a massive cyber attack!"

*　　　*　　　*

Mike rolled up to his rental listing on Oregon St. exactly on time. The potential tenant did not offer him the same courtesy. After twenty minutes of standing outside in the roasting heat,

Mike relocated himself into the unit. It was an oversized one-bedroom shotgun apartment that had been freshly painted and the AC was working like magic. Asim Ur, the Tunisian owner, had bought the building from the city housing authority during the Great Recession. Via Federal grants, city handouts and state tax credits, he had renovated its five residences for virtually no out-of-pocket expense. "That's how millionaires become billionaires!" Asim would repeat ad nauseam to Mike.

Standing in the apartment's living room, Mike reviewed the applicant's file. Carrie Jones, twenty-five years old, female, single, government job and solid credit. This was the kind of dream tenant any landlord would want. Mike's only worry was that she might not want to live in this part of town. After all, it still had a Wild West feel to it, even if the coroner's van wasn't as frequent a Saturday night visitor as it would've been five years ago.

Exactly thirty-minutes late, Carrie rolled up in a gray Dodge Charger with blacked-out windows. She was a well dressed, African American woman, diminutive in stature and weighing no more than one hundred pounds. Carrie was chaperoned by a large Black man called Ted, who wouldn't have looked out of place on the O-line for the Kansas City Chiefs. Carrie called him "The Bear" and described him as her "protection, chauffeur" and "blanket." She was quick to point out that he had his own place and wouldn't be living with her.

Mike gave them the apartment tour, highlighting the amenities: ice machine, deck, ceiling fan, generous storage and original hardwood floors. Carrie asked about the local crime and Mike, as per realtor rules, gave her the standard "look up the public reports" answer. With all the positivity Mike could muster, he pitched this apartment as if it were a beachfront pad in Malibu. In the back of his mind, he was hoping his next listing would be just that.

Carrie told Mike she loved the place. She took the application and said it would be submitted by day's end. Carrie and Ted roared off along Oregon St. in the Dodge Charger. Mike felt a sense of relief. This rental would be off the books and he would have a little bit of incoming cash on the way. *The drought is over,* raced through his brain, as he locked the apartment door.

A shadow descended on Mike and he could sense someone behind him.

He turned around slowly and nervously prayed he wasn't about to be robbed. When he saw who was standing next to him, being mugged might have been preferable.

"Mr. Ur, I didn't expect to see you today," Mike said to the rental unit's owner. Asim Ur was a short man who was well into his eighties. He dressed like a homeless bum but actually had a vast portfolio of residential real estate worth millions.

"I was watching you giving those two people a tour. You know every one of my places is like a child to me," Asim replied.

"I found you another amazing tenant so your little baby is once again going to be in safe hands," said Mike, gesturing towards the apartment's front door.

"I ask you, Mr. Love, what kind of profession are they in?"

"Carrie works for the government – safest job around. No problems collecting rent from her."

"What about the man who was driving that beastly car? What does he do?"

"Just a friend of hers; he's not part of the package," Mike replied.

"Come on, Mr. Love. This man brings her over, drives her around. He will be visiting often. A young lady like that is not chaste like they were in my day. She has needs, U-R-G-E-S. He will be turning up in that gangsta car destabilizing the peace and harmony of my community," Asim said.

"He seemed like a decent guy. Raised in Jennings. I know one-hundred percent he has his own apartment. He told me where he stays; he lives on Goodfellow Blvd.," said Mike.

"Nothing *good* ever happens on *Goodfellow.* Find me someone else, someone better. North County folk are BAD. They bring drugs, crime, problems. I want a clean, single gal. Quiet, no bother!"

"I'm not liking the way this conversation is going. We're getting into housing discrimination territory," said Mike, who was dreading the talk he would need to have with Carrie. Ted, *'the blanket,'* was unlikely to be warm and comforting towards him during that conversation.

"You realtors don't care about who you find. You just want to collect your commission and move on to the next project. I am the one who will have to deal with all the ghetto problems that come with *THESE PEOPLE!"* the landlord said.

"I'm going to pretend I'm not hearing any of this."

"Why's that?"

"It sounds racist," Mike said.

"Mike, I am from Africa. How can I be racist? If I don't like the look of someone, I won't have them in one of my properties," he replied, laying down his law.

On the face of it, Asim had a point. It would be hard to label a Black man from Tunisia as being racist to other people of color. However, in Mike's experience, the racial hostility between African Americans and first-generation immigrant Africans was some of the worst he'd encountered. African Americans often viewed the new arrivals as backward. The new arrivals saw the established domestic Black community as lazy and forever complaining about historical injustices. This was another miserable version of modern American race relations, and one that anxious white liberals pretend doesn't exist.

Mike bent down, took the keys out of the lockbox, and tossed them to the owner. "I cannot work with you anymore. And, yes, I will say it before you say it: 'If you throw a rock into a crowd of people, that rock will hit a realtor in the head.' I know you can easily find someone to list this unit," Mike said, using the same lines that Asim would spew out as a negotiating tactic to set a reduced commission.

"Fucking millennials always need to get in the last word," Asim could be heard saying, as Mike headed to his car.

Mike's minor triumph of filling the rental had evaporated before his eyes. He was officially without listings and was now juggling nothing but thin air to an empty audience. Lizzy would be expecting baller tales of all the conversions he had made this week, not some dirge about an $800 listing going belly-up. Mike needed to flip the narrative and transform himself quickly into a rainmaker.

The day was still youngish and the alternative of hunting for business was going back to Missouri Towers and having a difficult conversation with Gloria. Mike came up with a back-of-a-napkin plan.

Mike rolled down Arsenal St. and pulled up to Benton Park's central green space. From the minor tragedy of this morning, he would attempt to bounce right back.

*   *   *

With the windows boarded up and the IT systems down, Daris Ballic felt helpless in the Spitfire office. He told Pam and Puffman that he had an appointment and would be back later.

Daris's usual rides were flashy and far from discreet. In the basement garage at the office, he stored an alternative car for stealthy missions when he didn't want attention. Daris pulled his generic SUV with blacked-out windows from the underground parking garage and headed east on Washington Ave. He planned to conduct a boots-on-the-ground operation.

For some reason, the radio had been tuned in to the local public station the last time he had driven the car, and it was still on that channel when he turned the ignition. Public radio used to be something that if you listened to it long enough, eventually a show would come on that explained your nervous tick, odd habit, kooky obsession and ultimately achieved the goal of making you feel special. Some time in the last couple of years, however, it had been hijacked by equity zealots whose purpose was to make you feel depressed and convince you that you are living in an unjust, racist world. Daris felt this just wasn't what America was all about. He switched to a station where a raspy-sounding lady with a zany gang of co-hosts dished out folksy stories and classic hits.

Daris parked up across the street from the New Berlin office. He jumped into the back seat and got out his binoculars. The first thing he noticed was that they didn't have agents chain-smoking outside the front door. He would fix that policy at Spitfire straight away. He could see Alexi Coklande's car parked out front. *No loyalty*! he thought. The office did look slick, though. He watched the easy-on-the-eye agents going in and out, conducting their business.

Daris observed across the street a middle-aged man exiting a tattoo parlor, sporting arm tatts wrapped in a fresh sleeve of plastic. The midlife-crisis tattoo was the new midlife-crisis ponytail that had long surpassed the midlife-crisis sports car as a bleak symbol of male desperation. No doubt this sad sack would head straight to his favorite bar thinking the credibility his edgy Celtic script ink exuded would translate into scoring with women half his age. Watching the ensemble of pedestrian traffic milling around downtown was about as uplifting as the cash-checking line at Walmart on payday. Much more of this and Daris would need to hit the bar.

Just as he was about to give up and walk over to Jack Patrick's for a beverage, he spotted what he was waiting for. Thomas Trinkenschuh, New Berlin Real Estate's broker of record, pulled out from the parking lot in a Benz that made

Alexi Coklande's ride look shabby. Daris began following him at a respectful distance.

For a powerful car on wide-open roads, his target drove at a timid pace. Thomas took Market to Grand, then headed south. They passed the Tower Grove Starbucks and the drive-through line, as always, was spilling onto the street. Daris viewed this spectacle as the epitome of everything that's wrong with the modern way of life. Squeezed into gas-guzzling cars bigger than anyone would ever need were people with too much self-created girth, buying supersized sugary drinks with money borrowed from credit cards that in many cases were a swipe away from being maxed out. These same people would roll into the office wondering why they couldn't qualify to buy a home. Somewhere, the self-starting triumphant American was far along the path to becoming a slouching second-rate citizen of the world. The work ethic that had once created unrivaled exceptionalism had been pissed down the toilet one venti frappuccino at a time.

Daris spotted floundering real estate agent Mike Love driving in the opposite direction in that Sonic car he refused to give up. *I wonder what he's up to?* Daris mentally asked. Had he not been busy he would have done a U-turn and followed him. Daris would love to know how one of the most unproductive agents in all of his offices filled his days. Daris carried on with the pursuit of Trinkenschuh's car until it reached an industrial building on Morganford Rd. in South City.

Trinkenschuh let himself into the building with a remote-control opener. Daris pulled his car up, logged onto the Realtors' Association website, and ran the ownership details for the property. "Finally we are getting somewhere," he said to himself loudly, before adding in a distinctly Churchillian voice: "This is not the end. It is not even the beginning of the end. But it is, perhaps, the end of the beginning."

*   *   *

Nick Pipeman and Lizzy Winslow both used the expression "find your lane" when referencing Mike's career trajectory. Mike's current real estate lane was clogged with cheap rentals, slumlords and imploding transactions. Somehow he needed to get off this freeway of meh and find an expressway of deals.

"Emulate success" was something he recalled from the realtor manual. Clint Cummings, one of Spitfire Real Estate's shining stars, made his money on selling homes to people getting married, having children and expanding their families. It's what he called, "The Circle of Life." If a very gay Clint, who didn't exactly ooze heartland nuclear family, could win over this subsection of buyers and sellers, then so could Mike. He just needed to implant himself where there are people with children, and then work his salesman magic. Mike concluded his best option would be to go to a kiddie playground.

The Benton Park neighborhood, with its gourmet deli and newly opened artisanal gelato shop, had all the amenities of a hipster haven. There were still a few holdouts from its grittier days, but most of the residents were now young couples who self-described as mold-breaking individualists. To Mike, though, everybody looked like clones. The men all had well-groomed Confederate General facial hair, Yakuza-worthy arm tatts, drank craft beer and played Pickleball at weekends. The women were a similar army of groupthink clones who donned a standard uniform of black stretchy pants, obsessed over their social media pages compulsively, and talked nonstop about schools for their children. Mike, lacking any hipster urbanist DNA, for this reason usually gave this part of town a wide berth.

It was mid-morning and approaching 90 degrees, but there were a solid number of kids and parents at Benton Park's playground – and all of these families were potential clients. Mike sat himself down at a bench next to the jungle gym and scoped out the scene.

Watching the children running around drew him back to Gloria. She was desperate to start a family and had been up-front about this from the start of their relationship. Could he really drop her and run off to California with Lizzy? Then he reminded himself that getting set up in a big real estate market on a top team was something he shouldn't pass up. Lizzy's nocturnal delights were the icing on the cake – and he needed no reminding of that.

Whatever he was going to do, he needed to execute some business this week. Mike, with liquid-courage-like confidence, walked up to a group of parents he could hear discussing the napping routines of their spawn. From the gist of it, Shane was down from two naps a day to just one, and Lucy no naps at all. A sour-faced woman in athleisurewear told the group, with a hint of glee and plenty of one-upmanship, that Jill, although now three, had two sleeps a day for a solid ninety minutes each and would go down at 7:15 for bed every night. They all agreed she was one lucky mom.

With a priestly air of assurance, Mike intruded into the chat and said, "My guys all nap at different times. It's total hell!"

"How old are they, man?" said the lone male among the gaggle of parents who Mike could now smell had a musty odor coming from his raggedy crop of facial hair.

"How old are they? Great question... six, four, and two," said Mike, deciding to stick with even numbers.

"Difficult ages," said a woman in skin-tight yoga pants, who had no issues flaunting the tight ass she had earned at the gym.

Riding the sympathy angle, Mike added, "No peace, and up to our elbows in poopy diapers all day long. Manic being a parent these days."

"Your four-year-old *and* six-year-old are still not potty trained?" the sour-faced woman asked.

Mike had quickly found himself out of his depth with parenting knowledge. "I guess not. But the six-year-old has developmental issues and the four-year-old is a late bloomer," said Mike, thinking on his feet before adding, "The two-year-old is supersmart, though, and very advanced for her age." He was now sounding like a typical parent with a very special child.

"What are their names?" asked the boney-assed MILF.

"Names, names, names," replied Mike, again stuck for words. He then spewed out, "Little Jack, Hazey Davey and Outlaw Pete." These were all characters from Bruce Springsteen songs but in a pinch it was all he could come up with.

"Cool names bro," said the bearded man.

"Which one is the girl? None of those names sound girlie," asked the sour-faced woman.

"They're all boys," Mike replied.

"You just said your two-year-old was a super smart girl," pointed out the sour-faced woman in the athleisurewear.

"Do you guys rent or own?" Mike pitched out to the group in an attempt to change the subject.

"Where are your children? I didn't see you arrive with any," asked Mrs. Sour Face, who had no interest in discussing real estate and was clearly suspicious of Mike's story.

"Over there," Mike said, pointing in a direction where several children were playing.

"Those are our children!" said the lady who rocked the yoga gear.

"Not those kids, of course. Mine are playing together down at the lake. When you have three kids, they kind of look after each other. *Laissez-faire* parenting," Mike said.

"You have the developmentally challenged six-year-old who isn't potty trained supervising the other two by a dangerous body of water?" asked the bearded man with the ripe scent.

"Hazey Davey, the advanced two-year-old, is in charge. He is very good around water. The grandparents have a pool," replied Mike calmly.

The sour-faced woman, who was the type of lady who promoted her parenting skills on social media with the slogan,

"Dedicated Mother," looked towards the lake and said, "I don't see any children there. I don't think you even have kids!"

Mike looked over to the lake. There were no children present.

"Shit, you're right. They're not by the lake. I left them in the car. Totally forget to take them out."

"Dude, that's really dangerous on a hot day. They could be dead by now," said the man, with serious daddy concerns.

"Keep your beard on man. Everything's going to be OK! I left the keys in the ignition and the AC on."

Mike then ran off as quickly as he could. He chose the opposite direction of his car just in case anyone called the police.

That didn't go quite as Mike had planned but he decided not to give up just yet. He would reboot his strategy and try again at another park.

If there was one thing St. Louis had an abundance of, aside from crime and potholes, it was parks, made even more evident by the fact there were obviously not enough city workers on the payroll to adequately maintain these parks. This was noticeable when Mike pulled up to the Fox Park neighborhood playground. The toilets were locked, the trash cans were overflowing, and much of the play equipment was broken. In spite of this, Fox Park was an area popular with parents with young children. Once these parents were in need of good schools they would all flee to the suburbs. The real estate potential on offer at Fox Park was the beautiful double transaction. Find a client a new home and sell their old one.

The Fox Park neighborhood was a few years behind Benton Park in terms of the forces of gentrification. The moms were perkier and the dads had a more blue-collar vibe, as displayed by less arty tattoos. The area holdouts – unlike Benton Park – weren't aging immigrants from Poland but third-generation African Americans who had their houses passed down through the family. The juice bar may not have found its natural home yet, and the coffee might be stuck on second wave, but the hardcore ghetto was firmly in the rear-view mirror at the Fox Park neighborhood.

Mike's Achilles Heel earlier that day had been inserting himself into a conversation about parenting. This was a subject he knew little about and wasn't prepared for, hence he was quickly spotted as a fraud. Nobody is going to want to buy a house from a fraud, let alone entrust a fraud to sell one. What he needed this time was to establish that he was, without a doubt, a member of the parent gang. In order to do this, he needed props – a prop child to be precise. Where was he going to get a prop child in a pinch? In Japan you could rent faux family members by the hour. In Japan you could also buy dirty schoolgirl panties from vending machines. Here in St. Louis, he would need to improvise, adapt and overcome. Mike would have to borrow one from a parent. Tapping up an aspirational hipster for the loan of their child was going to be tough. He scoured the park looking for options.

On a bench he saw a young Black mother with three children. She was more into her phone than her kids. Mike thought a Black child would be a great option. It would give him a modern and diverse branding that crossed racial lines. Aging Hollywood celebrities did exactly the same thing, plucking kids from third-world orphanages and relocating them to their mansions. Another bonus is that no one would dare call him out as not being the kid's parent. Doing this to a multiracial family would risk them being tagged as racist or, even worse, a "Park Karen."

Mike thought honesty with the mother was the best option. No messing around, get straight to the point. He walked over to the bench where the lady was sitting, with forty dollars in his hand.

"Good afternoon ma'am. This might sound odd, but I would like to borrow your child for a project I am working on. I will compensate you. The young one who doesn't talk would be perfect. Just for half an hour...."

She was quick to cut him off: "Are you off your fucking mind? You think that just because I am Black I'd rent out my kids? What are you crackers smoking these days?"

"Hold on, let me explain! I'm a realtor and I just want to use one of your children to assist me. Help me talk to other parents with children to get some business," he replied.

"You're a disgusting sicko," she screamed loud enough that some of his intended clients started looking in his direction.

"I only want to push them on the swings. I'll hold their hands when they go down the slide, if that makes you feel better."

"Is that how you get your kicks?" the mom yelled.

"There's nothing sinister. I was merely asking nicely if I could rent your kid. I'm sorry I disturbed you, my mistake,"

Mike said, realizing he had poked a bear with an inadequately-sized stick.

"Big mistake! *YOU PEOPLE* are gross!" she screamed.

The lady made a call on her cell phone. "Jamus, I'm at the park, a pedo wants to rent our kids. Get your ass down here and give him a whooping?"

The other parents in the park were now staring at the commotion. Mike, on hearing about the whooping Jamus was on his way to administer, ran as rapidly as he could to his car. He jumped into the Sonic and screeched away from Fox Park as fast as the vehicle's 1.4-litre engine would take him.

So much for being upfront and honest, Mike contemplated, as he headed west on Sidney St.

0-2 today, but Mike wasn't quite ready to give up on his efforts. He needed to set his goals higher; he needed to think big. Why waste time chasing people looking to buy $200,000 houses when he should be looking at buyers in higher price ranges. In California, a starter home is a cool million. Mike kept on driving until he reached the upscale suburb of Clayton.

He pulled up at Shaw Park. The physical distance between downtown Clayton and downtown St. Louis might be ten miles, but the two worlds were light-years apart. Looking at the manicured lawns and new playground equipment he could see exactly why the county folk were not eager to merge with the city into one big, "better together" family.

Mike walked over to a bench and sat down. The park was full of hottie mommies and nubile nannies. The only way to figure out who were the hired hands and who were the bankrolled housewives was by looking at the left-hand ring bling for rock size.

Mike was watching the hot moms walking around. He was being generous today, pardoning most of the ladies on the wrong side of twenty-one for wearing age-inappropriate yoga pants. Between their good DNA, healthy diets and hardcore exercise regimes, few fashion crimes were being committed.

A man in workout gear, wearing an expensive-looking timepiece and conversing on a cell phone, sat down next to Mike. He had on a distinct pair of wire glasses that were a hybrid of early Bolshevik and late John Lennon. He was talking to a contractor about home renovations. Mike's ears perked up when he mentioned Spoede Rd. He knew this particular street exists in nothing but good zip codes. Putting all the pieces together, Mike could tell this man was a high net-worth individual.

A very attractive woman in a miniskirt walked past the bench. Mike could sense his seatmate was also checking her out. The man ended his phone call and Mike grabbed the chance to engage the stranger in the one arena of commonality that, at this precise moment, they shared.

"Either her skirt was shrinking or the legs were getting longer. I couldn't work out which it was, but the view was admirable," said Mike to his seat partner, in reference to the hottie with the barely-there skirt who'd just walked past.

"No shit. This place is full of bored housewives and fresh divorcees looking for fun. Either right here or the salad bar at Straub's Market are your best options," said the man.

"I have enough women problems without finding more," said Mike.

"I've been married for years and am always looking for more," he replied, exuding the unmistakable whiff of an alpha male. He then introduced himself: "I'm Mike."

"That's a coincidence, I'm Mike too."

The two men shook hands. Stranger Mike had an odd handshake that may have been Masonic.

They both watched a college-aged jogger in a tight sports bra run past.

"I couldn't help but overhear that you are rehabbing a house," Mike Love said.

"Building one. We're pretty close to completion," said stranger Mike.

"Have you sold the old house yet?" Mike Love asked.

"No. We're getting ready to list it. My wife is interviewing realtors this week."

"Your lucky day! I'm a realtor," Mike Love said, as he thrust a card into the stranger's palm.

High-flier Mike's face dropped, realizing he had been suckered into a sales trap.

Spitfire realtor Roxie Johnson had a good strategy to hold onto these types of potential clients looking for an escape. Bombard them with niceness and make them feel awkward and uncomfortable if they resist your pitch. Mike, with all the yappy-dog persistence of Rottweiler Roxie, spent the next twenty minutes sitting next to his new best friend, smothering him with lashings of niceness. Mike Love eventually ground high-flier Mike into submission. By the time the stranger had run off in the direction of Straub's looking for dates, Mike had snagged himself a listing presentation. And no women or children had been harmed in the process.

Mike Love raced back downtown to share the day's highlights and lowlights with Gloria. All this roaming around parks and watching parents with children had got him thinking about the two of them. Maybe he *had* found his lane after all and it was right here in St. Louis, not in Los Angeles. If he could crack the Spoede Rd. set, the world could be his oyster. Gloria, children, and a future selling robber baron mansions wasn't so shabby a life.

Mike parked his car in the garage of Missouri Towers and took the elevator straight to Gloria's floor. He rang her doorbell with his signature ring sequence.

Zoe opened the door. In his eagerness, Mike ran straight past her and into the apartment.

"Gloria, you have to hear about my day. I have an amazing listing presentation in Central West End tomorrow. The house is worth just under...." He stopped suddenly mid-sentence.

Gloria was sitting on the sofa and didn't look happy.

"Is there something wrong, Gloria?" he asked just as he noticed cards displayed on a bookshelf.

Fuck! It was Gloria's birthday and with all the disruption Lizzy had brought into his life he had totally forgotten.

That's why she had invited him to breakfast this morning! *This is really terrible,* he kept thinking to himself, the thoughts hurtling through his mind.

"I told you he had forgotten and wouldn't bring you flowers, let alone a ring," Zoe said to Gloria, with an air of disapproval.

"How could you not remember my birthday?" Gloria asked

Mike was speechless.

All Gloria could think of was teary-eyed Samantha Baker in *Sixteen Candles* moping around as all those she loved had forgotten it was her birthday. How could this happen to her? This was certainly not the prerequisite for any happy ending. Gloria had actually been expecting this was the day Mike would finally propose to her.

Apartment #1711 Gym-Tan-Drink

It was midnight by the time Gloria McKendrick had stopped crying. No ring, no flowers, and the realization that Mike Love was most likely not going to become her fiancée. There were a lot of thirty-plus unmarried women in Missouri, but most of them were divorced at least once, if not twice. At this point she would gracefully skip the walk down the aisle and go straight to the registry office to get that ring on her finger. *What has gotten into Mike lately?* was the only thought going through Gloria's mind.

"I can only hope my second day of being thirty-two is better than the first," Gloria muttered to herself after getting out of bed.

Meanwhile, Zoe was prancing around the apartment getting ready for tonight's date with Nick Pipeman. "I need some fresh air," said Gloria to Zoe. She didn't want to chance it bumping into Mike, so with coffee in hand she headed up to the Missouri Towers roof deck – the one part of the building he didn't frequent. This area used to be a fun summer hangout when the pool was usable, but at least the viewing platform was still open.

Gloria exited the elevator and walked past the swimming pool's turgid-looking body of water that, for some reason, management refused to drain. To the east of the pool, a spiral staircase led up one more level to an open-air viewing deck. She walked up the staircase and sat down in a chair. The vista was spectacular. A coal barge was chugging down the Mississippi, a tourist helicopter was circling the Arch.

Gloria was sipping her coffee, admiring the view and reflecting on the day ahead when she was interrupted by the sound of a cough. She wasn't alone on the deck and looked towards the direction where this noise originated. In the far corner, a lady who had been lounging on a chair sat up. The woman, who she now realized was sunbathing topless, took a cigarette from a packet. "Morning," she shouted to Gloria, before sticking a smoke in her mouth.

"Hi," replied Gloria.

"I don't like tan lines," the stranger replied between drags of her cigarette, indicating she wasn't going to put a top on for the sake of company.

Gloria took a better look at her deck partner. The leathery, overly tanned skin threw off an exact age. This woman could be anywhere from forty-five to sixty-five. Gloria tried not to look at her breasts but it was hard. All she could think of was that even her perky lady bits would end in the same sorry state with enough time and gravity.

"Beautiful day," replied Gloria.

"This is my happy place," said the topless lady, who was now sucking on a straw from what looked like a pint-sized cocktail.

"I'm Gloria McKendrick, nice to meet you."

"Madison Stone. Come over girl, you look like you've got something on your mind."

Gloria took a seat on a lounger next to Madison. If she thought the lady might put on a shirt and cover up, she was mistaken.

"What's your story? Everyone's got one," asked Madison.

Gloria finished off her coffee before saying, "Where do I start?"

Madison, sensing this was going to be a long tale, pulled out a pre-made cocktail from a cooler of the same caliber as hers. She handed it to Gloria. If she was ever going to cover up her upper torso, this would've been the time, but she didn't.

Gloria began to recount the current predicament she found herself in. Madison was a good listener and an excellent shoulder to cry on.

"Let me tell you my story," said Madison, as she plucked a fresh cocktail for herself and lit up another cancer stick.

"St. Louis, as you know by now, is one stuck-up, snobby place. I grew up living and dreaming that shit. I went to the right high school. I was even crowned the fucking "Queen of Love and Vanity" at the Shroud of the Genie Ball."

Mike had told Gloria about this secret local organization. It was an elite, high-society marriage club masquerading as a St. Louis business booster group, open only to people who went to the best schools.

"The high school I went to was nothing more than a girl's finishing school. In kindergarten, they taught you how the lady introduces herself to the gentleman. From then on the education was one long, expensive course in becoming the ultimate housewife."

Gloria, looking at bare-breasted Madison with a cocktail in hand and cigarette in mouth, could only hope her parents had been refunded a portion of their school fees. For sitting in front of her was a living, breathing prairie fire – about as far as you can get from being a well-formed example of ladyship.

"My debutante ball date was an heir to a local chain of supermarkets. We were engaged shortly after we began dating."

"That would've been handy," said Gloria, who was buzzing after downing half her cocktail.

"Not naming names but it wasn't the big well-known grocery store. It was one of the smaller chains with amazing gift baskets. As all good, born and bred St. Louisans a few grades short of Ivy League acceptance, we both enrolled at Mizzou. He studied business, I studied English literature. Our time at college was amazing, although we never really ventured too far from our bubble of high school friends. I spent most of my senior year planning our nuptials. The wedding was going to be a huge five-day affair at a vineyard his family-owned. After that, our futures were set: he would work at the family business, and I would be the happy housewife. Charity work and children were the extent of my expected duties."

By the time Madison had fleshed out her backstory, Gloria had finished her drink. Her hostess pulled out another one from the cooler, which seemingly had an infinite supply. Madison had called the viewing deck her "happy place." Gloria quickly figured that whatever was in these drinks was the essential ingredient to happiness.

"I'm guessing things didn't turn out as per plan," said Gloria, now sitting next to a woman who looked more like a down-and-out wino than a well-kept Webster Groves' housewife.

"The wedding was set, invites were mailed, dresses made, cakes ordered. Everyone and anyone from the monied St. Louis classes was going to be at the event of the year. At the last minute, everything changed."

Madison, for a brief moment, stared towards the Eads Bridge before continuing. "My bachelorette party was of course in Nashville, and I mostly avoided anything too out of control. The same couldn't be said about my fiancée. He came back from Vegas a changed man. All of a sudden he was demanding sadistic sex, wanted to bring others into the bedroom, and had started taking hard drugs."

"What happened in Vegas didn't stay in Vegas," Gloria said.

"I was twenty-two, naive and my school hadn't prepared me for this. Now I know a little more and most likely my man was ahead of his skis in terms of where marriages in high St. Louis society eventually go. This kind of activity is common, but usually not until three children have been reared. By that point, the wife is busy in full-force mommy-mode and turns a blind eye, or joins in."

"So what did you do?"

"I got over my initial shock and put it down to us both pretending to be people we were not. Maybe we both wanted something outside of what had been planned for us. We agreed to go our separate ways. Official line was that we were too young and the wedding was postponed."

Madison stubbed out a cigarette and lit a fresh one.

"I'm intrigued how you ended up here," Gloria asked.

"My all-girls' school may have on the surface been in the business of producing perfect wives, but they did also teach you a few useful life skills. In senior year the capstone class was essentially: "How to marry well and divorce better." The theory was that a high percentage of marriages, for whatever reason, don't work out and "you fine ladies" deserve to be taken care of, at the very least. My fiancée's family paid me off. Not a fortune but enough that if I lived somewhat frugally, drank excessively, and smoked at least three packs of cigarettes a day, I will never run out of money."

"You retired to Missouri Towers at the age of twenty-two?" asked Gloria.

"Exactly. And I'm happy in my little corner one-bedroom apartment with an amazing 17th-floor view of the Arch. I might not get invited to school reunions, or mix in the right circles, but I enjoy life. Gym, tan and drink is how I fill my days. I don't even care that the pool has been closed for over a year. I never went in it anyway. Now the rooftop is less busy and clothing is optional," said Madison, jiggling her bare breasts.

"Would you ever think about getting married in the future?" asked Gloria.

"Sure, if the right person strolled into my life. I'm not really too fussed, though, and never seem to run out of men."

The ladies shared a moment of reflection.

"As for your situation Gloria, 'fail to plan, plan to fail.' You need to nail down Mike."

"Take control," said Gloria, as her cocktail intake had given her a self-assertive stance.

Madison lit another cigarette before saying, "A charging bull only looks at the red cape and never at the man holding the sword."

Gloria had no idea what this meant and possibly thought that by now Madison was too drunk to make any sense. She did, however, know that she would have to find out what was going on with Mike. There was no way she wanted to end up in the same "happy place" as Madison.

*   *   *

Mike, fired up for the listing appointment, left his apartment and called the elevator. Nick Pipeman and a random person he had never met were coming down. Mike wasn't happy to see Pipeman but was relieved he wasn't sharing the ride with Gloria.

"Where are you off to all dressed up?" Pipeman asked Mike.

"Listing appointment."

"Do you need help?" Pipeman asked, wanting in on the commission. The random person in the elevator stared at his phone screen and kept to himself.

"I have it under control," replied Mike.

"Just like I'll have Zoe under my control on tomorrow's date," said Nick. They stepped out of the elevator together.

"That reminds me; we need to talk about Zoe," said Mike, who had totally forgotten to have a few important words with Nick. Lizzy parachuting back into town had put this delicate man-to-man chat on the back burner.

"Zoe is a nice girl," said Mike, now stalling as he tried to think of the phrasing to convey his message.

"And I am a good guy," replied Pipeman, not knowing what Mike was angling at.

"Where do you intend to take Zoe?" asked Mike.

"Bridge Tap House on Locust," Pipeman said, referring to the restaurant where Mike and Gloria had their first date.

"When you go in, you will be taking the front door. And if so, may I suggest that wherever else, or whatever you do with Zoe, stick to the front entrance," said Mike.

"How else would I get in?" Pipeman replied, with a strange look.

"The back door! The tradesman's entrance!"

"Why would I do that? I don't even think Bridge has an alley entrance," Pipeman said.

"Nick, you are a strange man and I want Zoe to be treated like a lady." Mike couldn't sense if Pipeman had worked out what he was alluding to.

"All I am doing is having dinner with Zoe, and if things go well we might walk over to Busch Stadium for a Cardinals game."

"Baseball is wonderful, wholesome clean fun. I like that plan Nick. Just stay away from the dugout or going for a fifth-base, home run after the game," advised Mike.

"I'm lost," Pipeman said, shaking his head.

"Nick, you are known around the office not as Pipeman but as Assman. Please, I beg you, don't ask Zoe for anal sex!"

"That was only once, and I was really just a little off with my directions. Took the OFF RAMP instead of the ON RAMP, if you get my drift," said Nick now playing defense.

Nick was referring to an office party hookup with a rookie agent. The poor girl was never the same after this shameful encounter and quit soon after. Pipeman, although fessing to this one incident of forbidden love, wasn't telling the entire truth. He was not only known for hitting up women on first dates for "backdoor-billy" but was notorious for seeking it out in strange places with strange people.

The rumor was that his obsession with gals' rear ends had been formulated as a boy after watching *The Goonies* movie. Director Steven Spielberg had the film's hottie Andrea

Carmichael, who was everyone's crush, running around throughout in a barely-there cheerleader outfit. As the story progressed you were treated to an increasing amount of thigh exposure and eventually the occasional "accidental" panty-peek. The climax of the film had the cheerleader fully compromising her modesty with several underwear-revealing butt shots. After watching *The Goonies,* poor 'ol Nick Pipeman was never the same again and became addicted to all things women's ass.

During his twenties, Nick was infamous for his horn-dog stalking of ladies at the annual Christian Convention – the kind of ladies who wore purity rings and were saving themselves for marriage. He had convinced many a beauty with hair down to their knees that "The Missouri Compromise," as he termed it, would leave their virgin status intact before the eyes of God. Recently, Pipeman had been spotted at Missouri's one and only abortion clinic sharking for women, his theory being that the ladies protesting the sanctity of life weren't going to chance it and put themselves at risk of needing abortion services. The love Nick offered was one hundred percent safer than any birth control.

Mike hoped Nick got the message and would be the perfect gentleman with Zoe. Otherwise, he was going to be in hot water with Gloria, who had no idea about the full extent of his uncouth mannerisms. With that off his chest, Mike proceeded to his listing appointment.

Spacious architectural gems of houses, at reasonable prices, were an upside of living in a city that experienced rapid economic growth and subsequent lightning-fast decline. As the wealthy population migrated west, left behind were underappreciated robber baron mansions and stately piles that in other cities would have been subdivided into apartments or, if left intact, now inhabited by the top one percent of the one-percenters. Mike's listing presentation of high-flier Mike's house was located on one of those streets in the Central West End area of the city.

Mike turned onto Washington Pl., a tree-canopied private road littered with gorgeous houses, any of which would make a perfect cinematic backdrop. It took little imagination to conjure up a heartbroken Molly Ringwald character slamming the front door behind her as she ran out of one of these homes in tears. Or a predatory Mrs. Robinson sitting on the porch with a martini in her hand, plotting how to seduce the next Benjamin Braddock. Washington Pl. was the quintessential picturesque street that anyone would aspire to live on.

Mike had driven Gloria down dozens of similar enclaves. Each time she would pick out her chosen mansion and plan a new, exciting life in it. She seemed to think residing on a street like this were only people without problems and she wanted in. Mike told her that with enough Prozac, these people are superficially without problems, but without the pills, it's the same bullshit, only with a better view. But for Mike, even a Mormon family-sized pack of valium couldn't numb the pain from the amount of upkeep these homes required in order to thwart gravity.

Of course, in St. Louis there's a dark side to every Shangri-La. In the case of Washington Pl. it was the dangerous and depressed neighborhoods a short distance to the north. On this manicured block, teen angst might be expressed by playing Nirvana at full blast after curfew; a few blocks away the same teen angst was often settled with guns. It wasn't uncommon for the owners of Central West End mansions to find bullet shells in their backyards. And on New Year's Eve, when the local celebratory rituals marking the occasion are emptying your gun clip into the sky, you best be taking cover.

While researching price comps for this home, Mike couldn't help but notice that the area's property title records read like a PBS Newshour sponsors' list – hyphenated kosher names and long-winded, tax-avoidance trusts with mailing addresses to law offices. As well as the irony of residents in one of the most liberal parts of the city trying their hardest to avoid paying their fair share of taxes was the irony of the security protocols these private subdivisions adopted. "Defund the Police" is a less noble cause to tout when you have your own well-funded private militia on the payroll. And the gates and walls these ritzy residents hid behind were in the arena of a "do-as-I-say, not do-as-I-do" ethical conundrum. For if Donald Trump could replicate the barricades enclosing the private streets of St. Louis on the southern border, he would now have the "Big, Beautiful Wall" he promised firmly in place.

Selling real estate is about projecting a confident image to all. Rolling up to meet a client in a car that everyone upgrades when offered as a rental at the airport doesn't portray the allure of success. For this reason, Mike parked his Chevy Sonic at the end of the block alongside the visiting maids. Mike had done his research and had an accurate grasp of how much high-flier Mike's home was worth. He was wearing his fighting suit and lucky bolo tie. This listing was for the taking, he told himself.

Mike stood in front of high-flier Mike's house. It was a tidy three-story Georgian just over a hundred years old. The symmetry was a little askew, with an odd vinyl siding addition, but aside from that it was cute. He took out his notepad and made fake scribbles. This was just in case Mike and his wife saw him from their window standing on the street. He then took out his cell phone and snapped a few pictures before making additional pretend notes. A continuation of the sly trick that he had been taught by Mindy Playpus. "Make yourself look like a pro and seem like you are working the job before you even have the job," she would say.

From the corner of his eye, Mike noticed something out of place. At the faux Tudor to the left of the house, a woman dressed like a dystopian housewife from *The Handmaid's Tale* was removing a Black Lives Matter sign. These lawn placards seemed to be built from the same Teflon-like substance that created President Trump. Just like "The Don" could weather any political or personal firestorm without consequence, so could the mighty virtue sign of the champagne socialist classes. To prove his theory, Mike would tell anyone to drive down a street following a big storm or crazy weather event. You will see trees down, roofs lifted off, powerlines shredded, and realtor signs relocated by the forces of nature blocks away from their listings. However, the Black Lives Matter signs somehow defy the elements and, like Old Glory on the roof of Fort McHenry, are unmovable by anything.

There is, however, one event in Mike's experience that will see these signs withdrawn from their perches. When a house is being cleaned up to sell they tend to vanish, more often than not under the cover of darkness. Virtue-signaling has its limits of acceptance; in this case, offending potential buyers and hitting the homeowner in the pocketbook. It's as if the symbol of capitalism, the For Sale sign, and the symbol of pseudo-Marxism, the Black Lives Matter sign, aren't designed for co-existence.

Mike Love straightened his bolo tie and rang the doorbell. High-flier Mike opened the door; he was wearing a pair of crisp slacks and a shirt made of the finest Egyptian cotton that had been designed to be worn untucked. He ushered Mike Love into the great room of the house.

"Nice to see you again, Mr. Mankey," said Mike, who had obtained the owner's last name from ownership records.

"Call me Mike. My wife will be down soon, she's just putting the toddler down for an afternoon nap," he replied.

Mike Love took a walk around the great room. "Do you mind if I take some measurements?" he asked Mike Mankey.

"No problem."

Mike made himself look busy pretending to measure the room. This was really a bit of clandestine bluff; he just wanted to scope out the various family photographs on the walls.

"Looks like you did some modeling in your youth," said Mike Love after seeing a framed picture of a younger incarnation of Mike Mankey in a JC Crew advert.

"Yeah man! Paid my way through Mizzou doing that. Easiest gig in the world, and better than working." He then added in a low, hushed voice so his wife upstairs couldn't hear, "And the lady models, oh my God! See the hottie next to me in the picture. I fucked the living daylights out of her after that shoot...." Mike Mankey continued in graphic detail, recanting more of his sexploits with numerous girls he had bedded.

The women at Mike Love's Community College were certainly not in the same beauty league as that JC Crew model. *That's the way to do college,* Mike thought, trying to tune out some of the kinkier details of the tales he was being told.

Mike glanced over at a wedding picture of the Mankeys. It was dated 2009 – ten years ago. The wife had a slender body but an unfortunate horse face, with a set of teeth that looked like they could eat an apple through a chain link fence.

Next to that picture was one of Mrs. Mankey and her bridal party. Her four bridesmaids were positioned like a perfect row of Matryoshka dolls, descending in girth and height. Each well-nourished, tresseled-haired lovely was a little chunkier than the one standing next to her.

"Do you mind if I go and look at the kitchen?" Mike asked, hoping Mike Mankey would curtail the war stories from his modeling days.

"Sure, it's that way," the homeowner replied, pointing towards a heavy-looking wooden door.

Mike walked into the kitchen. It was loaded with Viking and Wolf appliances and would be a great selling point.

"This has to be one of the most awesome kitchens I've ever seen. The granite counters are exquisite," said Mike, trying to make high-flier Mike feel like he had a very special home.

"My wife designed it. Cost a fortune."

The view from the kitchen window overlooked the backyard of the Tudor home next door. "Your neighbor has a big pool," Mike commented.

"They're talking about moving to Nashville," Mankey replied.

Mike Love's hunch about the virtue sign being stashed as a precursor to selling had been spot on.

"Swimming pools are worse than boats," Mike Love tossed out before expanding on his statement as he stared out the window directly at the body of water. "They say *boat* stands for "Bring Over Another Thousand," but with pools, it's more like "Bring Over Another Ten Thousand." Owning a swimming pool is like being married to an extremely beautiful woman. Expensive to acquire, then once you have one everybody wants to be your friend and invite themselves over. Once they're at your place, all they want to do is dive in face-first and fool around in that delightful wet hole. The pool, not the wife of course," Mike added with a sliver of comedic timing before finishing off his monolog with further sage advice. "And just like every glamorous trophy wife, swimming pools are expensive to maintain, don't age well, need their filters flushed once a month, and without professional supervision get nasty chemical imbalances and go funky on you. Your neighbor thought buying that house with the pool was the happiest day of his life, but he was wrong. The day he sells that house, he'll soon realize he is a happier person."

"The new home we are building on Spoede Rd. has a pool," interjected Mrs. Mankey, who had apparently finished putting the toddler to sleep and was standing behind Mike, listening to his views on swimming pools.

Mike Love turned around and tried to think of a way to climb out of the Olympic-sized hole he had dug for himself.

"Mrs. Mankey, nice to meet you. I am Mike Love," he said as he handed her a business card.

"Mrs. Bridgette Mankey-Trowbridge is the name I prefer to go by," she shot back.

Mike took a good look at her. Well-dressed, albeit a little curvier than the wedding pictures, but her facial expression in real life, as opposed to the photographs on the wall, was less horse face and more what he termed, "resting bitch face."

"You have a wonderful home, Mrs. Mankey-Trowbridge," said Mike, who on hearing her full name knew exactly who was bankrolling this household. Bridgette's hyphenated moniker wasn't a feminist clinging to a maiden name but a toast to a glorious, aristocratic West County dynastic family. The Trowbridges were one of the richest, old-money clans in all of Missouri. They had originally made their loot in dangerous lead mining in the 18th century, then moved onto slavery and cotton plantations in the 19th century, and were now heavily involved in medical insurance billing services.

"How exactly do you know my husband?" she asked Mike.

"Squash club," Mike Mankey said before Mike Love had a chance to give the real answer.

With his detective hat on, Mike quickly put the pieces together and worked out the family dynamics. Bridgette the heiress held the purse strings and called the shots. Mike was obviously in the relationship for an easy ride but was kept on a tight leash. The last thing Mike Mankey wanted was his wife to discover that yesterday he was sharking the deli line at Straub's looking for divorcees in need of comforts. Knowing Mike from the squash club was a safe answer that avoided further questions. If Mike was going to get this listing, he needed to focus his efforts on Bridgette Mankey.

"Mrs. Mankey, why don't we take a look at the rest of the house. If it looks as splendid as the kitchen, I think I will find you a buyer very quickly," said Mike.

Mike, with a realtor training manual level of exceptional professionalism, toured the home with the Mankeys. He was on top form, and even to an heiress and a corralled lothario sounded as if he knew the business of real estate. Mike didn't even let Bridgette, who was continually checking her watch, distract him. After fifteen minutes of walking around the three levels of the home, they were back in the great room.

"Thank you for your time," Bridgette said.

"I believe you mentioned a finished basement. I should really take a look at it," suggested Mike, trying to keep the dialog flowing.

"It's more of a creepy unfinished basement than anything you need to see," said Bridgette, shepherding Mike toward the door.

"I have a listing contract for you to review," said Mike, handing the Mankeys a stack of paperwork.

"Thank you," said Mike Mankey, taking the documents.

"We will be in touch," added Bridgette.

With that, Mike was coerced out of the door and back into the blistering heat.

Mike walked to the end of the block and entered his car. Mrs. Mankey might not have shared his views on pool ownership, but the rest of the presentation, in his opinion, had been a slam dunk. He was confident he had the listing in the bag.

He checked his phone for messages. The office systems were still down but at least they had rigged a secondary internet source, so it was possible to work at Spitfire HQ again.

A text from Gloria had come through. It simply stated, in full-throated caps: *WHAT ARE WE DOING WITH OUR LIVES!* He tried to analyze if the "!" punctuation mark where a "?" should be, held any latent significance.

Lizzy had also texted with a less dramatic, *Looking forward to Friday night XXX.*

Mike sat in the Chevy Sonic gathering his thoughts and dwelling on his women problems when he viewed a devastating sight. Rumbling down Washington Pl. was a convoy of zebra-print Land Rovers. The cars, part of the Lyon&Rore team fleet, pulled up in front of the Mankey residence. Exiting a Range Rover Sport was boss-lady Linda Lyon. She was dressed in a more subtle outfit than the bright pink moto jacket she had been wearing at Sunday's open house. Over her shoulder was slung a computer bag, and in her arms, she clutched a stack of glossy brokerage brochures. From the other SUVs descended two "cubs," as assistants were labeled within the team. These easy-on-the-eye girls were dressed in microminis, loose blouses and teetered as they walked along the sidewalk in outrageously high heels. Mike watched the team storm towards the house in perfect attack formation: Linda Lyon and the paperwork at the vanguard, and a young stunner on either flank.

Bridgette and Mike greeted them at the door and ushered them in.

As Mike eyeballed the rival team roll into the Mankey-Trowbridge residence, his heart sank. He figured Linda Lyon was using the tried and trusted power team tactic of choice. Swarm the house with a snappily dressed crew and portray to your potential clients the allure of an efficient full-service concierge team that lives and breathes real estate success. This show of force would wow Bridgette and Mike, and they would give Lyon&Rore the listing.

But Linda Lyon was a cunning and sophisticated operator whose success wasn't built on any standard playbook. Linda was not only a Lyon by name, she had the killer instinct of a lion by nature – and she had a more devious way to snag this listing in a way that wouldn't leave the door open for any other realtors to have a chance.

Linda was well-connected in St. Louis' upper echelons of society and could find out information about anyone. Via her contacts, she was able to ascertain that Bridgette bankrolled the family and was the decision-maker. A little more digging with her extensive country club sources revealed the extent of Mike Mankey's wandering eye and constant philandering. It was for this precise reason that Linda recruited the two hottest girls on the team as her wingwomen for the mission.

Had Mike Mankey been the power and money behind the couple, it would've been easy for the girls to use their charms and land the listing. After all, Mike's brain was mostly housed between his legs and he wouldn't be able to say "no" to the "cubs." But for this situation, the girls were merely bait to lure Mike into a trap he would self-create. Just as Linda figured, it became apparent quickly to Bridgette during the presentation that Mike was behaving like a dog in heat around the "cubs." The final straw for Bridgette wasn't Mike not so subtly peeking up the ladies' skirts on the steep stairwell to the third floor, but Mike offering to give the "cubs" a private home tour the next day when his wife wasn't home.

Bridgette became enraged at her husband's flirty behavior, and a blowout domestic argument commenced. Mike was tossed out of the house and a sobbing Bridgette left alone with Linda and her team. The supportive women, with tissues on hand and relationship advice to offer, provided the perfect shoulder to cry on. During Bridgette's moment of weakness, Linda made sure she signed a listing contract.

With the paperwork completed, it meant the door was closed for any other agents. Linda Lyon, with her "divide and conquer" tactics, had created the perfect situation in which Bridgette couldn't say no. "Take a bite out of real estate with us" was the motto at team Lyon&Rore, and they would be feasting on this listing commission for some time.

Mike hadn't been back at Missouri Towers long when he had an apologetic text arrive from Mike Mankey. *Sorry man, but Bridgette went in another direction. I am up for squash if you ever want to play.*

Mike had to Google what squash was. He learned it was a game played mainly by foreigners, Ivy League colleges, and people in St. Louis who went to the right high schools.

Mike had been on top form today (swimming pool faux pas aside) and had still come up empty-handed. There were no silver medals for real estate agents; just winners and losers. Life in Los Angeles on Lizzy's team was becoming even more appealing.

*   *   *

Daris was holed up in The Bunker alone. Usually, for big corporate decisions, he liked to take counsel with his trusted team of Pam Hardings and Brad "Puffman" Thrust. However, for the operation he was in the midst of planning, the fewer people involved the better – if for nothing else, for their own personal safety. "Give us the tools and we will finish the job," said Winston Churchill as he begged for weaponry from America to defend against the Nazis. Daris had en route his own very special tools. If need be they could easily finish the job. For the sake of all parties involved, he hoped it wouldn't go that far.

Apartment #1811 Mr. Brightside

Internet dating is all about bogus, overly flattering pictures and not letting anyone know until the third date that you have shit credit, two kids from a previous marriage, and a nasty case of the clap. By the time they realize the truth, you can hope that second-date shenanigans has been good enough to overcome any perceived problems, and that all parties will go on to lead a happy and fulfilling life together.

Selling a house is a similar hustle. To get the first date, empty your grubby home of the sinews of everyday life and spruce it up with fresh paint and new carpets. Then craftily curate the residence with a select amount of undersized furniture to make the rooms look larger. Next, get a photographer to shoot a pretty selection of oversaturated, high-definition pictures of your perfectly staged home. If it's a bad weather day, be sure they Photoshop the sky blue, and for extra feel-good place a rainbow into the background. Then word herd a few paragraphs of cheery verbiage pointing out all the features that this "very special home" boasts. Now all that's left is to list the property and wait for the swipe-right matchmaking to begin.

The real estate version of the second date is for the hopeful buyer to come on over, poke around your home's nooks and crannies, and become more intimate with their potential pad. They will walk around the property, test the toilet flushers for effectiveness, and see how loud footsteps sound from the second floor to the first. Is the master bedroom closet big enough? Can the lady of the house fit an adequate table in the dining room to seat everyone for Thanksgiving? Will the basement make a decent man cave? This journey of exploration is the make-or-break point of the fledgling relationship. If all goes badly, the prospective buyer moves on and looks for other opportunities. If it goes well and things gel, there's a contractual consummation and the relationship is taken to the next level.

Escrow, that time between having the contract accepted and getting the keys to your new house, is just like those third-date discoveries. By this point, you have some financial skin in the game, with money invested on inspections and surveys, and an emotional investment with the effort you've spent mentally placing furniture, planning the refinishing of floors, and envisioning your happy new life in said property. So when halfway through escrow and you find out the basement has a leak, the roof will need replacing in three years and the neighbor's garage is four feet onto your property line, you're not only balls deep into the process with no desire to pull out, but you are also totally in love with this home. So after getting over your third date wobble, you are the owner of not only the most expensive thing you'll ever own but also the biggest money pit you'll ever be tied to.

Buying a house, much like getting married, is much easier than selling a house or getting a divorce. Nick Pipeman, unlike a divorce attorney, was in the fortunate position of making coin on both ends of these deals. Not only did Nick do this well but he was a master of his craft and the top-producing real estate agent in all of downtown St. Louis.

Enriched with newfound knowledge from an educational class on gender pronouns, Nick was at his home office desk updating his website biography. Nick had always resisted portraying himself as a man who was in sales, even if that was exactly what he was. His current blurb poetically labeled him as a "marketing maven" and "real estate concierge." Pipeman was struggling with the choice of new terms he should puff his bio with. Today's agents were overly clever with self-promotion and he didn't want to be "that guy" advertising himself with an outdated set of skills.

The headshot accompanying Pipeman's digital presence was distracting his concentration; he thought it might be time to reimagine this stock photograph. The bootstrap beard and two decades past its prime soul patch were, in Nick's opinion, fresh as a daisy, and he wouldn't want to mess with something not broken. However, the Cardinals baseball cap he wore in the shot to conceal his chrome dome was ripe for an update. It was now all about the trophy-winning St. Louis Blues hockey team and not the so-so Cardinals baseball club. Nick made a note to book a session with a portrait photographer and shoot fresh snaps wearing a Blues hat. For added pictorial aesthetics, he would get himself one of those oversized hockey shirts that suburbanites donned like a mandatory uniform to games.

Following the recent class, Nick had settled on using the pronouns "he/him/his" on his realtor biography. "Ze/xis/xirself," although having a certain air of dynamism, risked causing branding ambiguity in a city with a population easily confused by newfangled terms. After saving his bio with the gender moniker, Nick picked up a thesaurus and began to hunt for exciting new buzzwords. *Always be the sizzle and not the steak,* he reminded himself as he flicked through the pages searching for inspirational phrases.

At Nick's feet slept his dog Rollo. This pooch was legendary in realtor circles for having the uncanny ability to sniff out home-buying clients in need of real estate services. The dog for Nick was not only an essential driver of profit but also a qualified tax write-off. Pipeman had recently been researching ways to capture Rollo's molecular DNA in order to clone a successor. Without that dog he would need a new game plan or a new career.

Pipeman's desk was much like his entire apartment: minimalist. To the left of his sleek laptop was a scaled model of the St. Louis Arch. Many would point out that this was redundant, due to the real St. Louis Arch being clearly visible from every single window of Nick's spacious corner unit. To the right of his computer was an enormous ceramic urn full of pennies; not just any coinage, but what Nick, with a fundamentalist zeal, termed "lucky pennies."

Pipeman had been sticking the one-cent coins he found on the ground, or at random places, into this heavy-duty tub for the last twenty years. He'd check each new coin he found to make sure it wasn't a valuable Indian head penny; this had not yet occurred, and he wondered if it was a myth that they even existed. He would then rub the coin three times on his forehead and proclaim the penny as being certifiably lucky. Upon the conclusion of this ceremony, he placed the newfound penny into the special jar on his desk.

Nick had been a blessed guy throughout his life and superstitiously attributed this to his penny-collecting rituals. Pipeman had found so many coins that he would soon either need to bank the cash or find a second storage container. He had yet to decide, as any change in his ritual might turn into a jinx.

How anyone ends up as a realtor is always a story, but how Nick found himself with a license was slightly more nefarious than most – and certainly nothing he would include in any biography. Nick was born and raised in Bellefontaine Neighbors. This St. Louis suburb holds two distinctions. First, with a grand total of twenty-two characters, it has the longest name of any municipality in the United States. Second, this city played a starring role in the sorry saga of block-busting and the subsequent "white flight" that this practice fueled.

As a boy he clearly recalled a sharply dressed real estate agent with a fancy car banging on the door of his family home. This man told his father, "The Blacks are moving around these parts, and this is your last chance to sell up at a decent price." He then added as good news, "I'll find you a nice home in St. Charles to move to."

Nick's father liked his house and the community and had no intention of leaving. Besides, what he was being offered for the property was substantially under value. The unscrupulous agent who hustled the Pipeman residence had quite the convincing spiel and bought up many of the surrounding homes. Working with a crew the properties were updated and sold to Black middle-class families who were fleeing the inner city. The agent had created a sense of panic where there was none, and used it to buy the properties at a discount. He then targeted a group of buyers with the homes at greatly inflated prices. An unethical illegal scam, but as Pipeman's father could see via the numbers, it was also a lucrative business model.

Nick and his family didn't have one drop of racist blood in them and embraced their new neighbors as they had the old. The people moving in were good folk wanting to leave the crime-ridden projects and make a better life for themselves in the suburbs. Within a few years, the area demographics had shifted and by the 1980s, when Nick attended high school, he found himself to be a minority within a predominately African-American cohort. The white flight of Bellefontaine Neighbors was one small example of a de facto segregation that persisted throughout the region.

Being sucked into the wicked world of block-busting and witnessing the resulting destabilization of a community had a life-changing impact on Nick. These events would ultimately steer him towards the real estate business. A better man than Nick could've channeled his energies for the purposes of good, possibly embracing the real estate industry as a way to assist minorities in navigating the complexities of buying or selling a home. Maybe Nick might have become a mortgage broker to help these same people who were often targeted with predatory loans. Another option was to involve himself with one of the numerous non-profits that were revitalizing urban blight. There were many avenues of positivity Pipeman could've traversed within the industry. Nick, however, was not that better person and had his own deviant agenda for becoming a realtor.

Upon first encountering the sleazy agent, Nick was less bothered about his illegal actions and more intrigued by the slick suit he wore and the fancy ride he drove. Nick wasn't that into cars or designer clothes but he saw them as a means to an end – and that end was getting laid on a regular basis with good-looking girls. He knew the block-busting agent was making big money and due to this fact had an upper hand with females. Pipeman, even back in the day with his illustrious head of hair, was an average-looking blue-collar kid with an education from a mediocre public high school. He was without sporting talent, had no college ambitions, and lacked family connections. Paycheck to paycheck, menial low-level jobs and a tract home in a second-rate township was about as good as life would get for a nobody like Nick. The real estate business offered Nick an olive branch to escape a mundane life in North County. Of more importance to Pipeman, it gave him a way to make the money needed to improve his odds of attracting the ladies. All Nick wanted from life was an in-the-flesh version of Andrea Carmichael's glorious *Goonies* ass, and this route was his best chance of getting it.

Successful realtors refuse to retire and unfortunately don't just fade away. Like a bad heroin addiction, the buzz of closing deals and the cashing of hefty brokerage checks is something hard to quit. Nick vowed he would never turn into one of those surgery-enhanced, long-in-the-tooth agents that hustle until the day they die. Suffering a stroke while holding an open house, or dying of a heart attack hunched over a computer writing up a counter-offer, wasn't his exit plan. Nick was working his nuts off with the aim of stashing away as much money as possible. His ultimate goal was to retire in Florida within five years. He just needed to stay at the top of his game between now and then and bank the dough.

For obvious reasons, Nick omitted most of his life story in his new bio. After all, who wants to know that the guy who has the keys to your house is a perverted desperado obsessed with women's ass. He was also careful to never allude to wanting to jack it all in within half a decade. Nick's sales pitch was always along the lines of, *my job is my life's mission and I will always be there for the client.*

After an hour of brainstorming, Nick had jotted down a selection of nuggets he wanted to splice into his resume, and a few already in there that he would redact. "Analytical" was cut – it was so last year. "Amped," on the other hand, had a certain postmodern vibe and was added. "Concierge" and "maven" were eliminated because every bored housewife turned realtor included those words in their "get-to-know-me" section. Pipeman also extracted any reference to selling or buying, and almost any notion that his line of business involved houses or homes. Nick deleted his old opening line: "I deliver tools, emotional support, and professional guidance from the day the sign hits the yard until the moment you get your keys at closing." His buzzy new intro read: "A creative player who humanizes habitation domain transactions. I innovate and thrive on success. I separate signal from noise. I cruise the margins of counter-culture and urban energy, where the fault lines of high and low collide. 'NO' is simply not in my vocabulary."

"Fucking awesome! They don't call me Mr. Brightside for nothing!" Nick yelled after reading his new bio opener aloud.

The more Nick could detach himself from the grubby business of selling homes, and market himself like a TED Talks headliner, the better. He might not have the looks of a hot blond with a $200-a-pop haircut, but he could keep up with the best of them in the realm of high-octane bluster. This was 2019 after all; the less you knew about the nuts and bolts of a profession and the more you know about marketing fluff, the better. Modern real estate wasn't an industry geared around knowledge but a smoke-and-mirrors exercise in nonsensical self-promotion.

Thrilled with his updated bio, Nick powered down his laptop. He could now focus his efforts on tonight's date with Zoe. "Stay away from any back door topics," Mike had warned him.

Nick walked into his bedroom and opened the closet. He was unsure exactly what he was going to wear tonight. But from a glance in his Marie Kondo-inspired tidy wardrobe, the chances were high that he would be dressed like Sonny Crockett in his *Miami Vice* season three prime.

*   *   *

Realtors are loathed to pass over a nickel's worth of business to anyone if they can avoid it. Mike laughed when agents who worked listings at all price points, in all parts of the metro area, suddenly had a project that didn't fit with their skillset and wanted to hand it off. Odds were that it was a dump of a house in a high-crime neighborhood or a client with mediocre credit looking for a cheap rental. The cutthroat, self-serving nature of the business made it standard operating procedure to have no qualms about passing dangerous, poorly compensated projects to colleagues. For this reason, Mike was wary when anyone else in the office offered him a lead.

However, there was one exception to this general rule. A referral from fellow Spitfire realtor Harry Muff always had the potential to be something decent. Harry was overly selective with the clients he took on, and due to this selectivity passed over many solid projects other agents could only dream of. In fact, the list of projects that Harry *would* work on was far shorter than the type of client or listing he declined. For Harry avoided representing doctors, lawyers, and architects because, as he'd say, "it always ends in tears." He wouldn't work in any areas north of Delmar Blvd. as that was "too dangerous." He wouldn't get involved in transactions worth less than $500,000 as "the commission wasn't worth the paperwork." He didn't want to get entangled in properties deemed architecturally ugly because "life's too short to waste your time on crap." For the same reason, he wouldn't represent ugly people, as in Harry's words: "People tend to buy homes that look like them, and ugly people purchase ugly houses."

A recent update to his no-go list was millennials, who due to their "lack of concentration" are a pain in the ass to work with. Clearly there was a method in Harry's madness, as not only did he have the lowest blood pressure of any agent Mike knew, he also managed to make an amazing living selling real estate.

So when Harry called Mike and passed over to him a couple who were flying in today from San Francisco looking to buy, he was quick to jump on the lead. The reason Harry told Mike he had eighty-sixed them was because they were from California. "People from Cali go around the business of buying a house in the Midwest like Missourians haggle over the price of a taco in Mexico. They have pockets of cash but refuse to spend it. It's plain rude and insulting!" said Harry as he handed Mike their contact details and loan pre-approval letter.

Mike learned a little bit more about the clients and the type of property they were looking for over a Skype call. Greg Smith and Jenny Lui were Silicon Valley software engineers. They were married but Jenny said she'd kept her maiden name to honor her Asian heritage. They had two children: Otterly, who was eight years old, and Rio, who was six. They proudly confessed that they had given their children gender-neutral names to allow them the freedom to embrace whatever identity they might choose. Mike just figured they were coastal, artsy names to compensate for the boring middle-class names that Greg and Jenny had been saddled with. They would both be working remotely in St. Louis for their Bay Area start-ups. And before telling Mike "We want a deal!" informed him they would be keeping their big California salaries. Greg and Jenny had a generous budget and could spend up to $800,000 (an amount that buys a lot of house in St. Louis). They had a down payment sitting in the bank, and with their loan in place were in a position to submit offers as soon as they found a property.

Their home criteria was at least four bedrooms, a minimum of three bathrooms, and enough square footage to carve out two home offices. Jenny wanted a space to create a yoga studio and Greg wanted a quiet area that could become his meditation zone. They both wanted a yard big enough to install a dry rock zen garden, and the roof had to be suitable for the installation of solar panels. Non-negotiable was a garage spacious enough to accommodate a Tesla Model X. Throughout the conversation, Jenny and Greg said on numerous occasions that they wanted to live in a "diverse neighborhood."

Mike was up until the early hours of the morning booking viewing appointments for eight perfect homes that fitted Jenny, Greg, Otterly, and Rio's needs. This tech couple with their California cash was the big whale he had been awaiting.

It was a little past 1 p.m. and Mike was waiting for the clients to arrive for the first showing on the list. He was dressed to impress in his one and only suit and matching bolo tie. The house Mike picked out was a stately Victorian on Westminster Pl. It ticked all their boxes and at $695,000 left enough room in the budget for not only solar panels but also a live-in housekeeper that would fit neatly into the original third-floor servants' quarters. Jenny, Greg, and the children had all flown in this morning from California but had texted Mike that they were running late. He had left a little bit of room between each showing, but if they didn't come soon it was going to wreak havoc with the planned viewing schedule.

At 1:15 p.m. they finally pulled up to the house. Jenny and Greg both had venti-sized Starbucks drinks in their hands. *Fucking hell! I am standing here waiting like a fool while they're at Starbucks,* thought Mike.

"Sorry we're late!" Greg said.

"We've spent the last hour hunting for a place to buy camel's milk," added Jenny in a grating, nasal voice between sips of her beverage.

"Rio only drinks camel's milk. It helps keep his stress levels down," Greg added. Rio was sucking some white liquid in a glass bottle through a straw – no doubt the camel's milk.

Rio had been referred to as "him" by his parents, settling one nagging question for Mike, especially as both kids had long hair and dressed in what Mike believed in California-speak was "a nonbinary style."

Greg and Jenny were a curious couple. They were in their early thirties. Greg was a bulky 6ft 4in white man wearing a Stanford T-shirt, plaid shorts and a pair of orange Sperry deck shoes. Jenny, in contrast, was 5ft 2in, could not have weighed more than 105 lbs, and with the high-waisted pants and oversized glasses she wore had the look of a Wellesley College gender studies Ph.D. student who didn't ever want to graduate. Mike had heard that all the tall, successful white tech guys had petite Asian wives and girlfriends. It was a status symbol in Silicon Valley. Maybe it worked both ways and tall white women sought the short Asian guys. Mike doubted it, though, and figured there were just a lot of bitter tall white women upset that all the tall men had found other interests. Mike thought that might explain why California had so many women who didn't shave and had found comfort with other gals.

"No problem guys. It's great to finally meet you, and I'm really happy you made it to St. Louis safely," said Mike, using an introduction line lifted from the realtor training manual as he handed Jenny the house spec sheet.

"We like the look of this area," Jenny said, gazing down a picture-perfect street lined with starter castles originally built for the turn-of-the-century merchant classes.

"Lots of Black Lives Matter signs. We like that too!" said Greg, reinforcing his woke values.

"This is a very walkable and diverse area that I think is highly suitable for your needs," said Mike, who knew from experience that the streets with the most Black Lives Matter signs tended to have the least actual diversity.

"We thought we might see Trump banners everywhere, being, like, in Middle America and all," said Jenny in a full-throated West Coast squeal.

"This is a very liberal area. Think of it as San Francisco with less fog," replied Mike, who with the never-ending heat could only dream of cool mist rolling in.

"Question for you Mike. The sat-nav took us a little out of our route," said Jenny, before Greg interrupted with: "I told you Apple Maps aren't good."

"We work for a rival company and Greg is always ribbing me for using Apple Maps. Anyway, we were about three blocks north from here and the neighborhood looked like it had recently burned down. Was there some kind of accident or problem over there?" asked Jenny, pointing in a northerly direction.

Greg, Jenny, and the spawn had made the mistake of crossing the other side of Delmar Blvd. This was known locally as "The Delmar Divide." From one side to the other of this thoroughfare was the greatest wealth disparity in the entire nation. Jenny and Greg, although only three blocks away from this mansion-lined street, had mistakenly wound up in one of the poorest and most dangerous census tracts in America.

Mike, on top of his game and not wanting to advertise the ghetto that was a football field's distance away from a house he was trying to peddle, shot back: "That's another diverse, fast-transforming area with a lot of development underway."

"Good to know, as we are super-big on equity and inclusion but personally we don't want to live too near the hood," said Greg, indicating the limits of his progressive values.

"The wagons of gentrification are circling all around us. Everything is a good investment in this area," Mike said, trying to steer the subject away from their brief diversion to the wrong side of the de facto tracks.

Jenny was reading through the spec sheet when she asked, "The price listed is $695,000. Do you think the sellers would take $650,000?"

These guys roll up late and are already haggling. Harry Muff was spot on, thought Mike.

"I have the keys here. Why don't we check out the house and see what you think? Then, if you like it, we can talk about what to offer. After all, I doubt you could even find a two-bedroom condo in the Bay Area at this price point," said Mike, trying to get the show rolling.

"That's one of the reasons we want to move to the Midwest," said Greg.

At this moment, Mike heard a familiar noise. He was so certain what it was that he didn't even have to play St. Louis' favorite game of, "firecracker, car backfiring or gunshots."

In an effort to drown out the sound of small arms popping off nearby, Mike began talking loudly, offering a few nuggets of local history as a distraction. He'd just started talking about the first-ever use of an ice cream cone during the 1904 World's Fair when he heard a screeching car coming down the street at high velocity.

"What's that?" said Jenny, as the family from San Francisco looked in the direction of the noise.

A gold-colored Dodge Charger with a blown-out front tire hurtled down Westminster Pl. towards Mike, Greg, Jenny, Otterly and Rio. With sparks flying from the rim of the wheel, the car then lost control fifty yards away from their position. The vehicle sideswiped two parked cars before completing a 180-degree spin and coming to a grinding halt about twenty yards from where they all stood watching.

"Should we go and check to see if the driver's OK?" said Greg.

Before anyone could make a decision on what to do, the Charger door opened and a man in a hoodie exited. He had sustained an injury and was hobbling down the street. He was now in the middle of the road and parallel to where Jenny was standing on the sidewalk.

"Sir, do you need help?" asked Jenny.

"Let me call an ambulance!" added Greg.

The roar of a black Cadillac Escalade with a St. Louis flag in place of the front license plate drew everyone's attention away from the man in the hoodie. This second vehicle careened down the road, coming to a dramatic halt about the length of a tennis court away. The hobbling man looked back and upon seeing the other vehicle approaching pulled out a 9mm pistol from his waistband and started shooting. The SUV's front window cracked and multiple other shots ricocheted from the hood. Emerging from the Escalade's sunroof appeared a man brandishing an AR-15 semi-automatic rifle. Upon seeing the second gunman and realizing he was in the middle of a shootout, Mike dove onto the ground for cover. A screaming Jenny threw herself behind their rental car and Greg grabbed both children to shield them. The second gunman, leaning out of the sunroof, let rip with the AR-15, blasting off dozens of rounds. As the mayhem unfolded, Jenny screamed, Greg pissed his pants, Otterly started bawling and Rio dropped his bottle of camel's milk, which smashed as it hit the ground. Bullets sprayed the street in all directions, hitting trees, cars, and the tarmac. The hobbling man with the hoodie fell onto his butt as a result of multiple bullets hitting him in the stomach. He managed to unload the rest of his pistol clip before rolling over and slumping to the ground. The Escalade then reversed down Westminster Pl. at high speed before roaring off north.

Seeing that the second gunman had driven off, and not hearing any more bullets being discharged, Mike finally stood up. He dusted off his suit, straightened his bolo tie, and assessed the situation around him. Jenny, Greg, Otterly and Rio were still cowering in terror, but none had been hit. The last thing he wanted was for a client to die on him.

Mike took some consolation that his Chevy Sonic, which he had hidden two blocks away, was out of bullet range and so unscathed. Unfortunately, the man in the hoodie was on the ground, with blood streaming from him. He was likely dead.

Mike pulled out his phone and dialed 911. The first two attempts were met with a busy signal. After the third try, he got through. By the time he had finished his call with the police dispatcher, the blood from the man lying in the middle of the road had trickled down to where he was standing and merged with the puddle of camel's milk. The fusion of milk and blood made a beautiful, delicate swirl pattern that to Mike looked like the topping of a fancy European cake.

*   *   *

Like a married couple, Sam and Alice had fallen into a regular routine. Sam would come home late from work and Alice would have dinner ready. They would eat together and share their accounts of the day. They would then sit on the sofa and watch movies. And just like the best of married couples, they would make their excuses of being tired or needing to be up early and go to bed without any anticipation of sex.

But Sam and Alice were *not* a married couple. She was a hired lady, and for the cash she'd taken had every expectation of being used and abused by Sam in all manner of vile ways. Alice was shipping out the following day and felt like she had cheated Sam. How could she take his $1,600 plus expenses for simply making dinner and keeping him company?

Sam and Alice were sitting next to one another on the sofa watching the 1940s film *Mildred Pierce*. After nearly a week together, she was almost *too* relaxed in his company. Come to think of it, she hadn't had a dream about being eaten by a snake for days. Instinctively, Alice began to snuggle with Sam as they watched the film.

"This is my last night," Alice said.

"I know," Sam replied nonchalantly.

Alice began stroking Sam's thigh. She could feel him tensing up.

"Is there anything special you want to do tonight?" she asked

"No."

Alice switched off the television and grabbed Sam's arm.

"Sam, the contract you had me sign was pretty blunt on what you wanted from me. I've been here for nearly a week and you haven't touched me. Am I a disappointment to you?" asked Alice, nearly in tears.

Sam turned to Alice and explained his extenuating circumstances in full detail.

Alice woke Sam up the next morning before his alarm clock went off. They had both slept separately – just as they had every other night.

"Sam, would you like it if I stayed another day?"

"I would, but I can't afford it," he said.

"If you pay the fee to change my ticket, you can have a freebie bonus day – but on one condition."

"What?" he asked.

"Call in sick and spend the entire day with me."

*   *   *

The shootout on Westminster Pl. yesterday wasn't the first time Mike had to dodge bullets on the mean streets of St. Louis but if he moved to Los Angeles it would be the last. The police rolled up within ten minutes and cordoned off the area with yellow tape. The man in the hoodie was pronounced dead at the scene. He had been hit by six of the forty-eight bullets the cops said had been fired. Mike added this homicide to his murder log, which now stood at 149. Zoe would've loved the casings for her jewelry line but they were all taken by the homicide squad as evidence. The police said it was a turf battle between two drug gangs. This run-of-the-mill carnage would be lucky to get a couple of paragraphs in the *St. Louis Tribune.* Black people killing other Black people didn't seem to get anyone riled up.

Greg, Jenny, Otterly, and Rio were in a severe state of shock after their near miss. Their rental car had two bullet holes in it, but aside from Greg's soiled underpants and the spilled camel's milk, they were all physically unscathed. The family bailed out on the rest of the viewings and headed straight to the airport. Jenny told Mike she had overestimated their appetite for living in a big metropolitan city and was now considering rural Maine as an option. Greg told Mike he had misjudged his eagerness to live in the vicinity of a transitional neighborhood and was going to put his quest for embracing diversity on hold. For Mike, this was another potential payday that had gone up in smoke.

With all the bad luck Mike was having this week, it really felt like the gods were telling him to make a new start in California. Mike drafted a resignation letter to Daris Ballic. He also needed to have a talk with Gloria – and he knew it would be tough.

Mike hadn't seen Gloria for two entire days. Missing a girlfriend's birthday is the second shittiest thing a boyfriend can do; worse is cheating – territory that Mike was now stumbling into.

Mike banged on Gloria's door. She answered; there wasn't the usual kiss or display of affection. Gloria instinctively brought Mike a coffee from the pot. On her living room television, the romantic drama *An Officer and a Gentleman* was playing. Mike knew this was research for work and she wasn't looking for fictional romance to supplement his dereliction. From the empty Twinkie box, though, she may have been looking for solace in food.

There was no sign of Zoe at the apartment. Mike was curious how her date with Pipeman had gone.

"Zoe around?" Mike asked.

"Running errands," Gloria replied.

"How did the date go? Did Nick say anything weird?"

"It went well. He was quite the gentleman."

"No strange requests from the Pipeman?"

"He did ask her if she's open to anal sex," said Gloria, in a matter of fact way.

Mike just about spat out a mouthful of coffee. He couldn't believe Nick hadn't heeded his advice.

"Her reply?"

"Zoe yanked up her skirt and said she's 'adventurous.'"

261

He didn't know what to say. This was the kind of topic discussed with a mistress, not a girlfriend. *Chasing the brown clown around town!* he thought to himself, deciding not to share these thoughts with Gloria.

"It was a test!" Gloria added.

"Who is testing whom?" Mike asked.

"You remember our first date, I asked you if you thought I should lose weight. You said, 'No you're perfect!' Had you told me, 'You could always lose a few pounds,' I would have sent you packing. This was his version of that first date test."

Mike clearly remembered that trap on their date, only because he had fallen at the same hurdle before with another girl. On that occasion, he hadn't given the answer required, and the date imploded. Tough lesson to learn. Women and their body weight was obvious, but what kind of twisted hurdle jump was Pipeman setting up?

"I am lost as to what this test is about," Mike said.

"Nick is quite the romantic and is looking for long-term love, possibly a wife. His theory is that in all relationships, at some point, "the love that dare not speak its name" will be discussed. So on every first date, Nick puts it right out there. Kind of a *The Princess and the Pea* scenario, where Nick is looking for his perfect woman and how the candidate answers will determine if she is it," Gloria replied.

"Like I said, Pipeman is an acquired taste, but it sounds like he has found his soulmate with circus clown Zoe," Mike said, trying to get away from any more talk about Pipeman's ass fetish.

Mike walked over to the living room window and looked out towards the Arch.

"I heard about your brush with death," said Gloria.

"It was scary and got me thinking about the future."

"I was expecting you to make a move towards 'our future' on my birthday, but a few days' late is fine."

Mike turned around and looked towards Gloria. *Shit, she thinks I am going to produce a ring from my pocket. Shit, why didn't I think about producing a ring. Because I am thinking of running off to California with an ex!*

Gloria sat on the sofa waiting for Mike to make a move. All Mike could think was, *Can I really do what Lizzy did to me and break Gloria's heart?*

Mike was spending too much time staring out the window and Gloria could sense no ring was forthcoming. From the expression on her face, Mike realized he had managed to suck the air out of the room and Gloria was suffocating from his inaction.

"I have a job opportunity in Los Angeles," he finally fessed.

By the look of her expression Gloria was horrified.

Adding details, he said: "It's with a team on a big brokerage. They will set me up; they have more work than they can handle, so I won't be hustling for leads."

"When are you thinking of going?" Gloria asked as she tucked her legs up into a ball on the sofa.

"A few weeks."

"Realtors in Los Angeles don't drive Chevy Sonics," Gloria said.

"They're going to lease me a new ride. You know I have been talking about moving to California since the day we met."

"I'm settled in St. Louis. I'm not sure I want to move again. Certainly not pack up and leave in a few weeks," she replied.

Mike didn't say anything. He walked back over to the window. He knew he would miss the Arch.

"Oh! You were not asking me if I wanted to come as well. You came here today to tell me you are moving without me," Gloria said, gasping for words.

"It's complicated. I've been trying to make it work in St. Louis but nothing goes right for me here."

"Screw the real estate gig. Get a different job."

"Back to the tire shop! Working for the man! That's my station in life, like a bad character in a Bruce Springsteen song."

"You could do real estate on the side," she said.

"I have the chance to be set up in Los Angeles. Working million-dollar listings and taking home big paychecks. Or I could stay in Missouri and work in the tire shop and as a side hustle sell vinyl-sided houses on Sundays. What would you do Gloria if you had that choice?" He asked.

"You're forgetting about me. I'm here in St. Louis. I thought we were a team. I thought we were made for each other. We were going to do our own part in enhancing the local gene pool with my cosmopolitan Kansan DNA. A little cross-pollination could certainly benefit the regional stock."

He looked at Gloria. Was he crazy even considering leaving her? She was perfect.

Sensing Mike's unease, Gloria went on full attack mode. "There's something you are not telling me about this offer. Who would hand you a job that sounds too good to be true. A gig that comes with a fancy car. A position in real estate that doesn't involve scrounging for business. There's got to be a catch. What's the name of the team you are working for?" Gloria grabbed her computer from the kitchen counter in anticipation of doing a little research.

"Someone I did a deal with last year in St. Louis. They moved to California. They're looking to bring select agents to their team," said Mike out of character, telling Gloria a lie.

"NAME PLEASE!" shouted Gloria.

They had always been honest with each other up until today, so Mike put one foot back on the truth train.

"Elizabeth Snodgrass, from City of Angels Realty," said a Mike short on details and long on deception.

Gloria pumped the names into a web browser and carefully sifted through the results.

"She has a lot of makeup on in the headshot," said Gloria, who scanned the pictures before delving into her bio.

Gloria was hunched over her computer with multiple browsers open tapping ferociously at the keyboard. Mike knew he was in trouble. Gloria would have become a forensic tax inspector or private eye if she hadn't pursued the circus. Her eyes darted between windows and at times she would jot down her findings. After only three minutes of sleuthing a smug looking Gloria looked over to Mike.

"You're busted. I know who she is!"

Mike froze in panic, there was nothing he could say as Gloria delivered her damming judgment.

"You can take the girl out of St. Louis, but you can't take St. Louis out of the girl. Women around here are so predictable, destined to marry their high school boyfriends. Even if it's on the second go around! Your dream job offer is from no other than a Miss Lizzy Winslow!" Gloria screamed as she turned around the computer screen to reveal a picture of Lizzy and Mike together at prom.

"The two of you dated in high school. This must be the same girl that you were still reeling from when we first met. She dumped your ass, broke your heart. Did she just call up and say leaving you was a big mistake? Come to Los Angeles, I'm going to make it up to you!"

"Sort of!" said Mike, before adding: "She actually walked into my open house on Sunday."

"That explains why you have been strange all week. That's why you forgot my birthday. And why you were asking about what I would do if Advik reappeared."

"Some of that was down to Lizzy, the rest a tough week of work," said Mike, angling for sympathy.

He didn't get any. Instead Gloria burst into tears and bleated between sobs: "Why are you doing this to me? This bitch emerges from nowhere and you are willing to lose everything we have for her?"

Mike went over to hug her but Gloria pushed him away.

"Take a step back, forget about me. Think about where you're going. You've never been to Los Angeles. I have and it sucks," said Gloria, who had traversed California during her circus days. She continued "The weather's great on the surface, but once you've been there for a while, it's boring. Sunny and seventy-five every single day."

"I could get used to that," Mike said, as he thought about how it could be eighty degrees one day and snow the next in St. Louis.

"Los Angeles is populated by rude people with barren lives continually boasting about their multiple useless college degrees. After a week in California, you'll realize how nice people in the Midwest are. Tell anyone you voted for Trump and that will be the end of your career. They talk about free speech but they don't practice it."

"I've braced myself for the equity zealots," said Mike, who knew from watching Tucker Carlson that California served out lashings of liberal hypocrisy to all.

"Forget about driving anywhere in twenty minutes. It's more like two hours of gridlock. You'll pay for parking everywhere. When was the last time you paid for parking in St.

Louis?" She asked knowing Mike didn't ever pay for parking. She then added, "Let me tell you about parking tickets. A parking ticket in Los Angeles is eighty dollars not fifteen bucks. And they even give you tickets for not having your wheels facing the curb. Another ticket for no front license plate. When did you ever get bothered in Missouri for the missing plate on your Sonic?"

"I'll budget for it. They have beaches in California – that's something I'm looking forward to," said Mike.

"Enjoy the beaches but you're going to freeze if you dip more than a toe in the ocean. The water isn't like a lake in Missouri. It comes from Alaska and it's cold."

Mike paced around the room like a caged lion but was still unable to form a reply.

"You might think you are like Bruce Springsteen running off to the promised land, but you know he himself never left his self-proclaimed "dead man's town." The guy may sing about being a blue-collar hero and escaping, but he still lives a few miles from the hometown where he grew up. Mike, HE NEVER LEFT New Jersey! He STAYED! All the talk about running away is marketing. Real life is not a Bruce Springsteen dirge. Los Angeles is not a PROMISED LAND! Think about what you are doing. Think about me. Think about us. Think about all that's good in St. Louis. Gooey butter cake, pizza with stupid cheese, empty roads, cheap housing, and if nothing else someone who loves you. Someone who loved you from the day we met until now. Not someone who comes back years later with a sob story about making a terrible mistake. You and I are meant to be together. YOU KNOW IT!"

The clarity of Gloria's words made perfect sense and Mike felt like a monkey surfing on an ironing board in a torrent of raw sewage. At some point soon he was going to wipe out and be submerged in the sea of shit he was riding on. Gloria was everything he could ever want, but Lizzy had made him an incredible offer. He didn't know what to do. Gloria's charms and passion in this moment were mightily persuasive.

"Gloria, I just said I have an opportunity in Los Angeles I am considering. Nothing is set in stone."

"Now you sound like Stan Kroenke. And we know how that went," she replied, referencing the owner of the NFL Rams who relocated the team from St. Louis to Los Angeles.

"That's below the belt," said Mike, who took offense being likened to the local public enemy number one.

"Below the belt? Well, I'll tell you what's below the belt. Having a boyfriend who should be your husband but who is instead considering leaving you for an old flame. Where's my ring, Mike? We should have children by now. I should be a West County wine mom and not a pending singleton about to dust off her Tinder profile," she said in full rage mode.

"I'm sorry," is all Mike could muster.

"You know something Mike? You have dreams of Los Angeles. Well, I also have dreams. I would've loved to have gone to India and lived in a fucking palace! Have servants wait on me. Or at the very least a big house and a nice car in a sophisticated city with a handsome man like Blane. Do you think I thought I would end up with a Duckie in St. Louis? I DIDN'T! But I love you, I tried to make it work. A Blane wouldn't forget my birthday. A Blane wouldn't contemplate running off and leaving me here alone. A Blane wouldn't get sucker-punched by a girl who dumped him. I wanted a Blane, what did I end up with? A Duckie. And my Duckie didn't even see it through," she replied in hysterics, referencing the characters in the movie *Pretty in Pink* to explain how her life trajectory was no fairytale.

Mike was shocked at Gloria's rant and shot back without pause. "I've watched *Pretty in Pink*, it's unbelievable bullshit And you know why? It's not because everyone lives in fancy houses, has good hair and drives unpractical cars. It's because it's just plain stupid. And here's why? It's the ending! John Hughes wrong-ended the script. Andie should've stayed with Duckie. He was cute, funny, loving and cared for her. Andie and Duckie were perfect together, they're made for each other. Duckie was everything Blane would never be. I'm sorry you feel like you were cheated out of a Blane, and forced to settle with a Duckie. I came here, to be honest. Honesty is what our relationship was built on. I've tried to make it work for us. And I'm sorry I failed miserably in my attempt to earn a living here. But all you've done today is prove there's nothing left for me. I'm done. We're done! Your Duckie is going his own way."

Gloria sobbed uncontrollably on the sofa as Mike left her apartment as fast as possible.

*   *   *

Churchill once said: "If you have an important point to make, don't try to be subtle or clever. Use a pile driver. Hit the point once. Then come back and hit it again. Then hit it a third time – a tremendous whack."

It was 10 p.m. and Daris was solo in The Bunker, waiting for confirmation that his point had been made. Like Churchill, he had opted for a night attack. Unlike Churchill, he was not going full-on Dresden, and as much he would've liked to obliterate New Berlin Real Estate, he opted for a precision strike. For one reason, the situation he found himself in was nuanced and complicated, and thus there were reasons to show restraint.

Daris's phone rang. The incoming call was from a number with a 718 area code. This was the update he had been waiting for.

Apartment #1911   St. Louie

Tyrone Booker was an old-fashioned cop. He had joined the force long before diversity training and restorative justice were part of any police academy curriculum. He knew his beat, he knew the community and, more importantly, he knew all the local troublemakers. From the saddle of a bicycle Tyrone worked the streets dressed in shorts. He was a firm believer that policing was best practiced with human interaction and not by hiding behind the blacked-out glass of a police SUV.

It hadn't always been that way, though. In a previous incarnation of his career, Tyrone was a detective in the Police Criminal Intelligence Division. It was tough, grueling, dirty work. But he would be lying if he said he didn't miss the thrill of an early-morning bust. The sound of a breaching gun taking off door hinges, the thud of a battering ram decimating an entryway, the smell of flash-bang discharges, the commotion of dragging bad people from their refuges and having them lined up face down on the ground. It was pure adrenalin.

The perps always protested and pleaded they'd done nothing wrong. The North City gangstas, seeing he was a Black man with a police badge, would curse him out and call him an "Uncle Tom." Of course, if he had a white man cuffed up, their taunts were more direct. They knew there was nothing he could do but suck it up and try not to lose his cool. This, after all, was St. Louis, and it was always going to be an "us and them" situation when people of different color faced off.

St. Louis was one big rotten city that made *The Wire's* Baltimore setting look like Disneyland. A colleague with military experience had an apt saying that the Marines used: "Order, added with counter order, equals disorder." This expression accurately summed up the mess that the business of policing is in a city as fucked up as St. Louis. A police force split along racial lines by its union, keeping order in a city geographically fractured by the skin color of its inhabitants. A City Hall administration riddled with corruption. Equity crisis, affordable housing crisis, racial injustice crisis, climate crisis, food crisis. Call something a crisis and not too far away, someone with close connections to power is getting rich off servicing and nurturing that crisis. Follow the money and, more often than not, it will eventually lead directly to a paternalistic elite dishing out diversity with a nod and a wink – one Black Lives Matter sign at a time.

How do you quit the gang, but feet first? was the thought that went through Tyrone's mind before every operation during his detective days. A bullet in the arm while raiding a drug dealer holed up in a modern house that had been sacrilegiously planted on the grave of a derelict 19th-century mansion was his wake-up call. Tyrone survived, but after years of being married to his job this was the last straw for his ex-wife. A year away from retirement, Tyrone and his high-octane detective slot had been traded for beat cop duties, and his suburban married life swapped for a rented bachelor pad in Missouri Towers.

He missed his tidy garden in his old South City house. He might have missed his wife if he had ever really known what regular married life was like. He was in a safer police position now; he just had to survive one more year to collect his pension. No flip-flop paradise for him; he had Colorado picked out. The plan was to open a bike shop in a Rocky Mountain town.

Tyrone had effortlessly settled into his new role on the city's bike patrol squad. In many ways, it was back to the future for him – like being a rookie all over again. It was a gig made easier by the lack of political will to prosecute actual crimes in the city of St. Louis. Writing up tickets for building owners with a tardy schedule of tuckpointing was about the only offense the current district attorney chose to prosecute, although Tyrone had seen many a brick fall from a downtown building – and the deadliness couldn't be underestimated.

At the start of every shift, the first thing Tyrone would do was ride up to Park Ave Coffee on 10th St. for a jolt of caffeine. For one thing he liked the coffee; for another he had an ongoing flirty romance with Stella who ran the art gallery next door. This courtship had been going on for months. They enjoyed candlelit dinners and boat cruises, and he was on occasion a welcome overnight guest at her loft. She was nothing like any other girl he had dated; she was old-school, hard to gauge. He put that down to her living in Montreal for five years. They had real-life French people there. The Frenchiness had made her strange.

Tyrone grabbed a copy of the *St. Louis Tribune*. Front page news was a little different from the usual weekday murders that traditionally spike during the heat of summer. *Local Real*

Estate Brokerage Attacked! roared the headline. The story explained, *In a systematic wave, recent entry into the market, New Berlin Real Estate, had every yard sign from its listings decapitated and its satellite offices fire-bombed. In a strange twist, the main office on Locust St. was unscathed.* It was hinted in the story that this was due to the mayor's new policing initiative for downtown, which had created a less dangerous urban core. Tyrone would call bullshit on this. He knew the mayor was all talk, and like all the others before him didn't give a shit about downtown.

Tyrone carried on reading the story. *Graffiti was sprawled across its various offices that read 6 Percenters. City detectives have a hunch that this is a clandestine community organization thwarting gentrification, which they believe to be promoted by the real estate industry.* The story concluded: *Police were carrying on with their investigations but so far had no solid leads.* Tyrone folded the paper and said loud enough that the people on the table next to him could hear: "Knuckleheads in the Investigations Department. This is a real estate turf war, and it's about commissions. Community action group resisting gentrification my ass!"

Tyrone then thought to himself, *no wonder we have so many unsolved murders in St. Louis if they can't even clear up this obvious case!*

Missouri Towers' neighbor Nick Pipeman walked past Tyrone's table with an unusual bounce in his step. For once he didn't stop and try to talk Tyrone into buying a loft.

Stella arrived at the gallery and Tyrone's heart skipped a beat. She smiled when she saw Tyrone and his mind suddenly deviated from solving crime.

Stella's art was deep and meaningful, wasted on the downtown crowd, Tyrone would tell her. She made a living mainly through grants and fellowships, less so by selling paintings. She loved what she did, and Tyrone had confidence that she was no more than a bit of luck away from hitting it big.

"How's my beautiful Miss Stella today?" asked Tyrone as he walked over to give her a kiss.

She moved away to avoid the display of affection. "You know my rules," she said.

"No public kissing. You're telling me none of the Frenchies in Canada kiss in the open?"

"Not with tongue like you." She said unlocking the gallery.

They both walked in. Stella brought with her a newly completed series of paintings and immediately hung one on an open wall.

Stella's work tended to be dark, highly technical and highlighted her years of formal art school training. However this piece was pure kitsch, a vibrant painting of a pink flamingo, in the style of Pop Art. Tyrone was lost for words.

"Irony masterpiece!" is what I am calling this, said Stella, who then unpacked five other similar paintings from the set.

"It's not your usual style," the cop said, as if about to start an investigation.

"I'm lucky if I sell one painting every three months. I thought I would try something different," Stella replied as she hung the rest of the series up.

Tyrone stood back and stared at the flamingo paintings. The art gave the drab wall an injection of color.

"My usual art is fit for museums. This is fit for the third bathroom in a Chesterfield McMansion. There are more West County powder rooms out there than procuring galleries of masterpieces, so I am diversifying," she said.

"Women make the rules," Tyrone replied, shrugging his shoulders.

*   *   *

Nobody ever texted in Bruce Springsteen songs. In fact, Mike hoped Springsteen never incorporated cell phones or any other tech device in any future body of work. Dirges of desperation wouldn't poetically flow if the parties were corresponding in real-time speech bubbles. Mike had been broadsided by texts from both Gloria and Lizzy over the past twenty-four hours. However with Gloria's, due to them being sent from her computer and not her archaic flip phone, there was a time lag between outbursts.

Lizzy had been sending long, thoughtful soul-searching texts. She blamed the influence of her mother for splitting them up all those years ago. *I am my own woman now,* was a phrase she repeated constantly. Everything Lizzy had been telling him made perfect sense. Mike almost felt as comfortable with her now as he had when they first dated, and somehow had managed to get over being dumped by her.

Gloria's texts were more sporadic. First she apologized for calling him Stan Kroenke. Then she took back the apology and said that if he moved to Los Angeles his life would be cursed, and just as the Rams will never win a Super Bowl, Mike's career will also be doomed. Then a few hours later she apologized again and said that looking at the Ram's talent roster, they had a good chance of grabbing the Vince Lombardi trophy within five years. "Is she apologizing to me or Stan Kroenke?" Mike asked himself.

Settling for Duckie? Mike thought about how they ended their nasty conversation. He was always restrained with his responses, and being a sassy millennial he knew that letting an argument escalate via text was deadly. A few hours later, Gloria messaged again, now agreeing that Duckie was a better fit for Andie in *Pretty in Pink.* She added that John Hughes changed the movie's ending after test audiences wanted Molly Ringwald's character to run off with the handsome preppy boy and not the nerd. *I am happy with my Duckie,* texted Gloria, in a sign of relations getting better.

But the thaw was short-lived. Next came the text that Mike had been dreading but expecting – the final ultimatum from Gloria. As one might predict it arrived in the middle of the night, in full caps, and with a disclaimer that this would be the final communication sent.

NO MORE WAITING! IF YOU HAVE NOT MADE UP YOUR MIND BY END OF FRIDAY WE ARE DONE!

Friday, Lizzy was coming back from Jeff City. She was expecting dinner, a ride to the airport, and confirmation that he had started packing for Los Angeles. Gloria had drawn her own red line in the sand and Friday was also her deadline. Mike was certain there was a Bruce Springsteen song where this same thing happened, but for the life of him, he couldn't place which one it was.

*   *   *

Nick Pipeman was on top of the world. His date with Zoe went wonderfully, and he had been on two more outings with her since. Ideally, he would've liked a younger girlfriend, but maybe the age-appropriateness of their relationship would, for once, lead to longevity. It had been some time since he had been in a proper relationship. It had been some time since he had strung more than three dates together with the same person. He was determined to make it work with Zoe.

As Nick got older, he noticed that his kinkiness and quirks weren't received with the enthusiasm they once had been by prospective partners. His market analysis of the dating inventory had put this down to most of the offerings being recent products of divorce. Their first-date banter was stacked with prior marriage woes and what they were now looking for in a partner. Sweet companionship, stability and maybe a little fun was about the extent of it. Pipeman's first-date topics were in the arena of long-term commitment requests, marriage in the near future, and of course his curveball chatter of all roads leading to the "back door."

He was kicking himself that he'd never previously thought about finding a clown convention to sniff around for lady action. The stories Zoe had told him about the circus world had highlighted a missed opportunity. It had also given him a newfound respect for Mike Love. What he couldn't do in the field of real estate he was now certain he'd compensated for in the boudoir with Gloria. After two days of hearing Zoe's debaucherous tales, he didn't doubt the trapeze artist cohort was just as wild.

Nick lost a day to puppy love but he was now back to the business of real estate schill. He had spent the early morning at the Spitfire office, organizing a showings tour for two clients in need of a downtown loft.

Devonte and Trisha Jones were relocating from Atlanta to St. Louis. It was a referral from an agent in Georgia but Nick was happy for a solid lead. The Joneses were only in town for a day and had told him they were determined to find something.

Nick had whittled down their top ten properties to just three. One at Louderman Lofts on 11th St. and the other two at Mappers Lofts down by the baseball stadium. Nick would start at those two residences before taking his clients to the final listing, which was closer to the office. There was no way he was going to let Mr. and Mrs. Jones get back on that plane to Atlanta without writing up an offer for one of these fine properties.

He exited Spitfire's Washington Ave. locale and walked into the outside heat. He was glad his clients were from Atlanta as this relentless steaminess would've sent most out-of-staters straight back onto the plane upon landing. Nick took a right on 10th St. and walked towards the art gallery and coffee shop. Tyrone Booker was sitting outside reading a newspaper. He didn't have time to talk with Tyrone so he pretended he didn't see him and kept on walking. He felt sure Tyrone would one day be persuaded to buy a property.

Nick continued down 10th St. The owner of Jack Patrick's was busy opening up his bar. Nick, who was used to scanning the streets for lucky pennies, was now also keeping an eye out for bullet casings. He was amazed at how well Zoe had been doing with her side hustle in jewelry-making. *Girl was a genius marketer!*

Nick was on such a love high that he had pinched himself several times over the last twenty-four hours to make sure it wasn't a dream – although his dreams were more akin to hardcore Dutch porno than happily ever after rom-coms. He really did think, though, that he had found his forever girl this time.

Zoe loved animals and was an instant hit with Rollo. She was even on board with his plan of ultimately moving to Florida – although in the interim she wanted to buy a house in the city. Nick, seeing first-hand what a ball-ache it is to buy and sell real estate, vowed to always be a renter. But he could compromise; after all, that's the foundation of a relationship.

By now he was walking through the ever-manicured City Garden. This two-block, art-filled, privately run park was one of the highlights of downtown. With the searing heat, paddling pools and water fountains were in high demand.

Then, from the corner of his eye, Nick saw a familiar site: a gleaming lucky penny. There was a bit of a trick to retrieving orphaned coinage in highly peopled places so as not to look like a desperate down-and-out. Most people wouldn't even stop to pick up such a small article of change. Many would just walk on. *Let a homeless guy have it, they need it more. What am I going to do with a penny? I pay for everything with plastic. That penny is covered in germs. That's gross, I'm not touching it,* were a few of the thoughts that go through people's heads when they encounter a random penny. Nick would not begrudge their choice of actions, even if in purely financial terms it was irresponsible. "If you watch your pennies, the pounds will take care of themselves," Benjamin Franklin said. Over his years of collecting lucky pennies, Nick had not only a boundless amount of good luck but also several hundred dollars worth of pickings. There was no way he was going to leave this penny behind for someone else.

He homed in on the solo penny, making sure no one else was about to pick it up. Once at its location, he stood on top of it and looked at his watch. He then bent down and pretended to tie his shoelace. At this moment he grabbed the penny and was just about to perform his good luck ritual when he heard a voice behind him say, "Hey man, what did you pick up there?"

Nick turned around. It was the City Garden security guard, affectionately known as Crockett. Next to him was his beat partner, who was jokingly referred to as Tubbs. The pair resembled detectives Sonny Crockett and Ricardo Tubbs of the eighties TV show *Miami Vice* – albeit an older and much less glamorous Missouri version. These guys had been working security at City Garden since its opening day in 2009.

"Nothing," said Nick, not wanting to get into a dialog with any rent-a-cops.

"I saw you pick something up," said Crockett.

"What you hiding?" asked Tubbs.

"Lucky penny," said Nick, showing them what was clutched in his palm.

"How do you know it's lucky?" asked Crockett.

"By virtue of me finding the penny in the street, it's lucky," replied Nick.

"That's not always the case; just cuz you find a penny doesn't automatically make it lucky," said Tubbs.

"Sometimes a penny escapes the pocket of a bad person for good reason. Although it's lucky for the penny to be liberated, the penny itself is possessed by bad karma. And you wouldn't want to pick up a penny like that," said Crockett with a lot more conviction in his voice than he ever projected in the arena of security services.

"I think you guys are overanalyzing the situation. This is a lucky penny. I've been collecting them for years and never had any bad luck," said Nick, now agitated that he was even entertaining this banal conversation.

Crockett shot back: "I don't know man what you want to do with that penny, but if I were you I'd throw it into the nearest fountain."

"Wishing fountains have the ability to turn bad pennies into lucky pennies," chimed in Tubbs.

"Although you never want to retrieve a penny from any kind of wishing well, as that in itself risks the chance of creating an unlucky penny," Crockett said, sharing more lucky penny mythology.

"I don't want to waste any more of your time as I'm sure at the other end of the park there's a skateboarder you need to shoo away. So if you gentlemen will excuse me, I'm late for an appointment. Have a nice day," said an exasperated Nick, tired of unhelpful chatter with Crockett and Tubbs.

"Runner statue in Kiener Plaza is your nearest safe place to discard that penny. I wouldn't chance it," shouted Crockett as Nick scurried away.

Nick walked across Market St. and over to Mappers Lofts. His clients were outside the building waiting.

"Morning," said Nick.

"Man, you got some heat here in *St. Louie*," replied Devonte, with a little tourist mispronunciation of the city's name.

Devonte and Trisha were a good-looking, professionally dressed, African-American couple in their early thirties. Devonte, who was currently working for Coca-Cola in Atlanta, had landed himself an executive gig at Budweiser. Trisha was an elementary school teacher and was going to transfer to a school in Clayton. The couple were prequalified. With a taste for flare, they knew roughly what they wanted and absolutely what they didn't want as their next home.

Nick gave the couple a little background about the area and the building they were about to enter. Its proximity to the ballpark was a big selling point for them as they were both baseball fans; Nick ribbed them, saying they had better not be wearing their Braves gear around town.

He punched the security code into the keypad to open the building's front door. Mappers Lofts' lobby was tidy and contained an old map-making machine that harked back to the building's former use. The units the couple were viewing were both on the 8th floor.

They exited the elevator on floor eight. The corridor was windowless and the low lighting, in combination with the long thin hallway, made for a gloomy space. Someone in one of the units on this floor was blasting out a Nelly song.

"Are these places always this dark? I need a flashlight to even see where I'm going," said Devonte.

"The good news is, you aren't going to be spending much time in the hallway. You will get used to the lighting. Wait until you get inside. The units in this building are spectacular. Walls of windows, tall ceilings, and the finishes are exquisite. Prepare to be blown away," said Nick.

"If they all look as good as the pictures, the only problem we are going to have is deciding which one we pick," said Trisha.

"Hold on guys, I need to retrieve the keys from the lockboxes," said Nick.

He walked down the corridor and out of the fire escape door. It was common for real estate agents in big buildings to stash keys in lockboxes chained to a stairwell railing. Nick found a gaggle of boxes. Via his Bluetooth phone app, he retrieved two sets of keys and returned them to his prospective buyers.

"Trisha, which apartment do you want to see first?" asked Nick, who knew *she* was the one who ultimately would decide which apartment they'd end up buying.

"#804, the one with the balcony," said Trisha.

"Let's go!" said Nick, walking down the hallway towards the unit. He had shown it before, so he knew exactly where it was.

Nick, as per protocol, banged on the front door, putting the key in the lock. He inserted the key but it would not turn.

He hated it when this happened and began to sweat. "I must have mixed up the keys. Let's try the other one," he said. The second key didn't fit. Nick turned on his phone's flashlight and looked at the keys. He had opened up a lockbox for a unit on the 9th floor instead of #804 by mistake. Easily done when your phone can open anything in front of you and agents group lockboxes for several floors in one area. Opening a box where you didn't have an appointment was a Realtors' Association offense. *I hope I don't get reported over this. Maybe that penny I picked up was cursed, after all,* Nick thought.

"I have the wrong key. I need to take this back and switch it out, so why don't you go down to #818 and look at that one first. It's vacant but nicely staged. You can be the realtor on this one Devonte," said Nick, handing the keys to his client.

"Does that mean I get the commission?" Devonte joked.

"State of Missouri rules dictate that only a licensed agent is entitled to commission, so you are out of luck," said Nick, heading to the fire escape door to sort out the keys.

Devonte and Trish walked down the dark hallway. The beats of Nelly were still blasting out.

Devonte put the key in the door but realized it wasn't locked.

"Last agent didn't lock up after they left," said Devonte, as he and his wife walked in.

"Wow, this is amazing," said Trisha, on seeing the inside.

Nick was halfway down the hallway with the right keys when he heard three gunshots fired. He ran to open the door of the loft his clients had gone in. Devonte Jones was on the living room floor with a stream of blood coming from his stomach. Trisha was standing over him screaming.

Nick grabbed his phone and dialed 911. The operator asked him for his address. He ran to the front door of the unit. "Oh fuck!" he screamed.

Devonte had walked into #813, not #818. In the low light he had misread the unit number and by chance the door he opened was unlocked. Unfortunately, it also happened to have an armed resident inside.

"Fuck! Fuck! Fuck!" was all Nick could say.

Tyrone Booker was the first cop on the scene. He was thankful the suspect hadn't resisted arrest and surrendered without incident. The shooter was an ex-cop who now worked in security. He waited for law enforcement to arrive with his hands up and his gun unloaded and out of reach. He also knew his rights, citing the "Castle Doctrine" and proclaiming he had done nothing wrong. "I was defending myself, brother," was all he would say in a cop-to-cop way. He was expecting to be home for dinner tonight, not languishing in any jail. In Missouri, his legal defense was solid, although Tyrone wasn't sure, looking at the scene, that the level of force used would hold up in court. A white man shooting an unarmed Black man would certainly not stand up in any court of public opinion.

Tyrone had seen a lot of shooting victims in his time. As he looked down at Devonte Jones being wheeled away on a gurney, he knew the odds of this man living were slim. In a city with simmering racial tensions that only need the smallest spark to rage, Tyrone knew this could get ugly fast.

Nick Pipeman was crouched at the end of the dark hallway with his head in his hands. He was in a world of pain. He reworked multiple times what he could've done differently that would have prevented Devonte from walking through the wrong door. For a start, he broke the golden rule – the client never opens up a property. He, the agent, was the only one who should've been unlocking doors. This was one hundred percent down to him. How did he let this happen? How would he ever forgive himself? It was that unlucky penny, it had to be. The penny was jinxed. Or maybe it was just because he'd forgotten to do his penny-blessing ritual. If Crockett hadn't been trying to shake him down with his folksy superstitions, he was sure none of this would've happened. *Fucking Crockett and Tubbs and their unlucky penny shit! That penny was lucky like all the others out there until they cursed it!* Nick took the penny out of his pocket and looked it over. He threw it down the dark corridor.

At the start of the day, Nick Pipeman felt like the king of the world. He was now in a deep world of hurt and his client was close to death. As Tyrone Booker walked over to him for questioning, Nick felt nothing but despair. The shooting was only thirty minutes ago but it was already hard for Nick to fully recall what had happened. Tyrone told him this was normal for someone in shock. Mr. Brightside is what they tagged Nick in the office. At this precise moment, he felt anything but that. All Nick Pipeman felt were dark and dangerous thoughts.

*　　*　　*

Sam Robinson called in sick and Alice Jones pushed her bus ticket back to Friday. Breakfast was the most important meal of the day, Alice chimed, as she cooked a batch of pancakes. As they tucked into their food, she outlined the day's plans.

First she booked Sam a trip to the barber. A fresh new haircut and a touch of color blended into his gray brought out his handsome. A return trip to *Ross Dress for Less* was next on the agenda. The broader-than-she-was-taller employee from last week made a beeline for Alice and greeted her like an old friend.

"You're back! And it looks like you brought your boyfriend. What can we find you guys?" the associate asked.

"New clothes for the gentleman. We need to freshen up his wardrobe," replied Alice.

The helpful employee gave Sam a once-over. "I think we can upgrade on this look easily." She then took Sam by the hand and escorted him to the men's section.

Alice browsed the aisles solo and in the bargain bin found a pile of old cassettes. Rummaging through them she struck gold: the *Pretty Woman* soundtrack.

The final stop on the journey home was Dierbergs supermarket in Brentwood. They picked up an array of exciting food. To the tunes of Roy Orbison and Roxette, a LeBaron brimming with bags pulled into Missouri Towers.

As the setting sun reflected off the Arch, Sam and Alice would turn back the clock and finish their journey how it began a week ago. Alice spent the afternoon preparing a magnificent meal to be served on a white cloth candlelit table. On the menu were chicken, mashed potato, and asparagus. For drinks, she'd splashed out on fancy wine.

Sam looked handsome and confident in his new clothes and made-over hair. Alice, just as she had done a week ago, glammed herself up in the black polka dot dress, matching hat and white gloves. She looked unashamedly gorgeous.

The conversation over dinner was fluid – easy and without pause. They discussed the week's highlights but never touched on their diverging futures. If nothing else they agreed their time together had been an adventure. They cleaned up the kitchen together and settled down on the sofa to watch a movie.

Alice took off her hat and loosened her hair. She put her arms around Sam and kissed him with tongue.

"I don't think that was in the contract," he quipped.

Alice slipped off her dress and, wearing just her lingerie, straddled Sam. They kissed passionately.

"You will get your money's worth tonight," she whispered into his ear.

Alice moved her hand to his trousers and unbuckled his belt. She placed her hand down his pants but Sam pushed it away.

"It doesn't matter," she said. They held each other tight.

"This is perfect, worth every dollar," Sam said, embracing the situation for what it was and not what it could be.

"This isn't the worst thing I have done in life; I'm a sinner in many ways," Alice said, presenting a hint of her troubled past.

Sam didn't want to dig deep. He knew when renting a woman for the week she was unlikely to come with an unblemished Mother Theresa-style resume.

"I don't need to know," Sam replied while stroking her hair.

"Do you think I deserve a fairytale ending?" Alice said in a nonsequitur to the flow of conversation.

"I'm not sure I believe in fairytales, but if it makes you happy, I will call you princess."

"Princess of St. Louis for the next fifteen hours? I will take it, my shining knight. It might be the only time anyone ever calls me that again," Alice said, realizing that by this time tomorrow she would be on a bus heading home.

Alice didn't know where to take the discussion from here. What she did realize, this was the deepest conversation she'd ever had with a man. Her usual guys were short on talk and heavy on treating her like a porn star.

"Sam, I cannot take your money. I feel like I didn't deliver my side of the contract," she said, with a combination of guilt and honesty.

"Don't be silly. You came all the way out here – you earned it. Anything that didn't happen was my fault and I would hate for you to get evicted," Sam said, being practical in light of the plight that had brought her to St. Louis in the first place.

"You Midwesterners are too nice," Alice said emphasizing her Appalachian accent.

They sat in silence, enjoying the moment.

"I wouldn't get evicted anyway. The money was never for my rent. It was for the church."

"What?" said Sam, who sat himself up in shock.

"God, through the mission, needed the money. This was the only way I could get what they asked for... What they needed."

"You guys do some crazy shit in the mountains. It must be the thin air," he said.

"I may have done bad things in the past; I am a sinner for sure, but I'm not a whore. I left your money in the kitchen stationery drawer. You need it more than the church does."

Sam went over to the kitchen and there it was. The exact same crumpled bills he had sent her.

"Count it if you want," Alice said.

Sam strolled over to the window and looked at the view. He was stuck for words. He paced back to the fridge to grab a Dr

Pepper but there was none left. If his ex-wife Becky had drunk all the Dr Peppers, Sam would have been angry, but in this instance he didn't say a word.

She sobbed gently on the sofa. This was the first sign of any trouble between them all week. He didn't know how to handle the situation. Then in a spontaneous move he put on a jazz CD. "Alice, this is our last night together – let's dance." He took Alice by the hand and they spun in rhythm to the beats of Duke Ellington.

The room was dark and the only glimmers of light came from the Gateway Arch and the candles burning on the dinner table. Alice, wearing only her lingerie with a backdrop of the shimmering Arch, looked amazing. A tear rolled down her cheek; it was unclear from whose eye it had originated.

The time they had spent together had been transformative. A mere seven days ago, either of them would have looked at the other and labeled them "sad and pathetic." Now they shared only mutual respect for each other.

In their close embrace, Alice realized Sam's "little guy" had made a shocking unexpected move. The two of them rapidly shed the rest of their clothes and seized the moment.

As Sam lay in bed enjoying post-coital bliss, the pieces of the puzzle all fell into place. Paying for booty had cursed him with performance problems. Somehow Sam, being hardwired with Midwestern sensibilities, had made it impossible for his brain to compute with his pecker when sex was a pay-to-play act. Alice returning his cash instantly changed the dynamics in their relationship. It was almost a *Princess and the Pea*-like story for the modern era – a fairytale ending for Sam Robinson, it could be argued.

Alice woke up in an empty apartment. Sam had bolted early for work. She couldn't say whether it was Sam's slow gentle touch or the "ribbed for her pleasure" condoms, but one way or another that night was unforgettable.

It was the end of the road for Alice's St. Louis adventures. Her contract with Sam had been fulfilled. She had done the right thing giving back the money; Sam was a good guy, screw the church. All that was left for Alice was to pack her bags and leave.

Apartment #2011 Dr. Gold Tooth

Danny Mango switched on the morning TV news. He usually regretted doing so, as nothing good ever happened during nocturnal hours in St. Louis. Today, though, he was looking to see if something specific had made the 8 a.m. broadcast. He tuned in as the weather report was wrapping up. After five years in St. Louis, he knew nothing good was ever reported in the local weather report either. The climate in this part of Missouri oscillated from one extreme to another. Snow storms, heatwaves, ice storms, thunderstorms, tornados – all dished out randomly from God's magical eight-ball. If you were lucky, a couple of weeks of temperate spring and a few days of glorious fall would be thrown into the mix just to keep everyone sane. St. Louis wasn't alone with the curse of bad weather, but at least other metropolitan regions presented their climatic experiences with eye-candy weather girls. The meteorologist currently waffling on about the heat had a body type that could best be described as "built like a refrigerator."

The morning news was heavier on the grim scale than usual, so much so that the regular Thursday night shooting sprees were relegated deep into the broadcast. The lead item was the unfortunate tale of an African-American visitor from Atlanta who had been shot by a white man at a downtown loft building. The police were saying it was a case of mistaken identity. But civil rights leaders, community activists, and assorted highly opinionated talking heads begged to differ. There were protests gathering outside City Hall, and rallies and vigils fronted by national civil rights leaders were planned for the afternoon. "The city is on edge," promised a stony-faced news anchor with glorious veneers as he salivated about what might kick off tonight.

What would have been top billing on a regular day was a strange also-ran on this newscast. Colton Chesterfield III, the local Prince of the Ponzi scheme, had gone missing. Friends and family said it had been several days since he had been seen or heard from, and it wasn't like him to not check in. The anchorman, switching to a concerned tone, alluded to Colton having plenty of enemies out there within the ranks of those he had "allegedly" scammed. The estimated losses for his wound-up company were just shy of $400 million the report stated.

News of the New Berlin Real Estates' fire-bombing and sign vandalization didn't get more than thirty seconds of airtime. It was squished neatly between a big-rig crash in Franklin County and a cheery reporter telling viewers how they could win a pair of tickets for tonight's Phil Collins concert.

This will make life less complicated, Danny figured. He needed to de-escalate the situation before it spun out of control.

At every stage of his early life, Danny Mango seemed to get royally shafted. He was the third child of a well-to-do New England family. The other two children before him were fine and beautiful examples of the human race. Although his parents were teetotal, Danny was born with what doctors described as a fetal alcohol syndrome-looking face.

Danny partook in the best education money could buy until the start of high school when his parents' fortunes changed. Due to "funding issues," he was transferred to a rough and shabby public school. With mediocre grades and lacking the family college savings his siblings had access to, he enrolled in a third-tier school for an undergraduate degree. He was, however, still determined to join the professional classes by any means. Some type of medical school he deemed the best bet. And this he did.

After four years of toil, and with a mountain of student loan debt, Danny graduated with a degree in dentistry from the University of the West Indies. Sitting at a Trinidadian hotel bar, racking up a cocktail tab that would be added to his growing debt, he had a "what now?" moment. Danny had borrowed so much money for dental school it was going to take a lifetime to pay it off – if he was lucky.

Most American dental practices tended to be skeptical of qualifications earned in developing countries. This would create an obstacle to getting hired – something he chose to overlook when applying for schools. Then there was the other problem: his looks. From birth until now, he had the kind of appearance that only a mother would love. Even she didn't seem to care for it greatly. Dentistry is a beautiful person's game and Danny, after his third cocktail, realized he might have a problem breaking into the business of American smiles.

A cricket game was playing on the bar's television. The West Indies were being thrashed by a team from New Zealand.

"West Indies used to be the best in the world," said an American-sounding man who came over and sat on the chair next to Danny. "You just graduated from dental school?" the same man asked.

"Yes," replied Danny, who knew it wasn't a pick-up line – that was the one thing his looks deterred.

"Where are you planning to work?"

"Good question," replied Danny.

"Loan repayments will start in thirty days," said the man.

The bar cheered as the West Indies batsman knocked the ball out of the oval and with it scored six runs.

"I've been where you are – I'm a dentist myself," said the man, who wasn't getting much of a response from Danny.

More cheering erupted as the home team scored again.

"Where do you practice?" asked Danny, in an attempt at politeness.

"St. Louis – know much about the place?"

"St. Louis... Arch, crime, that's where the Griswolds ask for directions in *American Vacation* and get their car ripped off."

"That's St. Louis!" replied the stranger, who dressed like a stereotypical Midwesterner on vacation. Danny introduced himself formally and thanked the man for the offer of a drink.

"Have you ever heard of Dread Pirate Roberts?" asked the St. Louisan.

"Did he sail with Captain Kidd?" replied Danny.

"Not quite."

"Never heard of him," answered Danny.

"My line of dentistry is gold teeth and cosmetic work. Ninety-nine percent of my patients are African-American. They drive in from hundreds of miles away, and line up around the block to see me. I don't take appointments; it's first come, first served," the man explained, as he sucked on his fruity cocktail.

Danny looked him over. He was one hundred percent white, which was odd for someone who made their living with the urban crowd. Danny now noticed something else about him: he had a slightly deformed face.

"How did you end up in that line of dentistry?" Danny asked.

"I myself am often surprised by life's little quirks. My name is Dr. Gold Tooth. Of course that's not my real name, but no one gets their golds done by a white guy named Kevin. You see, Dr. Gold Tooth is part one-man franchise and part aspirational brand. If you are Dr. Gold Tooth in St. Louis, it's a license to print money," said the man, who insisted on being referred to as Dr. Gold Tooth and not Kevin.

"Do you work on Fridays?" Danny asked.

"Dentists never work on Fridays," Dr. Gold Tooth replied.

"And evidently, being a white dentist doing cosmetic teeth for African Americans isn't an issue for you," Danny said, in a matter-of-fact way.

"Not at all," said Dr. Gold Tooth.

There was a slick double-play in the cricket game; the Kiwis dismissed both West Indian batsmen.

Dr. Gold Tooth carried on with his message. "Now you see, my friend, I've grown so rich that I want to retire. I am looking for a like-minded successor to train. You, Danny, could be the next Dr. Gold Tooth. Think of it as dentistry without the hard work. No fillings, no root canals, even better, no children. All you're doing is cosmetic treatments. You are paid in cash and you have a de facto monopoly within the region. The name Dr. Gold Tooth is the important thing; no one is going to get their golds from a guy called Danny Mango. Do you want to become rich, my friend?"

"What's the catch?" asked Danny.

*   *   *

There was no Churchillian New Berlin Real Estate "soft underbelly" to exploit, but once Daris had concluded who the enemy was, he knew the delivery carrier of his "message with meaning" had to be selected carefully. Two decades ago, the Italian families of The Hill area would've been the go-to service for message relay. The Italians retreated from that line of business in the early nineties. To be fair to their enterprising and organized nature, during their reign they never would've let an upstart like New Berlin destabilize local commerce. Their antics would've been nipped in the bud before anyone had even thought about rustling up private militias.

Northside street gangs in St. Louis were cheap to hire and had enough muscle, guns, and ammo available to conduct an operation on a large enough scale to facilitate a banana republic coup. They also had a tendency for a heavy touch on the trigger finger and were cursed with the aim of a *Star Wars* stormtrooper – as exemplified by their inter-gang turf battles and the numerous innocent bystanders accidentally taken out.

Daris wanted a measured response without civilian casualties.

Daris's typical outsourcing of special projects went to a collective of former Bosnian civil war fighters residing in St. Louis. They were thorough, improvised well, and were happy to serve righteous justice when called upon. Daris never had an invoice unpaid, if these guys showed up tasked with collections, you wouldn't say no. They didn't even have to pack heat like every other variation of Missourian pay-to-play goons. Most people would be crazy to bring a knife to a gunfight, but one look at a Bosnian Khanjar dagger is persuasive. For this job, against the old enemy – the Serbs – restraint for them would be impossible to maintain. Daris didn't want to play any part in reigniting old war grudges or turning the Mississippi River from brown to red.

Albanians – those European Muslim brothers and allies of the Bosnians – were selected as the perfect instrument for Daris's needs. The Staten Island-based Albanian mafia had a ferocious reputation for completing a mission, no matter what it took, and were always at a price available for hire. They hated Serbs just enough to carry out the task but had enough business acumen to not go overboard. Parachuting in the Albanians additionally gave Daris the element of surprise he needed in a town where secret operations are hard to keep under wraps.

New Berlin Real Estate, after the first salvo of night attacks, wisely reached out for a "sit-down," a matter promptly clarified by a call from the current regional arbitrator of all things dark and shady in St. Louis, Dr. Gold Tooth.

Although the premise was a sit-down, for a Bosnian, dealing with Serbs was never straightforward. Throw in the deemed hard-assed unilateral and unsanctioned escalatory strike against New Berlin, and Daris had broken multiple rules as dictated by the real estate quasi-cartel. The Serbs started it, they may have been undercutting the de facto six percent commission rate rule, but the collective required Daris to settle this type of dispute in-house. The real estate industry liked to remain as low key as possible and do its dirty work via highly paid lobbyists, not arsonists. Daris was on the precipice of taking this local disagreement and turning it into national news.

For Daris, attending a sit-down at Dr. Gold Tooth's wasn't optional. The situation that Daris had found himself in wasn't a clear-cut business dispute between two rivals. It wasn't even really about Bosnians against Serbs. This ran deeper. One way or another, it would be settled tonight, although there was a chance that Daris, through his actions, might have ended up arranging his own funeral.

*   *   *

Nick Pipeman hadn't left his loft in more than twenty-four hours. His phone was switched off and his voicemail was filled with unreturned messages. All Nick did was sit at his desk, refreshing the browsers of local news outlets, hoping for an update on Devonte Jones's condition.

He was constantly playing out in his head all the things he could have done differently. Letting Trisha decide on the order of their loft showings was his current fixation. If they had gone to #804 first, they wouldn't have been standing outside #813 waiting for Nick to retrieve the correct key from the lockbox. Devonte would never have walked through a random unlocked door. There were so many things he could have and should have done differently.

Across the local television outlets there were no updates on Devonte's condition. In contrast, the airwaves were filled with the sideshow that had sprung up around this tragic event. The world's media had descended on downtown St. Louis. "Ferguson Redux" is what they cynically labeled it. There were numerous famous civil rights leaders jetting in to hold peace rallies this evening. There were already groups of protestors outside Police Headquarters and City Hall. The mayor had publicly stated: "This is nothing like Ferguson. People, please stay calm! Please stay at home."

Nick sat at his desk with Rollo on his lap, staring at his jar of lucky pennies. He checked again to see if Devonte's condition had been updated. It hadn't.

*   *   *

Danny Mango jetted off to St. Louis and started his cosmetic dentistry apprenticeship. Dr. Gold Tooth's practice was indeed a local institution, and there had been numerous incarnations of the title holder during the past eighty or so years. The one constant was that the practice was always located at the same downtown Locust St. office. After twenty months of intensive training, Kevin retired and Danny became the next Dr. Gold Tooth. The transition was seamless, and many of the clientele didn't even notice the gypsy-switch between Kevin and Danny.

The Dr. Gold Tooth job was indeed lucrative, as promised, and Danny Mango was able to quickly pay off his student loans. Mango wasn't a great fan of St. Louis, but living in the city was a requirement of this position.

He rented a spectacular 20th-floor penthouse at Missouri Towers, and appreciated waking up to the magnificent views of the Gateway Arch and Mississippi River. This made life in St. Louis more bearable. For all those mandatory three-day weekends that dentists are unable to live without, Danny retreated to a vineyard he bought in Missouri's wine country. This gig in dentistry was better than anything Danny could've hoped for, and he was forever thankful for being granted the opportunity.

But there was a catch – an explanation as to why there was no competition in this lucrative, urban cosmetic-dentistry field in St. Louis. Just like the historical idiosyncrasy of the Spanish Bishop of Urgell also being a co-prince of Andorra. The title Dr. Gold Tooth came with a set of responsibilities. Every incarnation of Dr. Gold Tooth, as well as being a practitioner of dentistry, was also tasked with being the arbitrator of all disputes that occurred within the realm of what could be phrased, "St. Louis business enterprises." Dr. Gold Tooth's extracurricular role was part mediator of disputes, part keeper of the peace, and part local powerbroker. In return for this pro-bono side gig, no other regional dentist was allowed to enter into Dr. Gold Tooth's field of specialism.

The scope of Dr. Gold Tooth's arbitration saw no limitations in terms of business type or problems encountered. He was tasked with being the ultimate decider in the settling of disputes – everything ranging from low-level skirmishes between street gangs and other nefarious trades, all the way up the totem pole to the assisting and smoothing of relations between provincial captains of industry. The final word or call made on a subject or argument by Dr. Gold Tooth was treated as the last word by all parties. And nobody dared argue with, or protest against, Dr. Gold Tooth's verdict. For all intents and purposes, he was a one-man supreme court for the St. Louis business community.

The position of Dr. Gold Tooth was held in such high esteem that it was in equal importance to the Shroud Prophet, whose most visible responsibility was choosing and crowning the "Queen of Love and Vanity" at the annual Genie Ball. If you were the resident Dr. Gold Tooth, you mixed in the best St. Louis circles and would find yourself rubbing shoulders with sporting stars, entertainment industry icons and the heavy-hitters of the local merchant aristocracy classes. Dr. Gold Tooth, unlike the Shroud Prophet, would also find himself on first-name terms with gang leaders and on the VIP invite list to some truly wild Northside parties. Each incumbent Dr. Gold Tooth was one of the few people accepted with open arms in every quarter of a highly divided city.

On the wall of Dr. Gold Tooth's surgery were pictures of Danny Mango and all his predecessors. They were all male but of varying race, height and girth. There were, however, a few examples of conformity, which they all shared. All of them dressed for the photographs in depression-era dentist uniforms, complete with bow ties. This was a nod to the original Dr. Gold Tooth – James Goldman and his historical uniform. Of course, they all had amazing smiles, but interestingly none had any gold teeth or dental cosmetic work themselves.

If you looked at the line of pictures en masse, the one thing you would notice was the facial features of each dentist. For every Dr. Gold Tooth had some kind of deformity, or what could be politely tagged, as "an unconventional look."

This was no fluke but dated back to the first holder of the title, Dr. James Goldman. He was known as a calm, honest man who was liked and trusted by all. Mediating over a street dispute between two rival shoeshine boys that turned to violence, James was struck by a bullet in the face. He survived, but his wound left him disfigured.

In honor of his service to settling arguments and keeping the wheels of local commerce rolling, city players awarded him an exclusive carve-out for his line of dentistry. In essence, he was offered a protected monopoly, and with it a de facto license to print money. He became rich so quickly that he retired young and sought a like-minded successor to whom he could hand over the business.

To keep the continuity of service, each time the title was passed on to the next dentist, it was done in honor of Dr. James Goldman. And awarded to a person with an unattractive or bizarre look – someone who otherwise wasn't going to cut it in the world of dentistry.

Danny Mango was sitting in his basement conference room, waiting for the others to arrive. The room was bleak and looked like a cross between a bootleg gambling joint and a lab where you might perform an alien autopsy.

"Why did this have to go down on a Friday?" Danny muttered to himself. Although his office was closed on Fridays for dentistry, his other services were to be made available whenever needed.

Dr. Gold Tooth's assistant popped her head into the room. "Daris Ballic is on his way," she said.

"What about the others?" he asked.

"Still waiting for confirmation."

Danny went through his notes. One thing Dr. Gold Tooth was required to do was know all the history behind whatever dispute he was about to administer. Living in the same residential building as Daris Ballic, he was familiar with him. The other party coming to the table he had never met.

Danny delved into the file and continued with his preparation. After reading through his notes, he checked the Glock 19 pistol he wore at all times on an ankle strap. It was loaded and he took off the safety pin. Danny's arbitration mandate was loosely defined and without legal consequences – another quirk of this job. One way or another, Dr. Gold Tooth settled every dispute and kept business moving. On occasion, though, it could get messy.

*　　*　　*

Butterfly was enjoying her time down in the Bootheel. Four consecutive days of not working was the longest she had been away from a strip club since her eighteenth birthday. At the cottage there was no television, so it was like being off the grid. Hikes in the woods and tubing in the lake had filled her time. She could have gone home days ago but decided that Reginald needed someone to take care of him. She would cook dinner for the two of them and each evening they would discuss what they had done during the day – she, about her adventures around the Kennet area, and he, the work he was performing on the crematory retort. They were kind of like a happily married couple, but without anyone having to pretend they had a headache at bedtime. Butterfly wouldn't even dream of trying to make an advance. For one thing, she'd had enough man action to last several lifetimes. For another, she could see Reginald was still pining for his deceased wife Cynthia.

Butterfly, come rain or shine, needed to be back at the club Friday night. If she missed her dancing slot, they would relegate her to a less lucrative time. Besides, she had regulars who came for her show and many who stayed for a little extra private action in her booth. Lap dancing was where the real cash was made.

Colton had just spent his fifth night in the cellar. His rations were limited to Snickers bars and water. He was starving in a musty prison that stunk of his own festering urine. The only good news was that, due to a lack of food, he hadn't taken a crap since Sunday afternoon. The smell of shit down there would have been overwhelming.

Each time Reginald delivered a Snickers bar, Colton would plead for real food. "You'll get that when I get my money," Reginald would always reply.

"Government took it all," was Colton's standard comeback. Although each successive day his answer sounded less convincing.

Reginald came down to Colton's holding cell. "Well, Colton my friend, today is Friday, and you know what that means? PAYDAY!"

"Government took it all," Colton replied as usual.

"Then today is the day you meet your maker. You see Mr. Chesterfield, I have spent this week prepping the retort."

"Uh, what's that?"

"Let me show you."

Reginald, with shotgun in hand, escorted Colton to Safe Haven's cremation room.

"This is what I will do. I will put you in a coffin and wheel you into that chamber. Which, by the way, I've managed to get back into working order after much laborious work. You will die quickly. Almost too quickly, in my opinion, as the initial temperature will be 1500 degrees when you enter. It will then rise to an excruciating 1800 degrees. Two-and-a-half hours later, what's left of you will fit in an urn. I will dump your remains in the Mississippi River. You will be untraceable. GONE!"

Colton looked at the retort. With the roar it made, the machine looked convincingly dangerous. "Ummmh!" Colton said.

Reginald pulled out a coffin on a wheeled table and asked Colton to get into it. Colton refused.

"With your lack of nourishment, you're weak. I can easily drag you into the casket, but what I would do instead is shoot off your legs. It will be messy, but what the hell," said Reginald, now cocking the shotgun.

He then pressed buttons on a control pad. Music came out of speakers and the curtains at the entrance to the retort chamber peeled back.

"Here we are, Colton Chesterfield III. Payday or the day you die? I know you manage to squirm out of most scrapes, but this situation is quite linear."

"How much do you say I owe?" the criminal mastermind asked.

"One million, two hundred and thirty-two thousand dollars."

"How do I know that if I got you that money, you wouldn't put me in the crematorium anyway?" asked Colton.

"My word is my bond," the funeral director confirmed.

"Will you get me something to eat?" Colton asked.

"Pay me back now and you get food, and I won't turn you into dust."

"Get me a computer."

Reginald had an iPad, which he handed to Colton. With a bit of tinkering around and the inputting of strings of digits, Colton accessed a Bitcoin wallet. He then transferred the money into Reginald's checking account.

"You pretty much bled me dry, man," said Colton.

"What goes around comes around," Reginald said. Once again, the slimy conman – with his seemingly Teflon invincibility – managed, by the skin of his teeth, to stay alive.

Reginald ordered takeout delivery from a local burger joint.

Twenty minutes later, the food arrived. Colton took one look at the packaging and said, "That looks like crap."

"Don't eat it, see if I care," said Reginald, who then informed Colton he wasn't getting anything else – unless he wanted another Snickers bar.

Colton chowed down the greasy meal.

"For terrible food, you sure have a solid appetite," Reginald said.

"You have your money, why not let me leave? We'll call it even and go our own ways," Colton spewed out through a mouthful of burger.

"This was never just about money."

"It wasn't? So why have you kidnapped me and held me captive for days? It was always the cash you demanded. 'Get me my money or I'm going to turn you into ashes!' All you wanted was money. So what else do you want from me, man?" Colton asked.

"Justice!" Reginald replied.

"I have served my time, paid you back, and now you want justice?"

Butterfly walked into the room, fresh from a stroll in the woods.

"How's he doing?" she asked. "Same arrogant prick as always?"

Colton wolfed down his food. As crappy as it was, he hadn't eaten properly in the best part of a week. The two-Snickers-a-day meal plan hadn't been good for his energy levels.

Colton, with the sun on his face and food in his belly, felt satisfied. Technically, this moment had cost him one million two hundred and thirty-two thousand dollars. But along with not being killed, and in light of the laws of supply and demand, this was in his opinion, a deal. With the money transferred, Colton was down to his last fifty grand. But he was young, time was on his side – and he would bounce back whatever. That was the American way for a member of the criminal class.

"Is there anything to drink aside from water?" Colton asked, as he ate his last French fry.

"I'll get you something," Reginald said. He went to the house and returned with a glass of soda.

Colton chugged it quickly before demanding. "Can you drop me off at a Greyhound station? I want to get back to St. Louis!"

"Relax, there's no hurry," Reginald replied.

One minute Colton was on a post-soda sugar high, the next he was feeling dizzy.

"I don't feel good," Colton called out.

"You ate too quickly," the undertaker replied.

"I think you're right," Colton said as his head began to spin. Thirty seconds later, he slumped to the ground.

Butterfly watching on said, "That was quick."

"Where did you get that stuff from?" Reginald asked her.

"Next to my Smith & Wesson, the best thing a gal can keep in her handbag is Rohypnol. You never know when you need to calm a man down," she said.

Reginald checked on Colton. He was totally out.

"Give me a hand," Reginald asked.

They dragged Colton's body towards a coffin next to Butterfly's car. They threw Colton in it and shut the lid.

"It's one of the caskets Merlin Investments sent us in lieu of money when their finances began to wobble. Cheap Chinese junk and not worthy of a valid Safe Haven customer," he said.

"Now what? Are you going to turn him into ashes?" she asked.

"That would be too kind, but I did make a promise I wouldn't cook him. We can decide on his fate when we get back to St. Louis. It does seem unfair to unleash him again into society, though, don't you think?"

They loaded the coffin into Butterfly's SUV.

"I have something I need to take care of," Reginald said.

"You know where I'll be tonight. Come and see me perform," the pole dancer requested.

"Strip clubs are not my thing, but you never know!" Reginald yelled back, as he went into the house and changed for his next act of the day.

Butterfly looked at her watch and realized she needed to go. The plan was to get back to Missouri Towers and leave Colton at her condo – although she did wonder if, in all that heat, Colton wouldn't die in that box. Reginald had mentioned something about the cheapness of the wood making it more breathable than a quality product. Worst-case scenario, they could bring it back to the funeral parlor and turn him into dust. They had to do something with the smug little cock.

Gone Guy

Alice left Missouri Towers and headed in the direction of the Greyhound station, dragging her luggage behind her. The twenty-five-minute walk in the heat was brutal and she was kicking herself for not taking the train. Downtown was the busiest she had seen it during her trip. With her upgraded wardrobe, Alice looked more like a Phil Collins fan on the way to her hotel than a hooker on the way home.

In *Pretty Woman*, Julia Roberts' Vivian was rescued before she got on the bus to start a new life in San Francisco. As Alice took her seat on the Louisville-bound Greyhound, she knew her fate wasn't going to be flowers delivered to the sound of opera by any savior. Alice smiled at the fellow rider beside her but had already decided there would be no titillating show for him today. She was dressed conservatively in blue jeans and a white blouse and her flesh was well covered. Alice said her goodbyes to St. Louis as the bus crossed the Mississippi River and she took a final look at the Arch.

*   *   *

The back and forth with Gloria this week had been uglier than a bag of hairless cats. Time was running out on the game clock and Mike only had a few hours to decide the trajectory of his future. Not knowing what he was going to do, and not wanting to bump into Gloria, he decided to take refuge at the Spitfire Real Estate office.

Mike exited Missouri Towers. He wasn't sure what was worse, the stifling heat on the street or the screwball out-of-towners milling around downtown. Phil Collins fans and civil rights protesters made for strange bedfellows.

Mike arrived at the Spitfire office. The windows, boarded up soon after the hot war with New Berlin began now had a second layer of wood for added protection. Mike presumed this was in case tonight's peaceful protests in support of Devonte Jones turned kinetic.

Realtor Abby Wunderlich was the afternoon's designated duty agent and the lone person in the office. In the role of duty agent, she would get first rights to any walk-in clients.

"Afternoon Abby," said Mike as he passed her desk.

Middle-aged Abby was a colorful character, never without her menopause relief Bichon Frisé comfort dog at her side. She was a happy-go-lucky lady who had long ago embraced the curvy body that had escaped from her formerly waifish frame. Although in Mike's opinion, Abby was a little too comfortable dressing in sweatpants and thought she should, at the very least, make an effort when whoring herself on social media by caking on some makeup and wearing an outfit that fully covered her bingo wings. Strangely, though she had never been to New York and hadn't smoked a cigarette in her life, Abby spoke with a voice that sounded like an overly energetic Fran Drescher with a two-pack-a-day habit. Her realtor bio put great emphasis on a language degree from a big name liberal arts college and her obscure skill in being able to speak fluently in the virtually extinct dialect of Missouri Paw-Paw French. Abby specialized in selling tasteful rehabs in the fast-gentrifying neighborhoods of Marine Villa and Cherokee St.

"Mike, I'm so glad you're here. Or, more to the point, that anyone is here! Can you please take my desk duty spot? I'm going to the Phil Collins concert tonight and need to get myself ready. I have to do something with this hair," said Abby, tugging at her lifeless locks to emphasize the point.

Mike figured Abby was the type of person who couldn't pass up on the great man's visit. Actually, he expected that every dried-out woman of a certain age within a 500-mile radius would be heading to what the advertising blurb tagged, "A progressive rock extravaganza for the ages."

"Anything for a Phil Collins fan," said Mike.

"Thank you. I just hope he sings *Sussudio,*" shouted Abby, as she bolted out of the door.

Mike spent his first hour of desk duty trying to keep the strains of *Sussudio* from once again penetrating his inner cerebrum.

He peeked into The Bunker but it was empty. Daris must be leading the troops from the front today.

Sitting at his desk Mike contemplated his potential options. Both were amazing in different ways. Both were life-changing for not only him but the other party involved. But the emotional aspect of the decision he had to make was taking a toll on his state of mind.

For a split second, he thought he might have stumbled into the middle of that rom-com plot device of the lowest common denominator – a love triangle. Mike Googled love triangles. He veered away from Reddit stories, as they all seemed to lead down rabbit holes of limitless debauchery. But his research brought up some of history's greatest love triangles. Helen of Troy being fought over by Paris and King Menelaus. Mark Anthony, Julius Caesar and Queen Cleopatra. Butch Cassidy and the Sundance Kid were both in love with Etta Place. The Joey-Pacey-Dawson complex situation from *Dawson's Creek* was high on the deep and meaningful spectrum. Of course, the greatest love triangle of all time was the multi-season Ben or Noah conundrum that Felicity faced in the 90s TV show of the same name. To Mike, both Ben and Noah looked exactly alike, so it was a coin toss at best for weak-at-the-knees Felicity.

Then it dawned on him that usually it was two men arguing over a woman. Mike had found himself in the middle of a postmodern variation of a love triangle – although no one was actually fighting over him. It was he who was wrestling with himself. This made Mike ask himself, 'What's so special about me?' Suddenly he was overcome with an attack of self-awareness. Mike was essentially just another forgotten man of Trump country. There were millions out there just like him. What made him special? He pondered this for a solid hour.

By hour two, Mike had reminded himself why he hated desk duty. Years ago, long before he was an agent, office walk-ins were a good source of leads. So much so that it was a highly sought assignment, with agents drawing straws to get the best slots. In the modern era, web portals like Zillow scooped up most of the clients that didn't have representation. Walk-in conversions were now rare. The office was still devoid of other agents and the phone hadn't rung once since Mike had glued himself to the desk. Either everyone was getting ready for the Phil Collins concert, or they were giving downtown a wide berth in case of unrest.

He browsed through the *St. Louis Tribune* website. Black activist ministers from Atlanta, Chicago and New York had all flown in to hold competing civil rights protests tonight. The picture next to the story showed their various private jets lined up at Lambert. An airport spokesman said the last time St. Louis had seen this many out-of-town private jets arrive in such a short period of time was during a climate crisis convention. Looking at the size of the planes, Mike knew that the saying "there is a business behind everything" extended even to the burgeoning industry of civil rights outrage.

It was approaching 5 p.m. nearly closing time. Mike's stint of desk duty had been a total dud, just as the entire last week of real estate ventures had been. Rentals falling flat due to poor client credit and crazy heavy-handed landlords, open-house crashes, listing presentation burnouts, and then there was the bloody gun battle incident that scared away his California buyers. It could've been worse; at least none of his clients were on life support in the hospital. Mike felt bad for Nick Pipeman's predicament.

The week that Mike had endured was merely an extension of a miserable run of luck. Although, as Mike's hero Bruce Springsteen said, "Luck always favors the brave!" Maybe it was time for Mike to step up and be brave. Currently, not only was he making no money, but when his office fees and other related expenses were factored in, he was working his ass off to make a loss. Mike hated to admit it, but a good part of the appeal of heading to Los Angeles with Lizzy was having a slot on her high-flying team. He would be hitting the ground running and would earn money fast. The Los Angeles weather, the anonymity of big city life, and rekindling his romance with Lizzy were also tremendous pull factors. Today's placid stint of desk duty could be the final page of a bad chapter to the story of his life. Bruce Springsteen also said, "Brave are the people who follow their heart; brave are the people who take chances in life." *Am I brave?* Mike considered his choices and broke into a sweat with every pro and con.

His phone suddenly pinged. He looked down at the screen, thankful it wasn't Gloria or Lizzy. He still had no idea what he wanted to say to either of them. Abby Wunderlich had texted a picture of herself and her husband, all spruced up for tonight's concert. It looked as if she had spent a considerable amount of time and money on her newly tresseled hair. Abby's outfit was a shocking, gaudy eighties number that hadn't stood the test of time. The husband in the picture, who was a big shot in finance, had a slick suit, but that couldn't detract from the cheap haircut that gave him the look of an aging non-commissioned officer who is close to collecting his twenty-year pension.

You guys rock! He texted back, with an accompanying smiley face emoji.

Mike stepped outside the office to retrieve the "Agent on Duty" sign from the sidewalk. It was after 5 p.m. but the temperature was still above 90 degrees and muggy. The streets were now crammed with people who looked equally as appallingly dressed as Abby and her husband.

His phone pinged again. It was a text from Lizzy. *What time are we meeting tonight?*

A third option had just popped into Mike's head. Pack up the Sonic with whatever he could fit in it and drive away from St. Louis in whichever direction he fancied. Anything to escape this never-ending heat and avoid his personal dilemmas. As much as Bruce Springsteen liked to talk about being brave, he had made an entire career out of characters who ran away from life's problems.

Mike dragged the sign back into the office and sat down at his desk. He texted Nick to see how he was doing but no reply. He didn't dare text Gloria – he didn't know what he'd say to her. She would be heading off to City Museum shortly; best-case scenario it would be an unwanted distraction as she prepared for her performance.

The deadline Gloria imposed on him was about to expire, so he had to work on an answer, not be a jerk and let time on the clock run out. The least he could do was give her an explanation in person. He was about to text Lizzy back about their dinner plans when he heard the office front door open.

"Hello!" shouted an unfamiliar voice.

Mike looked up from his phone. A young couple with a dog were standing at the door.

"Good afternoon. How can I help?"

"We are looking for a realtor," said the woman, who was doing all the talking and looked to be in charge.

"You're in the right place. I'm Mike, step into my office." Mike beckoned them over to his desk in the vast but empty room.

"I'm Amanda and this is Angelo. We are looking to buy a loft. We want a penthouse with a deck and a view, we can pay cash," said the woman, whom Mike now got a closer look at.

Amanda was a beauty that ratcheted the looks dial firmly past eleven out of ten. She had a delicious oval face with smooth skin and long strawberry-blonde hair that had been tied into a ponytail. She was wearing a thin white T-shirt with the logo of a local all-girls private high school printed on the front. Mike knew it to be the one where the school buildings looked like castles and the girls were treated as if they were princesses. The exact same school where, back in the day, none of the girls would have ever considered talking to a boy from South County High.

Through the T-shirt, Mike could see a subtle glimpse of a luminous pink sports bra. The breasts were almighty alpine in structure. Mike couldn't decide who had bankrolled them; Dad for her sweet-sixteen, or the boyfriend as a present to himself. Whoever made the investment, the enhancements would yield Amanda a better rate of return than any property Mike could show her downtown. The rest of her outfit consisted of tight black yoga pants, white socks, and Nike running shoes. Mike judged she was in her late twenties, but with the body of a dedicated yoga disciple, he gave her a no-questions-asked dispensation on wearing the Lycra pants in public. In fact, Mike's only outfit regret was that Amanda's T-shirt was classily long enough to shield her curves.

Angelo was an outrageously good-looking man – a dead ringer for Brandon Flowers, the lead singer of pop band The Killers. He had picture-perfect olive skin and short, thick black hair. Angelo said he was originally from Rome and Mike estimated he was about Amanda's age. He was stylishly dressed in designer ripped jeans and a pink polo shirt. In his hand he clutched a packet of smokes. If he wasn't in Missouri, a state filled with chain-smokers, the cigarettes would have looked like a cliché Eurotrash accessory.

This was the nearest Mike had gotten to a sale in many months and he had to overcome his initial jealousy of Angelo's envious life (keeping Amanda satisfied in the bedroom) and focus on a possible deal that was there for the taking.

When Daris wasn't spouting Winston Churchill quotes, he would often toss out some good real estate advice. One of the things he had told Mike was that a real estate transaction is like flying a plane. Just like take-off and landings when flying, the start of a transaction and the very end of a transaction are the most difficult parts. Mike, at this precise moment, was like a pilot on the tarmac trying to remember every last sidebar in the training manual. He had to get "the plane" off the ground. Mike needed to make this deal happen like his life depended on it.

The real estate rule when dealing with a couple is working out who is the decision-maker. Mike's initial feeling was that Amanda was the boss. There were subtle non-verbal signs that hinted at this. Angelo sat slightly behind Amanda, was charged with holding the yappy little dog, and didn't interject much into the conversation. Mike was correct with this assumption. Amanda explained that Angelo was her fiancée and they'd met in Europe. She would soon be starting a law degree at St. Louis University and needed to be close to their campus. It would be her, or more accurately her father, who would be funding the purchase.

Angelo's position, Mike established, was the shaky middle-ground between European toy-boy and playboy lover. For this transaction, the beautiful Amanda would be making the calls.

Mike learned a little more information about the type of property Amanda wanted to buy: bedroom count, bathroom numbers and building amenities. He established quickly she was searching for something with a wow factor at the upper end of the downtown price range. As Mike knew the available inventory by heart, within ten minutes of meeting Amanda and Angelo he'd booked a showing for what he told them was, "something they had to see."

Before leaving to view the loft, Mike replied to Lizzy's text, *I have a showing and it looks promising. Talk later.*

Good luck. Seal the deal. I know you can do it! XXX, she pinged back.

*   *   *

Reginald drove to his wife Cynthia's grave to pay his respects. She had been buried in a family plot in the old French town of St. Genevieve – the oldest European settlement west of the Mississippi. Reginald had been lucky that the burial plot had been in the family for generations and her final journey wasn't mixed up with his failed business ventures.

The sun was setting in the west and dusk was approaching fast. Reginald was deep in conversation with the love of his life. At least on this occasion he had good news to share. He had finally gotten back the money they had lost in the Ponzi scheme. Reginald told his wife about his stripper friend Butterfly and the help she had given him in getting even with Colton. He asked Cynthia what she wanted him to do with the man who had derailed their lives and was surprised by her answer.

*   *   *

Butterfly had gotten stuck in traffic and was running late for her performance. The same seniority that bagged her this coveted Friday evening slot was a double-edged sword. One late start for work and she would quickly be replaced by any of the lissome teenagers waiting for their chance to shine. The thought of being shifted from a busy Friday to the mid-week lunch crowd would be enough to force Butterfly to consider retirement. Then she would need to find herself hobbies, and that could lead to trouble. Getting shit-canned for turning up late wasn't an option.

She stepped on the gas, but with the heavy coffin in the back, the vehicle wasn't zipping along at its usual speed. Ideally, Butterfly would've liked to do something with Colton before she went to work. Not that she knew exactly what to do with him. There just wasn't time available so he would have to wait. The thought that he might die in the heat, in a coffin, in a car with no AC on did briefly cross her mind. With less than thirty minutes before showtime, Butterfly screeched into the parking lot of Mound City Gentlemen's Club.

"Bitch!" Tiffany Choi had taken her reserved space. *No respect!* Tiffany, in her early twenties, had three decades on

Butterfly and was gunning for her lucrative slot. Tiffany had a face that looked like it had run a hundred-meter dash in a ninety-meter room. With an ugly mug like hers, in any other strip club in the world, she'd be cleaning toilets or mopping up beer. In the seedy world of Sauget's stripper scene, Tiffany, with her Korean looks was deemed exotic and was in demand by local clients who didn't see Asian women on a day-to-day basis. Parking in Butterfly's reserved space, Tiffany was little more than playing a psychological mind game with the aim of unsettling the veteran pole dancer.

Butterfly stormed into the back entrance of the club. Mound City's green room on a Friday had the same hustle and bustle you could find at an airport the day before Thanksgiving – albeit with more skin on display and smaller-sized bags being toted. Girls were coming off stage clutching wads of cash. Other ladies were lined up waiting for their turn to perform, taking a pre-dance drag on a smoke, or applying last-minute glitter on their lady parts. Tits and ass were everywhere, but nobody cared. In this green room, everyone was focused on one thing – making bucks.

As Butterfly entered her dressing room, she realized her parking space wasn't the only land grab attempted by Tiffany tonight. Her youthful nemesis was sitting in Butterfly's chair having makeup applied.

"Excuse me!" Butterfly said loudly.

Tiffany swiveled the chair around and squealed with a hint of left-coast K-Town squawk: "Didn't think you were coming tonight, boss gave me your dances old lady."

"BUTTERFLY is in the building, so you get the fuck out of here: BEAUTY before AGE!" The veteran spinner yelled back.

"Not enough time to make you over, oldie. Go and turn tricks at a truck stop. You're too decrepit for dancing!" Tiffany shouted.

Butterfly slapped Tiffany's face hard, grabbed her by the hair, and dragged her out of the dressing room. She then locked the door behind her.

"This place is worse than *Game of Thrones*," said Butterfly to the speechless makeup person before adding: "Do what you'd normally do in an hour, but do it in fifteen minutes. I'll have a house full of regulars and I need to look my best."

Butterfly lit up a Newport as the woman went about her work in silence. Mascara, filler, lipstick, curlers, pubic hair trimmers, baby oil, and a new outfit spliced and diced at Nascar pit-stop speed transformed Butterfly into her lubricious finery. With ten minutes before showtime, she was ready for center stage. Two smoked Newports later and right on cue, Butterfly pranced into the arena to her signature, Dolly Parton namesake tune.

It was Friday night – a packed house. Butterfly, like always, tuned out the faces and thought only about the money she would be extracting from these men. Part athlete, part artist, part acrobat, part dancer, Butterfly in sky-high stilettos began her show. Twirling around the pole with the agility of a younger woman, she never failed to give the crowd what they wanted. She might not have been as tight and perky as some of her boney-assed peers, but she made up for the sag of gravity with a mesmerizing show.

The clothes came off item by item: the hat, the gloves, the shoes, the bra, and then finally the thong underwear. At last, she was naked and the crowd roared in delight. Butterfly fed off the energy and for a brief moment felt like she was twenty again. If she was honest with herself, it was the dancing that kept her mind young. She didn't need any of the junk the kids they hired these days blew up their noses; for Butterfly, as long as she was arm's length from a pole, was on a natural high. Butterfly would dance until she died and would never retire by choice. She certainly wouldn't be shunted out by the Tiffany Chois of this world.

Down to her birthday suit, Butterfly made her way to the edge of the stage to make her regulars feel special. As she collected a crisp Benjamin from a gawking punter with his eyes fixated on her crotch, she noticed a familiar face. Reginald had come to the show. She only wished he had changed his outfit.

Strip clubs invariably attracted an eclectic clientele, but a man dressed in full funeral parlor garb was not enhancing the ambiance of erotica. Under the circumstances, she would give him a pass. If she didn't have time to appropriately deal with a possibly dead man locked in a coffin in her car, Reginald unlikely had the time to change clothes after visiting his wife's grave.

Butterfly switched outfits and came back for her second dance number. Following the *St. Louis Blues* Stanley Cup victory in June, she had retrieved from the vault an old routine to the song *Gloria* – a dance she used to perform back in the eighties. Butterfly did have to curtail some of the more adventurous moves due to less flexibility, but this number was a popular blast from the past for her fans. A few of the old-time regulars even remembered her performing it back in the day.

Butterfly watched Reginald sipping a soda as he took in the show. He looked uncomfortable in these rowdy surroundings. She could tell he was respectful with his eyes, which he kept directed towards her face. Although after thirty-plus years of flaunting her goods, she was beyond caring about anyone and everyone gawking at her treasures.

The smell of a funeral parlor is distinct – somewhere in the middle ground between the artificial scent of a hotel lobby and the sweet fragrance of a high-end florist. The smell of Mound City Gentlemen's Club tonight was distinct in its own way. Reginald detected a noxious mix of cigarette smoke, sweat, cheap perfume, and a slight hint of musky estrogen. Combined, these aromas made for an eau de toilette of white-trash debauchery.

Although a smorgasbord of delightful women parading in their panties was something Reginald usually wouldn't dream of passing up, in this moment he couldn't think of a worse place to be. Surrounded by in-your-face nudity in every direction was overwhelming for even his red-blooded senses. Maybe it was overstimulation; maybe it was the forceful element of the girls' sharp hustles. One way or another, he didn't feel comfortable and wasn't in the least bit turned on by the scenery.

He had originally come to see Butterfly perform; he was curious, if nothing else, to see her at work. He had to admit, for someone who would qualify for a senior discount at an early bird Florida buffet, she put on a good show. He did keep his eyes firmly focused on her from the neck up, or occasionally on his fellow club patrons.

Reginald thought the Missouri Bootheel crackers dressed strangely, but out here in the city sprawl, they had their own puzzling fashion sense. It was as if the typical St. Louis man never owned a baseball cap he wanted to wear forwards, a Cardinals' jersey that wasn't two sizes too big, or plastic sandals that, in the owner's mind, didn't look good without being paired with knee-length white socks. Your average St. Louis man dressed terribly, and the club tonight was full of them. Reginald had to put this into perspective as on the hottest day of the year, he was sitting in a strip club wearing his funeral director regalia.

The undertaker made eye contact with Butterfly and she acknowledged his presence. As much as she might think he had come just for the show, he hadn't. As much as he wanted to satisfy any curiosity in seeing a woman in her fifties swinging on a pole, he had something more pressing to discuss. And it could only be done in person.

After forty-five minutes of spinning, gyrating, and wiggling her ass, Butterfly took her final bow and left the stage. Two Newports smoked in quick succession and a dowsing of perfume to freshen up her money-making assets and Butterfly relocated to a private booth in another section of the club. A line of regulars had already formed to get a taste of her lap dance. One by one, the assortment of arm-tatt dads and denim overall-clad country folk exited her "office" with smiles on their faces and less cash in their wallets. Butterfly, for a price, was the fulfiller of dreams and never left anyone disappointed, or with anything less than a happy ending.

Reginald got to the end of the line. Tiffany Choi tried to tempt him away into her own booth. Her odd-looking facial features were improved with the application of fake palm-frond lashes and bright pink lipstick. To give Tiffany credit, what she lacked in the beauty category was made up for by a stellar body. Reginald sent her packing. She took her delights to a Japanese businessman who looked like he had won the lottery after being hit up by the only Asian dancer at the club. He was all too eager to shell over a stack of bills to get a peek at what was hidden inside Tiffany's mating-call hot pants.

A man wearing a "Play Gloria" St. Louis Blues shirt exited Butterfly's room and Reginald took this as his signal to go in.

"Give me a second," said Butterfly, who was teetering on a chair wiping baby batter that had found its way to the ceiling.

Butterfly tossed a soiled Clorox wipe into a trash can and turned around to face her next client.

Seeing it was Reginald, she gave him a hug on the house. She then led him onto her lap before saying, "Do you want the world-famous Butterfly special?"

"There's a problem," Reginald said.

"Butterfly is here to make all your problems go away," the dancer replied, with a standard make the customer feel wonderful retort.

"What did you do with Colton?" Reginald asked, with no hint that he was loosening his tie or taking his hat off in order to sample her delights.

"He's in the car, right where you left him."

"Dead or alive?" Reginald asked.

"Good question. I didn't check; I was running late for work."

"Colton's disappearance hasn't gone unnoticed. It's all over the news," said Reginald.

"Oh!" Butterfly exclaimed.

"Apparently, the story broke this morning and there's a state-wide search for him," said the undertaker.

"Do they have any theories?"

"A family spokesperson alluded to him having numerous enemies. The speculated possibilities of who might have a motive are endless. People he ripped off, people he served time with in prison, the husbands of wives he seduced, readers who gave his self-help book a bad review. The list of those who don't like him is extensive," said Reginald.

"But so far they have no idea where he is? And we haven't been linked at all?" said a slightly nervous Butterfly, who put a bra on and then lit a Newport.

"The strange thing is, they've had tips from the public, with Colton sightings in Barnesville, Hannibal, and Cape Girardeau. These are all Missouri towns where Gillian Flynn's books were set or their movie adaptations filmed. The media have tagged Chesterfield's mysterious vanishing into thin air as, "Gone

Guy." It's a play on the Missouri noir novel *Gone Girl*," explained Reginald, now having told Butterfly the latest developments.

Reginald was glad Butterfly had covered up her breasts. He'd seen plenty of bare flesh in his life – albeit most of the naked women were either family or about to be embalmed. But he found her ease with nudity distracting in light of the situation they were in.

Butterfly got up and poked her head outside her private lap dance room. There was a line of customers ready for their turn.

"Sorry guys, I have a baller out-of-the-club request that's going to take up the rest of my night. Plenty of ladies out there – go find yourselves some fun. Just stay away from Tiffany, she has a bad dose of the clap and you will end up with droopy dick," said Butterfly, who sent the customers scuttling off to fresh pastures.

Butterfly returned to the room and put on the rest of her clothes.

"It looks like it is down to the two of us to come up with an ending for the Gone Guy story," said Butterfly.

She and Reginald proceeded to discuss their options for the captive Colton Chesterfield III.

Comfort and Joy

When Mike showed Amanda and Angelo the listing sheet for the penthouse at XI Ave. Lofts, he told them, "Be prepared, as I promise you it's much better in person than it looks." The promotional pictures for the condo were dull, the blurb was folksy and the staging was more fitting for a Victorian townhouse than a chic industrial loft.

Mike had seen this residence in person during a brokers' tour and knew it was one of the most exceptional properties currently on the market in all of St. Louis. The reason it hadn't yet sold was down to sloppy presentation by an agent who didn't know the gem of a property he had on his hands, or how it needed to be marketed.

As Amanda and Angelo walked into the space, to say they were amazed would be an understatement for the ages. The split-level apartment with a balcony facing east and a huge south-facing patio deck was the embodiment of awesome. The three-bedroom, four-bathroom unit was spacious, open, airy, and bright, with original repurposed hardwood floors throughout. Exposed brick walls, tall ceilings, and a chef's kitchen kitted out with Viking appliances were just a fraction of its wow-factor offerings. An added bonus was the mirrors on the master bedroom ceiling that Mike, in full power agent sales mode, tastefully described as, "Adding a touch of glamor to the night chamber."

He didn't need to dig deep into the "closing the deal" section of the realtor training manual to sell the magic of this property to his clients. Amanda, within minutes of walking around the listing, said – in the manner of a woman who has gotten everything in life she has ever asked for – "This will be mine!"

Mike could only think, with a hint of envy, that Angelo was living the dream. With the irresistible Amanda by his side, he could soon be residing in this marvelous loft. All he had to do to earn his keep was look good, perform in bed and scoop up the Tootsie Roll-sized turds that Amanda's pampered pooch produced with regularity. Angelo was one overly lucky guy. Now, if this was one of the romantic comedies that Gloria and Zoe watched, the following curve balls should rightfully occur at this juncture in the script. Angelo would be revealed as a two-timing cad imposter who was conspiring to murder the dog. He would then, via a freaky accident, slip off the patio deck. Angelo wouldn't die but he would have a copious number of broken bones; this would keep him sidelined for enough time to allow Mike to unexpectedly promote his charms. Mike would somehow – within the essential rules of plot structure's "tension-climax-resolve" – battle the odds, fix all Amanda's tempestuous problems, and ultimately win her heart. Amanda and Mike would then live out their days together in this most amazing of lofts.

For a split-second, Mike wanted to flick a switch and be in that movie. Then Mike remembered he actually had the main role in his own, "Choose your own adventure" tale. And if he couldn't tie up his own loose ends, that story would end up more twisted noir than rom-com romance. He just needed to get Amanda into this loft and let Angelo live the dream.

Mike said his goodbyes to Amanda and Angelo, who were heading back to their hotel. He had a pretty good idea how Amanda was going to make Angelo work off his share of the earnest money. He hoped their bed had strong springs and, for the sake of the guests next door, the room thick walls. *Good work if you can get it,* ran through Mike's mind.

Mike returned to the office to write up Amanda's offer for the penthouse. Darkness had fallen and the walk from XI Ave. Lofts back to the office had a different feel to earlier in the day. Most of the Phil Collins fans were in the arena enjoying pre-concert drinks, and the hordes of protesters were no longer roaming the streets but at various rallies. All of the businesses along Washington Ave. were closed and boarded up. The one thing that didn't seem to change was the incredibly hot air temperature. As Mike approached Spitfire's office, he saw bike cop Tyrone Booker ride down Washington Ave. They exchanged waves.

The realtor sat down at his desk and began crafting Amanda's offer. On the verge of clinching a sizable deal, Mike had a feeling of euphoria that he hadn't experienced for months.

*   *   *

Locked and loaded, Daris left his apartment. The extreme heat that walloped him in the face upon exiting Missouri Towers made him regret tonight's choice of attire. Comfort over style needed to be the priority for the hot humid nights of August. Although if he was, as he suspected, walking to his own funeral, at least the undertaker wouldn't need to change him into an outfit fit for the event. For there was nothing finer than a suit from London's Henry Poole & Co.

The city had an extra layer of danger laced into the air tonight. From every direction Daris could hear noises he attributed to urban disorder. He was glad to be armed, for this wasn't a night to be walking city streets without protection. Daris strolled across Broadway to Locust St. He would never tire of downtown's majestic architecture.

There was police activity ahead and Daris didn't want to get mixed up in whatever was going down. He took a two block detour west and proceeded down Pine St. In the distance loomed the long vacant AT&T building. If that was still idle after Daris had completed his projects at Missouri Towers, he promised to make that his next mission. Only in St. Louis would a skyscraper with a metro station underneath it be vacant for so long. Daris had so many ideas for turning this building into a viable enterprise.

The sound of bullets flying over Daris's head brought him back to reality. He took cover behind an overflowing trash can before retrieving one of his own pistols. It wasn't obvious where the shooter was positioned. He was profusely sweating through his thick outfit. *Why hadn't I worn my Bermuda suit?* was all he could think.

Another two bullets hit the wall high above him. Daris fired three rounds in the general direction he believed they originated from.

Daris's cell phone pinged, *Are you running late?* came a text message from a number he didn't recognize.

Fucking Serbs and their sense of humor! They were messing with him with this little show of force. However, had they wanted to kill him they would have done that already.

Daris could hear police sirens coming his way. He ran as fast as he could up Pine St.

Out of breath, Daris arrived at Dr. Gold Tooth's office. He rang the buzzer on the door of the no-thrills operation.

"Can I help you?" rumbled from the intercom.

"I am not in need of golds!" said Daris.

The door was unlocked. Daris walked into the much cooler reception area.

*   *   *

Rock legend Phil Collins, for the last forty years, had looked exactly the same. That's shortish, baldish, and always dressed like an Iowan Greyhound driver with a facial expression that perpetually screamed midlife crisis. Somehow, this dimple-chinned avuncular everyman, in an industry dominated by youth, good looks and showbiz flair (all attributes it could be argued he lacked), had defied the odds and enjoyed a lengthy, illustrious and lucrative career. You only had to look at the packed audience this evening to realize that Phil Collins, to a crowd of mostly white, middle-aged Midwesterners, held living legend status.

Phil Collins' looks might not have changed radically, but his physical agility wasn't what it once was and he no longer drummed live. He could, though, still belt out all his trademark repertoire of sappy ballads and synth-pop hits. Mindy Playpus, a young blade she'd coerced for company, along with Abby Wunderlich and her husband, were enthusiastically watching the show from front row seats. The girls were in their element, dancing and screaming their hearts out to every hit. About an hour into the gig, Collins slowed down the tempo and eased into the ballad, *Against All Odds*. Upon the song's conclusion, he broke into a little banter with the crowd. "Good Evening St. Louis, I'm so excited to be back!" he yelled before telling his fans about his love for all things American. Mindy, as she gazed into Collins' eyes, reminisced about their dalliance all those years ago. "Screw in the loo!" is what she told everyone Phil had called the alleged lusty romp that no third party was able to verify.

And then, just like that, what everyone in the packed hockey arena was waiting for happened. The glorious funky opening beats of the great man's seminal hit, *Sussudio*, sounded out. The fans erupted with joy, and for many in the room this moment, along with the Blues winning the Stanley Cup, would be among the highlights of their lives.

And just as Phil was in his groove singing, and the fans were at their peak Collins frenzy, something strange and unexpected happened. In that brief interlude between Collins singing the words, "My love has just begun, Su-Sussudio," the sound system shut off and the lights in the arena turned on.

The PA system blared: "This is a public announcement. Due to civil disturbance, the St. Louis Police Department has declared a state of emergency. The concert has ended. Please evacuate the building. I repeat, the show has ended. Please vacate the building."

Phil Collins was ushered off the stage and the crowd was left in stunned disbelief.

"ARE YOU FUCKING KIDDING ME? They couldn't wait until *Sussudio* was over?" said Mindy, as she jumped off the seat she was dancing on.

"We were having fun! But I would hardly call 20,000 people grooving to *Sussudio* a riot," said Abby.

Abby's husband checked his phone for a news update. The civil unrest was downtown and not in the arena. As godly as Phil Collins is, he was no Guns N'Roses and couldn't start a riot in St. Louis. The report said a fire had broken out on Locust St. This was in addition to the three civil rights protests simultaneously taking place downtown. St. Louis police were on full tactical alert, and due to insufficient manpower, overwhelmed. The cops felt they couldn't safely monitor the concert and everything else that was happening, so the easiest thing to do was shut down Phil Collins.

The girls were in tears, Abby's husband was devastated, and Mindy's young, handsome date looked somewhat relieved.

As they started making their way to the exits, something wonderful happened in the arena that lifted everybody's spirits. In a spontaneous outburst, the entire audience began to sing *Sussudio.*

There's this girl that's been on my mind
All the time, Su-Sussudio
Oh oh
Now she don't even know my name
But I think she likes me just the same

Su-Sussudio
Woah oh
Su-Sussudio Su-Sussudio Su-Sussudio...

They kept on singing as they emptied the arena and hit the streets of St. Louis.

*   *   *

Mike fired up his desktop computer and got to work on Amanda's offer for the penthouse property. The price Amanda offered was $10,000 less than asking, which had already been reduced multiple times. Closing would be a quick thirty days.

Steve Flamingo, the listing agent from Arch Realty, was excited for any offer on his terribly marketed loft and had the owner primed for the good news. Mike filled out the Relationship Disclosure, Residential Sales Contract, Lead Disclosures, Condo Rider, Survey Waiver and sent them to Amanda for digital signatures. Just sixty minutes after Mike sat down to work on Amanda's paperwork, he had in his hands an accepted offer. The listing agent told Mike the owner was motivated and he saw no issues in this transaction going through.

Congratulations you are in contract! Mike texted Amanda, seconds before launching a triumphal fist bump into the air. Mike was back in business, and this $500,000 sale would not only clear his debts with Daris but put the wind back in his sails. Mike, with renewed mojo, felt like the king of the world. And if he'd had the time he would've done a victory lap around the empty office.

He looked at his phone and checked for messages. Pipeman hadn't replied, which wasn't a good sign. Nothing from Gloria; he had left things hanging with her in a bad way so wasn't really expecting anything. There was a text from Lizzy: *"Wait for you at our special place?"* Of course, the rabbit sculptures at City Garden where they had shared their first kiss was always their special place.

Mike locked up the office door and walked into the hot night air. Something must have kicked off, he realized, as he saw numerous helicopters in the sky. Three police wagons hurtled down Washington Ave. A firetruck with sirens roaring was speeding down Tucker at the next intersection. On this hot summer night, the pent-up rage from a city perpetually on edge was about to explode.

*　　　*　　　*

Daris was patiently sitting at the basement conference table, waiting for all the parties to arrive. Dr. Gold Tooth's assistant was situated at the back of the room and would keep the meeting minutes. She was currently struggling to decouple from a gigantum soda. *Odd for a lady who works in dentistry to consume so much sugary crap,* was the thought bouncing around Daris's brain.

The assistant's phone rang.

"I'll come up and let you in," Daris heard her say between swigs of the drink, which now sounded to be mostly ice.

A few minutes later, she reappeared with a person Daris recognized.

"Ian Lemon – we meet again!" said Daris across the room, to a weasel-faced man wearing an outfit best suited for selling bibles.

"You know it's pronounced I-ON LE-MAN and not Ian Lemon. It's French, not a line of Costco fruit," said the agitated person who, if given the opportunity, would bore anyone and everyone talking about his MBA from Wharton.

Ian was originally from Miami and was now the regional managing broker for a big corporate real estate chain. He was the "cartel" representative who would be reporting back to the various other brokerages the results of tonight's sit-down.

"If you send a damned fool to St. Louis, and you don't tell them he's a damned fool, they'll never find out," Daris said to Ian.

"Always the charmer and trying to win friends," replied Ian, who had never before heard Daris quote Mark Twain.

Daris and Ian had their own history. Lemon's big brokerage would always find a reason to reject contract offers from Spitfire agents. And the two of them had more than a few tête-à-têtes down in this basement before.

"I've dinner plans in Clayton. Do you know when the final party will be here?" Ian asked Dr. Gold Tooth, with one eye firmly looking at his wristwatch.

"Can you text them?" the dentist shouted over to his assistant.

Daris Ballic stared up at the basement walls. Pictures of every American president could be found hanging around the room. Daris became fixated on Bill Clinton, the incumbent president when Daris first arrived Stateside. Daris should've been a Democrat lifer, for all that this man claimed he had done for his old country of Bosnia. However, Daris had pretty quickly figured out that the Dayton Accords were not quite the selfish act of generosity as presented by then politicians. The immigration system was rigged and the veneer of compassion was no more than keeping the cheap labor pipeline flowing. The American Dream was a Ponzi scheme built on the backs of immigrant labor. Those fresh off the boat were in servitude to those who had arrived before. If the immigrants stopped coming, the whole American way of life would grind to a halt.

Bill Clinton, George W. Bush, Barack Obama and now Donald Trump. Daris had lived through all these presidencies. As Daris looked up at their portraits spread over the wall, his life flashed before him. Over twenty years of Missouri residency had gone by, just like that. The moment of realization that he'd been in the United States a long time came when the state of Missouri finally got around to executing the people whose crimes had happened a lifetime ago, but he could still remember firsthand.

Daris now glanced over at the portrait of president number forty-five: a beaming, smiling Donald Trump, in all his faux tan, combed-over hair, broad-shouldered, red-tied glory. Champion of the Midwestern rustbelt. Although if you looked at his business projects, aside from a hotel in Chicago, he was champion in spirit only. Trump was brash, vulgar, crude, possibly rich, possibly not. A phony man of the people, a philanderer, a cultural philistine, a cheeseburger-scoffing megalomaniac. In essence, he was the spirit and embodiment of all the constituents that make America great.

Only in America could someone like Trump fight his way to the highest office in the land. Only in America could I be what I have become, Daris mentally reassured himself.

Ian and Dr. Gold Tooth made small talk as the assistant shook the remaining ice in her drink while browsing a copy of *People* magazine. Her phone rang. "They're here!" she shouted over to Dr. Gold Tooth, Daris and weasel-faced Ian.

Daris straightened his tie and readied his posture in anticipation of meeting the person who had launched an all-out war on his empire. Daris could hear the footsteps in the room above. More than one person had entered the building.

"This is going to be an interesting twist," Daris muttered to himself. He had wondered if she would also show up.

When Daris pulled up the ownership records to the building New Berlin broker Thomas Trinkenschuh had entered, it was revealed who had been masterminding the attacks against Spitfire. Now Daris would be meeting with his old nemesis in person. One way or another, this beef would be settled tonight.

Dr. Gold Tooth, Daris and Ian all slowly moved their hands to various areas of their clothing. They did this in an intentionally subtle but of course obvious manner. They were releasing the safety catches on their weapons. Like every heavy-trafficked building in Missouri, the door of Dr. Gold Tooth's practice had a sign that read "No Guns" – something Missourians took zero notice of. Everyone in the basement was packing heat, and so was the party about to enter the meeting. Arming up was an anticipated, expected and regular part of St. Louis life. One twitchy finger and the meeting could go full Tarantino bloodbath.

The footsteps got nearer and finally the last entrants to the sit-down made themselves present. An imposing man with reptilian facial features, slick-backed greasy hair and sporting a dog-tooth blazer walked into the room. Behind him stood a slight, dark-haired woman with what Daris immediately recognized to be a second-trimester baby bump.

The new entrant walked up to Daris so there was a mere foot of space that separated them. Dr. Gold Tooth and Ian Lemon watched in anticipation of what might happen. If this was going to turn into a shooting match, now would likely be the moment.

"Zoran Milorad! Nice of you to try to kill me on the way tonight," said Daris, directly at the face of the person who had not only tried to destroy his life's work but had someone shoot at him this evening.

Zoran moved his hands outwards, which had the effect of showing the sidearm concealed under his blazer.

"Daris Ballic, or can I now call you brother-in-law?" Zoran said in an accent that sounded pure Hungarian hillbilly.

"And what did you do to my sister Sara?" said Daris, looking over to the woman who had arrived with Zoran.

"We are having a baby," said Sara, rubbing her belly.

"You are family?" said a shocked Ian Lemon to the two men.

"Family in the Slavic tradition. Hence, you interrupted my journey tonight with a little theatrical gunplay," said Daris in the direction of Zoran.

"All the best families fight," pitched in Dr. Gold Tooth.

"There's Dr. Phil family-angst fighting, but what you two are up to is full-on Missouri blood feud batshit crazy. You guys are busy smashing up each other's businesses, bringing unwanted attention to the real estate industry!" said Lemon.

"Pipe down MBA man," shouted Daris to Ian.

The receptionist was consumed at the back of the room taking notes.

Sara came over to Daris and gave him a hug. It had been years since the two of them had been in the same room together. Daris thought she was holding up well and exuding a certain pregnant glow.

Two fools in love as always, Daris thought to himself about Zoran and Sara's relationship.

Daris, Zoran, and Sara took their seats at the conference table.

"Daris never accepted my Serb blood into his family," Zoran said to Ian and Dr. Gold Tooth.

"How could I? What you people did to my homeland," replied Daris.

"That's the old world. I left it behind, and so should you," said Zoran.

"Daris never forgets anything. He holds grudges badly," Sara chimed in.

"You were too young to remember what happened. I witnessed things you would never forget. What the Serbs did to our village, our father's mutilated body. If you had seen them you wouldn't be married to one of them," said Daris.

"Move on," replied Zoran.

"He never could. He never approved of us," Daris's sister said with tears in her eyes.

"You are ungrateful Sara. You had it easy. I bankrolled your way through college. You didn't need to work for anything. And how do you repay me? Marry a dirty Serb, then go out and start a business in direct competition to mine. Where did you even get the money to start up New Berlin Real Estate?" Daris said in the direction of Zoran.

"My plumbing company made so much cash I needed to funnel the profits into something or I would have been killed by taxes. Why not real estate? After all, property is the linchpin of capitalism. And America is built on capitalism," said Zoran, channeling Daris's free market philosophy.

Guy isn't as stupid as I thought, Daris contemplated.

"I bet you wish you took on Zoran as a Spitfire agent when he asked," Sara said to Daris.

Daris was speechless and consumed with rage.

"To build may have to be the slow and laborious task of years. To destroy can be the thoughtless act of a single day," replied Daris, with a direct quote from Winston Churchill.

"It was the only way to get your attention. You offended me. You offended your sister. All we wanted was your approval. Your love," said Zoran being held back by Sara.

The situation looked on the brink of turning violent. The assistant stopped taking notes. Ian looked for a place to hide. Dr. Gold Tooth tried to remember where he had stashed the first aid kit.

"We all came to America for a new start, not to dwell on the past. You have grasped so much opportunity. Why can you not let go of history? Move forward, leave the old ways behind," said Sara, now pleading directly to her brother.

Daris stood up and walked to the other end of the room and stared at the wall of presidential portraits. George Washington was standing slightly cockeyed. Daris reached out and straightened him up. *Great man who could've become a dictator but took a different path,* thought Daris. He then looked over at his sister. Her child would be the first member of the family who could one day be added to this wall of pictures.

Ian Lemon stood up and shouted, "This is like a really bad family drama I don't want to be a part of! Tonight is meant to be a business sit-down, not a very special episode of a soon-to-be-cancelled daytime soap! Can we talk about real estate commissions? Six percent commissions to be precise. Can we at least agree to stick with that across all our businesses?"

"Man from the cartel, Real Estate Code of Ethics my ass – let the public be dammed. What's wrong with five percent? Can't we cut the man in the street a break?" said Zoran to Ian.

"Do your plumbers cut the man in the street a break when his turd-filled toilet is blocked up on a Saturday night?" replied Ian.

"Plumbing is a skilled trade," said Zoran.

"And you think real estate isn't?" shot back Ian Lemon.

"Six percent is the standard. We ought to stick with that," said Daris, veering away from blood feuds and back-to business talk.

"There's no such thing as standard: Sherman Anti Trust Act," said Zoran.

Dr. Gold Tooth now took charge of the meeting. "You are all correct. But let's just say it's better for everyone if we stick to the respected norms and magically all charge six percent. We in St. Louis are but a small pond that feeds into a larger sea. If we want our sea to remain unmolested by bad forces from the coasts, we need to follow the conventions. Let me just say some of the money in real estate flows back to Washington DC in the way of political contributions. Those donations keep the industry lightly regulated; the less regulation the better. All I want is for both of you to agree to maintain six percent commissions in this open and fair unregulated free market. So Daris, Zoran can we shake hands on six percent and no deviation on that?"

Zoran looked over to Daris and then to his pregnant wife. "OK, New Berlin Real Estate agrees to six percent," he said.

"We will of course maintain six percent at Spitfire," said Daris.

With the six percent commission issue settled Ian Lemon's work was done. The real estate industry could once again be assured the market was free and fair and not being undercut.

"Have a nice day GUYS!" said Ian in a manner that was a cross between the way women of the South say, "Bless your heart" and New Yorkers call an asshole "PAL!" Ian then packed away his computer and left the meeting for his dinner date.

Dr. Gold Tooth pulled out a piece of paper from his pocket and laid it out on the table.

"What's that?" asked Zoran.

"Back-of-a-napkin business plan for you two to work on," said Dr. Gold Tooth, who was of course aware of the family dynamics at play prior to the meeting.

"Why do we need that?" said Daris.

"You two knuckleheads are not in a business dispute; you are in a family dispute. And I am trying to end your senseless squabble," said the dentist arbitrator.

Dr. Gold Tooth presented his plan to the two men. "North City has untapped real estate potential. It's now a wasteland but look at what it can become. The new government geospatial agency is being built, an MLS team is in the works, a regional housing shortage. Thousands of millennials are ready to ditch wasting money on artisanal muffins and avocado toast and graduate into the world of home ownership. North City is ripe for gentrification. The "Delmar Divide" will be a thing of the past. You two with the pooling of your resources and skills have what it takes to become kings of the north!"

Daris looked over the plan. The two brokerages would merge together under the Spitfire brand. With the synergy savings they would expand northwards. As well as opening an office at the intersection of Goodfellow and Page Blvd., they would additionally get into real estate development. Dr. Gold Tooth, through his unrivaled connections, had already lined up meetings with architects, financiers, and Aldermen. It was in the interest of the local region to make a go of the northern districts. Local politicians knew that if this dream could be realized, it would raise their national credentials.

"This business plan is a hedge," said Dr. Gold Tooth.

"Yes, the development projects will thrive, even if the real estate business gets disrupted," said Daris, who knew that the traditional brokerage model wouldn't last forever.

"All these new residents in North City will have plumbing problems," said Zoran, thinking about the prospects for synergy with his other operations.

"If you can make this succeed, your families will be accepted by the local establishment," said Dr. Gold Tooth.

"No easy task when you didn't graduate from the right high school," said Zoran, who was well aware of how not going to the best schools was a handicap cracking the upper echelons of St. Louis life.

Zoran and Daris began to discuss how they would run their new venture.

Sara was happy to have her brother back and the comfort and joy of family around her. She texted her mother in Florida with the news about the détente.

Mission accomplished for Dr. Gold Tooth. He had once again carried on the proud legacy of business mediation with honor.

Daris Ballic pulled out a cigar from his pocket and lit it. "These are not dark days, these are great days, the greatest days that we have ever lived," he said to Zoran Milorad – a Churchill quote that he'd been waiting two decades to use.

The two men shook hands and began what they envisioned to be an exciting new venture.

*   *   *

Sam arrived home late after his double shift. The realization that Alice was gone hit him as soon as he walked through the door. Silence had replaced the noise of the old movies she would watch. The seductive aroma of home cooking and perfume was now just a trace in the air. By morning the smell of mold from the air-con would have reclaimed its throne as emperor of odors in apartment #1311.

"Sam took a look at himself in the mirror." He liked the new clothes. It gave him confidence. He would date again, no internet searching next time. Maybe he would join a bowling league, or start a trivia night; he had options. The week with Alice had retooled his machinery and he felt like he was back in the game.

Sam went to the fridge to see what he could rustle up for dinner. As he opened it up there was a pleasant surprise awaiting. Alice had prepared him a mac and cheese dish to warm up. Next to it, there was a note.

Dearest Sam

Thank you for a truly wonderful week. God brought me to you and God will take me home. Call me if there is anything I can ever do for you. Let's hope we all have our fairytale endings.

X

Alice

P.S. I am sorry I drank all your Dr Pepper. I bought two big bottles and they are in the pantry. Cans are expensive! Better to buy in bulk in the future.

Sam put the letter to his nose – he could smell Alice's hand cream. He then slumped into the sofa and turned on the television. The local channels were dominated by live feeds from the downtown protests. Sam couldn't help but think about Devonte Jones on life support. A guy who happened to be at the wrong place at the wrong time. Fate was a terrible thing.

He began to think about his own life. It had been dull. He had always aimed low and settled for the easy way out. Dating Becky, although the right thing to do, was a simple decision to make. She had asked him to prom at middle school. Once they started dating, it was certain they would end up married. That's just the way it happened in South County during that era. In hindsight, they should have both lived life a bit before settling down as two young fogeys – old before their time.

Aside from dipping his elbow into the hot waters of sex-for-hire debauchery, Sam had lived a dull life. His job at the utility company was safe but he quit it. His current gig was crap but he couldn't afford to quit it. He hadn't traveled much. Florida and the redneck riviera of Alabama was the extent of his worldly exploration. He was simply a guy who hadn't ever chased adventure.

Sam had to turn the news off – it was depressing. He poured himself another glass of Dr Pepper from the bottle Alice had left him. He tried not to dwell on his situation but he couldn't help himself. It was Friday night and he was solo in a studio apartment, in a building known by its residents as Misery Towers. There's an expression a friend had once used: "People build their own prisons." And this was true of Sam. He was in solitary confinement, a cell of his own making – although most prisoners would envy the beautiful view.

"What's the good news?" he said to himself as he placed his dinner bowl into the dishwasher.

The past week with Alice had been awesome, and Sam couldn't stop thinking about her – the way she listened to him, their candlelit dinners, that post-sex snuggle. *Why did I let her leave so easily?* he thought to himself, with the realization that the past week with Alice had been one of the best of his life.

He looked out the window. News choppers hovered over the Mississippi River. Again he thought about Devonte Jones. He thought about fate. He thought about life being short. He thought about life passing him up. He thought about Alice's long ride to Kentucky. He thought about fairytales.

"Alice!" Sam shouted, as his next thought was about breaking free from the prison walls he had surrounded himself in.

He bolted out of his apartment, headed to the basement garage, jumped into the LeBaron and fired up the engine. With the *Pretty Woman* soundtrack blaring he peeled out of Missouri Towers down Broadway. He followed the highway signs that took him to the Eads Bridge.

*   *   *

Nick Pipeman was in a dark place. His client Devonte Jones was barely clinging onto life. Any permutation of how events had transpired and Pipeman could only blame himself.

The media had drummed up this tragic situation as the next Ferguson and were milking it for all they could. All Nick could hear from the balcony of his apartment was the sounds of a city at war with itself. A terrible rage that his actions had ultimately created. St. Louis was burning and an innocent man was on life support. And it was his fault.

Nick Pipeman was standing precariously on the southern side of Eads Bridge, looking down at the water below. Nick's dog Rollo had followed him all the way from Missouri Towers and was anxiously watching his master's actions unfold.

He had contemplated jumping from the balcony of the 18th-floor apartment he called home, but he wouldn't want some unfortunate person to have to clean up the mess on the deck below. Jumping into the Mississippi River would be better for everyone. Easy, quick, no clean-up, and at least the catfish would appreciate him.

With both hands, Nick grasped a large urn that held all the pennies he had collected over his life. The container was heavy and with the heat it had been a herculean feat just lugging it this far from his apartment. Nick used to believe all pennies he found were lucky, but he had since learned that was not always the case. He was going to ditch the pennies.

Nick started tossing the coins into the river.

"Mississippi River, you have to be the greatest wishing well in the world. May you make all these pennies lucky for whoever finds them!" he screamed into the night air.

Pipeman looked over his shoulder as a gray, nineties Chrysler LeBaron blasting out a tune by Roxette roared over the bridge at immense speed.

Rollo barked at the car in a vain attempt to have its driver pull over and intervene. The dog could sense Nick needed help.

One careless slip and Nick would fall into the river below. He hoped that was how it would happen. It would be easier, with less theatrics and yield a zero chance to back out.

He scanned the city skyline. Helicopters were flying overhead and the sound of wailing sirens was constant.

Nick was now throwing coins into the river by the handful; he wanted to speed things up and be done with it. Be done with the pain he felt. Be done with life.

Rollo barked ferociously. Nick put down the urn and looked in the direction of where Rollo was facing.

His four-legged friend tried to warn Nick that someone was approaching. It was rare for pedestrian traffic on the bridge at any time, especially at night. The person was getting nearer and making a beeline for Nick.

Pipeman made a clear visual. Early twenties Black man with sagging shorts and a hoodie. *Only a gangsta would wear a hoodie on a hot night like this!*

"Hey buddy!" the man began to shout in what sounded like North City jive.

"Fuck me! Only in St. Louis do you get mugged moments before you are about to jump off a bridge," muttered Nick.

Rollo ran off in the direction of the city.

So much for man's best friend. Even the dog knows when to get out of Dodge, thought Pipeman.

Nick took his wallet from his pocket and threw it towards the approaching man.

"Take it please. There's a couple hundred bucks in it. I don't need it anyway," said Nick, still balancing on the ledge of the bridge.

The man didn't pick it up and kept walking towards him.

*   *   *

Colton Chesterfield III awoke to find himself in a nightmarish predicament. His most pressing concern wasn't that he was trapped inside a locked coffin with no apparent way to escape. His biggest issue was that he needed to take a crap. And not just any crap. He needed to expel a nasty-ass junk food shit that was rumbling in his belly. *If they had served food like that at the State Pen a riot would've ensued,* contemplated Colton, who would rather be locked up in prison than face his current situation.

During his prison stint, noises were something Colton paid attention to as if his life depended on it. The slightest sound that would be ignored in the outside world as unimportant in the slammer had meaning. It might offer respite from boredom or be interrupted as a signal of unfolding events. The thud of a guard's boots approaching, conspiratorial night whispers, cell mates getting their groove on, the sound of a shank being sharpened. Colton had a new appreciation of the slightest pattern of noise, and deciphering sounds was another arrow in his quiver of self-survival.

Colton's ears detected a change in his environment. He was no longer at the funeral parlor – that place had been quieter. The coffin he was trapped inside wasn't now in the old Hearse. Noise penetrated this vehicle differently. A large SUV, a Tahoe or Escalade were possibilities for the transportation. The sound of car doors slamming and remote lock chirps suggested he was stopped in a business parking lot. Not far in the distance, he could hear the rumble of big-rig trucks. He had to be close to a highway. If he could get out of the coffin, some kind of help was near. He had to make a move.

Colton began ferociously banging on the coffin lid and screaming as loud as he could, "Get me out of here!" After twenty minutes of trying to attract help, the banging and screaming was getting nowhere. Colton gave up. He needed to redirect his energies for the ongoing mission of holding back the ca-ca reservoir that was attempting to break free from his butt. As the seconds, minutes, or maybe hours dragged on, this became more challenging.

Colton tried to distract himself from his circumstances and made the mistake of letting his mind wander to a more delightful event. It was a dalliance with one of his former sales girls. He did the dirty with her in a plushly lined coffin; nothing like the piece of junk he was trapped in now. It was the one his customers thought they were getting as part of the deluxe package. Thinking about the fun he had with those perky breasts had the unneeded result of landing Colton a raging boner. He was contemplating the implications of self relief in a confined space without clean-up options when an even bigger problem presented itself. Colton's bowels could not be held back any longer and unloaded. A torrent of shit gushed from his ass, flooding into his pants.

"Either we live by accident and die by accident, or we live by plan and die by plan," Colton said to an audience of one as he recounted a motivational quip from his self-help book. The feeling of the soft serve consistency sewage collecting around his thighs was unnervingly gruesome. Oddly, though, the smell, which at first he thought would kill him instantly, was somewhat palatable after a few agonizing minutes.

Suddenly Colton heard the vehicle door open. There was hope.

Up Where We Belong

Gloria's dressing room was steaming hot; the air-conditioning at City Museum never abated the worst of summer's roasting heat. Gloria stared into the makeup mirror; her hair was in a sloppy, need-to-wash look, but with a little work she would soon be rocking her trademark perfect prom queen curls. She had recently started to feel old; gray hairs seemed to be reproducing without encouragement. Makeup tonight had discreetly defused the age lines on her face, but with the heat, she would be lucky if it didn't streak.

The new show she had been planning and prepping over many months was less than ninety minutes from its debut. As if though with the stress of this production she needed her relationship dramas with Mike. Settling down, marriage, children; in less than a week, all her dreams had been thwarted. She hadn't asked for much, only what every other Midwestern girl took for granted.

Mike wasn't perfect, but who is? Maybe she had been a little heavy with the pressure she piled on him? Binary choices sent via text in reflection are not always productive. The way Gloria's life was going, she would end up like Madison Stone – a daily routine of booze, gym and summers sitting by an algae-infested pool, harvesting cancer via sun and cigarettes. The only deviation to Madison's life was looking for one-night mattress-bouncers to bring home and offer redemption through the joys of post-nut clarity.

Gloria couldn't even contemplate jumping back into the dating pool. She had a lifetime's worth of tragic Tinder dates and might opt for the convent. Or she could go back to the farm. Maybe that was her true destiny. Maybe all the bad luck she had been served was karma for not knowing her station.

Gloria hadn't heard from Mike since she fired over her self-prescribed deadline. For all she knew, he was on the highway heading to California right now. Gloria was mentally preparing to have her heart broken a second time. For now, though, she had a show to prepare for. As for her personal life, she was bracing for impact.

*   *   *

Mike walked over to a line of electric scooters parked up on the sidewalk next to the office. He had a life-changing decision to make, and it had to be made now. Follow your head, or follow your heart; although it was far from clear which option was which. Mike hastily unlocked the first scooter in the nest and put one foot on the board and the other on Washington Ave.

Four blocks north, Gloria McKendrick was preparing for her performance at City Museum. She was perfect in every way and offered the natural order of life for a regular heartland guy like him. Could Mike smash her heart and run off to Hollywood? Gloria was tired of waiting and had told him so.

Seven blocks southeast was Lizzy Winslow, the prodigal sweetheart who had left him once before. It was a big mistake on her part and she wanted to take Mike back with her to California. Finally, he would have the chance to escape Missouri. Finally, he would again be with Lizzy, something he had dreamed about, and planned for, since the day they parted. Could he pass up a ticket to Los Angeles? Making it in Hollywood with your high school girlfriend by your side is the ultimate Midwestern fairytale ending.

Mike had made his choice. With the tune of *Thunder Road* playing in his head, he had finally worked out his version of a promised land. He opened up the scooter throttle and proceeded east on Washington Ave. He was headed to City Garden, where Lizzy was awaiting.

Mike had only progressed a block east to Tucker Blvd. before he realized the dangerous state of affairs developing in the city. To the north, he could see an army of sheriff's deputies putting on riot gear. Their insignias indicated they were from Jefferson County. For them, the chance to get out the big boy toys of law enforcement and collect overtime was like Christmas come early. To the south, squads of city bike cops were being briefed by their sergeants. Helicopters and drones monitoring from the sky softened the wail of sirens coming from all over downtown.

Mike crossed Tucker and rode down an eerie Washington Ave. void of pedestrians. A sprinkling of residents on loft balconies with cocktails in hand were watching for events to kick off. Mike took a sharp right down 10th St., cruising past the art gallery with its colorful flamingo pictures displayed in the window. At the intersection of Locust he stopped to let two muscle cars that weren't observing traffic signs race each other. Mike whizzed past Jack Patrick's pub; they hadn't boarded up and he could see it was brimming with customers. Nothing deters the regulars at Jack Patrick's!

He was fast-approaching City Garden's rabbit sculptures. Memories of dating Lizzy came flooding back. His heart was beating fast and he was nervous; it felt like being a teenager again. The park wasn't even officially opened when he had first come here with her. They were two kids in love and had hopped the construction fence searching for a make-out space. That made the event even more daring, risky and memorable.

He couldn't see Lizzy. She was most likely hiding behind the sitting rabbit. That was always her favorite spot; it was their special place, the place they had shared that first kiss.

Mike parked the scooter on the gravel next to the rabbit sculptures. The air temperature was stuck in the eighties and he wiped sweat off his forehead to stop it dripping into his eyes.

"Lizzy!" Mike shouted as he walked around the rabbits looking for her.

The sound of gunshots rattled from a spot too close for comfort. From Mike's estimation, the gunshots were coming from the far side of the AT&T building.

"Lizzy, are you hiding?" Mike shouted now, concerned for their safety.

Mike took out his cell phone and texted Lizzy. The lines were jammed and it wouldn't go through.

He jumped back on the scooter and cruised to the park's security guard house. He banged on its door.

Tubbs opened up and Crockett could be seen in the background eating a sandwich.

"Sorry to bother you, but did you see on the security cameras anyone by the rabbits recently?"

"Description?" asked Tubbs.

"Blonde, cute as a button, probably dressed like a tourist from the coasts," said Mike.

"No man!" shouted Crockett from the back of the room.

"Been dead here all night," said Tubbs.

"Stay safe out there!" Crockett shouted, before going back to the work of reading the paper and eating his sandwich.

There were more sounds of gunshots echoing off the AT&T building. A helicopter could be heard coming towards City Garden.

Where r u? Mike texted Lizzy. Finally the message managed to find itself a path through the jammed airwaves and was sent.

An anxious thirty seconds later, the reply arrived. *Top of the Arch! Our special place. Up where we belong!*

Mike looked towards the beautifully illuminated St. Louis Arch. Of course, Lizzy's version of what would be their special place was different from his. Mike, the latent romantic, thought all along that their first kiss had been behind the sculptures. Of course, Lizzy's rendering was the private time they shared on a ride to the Arch's observation deck that had made the monument their special place. Lizzy was always wild and he was amazed at what they were able to accomplish in that enclosed space. Those sticky teenage antics on the Arch ascent had Mike a base away from scoring a home run.

On my way, Mike texted back. He peeled out of City Garden and onto Chestnut. Flying overhead was a helicopter with searchlights on, scoping out the area. As he crossed 8th St., he could see police lights flashing and clouds of tear gas forming in the distance, on Washington Ave.

He cruised parallel to the open space that comprised of Kiener Plaza, to witness an astonishing spectacle. Thousands of Phil Collins fans en masse were descending. In unison they were singing the annoying Phil Collins song, *Sussudio.* Mike had seen videos of chanting soccer fans in Europe and this was on par with that – although this crowd was older and alarmingly more dangerous looking.

He continued down Chestnut past Hooters. At the eastern end of the plaza, a large crowd of protesters left from an earlier rally were milling around. A heavy police presence stood guard in front of the stately Old Courthouse.

Mike stopped at Broadway, waiting to cross the intersection. A convoy of police SUVs raced past him heading north. Coming the other way against traffic was a gang of motorbike riders roaring down the street. Several were doing wheelies and one was standing on the saddle as he rode. A few of the cops gave the bikers a thumbs up.

Two blocks north, on Washington Ave., Mike could hear the sound of flash bangs being fired by police.

Mike looked left and right and the road was clear. He opened up the throttle and darted across Broadway at full speed. The Gateway Arch was getting nearer by the second. A full moon could be seen emerging from between its span. Just as the scooter reached maximum speed, it stuttered and groaned and lost all power. He looked at the battery gauge; it was out of juice. In his haste he hadn't checked if he had taken a fully charged ride. The *Thunder Road* soundtrack that had been playing in his head seemed to be synchronized with the battery, as the tune faded along with his speed. Mike coasted for another twenty yards before grinding to a halt.

Mike tossed the scooter to the ground and started running towards the Arch as fast as he could. The last time he had self-propelled at this velocity was a track meet in high school. If anyone had been on the streets to watch, he would've looked like a disheveled Benjamin Braddock on his mission to make it to the church before Elaine said, "I do." If anyone was able to rustle Mike's thoughts, he was somewhere in the mental space between Harry Angstrom and Holden Caulfield, searching for clarity and trying to find a way to decipher life.

Somehow in the stifling August heat, Mike made it to the doors of the Gateway Arch without collapsing in exhaustion.

The air inside the building was frigid and the sweat dripping down his body now felt cold. The security line was empty. Mike made it through quickly. He ran down the stairs and through the newly renovated museum. The pictorial history of St. Louis was a blur on either side as he sprinted towards the tram that would take him to the Arch's zenith.

There were only a few people in line ahead of him. "Have your tickets ready," the attendant shouted.

"Shit!" Mike said. He didn't have a ticket. He left the line and ran over to the ticket booth. There were three people standing in front of him.

An announcement on the museum's loudspeakers broke the humdrum of late-night tourism: "Due to civil unrest the Jefferson Memorial Gateway Arch will be closing early. There will be no more tram tickets sold this evening."

Mike ran over to the tram line. "No more rides today. We're closing," the attendant told him.

"I have someone I'm meant to be meeting at the top. Can you please let me go through?" Mike pleaded, to no avail.

He looked at his cell phone. The reception was dead. He walked away from the line and paced for twenty seconds. It could take forever for Lizzy to come down and he wouldn't be able to wait for her as the museum would be closed. Anyway, Mike wouldn't even know which exit she would take. He knew Lizzy would be waiting for him on the observation deck as long as she could. That was just the type of woman she was. He had no choice, he had to get to the top of the Arch.

Mike walked over to the attendant manning the tram on the opposite leg of the Arch. He was busy roping off the area.

"Hey man! You aren't going to believe it but Nelly is in the gift shop, he's with Jon Hamm. They are looking at Arch snow globes and signing autographs. This is a crazy, once-in-a-lifetime St. Louis moment you won't want to miss," said Mike, lying about spotting two of St. Louis' greatest living legends.

"No shit!" the man replied as he took a phone out of his pocket and hastily walked towards the gift shop hoping to witness history.

As soon as the attendant departed, Mike seized the moment, jumped over the security rope, and ran towards the tram door. Unfortunately, the tram was already shut down. Mike was left with no choice but to take the stairwell.

One thousand and seventy-six agonizing steps later, Mike was standing six hundred and thirty feet higher than where he started. He wasn't sure if he was wobbling from the grueling hike, or if it was just one of those windy nights when the Arch swayed dramatically.

Lizzy had been waiting for Mike and was the last person left on the observation deck. She was busy looking out of a viewing window staring down at the city as Mike approached.

"I made it," said a beaten and battered Mike, who felt like he had just climbed Everest without the aid of oxygen or sherpas.

"I knew you would," Lizzy said looking at Mike.

As beautiful as ever, was the only thought that ran through Mike's mind. He moved closer to Lizzy. She was wearing a thrift store boho dress that somehow, on her waifish frame, looked like high couture. That face, even behind the geek glasses she had switched-out for her contacts, was stunning. A face with an unrivaled mercurial intensity that could launch a thousands ships. A face that with ease had sold millions of dollars worth of California real estate. A face that Mike had spent his life chasing. How had Mike managed to win a second chance with the ever-mesmerizing Lizzy? A second chance that he hadn't even had to wait fifty-three years, seven months, and eleven days for, as Florentino Ariza had for Fermina Daza in *Love in the Time of Cholera.*

They moved closer to each other. He could smell Lizzy's perfume; she was the same free-spirited, braless self under the flouncy dress that she had always been. He was slightly self-aware about his own sweaty-stinky state. But for Lizzy, even that would be an aphrodisiac.

She was wearing a third of the articles of clothing she had on the last time they rode the tram together, and that day they had quite the tryst. If her lusty eyes were any indication, what was on the menu for tonight's ride? A double home run on the way down wasn't out of the question.

Lizzy moved towards Mike and took hold of his right hand. For Mike, this was electric and his emotions raced. Lizzy then took his other hand and brought him closer. She whispered to him a quote from her favorite poet, T.S. Elliot, that spoke to the moment: "And the end of all our exploring will be to arrive where we started, and know the place for the first time."

Lizzy embraced Mike and began kissing his ear. Mike wanted to take her down to the banks of the Mississippi River. Watch the barges go by under the Eads Bridge. Listen to the trains rumble under the levee. Rewind the clock to where they left off the first time they had been together. Start planning their new lives. Somehow take a ride back to the future.

But he couldn't.

With tears in his eyes, he said to Lizzy: "I am not going to California. I'm sorry. It's not you, it's me."

*   *   *

Nick Pipeman was standing on the ledge of the Eads Bridge, frozen in panic. And it wasn't because one misstep and he'd go tumbling into the Mississippi. After all, his intention had been to become one with Ol' Man River all along. His greatest fear was that he was going to be mugged. It didn't matter that he wouldn't be in need of whatever material objects he was about to be relieved of; it was the indignity and the sense of violation that this action would present. Nick had lived his entire life in the St. Louis region and had never once been held up. To make it this far and then get mugged moments before you kill yourself could only happen here.

The man got within two feet of Nick. Technically, Nick had the high ground but that was worthless because one nudge from his would-be assailant and he would tumble into the river.

"Hey man, you threw your wallet at me. What's that all about?" asked the individual, whose accent was a cross between Tom Sawyer and Nelly.

"Because...," Nick said.

"Becuz you see a BLACK MAN walking towards you and ya think you're about to be ROBBED?" the man said angrily.

"Crazy kind of night!" Nick said, with the symphony of mayhem playing out in the distance.

"Get off the ledge, get down you dumb motherfucker," said the man, with the authority of a successful mugger before adding: "Ya fall off if you're not careful, I can't swim. I'm not fishing ya out."

Nick jumped down from the ledge and placed the urn of remaining pennies on the ground.

"What's your name?" the stranger asked.

"Nick Pipeman."

"I'm Rolex, but call me Flash." He reached out his hand and the two men formally greeted one another.

Nick picked up his wallet from the ground.

"What you doing on that ledge?" asked Flash.

After a long pause, Nick replied. "Had a bad day."

Flash, in a move only a professional athlete could pull off in one leap, jumped from the sidewalk onto the ledge of the bridge. He was now standing on the exact same spot as Nick had been.

"Kind of scary up here," said Flash.

Nick stood back and didn't know what to do.

Flash pointed over to the St. Louis skyline. "Nick, you see over there? That is the land of the living, and the river down below us is the land of the dead."

Flash then looked down at the Mississippi and watched a barge go by.

"And you know what the bridge is?" Flash said as he turned around with his arms wide open. "This is the 'bridge of love.' The bridge is the only survival, the only meaning. Nick, the best place is on the bridge, not in the land of the living or the land of the dead. Stay on the bridge tonight."

"Where are you getting this shit from? New wave rap gone all philosophical these days?" asked Nick.

"There you go again Nick, cuz I'm a Black man and wear a hoodie don't mean I'm going to mug you or know anything about rap!" said Flash as he jumped down from the ledge of the bridge and to a position in front of Nick. "It's literature Nick. Thornton Wilder, *The Bridge of San Luis Rey*."

"Never heard of it," said Nick.

"It's famous. Won a Pulitzer Prize."

"You are better read than me," said Nick.

"The message of the book is everything and everyone is connected in some way or another, but the biggest importance of all is love. The bridge in the book represents love. You were teetering on the edge Nick. You gotta remember there's no such thing as chance in this world. Everything happens for a reason. Whatever bad thing you did that brought you here tonight was out of your control and would've happened anyway, no matter what you did. So you can't blame yourself. We are all connected. From your neighbors in your apartment building to every single person in the city around you."

Flash could see Nick was deep in thought.

"Where did you go to high school, Nick?" said Flash, with the ultimate St. Louis get-to-know-you question.

"Not a good one, it closed down years ago."

"I went to the best high school in all St. Louis. The supermarket aristocrats and beer heirs and everyone who is anyone went there. Basketball scholarship, if you're wondering. I didn't graduate. They knew that was never going to happen when they plucked me out of the hood. But I can sure throw a ball in a hoop. I went to college; got kicked out for discipline problems. Talent-wise, I should be in the NBA now. I'm what they call a 'flawed prodigy.' Look me up: Rolex Flash. One big masterclass on how to fuck up your life. I've got kids all over the place and nothing going on basketball-wise. But that's fine. It was meant to be. It's all part of the plan."

Flash then pulled out a joint from the pocket of his baggy, sagging shorts. "I might not mug you, and I might not know a fucking thing about rap, but I'm still a North City hillbilly and I like to smoke weed," said Flash.

He took a drag of the doobie and passed it to Pipeman. The two men sat on the bridge getting high, discussing their lives for a solid half hour.

"I think your ride is here Nick," said Flash, pointing to a car.

It was Zoe who had pulled up. Rollo was riding shotgun.

"Nick, what are you doing here, in the middle of the Eads Bridge?" asked Zoe through the open window.

"Smoking with a friend on the 'bridge of *love!*" said a stoned Nick.

"What are you talking about?" she replied

"How did you even know I was here?" asked Nick.

"Rollo was scratching my front door and led me to the car and ultimately brought me here. This dog has some crazy sixth sense. We'd been worried sick about you for hours. We had given up searching."

Like Lassie finding Timmy down the well! That certainly wasn't by chance. Nick contemplated about his dog who had an additional talent on top of sniffing out real estate leads.

Nick jumped into Zoe's car. "Flash, can we give you a ride somewhere?"

"I'm good man. I like to walk." Said Flash as he disappeared in the rear-view mirror as they drove away.

*   *   *

Mike, who had planned all the amazing, different ways he would win back Lizzy, had never considered he would be in a position to turn her down. So stuck for carefully curated words to form a heartfelt message of rejection, all he could manage was to regurgitate Lizzy's phrase: "It's not you. It's me." After all, those words had been etched in Mike's psyche since the day Lizzy had used them on him.

Lizzy stepped back and tears rolled down her cheeks. She wasn't the sentimental type, so this was a surprise to Mike.

"Bad timing?" Lizzy asked.

"It's always about timing," Mike replied.

She wiped her eyes. Mike knew that sympathy was a counter-productive emotion, so as hard as it was he held back from showing any.

"My whole life, since the day I met you, all I ever wanted was to be with you. But it's too late. As much as I want to, I cannot do it. I don't think I can explain in words what Gloria means to me," Mike said, in support of his position.

"Nobody says *no* to me. I've always got what I want in life. What do I need to do to make this happen?" growled Lizzy like she was fighting to get a sales contract accepted on an in-demand listing.

"Nothing, this is one deal you're not gonna close!" replied Mike.

The allure of Lizzy and the offer she made to set him up in Los Angeles was everything he should've wanted. But he decided to turn it down. Mike and Lizzy would not grow old together as per their teenage dreams. For this saga, there would be no *Love in the Time of Cholera* ending.

Gloria, with her passioned Gettysburg-style speech, had tried to keep him on course, not by touting her own merits but by selling to him all the reasons to love St. Louis. In the end, what made Mike's decision easy wasn't what Lizzy, Gloria or St. Louis could do for him. It was what Mike could do with Gloria.

Mike finally, and in the nick of time, realized how awesome Gloria was as he toured the penthouse loft with Angelo and Amanda. Angelo, on paper, had a dream job; keeping beautiful Amanda warm at night and reaping the rewards of life as a kept man. Who wouldn't want that gig? The burning bush moment, however, came for Mike as he watched Angelo pissing around with the yappy dog and picking up its Tootsie Roll-sized turds. At that precise moment, Mike realized that if he chased Lizzy to Los Angeles, he would end up just like him. He would be the guy picking up the metaphorical turds, albeit in a place with better weather. Mike would always be a junior partner in any relationship with Lizzy.

The life Gloria offered was so much better. They were in a relationship of equals. What Gloria presented was much better than he could ever have with Lizzy. They were a team – and a great one at that. What was Mike even contemplating leaving Gloria? A head hardwired with Bruce Springsteen songs and blinded by dreaming about a *Love in the Time of Cholera* happy ending had led him astray.

The last piece of the emotional puzzle was his flatlined realtor career. Getting Amanda under contract on the loft had rekindled his confidence and spark. He knew on the back of this sale he could "find his lane." He didn't need to be handed business on a silver platter. He was good enough at his job to make it work as a realtor in St. Louis and would put down the previous week's catastrophes as a string of unfortunate luck.

To give Gloria extra credit on her pitch, she did an excellent job promoting the merits of St. Louis – one worthy of a Chamber of Commerce gold star. Los Angeles seemed like a nightmare place to live. The populace she framed as a narcissistic bunch of rude people, the beach, with its cold water, was worthless. Not being able to get anywhere within a twenty-minute drive was a tough concept for him to swallow, and paying for parking was even harder. Anyway, if it's good enough for Bruce Springsteen to stick around his hometown, then there's no reason for Mike to look for any other promised land than the one he now called home.

Gloria had possibly gone overboard in labeling him a Stan Kroenke, but he'd already forgiven her for calling him Duckie. Everyone knows Duckie was the choice Andie should've made.

The tram ride to the bottom of the Arch with Lizzy wasn't anywhere near as much fun as their third-base frolics the last time they took the trip together. Lizzy, who was never one to turn down the opportunity to get frisky if asked, even under these circumstances probably would've been up for a quick tryst. If for no other reason than just for old-time's sake, or to shake off preflight nerves. She was a wild, manic pixie dream girl who would never be tamed. Mike, as tempted as he might've been, just couldn't cheat on Gloria.

As they exited the tram car, Lizzy said: "I didn't expect that answer, but I respect your decision. I hope it works out for you. Gloria is one lucky lady."

Mike, pulling Lizzy's luggage, escorted her through the Arch grounds. The night air was relentlessly humid. In the distance they heard a myriad of sounds familiar to anyone who has found themselves caught up in urban unrest: chanting, smashing windows, the sound of plastic bullets being fired, and the never-ending sound of sirens.

A taxi was parked outside the Hyatt. Mike opened the door for Lizzy.

"Airport," Mike told the driver. He then gave specific instructions to stay away from Interstate 70 as there were too many shootings on that road of late. "Take 'farty' to 170," Mike told the driver in that strange way St. Louisans pronounce highway 40.

Lizzy gave Mike a final hug before stepping into the taxi, and for the second time in their intertwined histories, they parted ways.

He checked his phone. Gloria would be starting her performance any minute. She had given him until she arrived home tonight to make a final decision on what he was doing with his life, and from there she would decide what to do with hers. Mike wasn't even sure at this point that a future for them together was unilaterally his call. He tried to phone her but couldn't get a signal. There was no point messaging, Gloria's clunker phone didn't take texts. With the chaotic state of downtown St. Louis, he couldn't leave her to make her own way home tonight; she might never make it back. There was only one thing to do if he had any hope of winning back Gloria. Go to City Museum.

Mike scanned his surroundings looking for a scooter to commandeer but he was out of luck; they had all been cleared off the streets. He would have to walk the fourteen blocks. He crossed Broadway and made his way west on Pine. The street ahead was deserted of people. From all directions he could hear police sirens and the hum of choppers. Then, from the corner of 7th St., the sound of smashing glass alerted Mike that he wasn't alone. He could make out a gang attempting to break into a store. Criminal elements tended to tag along the fringes of civil rights protests. One of the gang members got a visual of Mike and the entire group of about six, some clutching iron pipes, began walking towards him. He wasn't going to wait around to see what they wanted. He ran as fast as he could towards Washington Ave.

The gang gave up following after two blocks. Mike hid in the entrance of a parking garage to catch his breath. A group of teens were spray painting a creative mural on the boarded-up windows of a bank. From his concealed position, he watched a muscle car driving against traffic looking for opportunities. Mike had never owned a gun but on a night like this he could see the appeal. Checking the street was clear, he started a brisk walk to Washington Ave.

He made it to High-Pointe restaurant. Across the street, a number of windows had been smashed out at the Convention Center. Several trash cans were on fire, and others emptied of their contents. Broken glass crunched under his feet. A police car screamed past heading east. Mike continued to trudge down Washington Ave. in the direction of Gloria.

He was making steady progress and had gotten as far as 10th St. when he sensed something was about to go down. Three men in backpacks were standing on the corner outside the Thai restaurant. They had hoodies and ski masks covering their faces – ominous attire on a hot summer night. This was the advance party; coming down 10th St. Mike could see hundreds of people marching. Among the group were men on bicycles, motorbikes and cars driving alongside. In their hands the mob clutched crowbars, baseball bats and pieces of iron fencing. Like a horde of modern-day Vikings, they smashed at parked vehicles, business windows and anything else breakable. Some members of the group pushed shopping carts, and items of value that could be plundered were loaded up. The one thing certain about this group was Devonte Jones on life support was just an excuse for them. Mike hid behind a bus shelter and watched the savages wreak havoc. A group splintered off and headed farther down 10th St. toward the art gallery. A chopper flew overhead and focused its searchlight on the crowd. Mike then heard gunshots.

*   *   *

Tyrone didn't scare easily, but from the chatter on his police radio, it was evident the city was out of control. A directive from the mayor's office earlier had forbidden the police force from placing itself on tactical alert. The mayor said the act of getting ready to fight a riot was an overreaction that would become a self-fulfilling prophecy and lead to a riot. The urban unrest, as every division chief predicted, happened anyway. Unfortunately, though, due to this the St. Louis police patrolling the streets today were dressed and equipped for crowd control at a Cardinals game and not civil disorder of the highest degree.

The heads of the two police unions, one for African Americans and one for white officers didn't agree on much. But tonight they were in total agreement, for reasons of safety, they weren't going to aggressively intervene in the melee that had broken out. In a joint statement, they proclaimed to be undermanned and without adequate equipment for the scale of unrest. The mayor, in full panic mode, called for mutual assistance backup from surrounding jurisdictions. The governor, seeing a political opportunity to show the pale blue dot of St. Louis what red state safety looks like, rushed in the National Guard. The city of St. Louis, with multiple descending regional militias and an out-of-control array of anarchists on the rampage, looked like an active war zone.

In numerous suburban inner-ring cities of St. Louis County, states of emergency were declared. They wanted the unrest in the city to be contained within its limits. Roads that crossed from the county to the city were blocked to traffic. The liberal-leaning private subdivisions of University City, Clayton and Central West End began to shut and lock their entry gates, and call in for extra backup from the private security firms they retained. The irony lost on the battening down the hatches inhabitants whose usual coffee shop banter was in the vein of defund the police and never let Trump build a wall.

When Tyrone heard on the radio that Stella's gallery on 10th St. was being attacked, his heart sank. He wasn't far away, but first he called her to check she was safely at home. Tyrone had instructed Stella this morning to stay in tonight. He couldn't get a cell phone signal so he cycled to the old Southern Bell building that still had a pay phone for posterity outside. He called the landline at her loft but there was no answer. "Where is she?" Tyrone yelled as he slammed down the phone. "She couldn't be," he said to himself like a crazy man. He then called the art gallery. Stella picked up after three rings. Her voice was panicked and he could hear the sound of windows smashing and gunfire. *Shit, Stella must have gone to protect her art!*

He cycled as fast as he could the five city blocks towards Stella's gallery. He stopped at the intersection of 10th and Locust. Dozens of city cops were standing on the corner. They were watching from a distance the marauding mob in action a mere block away. With crowbars and baseball bats, they were now smashing the windows of the coffee shop. Across the street, trash cans were on fire. A masked man lobbed a petrol bomb. Tyrone could see a looter running with one of Stella's paintings in his arms.

Tyrone had to get her out of the gallery. He looked for the commanding police officer of the group and approached him.

"Sir, I believe a member of the public is in the gallery over there," said Tyrone, pointing towards the besieged shop.

"We don't have the numbers. Our orders are to stand back," said the officer dismissively.

"There's at least two dozen of us here. I feel it would be a good time to fulfill a little of our 'protect-and-serve' ethos," said Tyrone, now bordering on rage, to his superior.

"Those are our orders officer," he yelled back over the noise of smashing windows and a helicopter in the air above. Another petrol bomb was thrown in their direction. It fell short.

"Sir, the optics don't look good. We the thin blue line are standing here watching a bunch of thugs smash up downtown. I believe someone is stuck inside the gallery. We have to do something!"

"We are doing nothing until we have reinforcements and regional backup. That's the end of it!"

Tyrone walked away from his battalion commander and a little closer to Stella's gallery. There must have been over fifty in the mob outside its door. He certainly couldn't go in on his own. He looked at his colleagues. He looked at the news chopper in the air. People were sitting at home watching the city being ransacked live on television as the police stood helplessly watching on.

Tyrone picked up his radio and put in a call for help that was a long shot but his only chance.

A few minutes later, the cavalry arrived. Tyrone had put an SOS blast to the entire downtown bike cops division. En masse, from all over the city, every on-duty member of the department cycled to Tyrone's position to offer assistance.

Tyrone explained to his colleagues that Stella was holed up in the gallery. With bare legs, short-sleeve shirts and only bike helmets for protection, the cops lined up in formation. They rode in unison to within fifty feet of the vandals and dismounted their rides. Upon the captain's signal, each cop picked up his bike and used it as part shield and part battering ram, and advanced towards the mob. With each step the officers yelled, "MOVE BACK." The crowd, with rocks and petrol bombs lined up, readied for a fight.

"Fuck you killer cops," the mob chanted as they hurled rocks at the police. The group's leader started a shout of, "Whose streets, our streets!"

The officer in charge of the regular police on the corner, seeing the bike cops unilateral advance, mobilized his troops. His officers began firing rubber bullets and smoke grenades towards the direction of the agitators.

A full melee broke out as the bike cops collided with the mob. They managed to push the looters half a block back before they lined up and readied for a counter-attack.

If the bare-legged bike cops and their rubber bullet-shooting backup hadn't been quite enough to deter this band of thugs, another force was about to enter the fray. Just like the Prussians came to Wellington's rescue at the battle of Waterloo, a fresh army to be reckoned with in the shape of an angry group of Phil Collins fans stormed into the theatre of action. Maybe it was chance, maybe it was genius, maybe the fog of war, or maybe it was the chorus of Phil Collins' hit single, *Sussudio*. Call it whatever you want, but what the Phil Collins fans brought to the battlefield changed the equilibrium. The mob of rioters scattered onto Washington Ave. and the bike cops secured 10th St.

Tyrone ran into the art gallery and found Stella locked in the bathroom. Some of her art was stolen and windows were smashed, but importantly Stella, aside from feeling scared and shaken, was unhurt. The only other damage was five holes in the ceiling when she had shot her pistol into the air as a warning against her attackers.

"I always tell you to leave that gun at home, Stella," said Tyrone as he walked her out of the gallery onto the street.

Stella's reply was not what he was expecting. She turned around and kissed him with tongue.

"Women make the rules," said Tyrone, in reply to her embrace.

*   *   *

Two blocks north of Mike's position, sheriff's deputies were forming a skirmish line; behind them water canon trucks readied as backup. Whistles were blown and the mobilized police in full riot gear proceeded to move down Washington Ave. They made it half a block before discharging a volley of tear gas rounds. This was also the signal for them to start banging their riot shields to a steady beat with batons. The chilling sound of the cadence march echoed from the buildings around Mike. The mob had been vandalizing the Thai eatery, seeing the cops move towards them, regrouped and readied for a fight. To the south, Mike could hear the distinct sounds of Phil Collins fans singing *Sussudio*. Above him choppers hovered.

Any one of the groups that were in Mike's vicinity – a marauding group of thugs, a formation of frothing sheriff deputies in riot gear, or a pissed-off cohort of Phil Collins fans, – were groups Mike wanted to avoid on the best of days. However, all these distinct bodies converging within a block of each other had the makings of a clash of civilizations-worthy extravaganza that he wanted no part of. He ran as fast as he could in the opposite direction.

Mike crouched on a corner behind an abandoned car with smashed-out windows. City Museum was a straight six blocks from there. He began walking towards his goal.

Mike made it a block farther when out of nowhere the sound of unmuffled motorbikes descended. Before he could escape, he had ten quad bikes encircling him at dangerous speeds. The bike's pilots were helmet-less men in hunting camouflage who performed wheelies and tricks as they swarmed. Mike felt like a helpless General Custer at Little Big Horn waiting to receive his fate. This went on for two long minutes, and as much as Mike hoped, no help in the form of the police arrived. He could only hope the bikers would get bored and take their display of masculinity elsewhere.

In desperation of being trapped by the redneck street bikers, Mike screamed over their engine noise: "Guys, you've had your fun! What do you want?"

After another thirty seconds of this display, a quad bike with a "Honk If You Eat Ass!" sticker in place of a number plate pulled up next to Mike. The rest of the gang continued circling. Mike readied himself to be mugged, bludgeoned to death, or any of the other miserable endings that earn you a square inch of newsprint in the *St. Louis Tribune*.

"Dude! You got a death wish? It's a dangerous night to be taking a stroll. Do you need a ride somewhere?" said the leader of the gang.

"City Museum if you're offering!" said Mike, who had just witnessed the unorthodox nature of a city of infinite contradictions.

He hopped on the back of the bike and held on for dear life. His free taxi launched from zero to what felt like 100 mph in seconds. They flew so fast through the intersection of Tucker Blvd. that they were lucky to miss crashing into a convoy of National Guard. With the fleet of bikes riding escort, Mike felt like one lucky kick-ass baller. And just like that, he was delivered by his new friends to the entrance of City Museum. He thanked the crew and watched them roar off into the distance.

Mike ran up to the doors of City Museum and attempted to open them. They were locked. He could see the second set of doors behind were boarded up with plywood. The entrance might not open, but as evident by the partying people on the MonstroCity outside area, this mad playhouse of a museum wasn't closed. It was in the midst of one massive lock-in for the ages. From the blaring noise and manic revelry Mike witnessed, what appeared to be going down was the most amazing St. Louis party you could ever dream of.

He walked through the parking lot looking up at the replica castle turrets that marked the museum's boundaries. Between these bastions was a set of interconnecting walkways. If he could get up there he would be able to traverse the bridges and tunnels of MonstroCity and arrive directly at the floor where Gloria's circus arena was located.

Mike could see National Guard Humvees pulling up in the parking lot. They were here to protect the museum. He needed to somehow scale the castle walls before they dug in. The music blasting out over the City Museum speakers was a cover of David Bowie's *Absolute Beginners,* sung by a sultry French woman. Mike looked over into the museum's main building. The party outside extended to all floors and even the roof deck.

He felt a Homeric feeling of adventure as he looked up at the daunting sloped castle walls that stood before him. Mike took a run and jumped at the wall in an attempt to scale the ramparts but slid straight back down. He looked over to the next tower. A tree was positioned to its side; it might just be climbable. He got near the tree, hoisted himself onto a car parked under it, and from its roof climbed onto the first branch he could reach. Following a little scrabbling for grip, he was quickly at the top of the tree, about two-thirds of the way up the turret. Below he could hear National Guard troops spilling out of their transportation. This was his only chance of getting into City Museum before they tossed him out of the area. He tried to reach from his location a turret ledge, but he wasn't close enough. He was now stranded in the tree with no way up, and below was the National Guard.

Mike was tantalizingly close to storming the castle; close but no cigar. It was only 10 feet that separated him from being able to get over the wall. He stood in the tree, trying to compute a way to make it happen. His thought train was disrupted by the telltale sounds of an amorous couple behind the battlements on top of the castle turret getting their rocks off.

"I can hear you!" Mike shouted up.

A head peeked out from the gap designed for a defender to attack from.

"What do you want?" the man with a very Americanized, Middle Eastern accent asked.

A soldier from below yelled up, "Is someone in that tree?" A flashlight was pointed in Mike's direction.

"Help me man! Hoist me up. I am late for a circus show," said Mike to the man in the castle.

Mike got a better look at the guy on the battlements. He was wearing a City Museum employee-branded shirt. Now a cute blonde woman peeked over the walls. From her shirt, he could see she was also on the staff. The sound of civil disorder in the night air had been the perfect tonic to get them in a frisky mood. And no better place than the top of a castle tower made all the easier when you have access to the keys that can block the area off from anyone else.

"Sure thing," said the man hanging over the battlement and extending his hand to Mike.

Mike jumped from his branch and grasped the outreached limb. He was in luck; his savior had arms that a Bulgarian wrestler of any gender would be proud of. Mike was pulled up and was finally on City Museum turf. He thanked his partially disrobed collaborators and left them to get their groove on.

He ran over the rickety bridges and up the staircases of MonstroCity until he found the doorway that led onto Gloria's floor. The building's organ was triumphantly playing *Absolute Beginners* to accompany the sultry French singer still blasting through the sound system. Mike looked around. There wasn't a person not clutching an adult beverage, and in all directions, bodies were dancing, making out, and having the time of their lives. This would be a Friday night never to be forgotten.

Mike ran past a billboard promoting Gloria's circus troupe performance tonight. The show was based on the classic Richard Gere movie *An Officer and a Gentleman*. The picture on the promo had Gloria playing Debra Winger's Paula Pokrifki character being hoisted by a man in a white naval officer uniform who was a clone of Gere's Zack Mayo. She had been planning this performance for months. Nothing was going to stop the show – not even a burning city and a near dose of heartbreak.

He rushed through the partying throngs and reached the windows of the circus arena. It was packed, albeit not the usual family crowd but 150 drunk people who looked like they had stumbled out of a Soulard Mardi Gras parade. Mike got a glimpse of Gloria. She looked stunning in a purple and gold sequin leotard while standing on a huge red ball juggling five bowling pins. On each side of her, another girl on smaller balls spun gold hula hoops from their bellies. The three ladies wore depression-era factory worker caps, as per Paula in the final scene of *An Officer and a Gentleman*. On a monocycle, a man dressed like Richard Gere in navy dress was riding around juggling white peaked officer hats. The mesmerizing performance played out against the Joe Cocker and Jennifer Warnes' slushy love song, *Up Where We Belong*.

Tales of Whiskey Tango

The City Museum circus arena was bigger on the inside than it looked through the windows. Designed to be a scaled version of a full-sized big top, it gave the illusion to the crowd they were in the real McCoy. Tonight's show was a dazzling Ringling Brothers-worthy display of smooth-flowing choreography. Mike snuck into the crowd and took a seat. With the stage lights in her eyes, Gloria didn't see him arrive.

A rope lowered from the ceiling and Gloria climbed halfway to the top of it. She twisted and turned and gyrated like the finest of those who call circus performing their craft. The booze-fueled crowd clapped in rhythm as the music ramped up in tempo. Hanging upside down holding onto the rope with one leg, she began her incredible finale. She rapidly rotated like a spinning top as her fellow dancers swarmed around her juggling. The naval officer performer jumped from his monocycle and awaited for Gloria to descend. He would then swoop her up in his arms and conclude the show.

As Gloria spun on the rope, with eyes closed, Mike moved to a position by the backstage entrance to her rear. The sound engineer, recognizing him and seeing he had made it tonight, smiled. Mike noticed a spare naval officer cap on a pile of props and put it on his head.

As Gloria's spin ended, she landed on the floor and looked towards the crowd. Mike made his move and walked up behind her. Something that everyone in the room but Gloria could see. The audience thought it was part of the show but the rest of the cast who could see what was about to happen knew better. Gloria glanced towards her Richard Gere lookalike co-star and awaited his strong-handed lift move. As Gloria stared into his eyes with anticipation, she felt a cool sensual kiss on the back of her neck that wasn't part of any script. She looked around; it was Mike. He had come! A beaming smile exploded from her face that said it all, and from within she felt an incredible sense of relief. Mike grabbed the sides of Gloria's head and kissed her on the lips. She in return put her arms around him.

With a full embrace, Mike lifted Gloria up and their faces became level. They spun as they passionately kissed. Over the continued soundtrack of *Up Where We Belong,* a co-star dancer yelled as she clapped, "Way to go Gloria! Way to Go!" The crowd cheered and the rest of the troupe smiled.

Mike, stealing the role of Zack Mayo, picked Gloria up and cradled her in his arms. As if on cue, Gloria's worker cap flew off and released into the wild her perfect prom queen curls. She then pulled Mike's naval hat from his head and put it on her own. Mike, with Gloria, held firmly in his arms, triumphantly exited the circus arena.

On a night like this, there was only one place where two crazy kids like Mike and Gloria could continue the magic – the roof deck of City Museum. They jumped into the elevator and went straight to the top. The outside air was hot and dripping with humidity. Gloria, leading Mike by the hand, pulled him into the middle of a dancing crowd. The Ferris wheel was packed and a couple were doing handstands below the giant praying mantis sculpture. The party scene around them felt like a wild St. Louis New Year's bash, only with tropical weather. Gloria pulled Mike to the old school bus that precariously hung over the side of the building.

They took their seats together and caught their breath. From the windows of the bus, they could see the chaotic city around them. In the sky, helicopters from news networks flew overhead. On Lucas St. ten floors below, police were in formation, holding off a rock-throwing crowd. Smoke was coming from a fire to the east. On every street, in every direction, Mike and Gloria could see emergency vehicles with lights on and sirens sounding.

The two of them didn't utter a word. They analyzed the surreal moment and the journey that had found them together, sitting in an old school bus, hanging off the side of a building, in a city engulfed in chaos. A few other faux passengers inside, sensing an unusual energy from the couple, gave them curious looks. Gloria stared back and then glanced over to Mike. She had found herself replicating the final scene of *The Graduate.* Now that was a rom-com noir Gloria had decided was destined for a not-so-happy-ever-after epilogue. Not wanting any of Benjamin and Elaine's likely curse, she quickly flipped the narrative. Before she had given herself any chance of humming along to *The Sound of Silence,* she dragged Mike from the bus.

Although not expecting the sudden yank, he was happy to be holding her hand. He would not protest wherever she wanted to pull him. As they stood hand in hand, taking in the air, a magical event happened. A drop of rain landed on Gloria's head. It was the first rain after many weeks.

"It's raining!" yelled Mike. All around people began to scream in joy. The sprinkle turned into a deluge but nobody on the roof of City Museum opted for shelter or complained. Within ten minutes, the outside air temperature had ratcheted down fifteen degrees and with it, for the first time in weeks, snuffed out the wretched humidity. Finally, there was an end to the cruel summer heat.

The city of St. Louis was engulfed in brutal mayhem. Riot police were charging crowds, anarchists were destroying property, gangs were stealing whatever they could find, and even a few peaceful protesters were still diligently pursuing a righteous fight. The one thing that unites all these disparate groups is the passion they hold for their causes. It was hard to get any of these factions to stop what they were doing of their own accord, or via strong-armed coercion. The city was out of control, even the governor drafting in the National Guard had not been able to put a lid on escalating events.

As the rain sprinkle turned into a thundering monsoon, it was as if someone had flicked a switch and instantly turned off the rage that flowed through the city of St. Louis. Fires were extinguished, cops took shelter in their wagons, looters ran home with their plunder, celebrity civil rights leaders returned to their hotel suites, Trustafarian anarchists retreated to their luxury rentals, and the anxious white liberals of West County regrouped at the wine bars of Clayton, Frontenac, and Ladue. The rain even managed to break up the rabid throng of *Sussudio*-chanting Phil Collins fans, as they all began to wend their way to all the specs on the regional map tagged "God's Country."

In the end, all it took was a downpour and a double-digit drop in air temperature to put a stop to undiluted crazy and restore the city of St. Louis to its regular semi-lawless state.

*   *   *

After nearly two days of touch-and-go on life support, Devonte Jones's vitals suddenly improved. The doctors told Trisha Jones they were amazed at his progress and said Devonte was a plucky fighter who had beaten the odds. The first person Trisha shared the news with was Nick Pipeman.

Nick was on the balcony of Zoe's apartment, watching the arriving storm when Trisha's call came. To say he was relieved would be an understatement. Just hours ago he was literally on the precipice, at the intersection of life and death.

Nick looked over at the Eads Bridge. He now saw it in a more spiritual light. "The bridge of love," is what the stranger had called it. Nick Googled the philosopher basketball player Rolex Flash, but no results could be found. All Nick could think about was his message: all our lives are connected and everything, for better or worse, is meant to be. Someone or something had been watching over Nick tonight, and Rolex Flash walking over that bridge was no accident of chance.

Zoe, with Rollo in her arms, came onto the balcony showcasing her new winter boots. Nick looked at the two of them. He then looked back towards the Eads Bridge. "The bridge of love," he shouted, before making a mental note to self: *I'm going to be just fine.*

*   *   *

Tyrone Booker and the heroic metro bike squad fighting off the mob to free Stella played out live on television. Courtesy of the eye-in-the-sky chopper cams, St. Louis was presented not only with the heroes it needed but the heroes it deserved. The St. Louis region for once had an exhibition of community policing that made national headlines for all the right reasons.

Thanks to the news camera footage of looters taking her art, Stella finally got the exposure she needed. Within hours of her work making it onto television, all of Stella's art had been snapped up by patrons and dealers. She was even offered a show at a prestigious local museum. From the tragedy of that ugly night came for Stella her own Warholish fifteen minutes of fame. Tyrone always said she needed a little luck – finally it came her way.

*   *   *

The wretched smell of human feces sucker-punched Reginald as he opened the trunk of Butterfly's SUV.

"He's shit himself, for sure. Likely he died and that was his final act," proclaimed Reginald.

"I thought about leaving the window cracked to let in air, but I was worried he might make noise. Suffocating to death is an awful way to die, even for a scumbag like him," Butterfly said, sounding marginally concerned.

"Our choices on what to do with him have been narrowed," replied the ex-funeral director with less dilemma.

"Get me out of here, dipshit," came the voice of a muffled Colton from the coffin.

"He's alive," Butterfly said, with a hint of regret.

"I shit myself!" Colton added in desperation.

"We can smell that, pretty boy," Butterfly shot back as she lit a Newport to mask the odor.

From his jacket pocket, Reginald pulled out an uncirculated JFK fifty-cent coin. He carried them with him for special funeral requests. The occasional customer's family adhered to the ancient custom of Charon's obol, burying the body of their loved one with a coin, so they could pay the ferryman to cross the Styx and enter the next world.

"Butterfly, here are the choices. We dump the coffin in a North City back alley. He has a fighting chance of seeing tomorrow, depending on who finds him. The second option is, drive down to the levee and set him adrift in the Mississippi, and he disappears. I propose we make a toss to seal his fate," said Reginald, placing the beautiful silver coin on his thumb.

"I call heads," Butterfly said after proclaiming her preferred option as Reginald flicked the coin into the air.

They both studied the half dollar as it landed. As the gods made their choice for them, Butterfly and Reginald said simultaneously, "Best of three!"

*　　*　　*

Sam Robinson pushed the pedal to the metal and took his LeBaron to the edge of its limitations. He could see dark rain clouds forming on the horizon but couldn't afford to lose time pulling over and putting up the roof. Sam had calculated with bush math, that if he held his speed to an average of 87 mph, he would intercept Alice's Greyhound bus at its stop in Mt. Vernon, Illinois.

Sam barreled straight into the storm. He was thankful for the ducktail spoiler he'd bolted onto the car and the extra speed it yielded. A fast, wet hour later he pulled into the Greyhound station and parked up. Sam saw the Louisville-bound bus waiting and ran over to it. The driver was in his seat as he boarded.

"Ticket please," the driver requested.

"I'm looking for someone," Sam replied as if he was using a Jedi mind trick to circumnavigate the bus driver's authority. Sam scanned the seats but didn't see Alice.

Sam, wet to his bones, walked over to the waiting room. The air-conditioning in the building hadn't adjusted to account for the cooler outside air temperatures, and it was frigid inside.

He looked around the busy waiting area. It was packed with people sheltering from the storm. He finally spotted Alice. She was sitting on a bench, drinking a bottle of Dr Pepper. She had headphones plugged into her ears.

Sam sat down next to Alice and put his arm around her. She split her headphones and put one into Sam's ear. Alice was listening to the *Pretty Woman* soundtrack.

"This has all the makings of a whiskey tango fairytale!" said a smiling Alice as she kissed Sam on the cheek.

*   *   *

"We shape our dwellings, and afterwards our dwellings shape us," said Daris Ballic, repeating a Winston Churchill quote as he strolled onto the rooftop of Missouri Towers. Daris looked over at the algae-infested pool and couldn't wait until he owned the entire building. He had so many plans.

The city in the distance sounded scary and dangerous. A storm was approaching from Illinois. He had decided to watch it come in from the viewing deck.

Daris standing on the deck, lit a cigar and looked into the sky. Overhead an airplane flew en route between the left and right coasts. Below in the river, a piece of wood that for a split second had a coffin-like appearance was dragged in the fierce Mississippi currents.

"Good evening," a voice said.

Daris looked over and saw a lady drinking iced wine from an oversized tumbler.

"Would you like company?" He asked.

Daris took a seat next to the woman, who introduced herself as Madison Stone. She poured him a drink. Together they watched the storm. When the temperatures took a double-digit drop, he loaned her his Henry Poole & Co jacket to keep warm.

*   *   *

Mike knew City Museum's rooftop by heart and knew exactly where to take Gloria. He took her by the hand and together they climbed to the top of a steel-framed tower known as, "The Russian Keg." As they made the ascent, they were treated in every direction to unobstructed views of St. Louis.

They eased themselves into the small metal cage at the Keg's peak. At last, alone together and with nowhere else to go. The rain was pouring down and they were drenched, but neither of them cared. Gloria held Mike's hand and sang to him his favorite Bruce Springsteen song, *Brilliant Disguise*. Mike looked into Gloria's eyes and knew this was it. There was only one word that could capture not only this moment but the futures they would share.

"Forever," he said.

The Author

James Aylott is a former sharp-elbowed Hollywood paparazzo and ruthless supermarket tabloid photo editor. His award-winning debut novel, *Tales from The Beach House*, was both critically acclaimed and a hit. His follow-up work of fiction, *Tales of Whiskey Tango from Misery Towers* is set in St. Louis, Missouri, one of America's most dangerous cities. The author took inspiration not only from the colorful characters he met while embedding himself in the real estate business but also from the mayhem of everyday life on the wild streets of downtown St. Louis. James Aylott is a graduate of the University of California, Berkeley, and King's College, London. He is happy to call a leafy suburb of St. Louis, Missouri his home.

Made in the USA
Las Vegas, NV
15 September 2024

95303975R00246